Review

All My Sunsets is a story of a man who sets out to recreate his future. While this is fiction, it also contains an inspirational message that asks two questions. What would you do if you knew you had only a few weeks to live? What would you do if you suddenly discovered that there is a reset button you can use to start afresh? The novel is cleverly plotted, beautifully written, and entertaining.

Readers' Favorite

Books by Stefan Vučak

General Fiction:
Cry of Eagles
All the Evils
Towers of Darkness
Strike for Honor
Proportional Response
Legitimate Power
Autumn Leaves
F/X-26
28th Amendment
Night Sirens
Broken Rose

Science Fiction:
Fulfillment
Lifeliners
All My Sunsets

Shadow Gods Saga:
In the Shadow of Death
Against the Gods of Shadow
A Whisper from Shadow
Shadow Masters
Immortal in Shadow
With Shadow and Thunder
Through the Valley of Shadow
Guardians of Shadow

Non-Fiction:
Writing Tips for Authors

Contact at:
www.stefanvucak.com

ALL MY SUNSETS

By

Stefan Vučak

Dedication

To Kristian Peraica ... for a future yet to be written

Acknowledgments

To Charlotte Raby for additional proofreading and insightful suggestions.
https://charlotteraby.wordpress.com/

Cover art by Laura Shinn.
http://laurashinn.yolasite.com

Chapter One

Andrew Payne was dying and knew it.

What was worse—if there could be anything worse—he did it to himself. Too much sun, surf…and girls.

To kick off at twenty-five, though, he figured it a bit rich. If only he could turn back time.

Shait.

He did not hurt much, unless he thought about it, which he preferred not to, or the thing ravaging his body. They still had him on checkpoint inhibitors, but gave up on interleukin-2. The stuff made him ache all over, induced drowsiness, and he felt bone tired all the time. Too far gone, they figured.

At least they did not have him in the ICU with tubes stuck in him, monitors blinking, tracing wiggly lines—one stared at him now beside his left bedside cabinet—and having to smell the pervasive antiseptic stink in the air, which would probably send him over the edge. They had done all they could, and would continue until all the yellow lines in the monitor flatlined. On the other cabinet, an electronic alarm clock stared at him. Numerals glowing pale amber, it said: 12:25 pm. Above it in smaller font, it announced, March 4, 2022. Like any of it mattered.

Whatever they gave him for pain left his mind clear, enabling him to think. Perhaps not such a crash hot idea, all things considered. There were moments, feeling weary and dejected, when he longed for stupor until it all sunded. He was too full of life for that, not prepared to give up just yet despite the odds stacked against him.

He did not fear death, although he did at first. Now, they had become acquainted, friends almost. It came to collect all of them eventually. What he considered unfair, death had come to claim him before he started serious work on his to-do list. Not that he ever prepared one, but still not fair. He had gotten over that resentment, wondering how the moment would actually feel when he got to see the naked face of eternity. Would he feel anything? Would there be an after?

Bright sunshine streamed into his private room through gauzy white curtains, making the colors sharp and vibrant. He turned his head and gazed absently through the wide window at rooftops and tall buildings surrounding the Institute. He longed to be out there, walk the crowded streets, listen to the sounds of rushing cars and hurrying pedestrians one more time, knowing it could not be.

The monitor gave a soft beep, which he ignored. The nurses on his watch did not pay it much attention either. Besides, the repeater at their station would alert them if something needed doing. Like zipping him into a body bag, he reflected sardonically.

A drip tube inside his left elbow fed him drugs and a saline solution to keep him hydrated. Efficient nurses wearing starched uniforms and mechanical smiles changed the bottle when the liquid ran down. He had a pitcher of water and orange juice beside him—he alternated with pineapple, apple, and a tropical mix—but procedure called for a drip. A damnable nuisance at night when he rolled over and the catheter tugged painfully at his arm.

The door opened and the attractive little Despina walked in pushing the lunchtime meal wagon, as he called it. His eyes followed her as she smiled brightly, adding to the sunshine in the room. Short black hair framed a pretty round face, bold blue eyes, and a mouth that laughed easily. She told him once the nurses were running a pool on how long he would last, but she confided that she thought he would pull through. A load of poop and both of them knew it, but the grim game had to be played to its inevitable end.

"Afternoon, Mr. Payne," she announced cheerfully. "How are

we today?"

"Andrew," he told her, which she ignored every time. Don't get involved, the order of the day. Maintain a friendly, but impartial outlook and survive. Getting emotionally involved with a patient meant whiplash of the heart, tears, and trauma. "We're doing good," he told her.

"Outstanding. Do you want anything? Any pain?"

"The pain is okay, but I could use fifty more years out there," he said tilting his head at the window.

She laughed and patted his shoulder. "Hang in there. It's not over yet."

With a bit of help, he sat up. Despina pushed an extra pillow behind his back, then swung a broad wooden tray across his lap. She laid out the plates and glanced at the drip and monitor.

"Need to go to the bathroom or anything first?"

He shook his head. "I'm fine, thanks."

Those chores at least, he could still do without help, and when he could not? Despina would be there, and she would tuck him in afterward. Better her than the stern-faced Mrs. Courtney who had his graveyard shift. The old matron projected doom and end of days by her mere presence. If she ever smiled, her face would crack and fall off.

"Buzz if you need anything." Despina pushed the meal cart toward the door, fluttered her fingers at him, and strode out.

Images of them stretched out on a hot beach soaking in the rays filled a pleasant moment of reflection as he gazed at the frugal, unappetizing meal that would leave a magpie hungry. Sun and surf is what got you here, he reminded himself. Anyway, Despina probably had a bronzed hunk to stretch out with. He used to be a hunk himself...when he lived life without cares. Now, skin and bone, and not much of that either.

He sniffed at the anemic slice of roast beef swimming in pale gravy, and frowned. Baby peas and a dollop of mash completed the menu. The yogurt and mixed fruit containers looked more inviting, so he started on the fruit. His appetite had taken a dive, which he figured could not be a good sign. He spooned the fruit and chewed slowly.

You won't have to wait long, Death.

He finished the yogurt and eyed the peas. He really should keep his intake of veggies. In the end, he sighed and leaned back. He'd had enough. Enough of everything. Getting moody did nothing to resolve his current predicament, but he felt he earned another moment to feel a little sorry for himself. In the mood for it, he might as well go all the way. Rant, rage, and shout at the unfairness of it all. He had a great life before the fates turned their backs on him. A promising career and a girl who adored him. All gone with one visit to a doctor to check an itch on his forearm.

His eyes strayed to the window. Silence echoed his gaze. It could not drown out the torrent of noise in his head, or the images it made. Images of his yesterdays and the dreams of his tomorrows. Forlorn images of what might have been. He tried to suppress them, shut them out, but they still came. After a few minutes, they faded. They always did if he waited long enough.

Andrew sighed and shrugged. His tomorrows might be gone, but he had today. The fates had not taken that from him. He glanced at his laptop and a stack of medical books beside the alarm clock, tempted to do more research. What was the point? He was already an expert on what kept eating his insides. Knowing more would not change anything. Perhaps not, but an interesting article he read in the current edition of the *American Journal of Medicine* prompted him to dig deeper. It offered a slender string of hope…or another delusion. He had nothing to lose either way.

Francis came in and cleared the dishes, piling them onto the cart. Andrew nodded to him as he pushed it out without a word. He knew the orderly. In the ten days he'd been here, they hardly exchanged a dozen words. He did not mind, not in a particularly talkative mood himself. With Despina, he could chat all day, but she had other patients who needed her sunshine.

Too bad they had not met when the sun still shone on him. Then he would not have found Adriana. Other images, pleasant and warm, made him smile wistfully.

The door opened and the formidable Dr. Gail Dalton strode in. Over the last eleven months, he came to know her well. Her conservative gray business jacket and black trousers hid a caring professional who, like the nurses, had learned early not to get emotionally involved. Although older, he would not mind going out with her. Another shattered fantasy.

About 165cm, long copper hair that fell halfway down her back when not piled up in a bun, delicate oval face with a flawless complexion, and brown eyes that cut like a scalpel anything they happened to focus on. Full lips he ached to kiss, she was also remote and unreachable. Another disappointment in life.

She shut the door with a backward shove of her wrist, dragged a visitor chair closer to the bed, and sat down.

"How are you feeling today, Andrew?"

"Not too bad. My appetite is shot. Probably all the drugs you've been feeding me," he added lightly. Another lie, but what the hell.

She cleared her throat and clasped her hands in her lap, clearly uncomfortable. Every time she cleared her throat, it meant bad news. Well, how bad could it get? For a fleeting moment, tempted to make this tough for her, both were past such foolishness.

"How long?" he asked softly.

Whatever she said, it would not be a revelation. He had known for three months the seeds of time running out for him had turned into a torrent.

"I'll continue the checkpoint inhibitors treatment, but the prognosis is not favorable. Your Stage IV polypoid melanoma has metastasized through all your organs, and they're slowly shutting down. The combination of drugs you're taking has slowed the progression, but has not stopped it."

"I wish you would stop feeding me those things, Doc. They're making me feel like crap."

"I cannot do that, but I can reduce the dosage."

"Well, that would be something." He braced himself. "How long do I have?" he asked again.

"Three weeks. Perhaps four. The pain threshold will peak in about eight days, then fall off rapidly."

He grinned without humor. "The old body deciding to settle its affairs?"

"We'll make you as comfortable as possible," she told him, her voice distant and clinical.

Don't get involved. He could almost hear her thoughts.

"It's okay, Dr. Dalton. I should have been dead months ago, but you wouldn't let me." He raised a hand to forestall her protest. "In that time, I came to learn quite a bit about melanomas. Wish I paid more attention before I got it. Never mind, it's done."

Her eyes strayed to the pile of books she gave him. "You *have* learned a lot. You should have studied medicine." Her mouth twitched in a faint smile at the thought, which made her face radiant. Then it firmed and the protective façade snapped back into place. "I'm sorry, Andrew. The Institute did everything it could."

"I know, and I appreciate it. Four weeks doesn't give us much time to beat this thing, but I want to try something. It is probably a doomed hope, but better than nothing."

"What have you found?"

"I came across an intriguing article in the *American Journal of Medicine*. Do you know a company called Broca Genetics?"

Her mouth pursed in a frown. "As a matter of fact, I do know them. A recent Silicon Valley startup researching the application of macrophages against various cancers. They've done some groundbreaking research. What about them?"

Andrew leaned forward. "They could help me. Correct me if I'm wrong, from what I've read, I understand macrophages are white blood cell types produced by the immune system to engulf and digest cellular bodies, foreign substances, microbes, cancer cells, and anything else that doesn't carry the type of surface proteins specific to a healthy cell. Right?"

"Accurate enough. Your point being?"

"I gather that macrophages can be in two states, the cell-repair and eat-me mode."

"That's right. In their cell-repair state, they can promote tumor angiogenesis and suppression of antitumor immune cells," Dr. Dalton added. "In their eat-me mode, they directly attack tumor cells and induce T-cells to recognize and combat them."

Andrew beamed and raised his index finger. "Now for the punchline. It says that programmed cell removal is a process of macrophage-mediated immunosurveillance by which cancer cells are recognized and removed. The problem is, cancer cells block the macrophage eat-me receptor used to clear apoptotic cells and turn the macrophage into its cell-repair state, at the same time inducing the phages to suppress the body's immune response and helps tumor cells metastasize."

"That's true, although macrophage functionality is not yet fully understood," Dr. Dalton remarked said wearing a slight frown. "You must also know that all efforts to extract macrophages from someone, switch them to their tumor-kill state and reintroduce them to fight cancers failed, as the tumor immediately switched them back to their cell-promoting state."

"Yes! This is where Broca Genetics comes in. Most researchers pursued development of a macrophage cytokine-secreting backpack that is supposed to prevent cancer cells switching off the eat-me receptor. Once the tumor cells are eliminated, the macrophage switches to its normal cell-repair state. According to the article I read, what Broca has done is tailor a macrophage for a specific cancer without the need to create a cytokine backpack. I want to try that treatment."

Dr. Dalton rubbed her chin, a characteristic gesture when concentrating. "For any treatment to work, in addition to blood, to tailor a macrophage for your condition, Broca would need a live tissue sample of your cancer."

"Fine. Another biopsy isn't a problem."

"That would not be necessary. We have sufficient cultures."

"Yes, I imagine you do."

"Mind you, Broca's research, although promising, is highly experimental. Even if they were willing to do something for you, I doubt they could do it in the time available. Such development takes months."

"You're probably right. Still, they claim an eighty-three percent remission rate in test primates."

"Primates, yes, but they are at least two years from conducting even preliminary human trials. I cannot sanction such treatment, especially one that might very well kill you."

"Kill me, Doc? I'm already dead. Besides, I don't have two years. Even if the treatment fails, it will give Broca and the Institute valuable clinical data."

"I don't know if the Institute's ethics committee would permit this."

"I'll sign a liability waiver to protect you, the Institute, and Broca from any punitive litigation. I have nothing to lose."

"You could lose your four weeks."

He snorted. "Wow, some risk when compared to the possibility of even partial remission? How about it?"

Her eyebrows came together in a deep frown. "Ordinarily, this would be against my better judgment, but as you pointed out, your condition is terminal and I am ethically bound to help you if at all possible." She stood, hesitated and nodded. "Let me make some calls."

When the door closed after her, he pumped his right fist.

"Yes!"

You are not getting me yet, Death.

He did not fool himself. His chances were thread-thin that Broca could develop something within the time he had left and the treatment to work. However thin, nevertheless a chance. Satisfied, he pulled back the connected tubing, wriggled farther down under the blankets, slid a hand behind his head, and allowed himself to sink into memories, for there were damn few tomorrows.

A year ago, life looked bright and full of promise.

* * *

For Andrew, 2021 started hot and continued through February. He clearly remembered that sunny day when he stepped out of the ANZ Collins Place tower elevator and gazed, nonplussed, at the lunchtime crowd packing the huge covered plaza that straddled the other tower. At the lower ground level, all the dining tables occupied. Popular, with a variety of restaurants and a fast takeaway food court, the plaza always packed…and noisy. He wondered how people could hear themselves talk. Probably tuned out everything around them. That's how he did it.

He strode toward the broad sidewalk and squinted. Bright sunshine beat down from a pale blue sky, the air thick. Cars streamed along the broad boulevard, tooting horns at daring individuals running across the tram tracks. A green Yarra Trams monster clanked its bell and hissed up Collins Street toward the state parliament buildings at end of the street. Tall maple and plane trees lined both sides. Sparrows perched on branches, twittering at people below. Enterprising pigeons pecked at crumbs and scraps on the sidewalk, unfazed by hurrying pedestrians around them.

He liked summer, and February most of all. He liked the hot, dry days despite the stifling oven winds that sometimes came from the central deserts. The winds were part of the package that came with living in Melbourne. Nothing to get excited about, although they were a diverting topic of conversation. Solution; ramp up the air-conditioning when they hit and ride it out.

Dressed formally in a pale blue shirt, dark orange tie, and navy trousers—he had to look professional as one of FutureTech's bright analyst-programmers—he walked across the plaza toward the sidewalk. He did not mind the dress code. Things generally did not get him worked up. Maintain an even strain, go with the flow the order of the day. He carried little worries like everybody else—rent, bills, running a car—but found life generally easy.

He missed surfing. A real bummer. That too came with the package of a full-time job. He turned right and strode briskly up the street.

Memory memo to self: Call Mark and Orwell.

Saturday only two days away, they might be interested in an outing somewhere along the Great Ocean Road.

Unbroken sea all the way to Antarctica, the water would be cold, but a light wetsuit would take care of that problem. Besides, none had married and could afford the time. The more he thought about it, the idea of running some waves, ogling sun-bathing girls, and being contemplated himself—at 174cm, square jaw, dark hazel eyes, he looked mature, and knew the girls liked him and his equally bronzed friends—it beat the hell of spending the weekend in his one-bedroom Richmond apartment. He had shopping to do, washing, and general cleaning up, but he could do that on Friday evening.

He scratched an itch on his left forearm and glanced at the black Rado on his right wrist: 12:52. Plenty of time to make his one o'clock appointment. He had a Motorola smartphone in his pocket that told time very well, but he had become attached to his Rado, a duty-free thing he purchased at LA airport two years ago before the COVID-19 panic shut down the world.

The 2020 lockdowns did not affect him all that much, as he worked from home on most days, glad to have a job as a new graduate. If he had not worked for FutureTech during his university summer breaks, he would probably be twiddling his thumbs now.

The media spewed out a lot of conflicting information about the coronavirus, and he often wondered if the news presenters knew what they were talking about. In his view, they were part of the problem with their 24/7 coverage. Didn't anything else happen in the world? He resented confinement in his apartment, unable to see family and friends, or go out. Pandemic or not, he wasn't a criminal to be locked up. Perhaps the authorities did know what they were doing, but he had his suspicions. There were other ways to control the spread without turning the country into a prison.

The world slowly climbed out of the economic hole it dug for itself, the struggle likely to take years before things returned to normal, whatever that meant. What concerned him was the ease with which governments savagely curtailed people's rights and freedoms, and were slow to return them. In places, they were not returned. Freedom or protecting societies from themselves, a thorny conundrum.

Ah, to hell with it. Right now, he had a hot and sunny, and his life looked bright.

He spotted the grimy, almost black stone façade of the narrow building and pushed open the heavy wood door. Usually, a boutique, jeweler, or takeaway joint would occupy the ground floor space, but most buildings in upper Collins Street housed well-heeled doctors, lawyers, and dentists. A business address in the Paris end proclaimed to everyone that you have beaten the system and joined the successful elite. It also allowed you to immediately double or triple your service fees. Someone had to pay for that Southbank condo, the BMW or Merc.

He walked into the cool foyer and headed for the single elevator. He pressed the request triangle and it turned white. The display above it showed it coming down and he turned to face it. The steel door opened and he stepped in. He tapped the fourth floor button and clasped his hands behind his back. A habit he picked up serving with the Melbourne University Regiment Army

Reserves while studying at the RMIT University. When he got his honors degree in November 2019, majoring in virtual design and programming, he received a commission as a first lieutenant and promptly resigned. Playing soldier became an exercise of youthful fantasy, although he had some fun along the way, but the novelty quickly faded into a dull grind of boring procedures. The few fun times he went out on field exercises and got to shoot off weapons and throw grenades did not make up for the numbing close-order drills and chores an officer candidate had to put up with.

In case of war, he figured the federal government could recall him.

The elevator door slid away. He turned left along a brightly lit corridor and stopped before a frosted glass door that had First Teeth engraved in gold letters. He opened the door and stopped before the reception desk. A young Asian girl he had not seen before looked up from her computer and smiled brightly.

"May I help you?"

"Andrew Payne to see Dr. Teller."

The girl checked her computer and nodded. "The doctor will be with you in a moment."

He took one of the visitor chairs and leaned back. An LED TV stuck to the wall silently showed the ABC news, the words displayed in subtitles. Everything around him appeared new, modern, and smelled faintly of anesthetic. A coffeemaker and sundries stood on a corner table beside the water urn. Given the fees, First Teeth did well for itself.

A side door opened and a young woman nodded to him. Her white lab coat enhanced the short platinum hair, deep olive eyes, oval face, and high cheekbones. Her small mouth showed even, perfect teeth. Figuring where she worked, he should not be surprised. Quite tall, almost 170cm, slim, her confident stance and frank gaze made him stare at a fantasy unlike anyone he had gone out with. Her air of maturity hung around her like a protective blanket. Friendly, but don't touch, it said. She regarded him with a slightly whimsical smile.

"Mr. Payne?"

He stood up. "That's right."

"I'm Dr. Teller. Please come in," she said and stepped aside.

Dr. Hendrix, his usual dentist, had the bad manners to be on leave. That is what the receptionist said when he tried to make an appointment. Fussy about who handled his teeth, but a hole in his lower molar needed treatment before it bored its way deeper and he would be up for a root canal job. He took care of his teeth, and it puzzled him how the hole developed.

As he strode past her, he could not believe she was a fully qualified dentist. The title 'Doctor' always cracked him up. They only had a bachelor honors degree, yet dentists were allowed to call themselves Doctor. One of life's inexplicable phenomena.

Teller led him to a compact treatment room fitted with all the latest support gadgets and a recliner seat comfortable enough to sleep on. A ceiling TV showed something from Channel 10. Beside the seat stood a short girl in a green protective gown. He could not see her face behind the white mask.

"Sit down. Mr. Payne," Teller told him pleasantly in subtle contralto, and leaned to peer at the computer.

Andrew made himself comfortable and the attendant tied a bib around his neck. Teller looked down at him.

"We'll get an x-ray first to check the extent of enamel penetration. Are you in any pain?"

"No, but my tongue keeps straying to the hole."

"A common reaction," she assured him with a grin.

She swung a portable x-ray head toward his cheek and made him bite down on a film slide. The thing done, she checked the computer.

"You're lucky we caught this early. It won't take a minute to fill. Your other teeth look good."

"I try to take care of them."

She slipped on her mask and gloves, and dabbed a cotton finger soaked with an anesthetic against both sides of his molar. He hated needles, but First Teeth did not use them for simple repairs, something he appreciated.

It only took a few minutes to drill out the cavity, fill, and seal it with a laser, as Teller promised. He rinsed his mouth and the assistant removed the bib. His tongue slipped over the filled tooth, liking the smooth surface.

"Thanks, Doc."

She nodded. "You're welcome."

He searched her face and made the plunge. The worst thing she could do was say no.

"Look, I haven't had lunch yet. How about we have one together? If you're free, that is."

She laughed with genuine mirth. "Is this your standard pickup line, Mr. Payne?"

"No, it isn't," he told her seriously, drawn by her captivating eyes. "I really would like to go out with you."

He could see the assistant smile behind her mask.

Teller bit her lower lip. "Mmm. Settle your bill at reception and I'll see you in a minute."

Searing heat surged through his body and he broke into a wide grin.

"Deal!"

They took the elevator down and Andrew opened the ground floor door for her. She stepped out and gasped.

"Wow. It's hot."

Dressed in dark gray trousers and white shirt, she looked regal.

"Since we're lunching, I would like to call you something else than Dr. Teller."

She smiled. "Adriana," she said and frowned. "Would you mind if we go somewhere close? Collins Place, perhaps? I don't have much time. Patients."

"Collins Place works for me, and it's only down the street."

"I often go there," she said. "You?"

"I work at the ANZ tower, and the food court provides good meals."

"You work for the bank?"

"I'm an analyst-programmer for FutureTech, a virtual reality games developer. It's a U.S. company based in Mountain View, Silicon Valley, and their Melbourne office runs the Australasian region."

"They must be doing well to afford an office there."

"Virtual reality is the future in games, and I have ideas for other applications. I'm just getting started there, and I'm reluctant to push on them yet." He glanced at her. "I haven't seen you at First Teeth before."

"I graduated last year and this is my first real job. I worked for them as a dental assistant, then a technician while doing my degree."

"I wondered how you managed to land a job with them. Most of the dentists there are past it."

She laughed. "They're choosy whom they take on, but Dr. Hendrix has been my family's dentist for years. When I told him I studied to be one, he became my mentor."

"I like Hendrix," he told her. "He's been looking after me for a while. Some people make you feel warm by their very presence, and he is one of them. Must be a great asset in your profession." He gave her a searching look. "You have that quality yourself."

Adriana's eyes probed him, and he felt his personality being peeled back, revealing the layers beneath. Normally, he shied away from such scrutiny, but he found he did not mind it from her. He wanted to peel away her layers as well to see what lay there.

"You've been with FutureTech for some time?"

"It's my first full-time job. I started last February before the pandemic kicked off, but during my final two years at RMIT, I had work experience training with them, and as a casual during the summer breaks. I'm glad I did that, as it opened my eyes to how real business does things. Universities don't properly prepare students for the job market and what the commercial world wants. The work experience program is the best thing they put into place.

"I thought myself an expert in VR design, but university projects are a far cry from real world applications. FutureTech taught me a lot, but I also gave them a lot. When I started with them, they sponsored my MBA at RMIT. I guess they see me as a prospective manager. If I keep my nose clean and work my butt off, I expect to graduate this November."

"You've done well."

"It's a pain, all the study. It cramps my social life."

She chuckled. "Ah, the sacrifices we make."

"If only you knew," he told her.

When they reached Collins Pace, he took her to the lower level and headed for Peroni's. Not quite upmarket, but he had eaten there before. Its quiet atmosphere and subdued lighting more satisfying than the gregarious, noisy ambiance of the open court outside. He normally booked, but well after 1:30, the attendant got them a back corner table.

Adriana ordered mineral water with her lamb cutlets and stir-fried vegetables. He got himself a dark light ale with his veal medallions, also with stir-fry veggies.

She looked around the full venue and nodded in appreciation. "I eat here often, but it's the first time at Peroni's."

"Lots of interesting nooks and crannies in the plaza. It's a warren. You just need to look."

"What else occupies your days when you're not a VR analyst?" she asked lightly, a glint of overhead lighting making her eyes sparkle.

"My two friends and I love surfing and being on a beach. Nice things to see there," he told her seriously, and she cracked a broad smile.

"I don't doubt it. And you took in all the sights."

He shrugged. "That's what it's for. Regrettably, when we started university, we were forced to sacrifice many of our extra-curricular activities. If we wanted to pass, that is."

"How you suffered."

"We did, but we're not letting this summer go to waste. As a matter of fact, I'll be arranging an outing with them for this Saturday." He cocked an eyebrow at her. "Would you like to come with me?"

She waved a hand. "Afraid not. I have things to do."

"Teller…May I ask where that comes from? Swiss, maybe?"

"Swedish. My father's parents came to Australia in 1956. Dad was born here, and Mom is Greek. What about you?"

"My mom is English. Came over with her parents and brother in 1992. My dad's parents are Americans. His old man saw service time in Queensland. After the war, he went back to San Francisco to pick up his wife and they settled in Sydney. A few years later, they moved to Melbourne, and never stopped complaining about our cold weather."

Adriana grinned. "Sydney *is* much warmer."

"It is, but when Dad was born, that settled it. Everybody stayed here."

"Your father's parents still alive?"

"Both were killed in a car accident last October. A speeding idiot ran a red light and T-boned them at an intersection."

"I'm sorry to hear that, Andrew."

He shrugged. "I liked them a lot. They apparently liked me, for they left me their South Yarra house. I'll be moving in at end of the month. That's when the lease on my Richmond pad expires. It will take me a bit longer getting to work, but having a place of my own will make up for it. Renting is giving money away."

"Anybody else in the family?"

"Only my sister Belana. She's almost eighteen and in her first year at Melbourne Uni."

The attendant brought their drinks and meals, and both concentrated on food for a while, making an occasional comment how good it tasted. Very conscious of Adriana's presence, he took pains to note her mannerisms and simply enjoyed being with her. He found her different from any girl he dated. He sensed a depth he wanted to explore, afraid he might not see her again, until he needed another tooth fixed, and he wanted to see her again badly. To feel such a connection at first sight somewhat new territory for him, and he felt a tremor of uncertainty at the prospect of possible long-term commitment. He liked girls, liked going out, liked the fun he had with them, but with strict understanding it was only a bit of fun. They had not wanted it any other way either. That is how it had been so far.

The situation he found himself in with Adriana somewhat bemusing. With her, he could not slip into his comfortable, tried one-night stand routine. This left him unnerved and puzzled as he tried to sort out his feelings, but also excited. Not the prospect of making a conquest, but a genuine desire to become closer with another person. He felt undeniable physical attraction, but he found that this time, he wanted much more. He faced his twenty-fourth birthday in a couple of months, and recognized that life had started to be serious at many levels. Was he ready to take such an important step with her?

Looking at her, he could not decide.

Stupid!

They were only having lunch, and he should not make too much out of it. His inner self jeered at him for being a coward. If she did not want to see him, his surfing weekend would be without her. There were other shells on the beach, but he wanted this particular shell.

He downed the last of his ale, and Adriana dabbed her lips with a napkin.

"I enjoyed that, Andrew, and our little chat. Time I got back to the practice."

"There is a lot more about me I haven't said," he told her. "To find out, you'll need another lunch or two, or a dinner."

Her eyes lost some of their brightness and she turned thoughtful.

"I am not sure I want to get involved with someone right now. My last boyfriend turned out to be one of those old-fashioned dominant types who thinks a woman should mind smelly babies and look after the house. His parents were polite but distant. I wasn't a Polish girl, and that earned me a black mark to start with."

"Am I coming on too strong?"

"A little, but I don't mind too much. You're not afraid to express your feelings, and I appreciate that. Right now, though, my job and a routine keeps me occupied. It's enough."

He fingered the beer glass for a moment, then looked at her.

"You have some very special qualities, Adriana, and that makes me nervous, because I never met anyone like you. Now that I did, I would very much like to know you better…if you'll let me." Silence lingered between them for several long seconds.

"What did you have in mind?" she asked at length.

"Lunch tomorrow?" he queried hopefully.

"You don't waste much time, do you?"

"Circling the wagons to stave off any possible competition." She laughed. "You're a dupe. Let me think about it, okay?"

Not what he wanted to hear, but she did not reject him either.

* * *

"I keep wanting to scratch it," Andrew declared, frustrated and concerned. Only a mole and he had dozens all over his back. Just thinking about it made his forearm itch.

Dr. Ananankos pursed his lips. "Any bleeding?"

His deep voice calm, measured, and reassuring, put Andrew at ease. Bushy hair almost all white, black eyes that missed nothing, a bulbous nose with a large wart on the right side, jowls sagging, the doc definitely did not project a poster GP image. What made his patients come back, and Andrew a regular from his university days, was loads of empathy. His mere presence and kindly demeanor dispelled anxiety.

"No. I'm not scratching that hard."

"Any dermis under your fingernails when you do scratch?"

"Sometimes."

"How long have you had it?"

"It appeared as a small mole last October."

Ananankos grunted as he pushed back his chair and rummaged through a desk drawer. He held up what looked like a large jeweler's loupe attached to a thick handle.

"Pull up your sleeve."

Andrew did and rested his arm on the desk.

The doc absently brushed back a wad of hair and leaned forward. He switched on the instrument and positioned it over the black mole. The examination lasted about a minute, with Ananankos making an occasional sigh, which did nothing for Andrew's disposition.

"Take off your shirt and stand up."

Puzzled, Andrew bit his lower lip and complied, not liking the doctor's frown.

He flinched slightly when the cold instrument touched his back. Ananankos took his time sliding the thing across his back. He sat down and shook his head.

Andrew buttoned his shirt and hung his tie around the collar.

"There's quite a collection of moles on your back," Ananankos declared sonorously. "Clear evidence of UV damage, but nothing of any concern. I would advise you to take greater care of your skin, though. Use lots of sunblock."

"I *am* using it," Andrew said unconvincingly.

The truth, he had not been very diligent when it came to sun protection. The best blockers made him look like a white ceiling or left him smelling of cheap aftershave. Neither went down well with the girls.

"Try harder," Ananankos told him firmly. "I'm concerned about the mole on your forearm. There are irregularities I don't like. I would recommend removal and a pathology examination. I can do the biopsy now if you like." He smiled. "It will stop the itching."

Andrew grinned back. "In that case, let's do it."

It did not take long. Ananankos jabbed him with an anesthetic, which made him wince, and carved out a substantial slab of tissue around the mole. It took four sutures to close the incision. He wiped excess blood and stuck a wide waterproof pad on the wound, sat back, and glanced at the computer.

"Come in on Tuesday at eleven. That's February 16. The results should be in by then. Next Friday at four, I'll take out the sutures. *Don't* remove the protective pad before then, okay?" he said and held out an appointment card.

"Got it." Andrew tempted to skip this part, but he had to know. "The mole…What do you think it is?"

"Hard to say. There is some discoloration not consistent with a normal mole, and the growth is irregular. It could be nothing, but we'll know for sure on Tuesday. I wouldn't worry too much about it."

Whenever someone told Andrew not to worry about something, that's when he started to worry.

"If the test comes back positive?"

"If it's melanoma, the report will tell us what kind, which will dictate the type of treatment. There are lots of tools in our bag these days to beat these things, but as I said, don't worry about it for now."

Andrew stood, tucked in his shirt, and extended his hand. "Thanks, Doc. I'll see you on Tuesday," he said as they shook hands. He strode toward the door, then stopped and turned. "I planned to do some surfing tomorrow. I suppose that's out now?"

Ananankos wagged his index finger. "Definitely, and anything else that might cause the protective pad to come off. Especially in the first three or four days."

"Got it. Thanks again."

Shait.

Memory memo to self: Give Mark and Orwell the grim news.

Outside the clinic, he squinted at the steel sky and glanced at his watch: 12:56. He muttered a pithy word and hurried up Exhibition Street. Collins only a block up, but he would still be late for his one o'clock lunch date with Adriana. He called her yesterday and she agreed to go out. He dug out his cellphone, scrolled down the Contacts list, and pressed the ring icon.

"First Teeth, Penny speaking. How can I help you?"

"This is Andrew Payne. I have a meeting with Dr. Teller outside the building at one, but I'm running a few minutes late. I would appreciate if you could please let her know?"

"Not a problem, Mr. Payne."

"Thanks."

"Bye."

Pedestrians crowded the sidewalk, some still wearing protective masks, and the street stank from car exhausts. He wondered how the maples along the central nature strip coped. He pushed the thought away…and his biopsy. Like the doc said, no need to get excited yet. Wait for the facts, *then* get excited.

Adriana came out as he approached the building. She spotted him and waited. Wearing a pale blue shirt, sleeves cut part way up the elbows, navy slacks, she had poise. Several men gave her a passing glance, as did some women. He saw that she did not appear to notice the attention, or accepted it as her due.

He stopped in front of her and smiled sheepishly. "Sorry to hold you up. A minor medical emergency. At least I hope it will be minor."

"Emergency?"

He lifted his left arm. "I had a mole cut out. It's been itchy for a while and I decided to check it out."

Her eyes lit with mischievous amusement. "That's what comes from too much sun, surf, and other things."

"Your sympathy is overwhelming."

She chuckled and patted the wounded arm. "The doctor knows best."

"You've been waiting long?"

"I finished up when Penny told me you were running late. Now, about lunch. There is a very nice Japanese restaurant at Collins Place, Heiwa Fun'iki. Means peaceful ambiance, or something like that."

"You've been there before?"

"A few times. I booked us a table. My treat this time," she added.

"Hey! I asked *you* out."

"My treat or I'm walking back."

"Fine. Japanese it is."

They merged into the crowd heading down the street.

Strong, independent, and knows her mind. Andrew liked that. Most girls he dated until now were quite happy for him to take charge. Apparently not Adriana. He needed to be careful how he handled himself with her...if she gave him a chance to go out again.

At the plaza, they walked down broad steps to the lower ground level, threading between lunch goers, trying to ignore the ambient decibels.

A Japanese girl in a white shirt and black trousers bowed as they stepped into the bright atmosphere filled with inviting cooking smells. Most of the small square tables were full. Judging by the animated conversation and free laughter, the patrons were having a good time. After confirming the reservation, their hostess led them to a table beside a ceiling-high plate window with a view of the plaza, and handed them menus.

"Sencha tea, please," Adriana told her.

"Same for me," Andrew added.

The hostess smiled, bowed, and steered her way between tables to the order bench. The place had no bar, not catering for such clientele. However, he did see several men drinking sake. He liked the rice liquor, especially when served hot, but as a working day, he needed to keep a clear head. Sake doesn't taste strong and it fooled many who thought it a soft drink.

His gaze lingered on Adriana's face, taking in every curve and feature. She did not look away, scrutinizing him in turn. Definitely a woman of character, he decided, feeling sorry for her last boyfriend, letting her slip between his fingers.

After studying the menu, she looked up. "Dreamed up any new VR games?"

"My team and I are finishing putting one together."

"Blood, gore, cannons everywhere, slashing swords?"

"Ouch, that hurt, but you're right. Interactive action games are the rage, I'm afraid, and bring in the money. However, I'm doing some coding at home to develop 3D rendering sets to make everything more lifelike. Computer animation these days is first-rate, but no matter how well done, the characters still look like dolls, and the scenery is lackluster."

"I know what you mean. I've seen clips on YouTube."

He leaned forward, allowing his enthusiasm to bubble. "And it still costs anything up to two hundred thousand or more to develop a good game. What I want to do with my rendering sets is produce characters and backgrounds first seen in *Avatar*, but without spending hundreds of millions James Cameron had to. Mine will be cheaper and better." He saw her bemused look. "Computer animation doesn't do anything for you, does it?"

"I don't know anything about it," she admitted, "but I'm fascinated by your enthusiasm."

Their hostess glided to the table and unloaded a large blue porcelain teapot and shallow cups. She poured for them, then dug out her tablet. "Ready to order?"

Adriana nodded. "I'll have the Ebi Furai prawns and the pork Tonkatsu."

"For me, the prawns as well, and the Tako Karaage," Andrew told her.

The hostess nodded, picked up the menus, and strode off.

Adriana mixed brown sugar crystals into her tea and sipped. "This is good. Must be a fresh batch."

Andrew tried his—no sugar—and nodded. "Not bad. If you don't mind me asking, how do you spend your days?" he said, then raised a hand. "I know. Teeth and more teeth."

"I'm afraid so. I'm glad to be spared some of the horrors one of my best friends puts up with. Susan works at a practice in North Melbourne not far from the Victoria Market. The things she tells me makes me shudder. Some of her patients come in with teeth that look like bombed-out buildings."

He smiled, images of Berlin's post-war skeletons jumping into mind.

"Some don't brush or gargle, and the kids…" She shuddered, then grinned. "Since we're about to eat, I better not go there."

"First Teeth patients obviously take care of themselves," he said.

"They do, and that's good." She took a sip of tea.

"Any other dentists in the family?"

"Just me."

"Brother or sisters?"

"My parents wanted a larger family, but when I was born, Mom had problems and couldn't have any more."

"I'm sorry about that," he said contritely.

"They adjusted, and their careers keep them busy. Dad is an

electrical engineer with Graff Construction. They do a lot of high-rise stuff and factories. Mom is a financial advisor at AMP."

"A lot of bloodletting there after the 2018 Royal Commission into banks and financial institutions."

"There certainly was. It demonstrated unequivocally that corporate greed does not pay in the long run," Adriana agreed. "The scandals left the banks reeling. It will take them a long time to build trust again."

Andrew sighed. "I don't know. They're monopolies, and most of their money comes from the corporate sector. The little people are an inconvenience they must put up with."

Adriana raised her eyebrows. "My, aren't we cynical, Mr. Payne."

"You think I'm wrong?"

"Sadly, I agree with you, as does my mom. Despite the Commission's findings, none of the recommendations are implemented yet, and the banks took advantage of that last year. With the pandemic raging, they cut back dividend payments, as did many large corporations, with tacit approval from Canberra. They needed to save money to survive," she added, rolling her eyes. "What the government and banks ignored is that those dividends make up a substantial portion of pensioner and self-retirees' earnings."

He nodded. "It looks like both of us hold a less than respectful attitude when it comes to the big end of the corporate sector."

"Despite what Michael Douglas said in one of his movies, greed is not good."

"You follow politics much?"

She crunched her nose. "With a very cynical attitude. You?"

"About the same. Every time I wake up, I'm hoping they haven't screwed things up further."

Their hostess showed up bearing two plates. She laid them down and nodded. "Enjoy."

"Saved!" Andrew declared, eyeing the deep-fried crumbed

prawns.

"We did get diverted into gloomy territory, didn't we," Adriana said and dipped a prawn into a side bowl of sweet chili sauce. She bit into it and sighed. "Yum."

"Not bad at all," he agreed around a mouthful. "What else occupies that probing mind, Doctor?"

"Are you after my resume, Mr. Payne?"

"Just curious. You interest me."

"Dupe. For your information, I like my mom's cat Fluff, but I'm not keen having one of my own. What about you? Are you a pet lover?"

"My mom has a black tomcat who tolerates me. That's as far as I go with pets. I live in a one-bedroom apartment in Richmond, which is no place to keep an animal, even if the landlord allowed them."

"How do you get to work?"

"I catch a tram. It drops me off at Parliament and it's a short walk to Collins Place. Last year a monumental drag with all that social distancing, and I'm glad things are more normal now." He looked at her. "What about you?"

"I live in Footscray and take a train. It stops at the Parliament underground and First Teeth is around the corner." Her eyes probed him. "No pets, but you must like something else instead."

"Oh, I read most fiction. Go out with my friends. Sun and surf." He glanced at his arm and smiled. "Perhaps not for a while. I'm an invalid for one week."

"So, the Great Ocean Road outing is off tomorrow?"

"Until further notice. I don't mind too much. My job keeps me pretty busy, and a quiet weekend might not be such a bad thing."

"What else interests you?"

"I like classical music. Orchestral mostly. I'm not much into piano recitals and stuff."

"Classical is okay, but it's not something I listen to a lot," she said. "Which is odd, as I play a violin."

He raised an eyebrow. "Interesting. I would like to hear you play sometime."

"We shall see."

They finished the prawns and were sipping tea when their hostess came to clean up and bring the mains. Andrew cut off a piece of octopus from his stick Karaage, dipped it into Worcestershire sauce, and chewed the tasty morsel. Adriana seemed to relish her pork Tonkatsu.

Conversation ebbed and flowed between them as they discovered each other, Andrew getting increasingly smitten with her. What she thought of him, he could not say. He hoped it was favorable.

She glanced at her watch. "Goodness! I've got to fly. I actually enjoyed this. Thank you." She raised her arm and their hostess appeared, tablet in hand.

Adriana settled the bill and said, "*Domo arigato.*"

The hostess beamed and bowed. "*Douitashi mashite.* Enjoy your day."

They walked out and headed up the stairs to ground level. As Adriana prepared to head across the plaza, he reached for her hand.

"I would like to go out with you again."

She appeared to think it over. "Perhaps," she said and strode briskly toward the sidewalk, swallowed by a wall of pedestrians.

For several long moments, he watched the space where she vanished, then shook his head and ambled toward the ANZ tower.

When he got to his bullpen cubicle, he turned on the powerful graphics computer and started Googling information about skin cancers and melanomas in particular. After an hour or so of intense reading, he knew much more about the subject than he wanted. Bad news whichever type someone got, with poor life expectancy beyond five years even if caught early. Melanomas were buggers whichever way he cut it.

His heart not in his work during the rest of the afternoon, his mind skipped from Adriana and a promise of seeing her again, and gloomy possibilities he did not want to dwell on.

* * *

Mouth dry, Andrew but his lip, sat down, and leaned back trying to relax. It did not work. He gazed at Dr. Anannankos, his stomach tense, ripples of muscle tension running up and down his body.

The old doctor frowned. "I wish I had better news, but you need to face the fact that you have Stage I polypoid melanoma. They grow deeply into the dermis and underlying tissue before any surface protrusion becomes visible. You said you noticed that mole in October, which means cancerous cells were present long before then."

Andrew sat there without saying anything. Now that he knew, the tension and nervousness were gone, but he felt nothing. The shock would come when all the pieces came together with the realization the bright future he hoped for now a fantasy.

"Polypoid melanoma...the most nasty kid on the block."

Anannankos sniffed. "Cancers damage the body in many ways: blocking digestive system processes, lung infection that prevents intake of oxygen, excessive calcium discharge if malignant cells get into the bones, disruption of liver chemistry, destruction of brain cells...The list is lengthy, and this one is particularly invasive."

"Since we last met, I've read something about melanomas, Doc," Andrew said woodenly.

"Then you're aware of the options to treat it. The Peter Mac-Callum Cancer Center, part of the Royal Melbourne Hospital in Parkville, has first-rate diagnostic and treatment facilities. However, many of their specialists are external consultants, not residents. What I'd like to do is send you to the Lyndon Cancer Institute in Victoria Parade. They're in Carlton not far from here. The Institute is one of the best in Australia. It's primarily a research facility, but they do have a hospital arm."

"What will they do?"

"You need a sentinel lymph node biopsy in your neck to determine if there is any spread. Treatment will depend on what they find. If there is no spread, you'll still need to take immune checkpoint inhibitors or targeted therapy drugs to contain the tumor. If any of your lymph nodes are affected, they would require removal. Your specialist will discuss this in greater detail and advise you after they do the SLNB. I'll send them your medical history and make an appointment with Associate Professor Gail Dalton. The Institute will call you when to come in. It is important to define the status of your condition quickly." Ananankos cleared his throat, not liking this anymore than Andrew did. He reached into a desk drawer and pulled out a small brown glass bottle. He took out a red pill and held it out.

"Tranquilizer. The shock has not hit you yet, but it will. This will help. I suggest you lie down for a few minutes and let all this sink in."

"It already has," Andrew murmured, took the shiny red pill, stared at it for a moment, then popped it into his mouth. It slid down easily, leaving a slight sugary aftertaste.

Ananankos gathered several leaflets and booklets off his desk. "Information on melanomas and treatment options. I would advise you to familiarize yourself with them. It will help counter negative psychological reactions."

Andrew shook his head. "Thanks, Doc, but I don't need PR glossies. What I want is hard scientific data, which I'll Google or get from the Melbourne University medical library."

Ananankos glanced at the brochures and placed them back on the desk. "I'll not shield you from the harsh reality that your life expectancy is drastically curtailed. However, there has been rapid progress with various gene therapies, and one of them might be tailored for your condition. Dr. Dalton will go into all this in greater detail."

Andrew exhaled loudly and stood. "You aren't much fun at all, Doc," he said with a wry grin.

The older man smiled faintly, stood, and offered his hand. "Good luck. See me any time…for anything."

Outside the clinic, patchy clouds were drifting in from the west. A warm mild breeze stirred leaves, making them whisper to each other. Traffic streamed both ways, and pedestrians clogged the sidewalks. A hot February usually meant a hot March…usually. This was Melbourne, and nothing could be taken for granted.

Enjoy what you have and don't bitch, he told himself. Did that apply to his melanoma as well? After some deliberation, he decided it did.

Life always dished out shitty deals, and he could be run over by a cement truck while jaywalking.

He felt numb, detached, without an anchor to reality. Must be the tranquilizer he took. Right now, he did not need any anchor. His situation real as it could get. He did not feel anger at the injustice and unfairness of it all. What did the fates care about one insignificant life among billions? Simply one more dust mote drifting aimlessly in the air, no importance at all. Life moved inexorably on the river of tomorrows. His had hit a minor eddy, but there were lots of other dust motes in the air. In the grand scheme of things, whatever that might be, his would never be missed.

He turned and started to walk toward Collins Street.

Behind him, shattered dreams fell as shards.

Adriana…

She needed to know. They were having lunch tomorrow and he would tell her then.

More shards.

My darling Adriana, too bad we're not going to have all those tomorrows.

He thought about ringing his mom, and decided to hold off until the Lyndon Institute had a go at him. She would get emotional if he told her now and that would make him emotional, and things would only get worse from there. Later, he decided.

When he reached the ANZ tower, he did not know how he got there, he took one of the elevators to the fifteenth floor. At his desk, he powered up the computer, checked his email Inbox, and groaned seeing two pages of mail. Urgent stuff every one of them, no doubt. Like anything mattered right then.

He stared at the list for a few moments, sighed, and opened the first item. Not dead yet, he still had a paying job to feed all those bills. Most were CCs for his information. Work done by his two team members and others affected by testing of his game. The QA people had gone through it in excruciating detail and identified a number of bugs. Nothing critical, but they must be eliminated before the game could be given to the beta test site prior to release. The site employed actual gamers, teens and some oldies, experts at ferreting out layout bloopers, logic holes in the game itself, or character inconsistencies. None could be allowed to slip through in the release version. FutureTech prided itself on producing bug-free games, their reputation justified. It took time to earn it, but it could be wiped out in a day by one shitty release.

His cellphone rang and he tapped the answer icon. "Andrew Payne."

"Mr. Payne, my name is Amanda Gregory. I am Dr. Gail Dalton's secretary. We received your medical records and arranged an appointment for three pm tomorrow, if convenient."

"Three o'clock is fine," he said.

"Very good. We shall see you tomorrow," Amanda said and hung up.

He saved the name and number in his Contacts list, figuring it would get some traffic.

He stood and made his way to a bullpen cubicle where Warren Kant managed three projects. Not a tall guy, and knew almost everything there was to know about VR games and how to put them together. FutureTech had a group of thinker-uppers in all their regional world offices who storyboarded every new game and conducted dry runs before considering a game for development. Before people like Warren got one, market analysts rated target players and sales potential. A game might be interesting in itself, but unless corporate figured it would earn them money, the concept ended up in the reject tray.

In his mid-thirties, totally bald, his boss looked up when Andrew leaned over a divider.

"How's testing?" Warren asked, as though he did not know. As project manager, he knew everything that went on with his three teams.

"*Tank War* will be ready for beta on Thursday," Andrew told him. "That's not why I wanted to see you. I need to take part of tomorrow afternoon off."

"Has it anything to do with the mole you had taken out last Friday?"

"It has. The Lyndon Cancer Institute wants to run some tests."

Warren raised an eyebrow. "Anything I should know?"

"I'll tell you once I know myself."

"Fine. I hope it's nothing."

"Me too."

He strode back to his seat and looked at more emails.

Glad when the day ended, Andrew followed the rest of the throng to the elevators, anxious to get out of there. Outside, he ran across the street and waited for a tram going to Richmond. It came, clanged its bell, stopped, and the doors snapped open. He pushed his way in, tapped the Myki card against the sensor pad, and grasped a steel stanchion, not a very happy man. He figured no one would begrudge him if he felt a little sorry for himself, and more than a little concerned. The unknown, not knowing, gnawed at his insides.

He stared vacantly at buildings crawling by, cars and pedestrians, to make time go faster. Across the Yarra River, he could see the Melbourne Cricket Ground and the tennis complex. For the first time in its history, they canceled the 2021 Australian Open, international travel still banned. Not into tennis, the cancelation did not bother him much. Cricket also took a hit, but apart from watching an occasional 20/20 game, his interest did not extend to dull five-day test matches.

On his left, sprinklers cast rainbows through the Treasury Gardens. Joggers gamely pursued winding paths, threading their way around occasional strollers. He saw a dad kicking a football with his son, the image lingering in his mind as the tram angled right onto Bridge Road. A few streets down, he pressed the red buzzer button. The tram sighed to a stop at Lennox Street and the doors opened. He tapped off his Myki and climbed out. A two-minute walk brought him to his three-story apartment block.

After a shower, he made himself a ham-cheese-tomato grilled sandwich and slowly ate as he watched the Channel 9 news, a tall glass of tropical fruit juice at his elbow. A smash on the Monash Freeway had caused chaos for drivers wanting to get out of the city, and the West Gate Bridge a parking lot as usual. The federal government assured people the Coalition had done everything possible to further stimulate the economy in the post-COVID-19 environment. The Labor Party blamed the government for everything, but had little to say how they would fix things. Premier Daniel Andrews congratulated himself for steering Victoria through the pandemic and revitalizing the state, after he first wrecked it. Really gripping stuff.

The bulky Peter Hitchener droned on. Andrew watched out of habit more than anything else. Something he did automatically every evening after work. Some images stuck in his mind, but most clips washed over him and receded like hissing surf.

He took a bite of the now cool sandwich and slowly chewed. A sip of juice helped the thing go down. His eyes strayed to shelves surrounding the TV and the rows of DVDs, CDs, and books. He had quite a collection, over two hundred. He read most stuff, but stayed clear of romance and vampire gore. He liked science fiction, but not the oldies like Asimov, Clarke, and Heinlein. Too dated for his taste. Baxter used to write some nice stuff, but his latest books were mush. Another author who lost it. He liked David Weber's early Honor Harrington stories, until Weber became dazzled with his literary erudition and his books became padded with rambling irrelevancies.

He conjured memories from stories he read and music he listened to, the TV forgotten. He felt lethargic and slowly slid into melancholy introspection. His eyes misted and he blinked back the sting. Something cold slithered down his back and his body shuddered. A tear slid down his cheek and his lips trembled from a surge of dark emotions. He sat there and more came.

All the things he kept bottled after seeing Ananankos burned their way to the surface, scouring everything they touched, his past and his tomorrows. Bile rose in his throat and he rushed toward the toilet, just making it. He threw up and stood there, gasping for breath. After a couple of dry heaves, his body settled down. In the bathroom, he washed his face and rinsed his mouth. Face wet, he looked at himself in the mirror. Hard hazel eyes stared back at him above a square jaw—not a boy's face at all. Nothing had changed on the outside, but he felt ancient inside.

He binned the sandwich remains and poured the juice into the sink. After standing for a minute in front of the droning TV, he pulled out a CD of Strauss waltzes and slid it into the player. With a tumbler of dark spiced rum in hand, he sprawled across the couch. *Tales From the Vienna Woods* filled the lounge with haunting strands and washed over him. When *The Blue Danube* started, he transported himself into *2001: A Space Odyssey*.

The tears began to burn again and he let them run as he

sobbed quietly.
Shait.

Chapter Two

Andrew carried a plate of toast and a bowl of mixed fruit he made himself—the canned stuff mostly sugar syrup—to the breakfast table. He fetched his coffee mug and turned on the TV to catch the seven o'clock news.

"This is ABC Breakfast, February 17, 2021. Good morning to all viewers, this is Michael Rowland. For those joining us, here are the main points.

"In a dramatic development, a Japanese Self-Defense Force destroyer sank a Chinese Haijing patrol boat escorting five fishing boats encroaching into Japan's territorial waters off the Senkaku Islands in the East China Sea. This followed a similar incident where a Vietnamese patrol boat rammed a Chinese fishing trawler off the Hoang Sa Archipelago. In response, Chinese fighters mounted a strike, badly damaging the Japanese destroyer."

Sitting beside Rowland, Lisa Millar looked suitably grave as she picked up the commentary.

"In response, the USS Nimitz carrier group destroyed Chinese facilities on the Subi and Mischief reefs, part of the disputed Spratly Islands group. Beijing has threatened 'a swift, proportional response for this unwarranted aggression'. Despite high tension in the area, there were no further exchanges."

Andrew stared at the TV, slowly shook his head, and switched off, not in the mood for more stupidity. Let them blast each other. Let it all end. His world had ended and he didn't care.

He cleaned up and locked everything. Outside, Melbourne always very much alive, the sun already warm, beating down from a clear sky. He would rather be on some deserted beach catching waves, but an office slave, he had responsibilities, which amused him hugely.

He managed to arrive at his desk by eight, his usual time. Sometimes, he came in much earlier, depending on the workload. He tried not to do it too often, as the practice could easily turn into an undesirable habit, which some of his colleagues fell into. He took his job seriously, but not addicted to it. As a junior project leader, he did not have *that* many responsibilities. Right now, he only had one: making sure *Tank War* got ready for the beta team tomorrow.

Predictably, the whole floor buzzed with the latest Chinese attack, everybody wondering what would happen next. He didn't give a damn.

Around ten, Adriana called, begging off their lunch date. A dental technician off sick, and she simply could not get away, promising to make it up to him tomorrow. Naturally disappointed, he understood, and made sure she did not feel bad about it. When she hung up, he also felt a mild flood of relief. With the Lyndon Institute appointment hanging over him, he would not be very good company. Before he forgot, he rang Hotel Windsor One Eleven restaurant and changed his booking to Thursday. He had never eaten in the classy place and looked forward to the experience.

A couple of fried dim sums for lunch, not feeling particularly hungry, he checked with his team, satisfied the game would be ready for handover. At two-forty, he told Warren that Elvis had left the building and headed for the elevators, something cold slithering in his stomach.

The tram clattered past the state parliament buildings, turned right onto Victoria Parade, and dropped him almost directly opposite the Institute. As he stood on the sidewalk, he looked up at the modern four-story building, the sun reflecting off its glazed windows, his thoughts mixed. The heavy transparent glass doors slid out of his way and he strode toward the security desk. The uniformed guard looked up and waited.

"Andrew Payne to see Dr. Dalton."

The guard checked his computer and held out a blue visitor pass. "First floor."

Andrew nodded and headed for the two elevators. When one came down, he got in and punched the first floor button. The double doors slid open and he walked into a bright, airy space that reminded him of an airport waiting lounge. A number of people were seated leafing through magazines or staring at nothing, absorbed in thought. Some wore masks, but social distancing no longer enforced. He strode to the reception desk and an attractive girl beamed at him.

"May I help you?"

"Andrew Payne to see Dr. Dalton."

"Have you been at the Institute before?"

"First time."

She handed him a metal pad and pen. "Please fill these out and I'll let the doctor know you're here."

He found an empty cloth-covered chair and scanned the list of questions. All standard stuff and he finished quickly. He dashed off his signature and returned the pad. About to take his seat again, certain of a long wait—he always waited everywhere— a striking middle-aged woman in a blue shirt and cream knee-length skirt, walked up to him and smiled.

"Mr. Payne? I am Amanda Gregory. Please come with me."

A jolt of anxiety shot through him. She led him down a wide corridor, stopped before a ceiling-high black door and knocked. Black for grim news, he figured. A muffled 'Come in' sounded from inside. Amanda opened the door and moved to one side.

"Mr. Payne, Doctor."

He stepped in and remained rooted. Expecting an elderly professor, he did not expect the young woman who stood behind the desk, wearing an easy smile that made her brown eyes sparkle. Tall, dressed in a perfectly cut charcoal suit, copper hair tied in a bun, she looked very attractive. Difficult to judge her age, though.

Twenty-eight perhaps. Her confident stance and an air of total authority made her captivating.

She held out a slim hand. "Welcome to the Institute, Mr. Payne. I am Professor Gail Dalton. I'll be your surgical and medical oncologist."

"Just Andrew, please," he said as he shook her hand, and sat down.

"Your condition has undoubtedly caused you a degree of anxiety…Andrew. A perfectly normal reaction. I'll try and explain as clearly as I can how I propose to treat you. This will help develop a positive outlook. Sinking into a depressed state will negatively affect your condition. If you have any questions along the way, don't hesitate to ask."

"Sounds good," he said, trying to calm his racing heart.

"Dr. Ananankos informed you that you might need a sentinel lymph node biopsy to identify possible spread of tumor cells. You know what are lymph nodes?"

"They employ immune cells called lymphocytes to destroy bacteria and cancer cells, and help fight infection." He knew all about lymphocytes and what they did from his research.

"That's right. Although we may need to do an SLNB at some point, I prefer to use a less invasive approach for initial diagnosis. What I want to do today is a sentinel node scintigraphy test to identify the extent of possible spread through your lymphatic system. This involves injection of a radiotracer to locate any tumor cell groups using positron emission tomography, PET, and SPECT-CT scans of lymph nodes in your arms and neck. The difference between the two is that the SPECT scanner detects gamma-ray emissions. The scans themselves normally take about fifteen minutes each. If there is identified spread, the procedure will take longer. You won't have to wait for the results. We'll know your condition immediately."

"Clear enough," he said, reassured by her positive manner.

"There is something else you need to know. Pathology examination of your melanoma biopsy tested for mutation of your BRAF gene. Among its many functions, it is responsible for regulating growth and cell division, and cell death. The gene can mutate under prolonged exposure to ultraviolet radiation, which causes it to be continuously active, allowing abnormal cells to grow and divide without check. It can also be inherited, but this has not happened in your case. Fortunately, there are no detectable changes in your c-KIT gene. If the cytokine receptor is altered, it can interfere with cell signaling, allowing uncontrolled expression—growth. Since your c-KIT gene is unaffected, this will simplify the treatment program."

"That's good to know. What do you recommend for treatment?"

"I will start you on an immediate regimen of checkpoint and angiogenesis inhibitors. Checkpoints are proteins on immune cells that are turned on to initiate a response. Melanoma cells often switch off these checkpoints to avoid being attacked. The inhibitors will help your macrophages and T-cells prevent deactivation and restore a normal immune response."

"Isn't chemo the preferred way to go?"

"Ordinarily, yes. I want to see the effectiveness of this treatment before resorting to chemotherapy and targeted radiotherapy, provided your melanoma has not spread into the lymphatic system. If there is cell migration, I'll carry out an immediate regional lymph node dissection. Immunotherapy is usually administered after a surgical procedure to excise the primary tumor site, but in its early stages, I found that preliminary application of targeted immunotherapy agents has yielded positive results."

"I'll not be having chemo?"

Dr. Dalton shifted in her seat. "Although chemotherapy is a proven treatment, there are serious side effects. Because it indiscriminately kills all rapidly dividing cells in the body, including cancer cells, it can cause nerve damage, loss of hearing, and increased risk of infection due to disruption of the immune response. Treatment is effective only as long as the drugs remain in the body. I prefer to use immunotherapy, which works with the immune system to recognize and destroy cancer cells. This option does not yield immediate results, as it takes the body some time to mobilize, but the effect is permanent with far fewer negative side effects."

"How long will the treatment last?"

She cleared her throat and rubbed her chin. "I'm afraid for life. These blockers are not a cure and don't lead to remission. They simply slow down the spread of tumor cells. Polypoid melanoma is particularly invasive, and survival rates beyond five years are not favorable, on the order of thirty to forty-two percent."

Although he knew this, the stark confirmation made him flinch. "I see. How is this treatment administered?"

"Checkpoint inhibitors can be taken orally. There will be some side effects, the degree depending on the individual. You may feel fatigued, develop a skin rash, diarrhea, and joint pain. These can be alleviated with appropriate drugs. A lot of progress has been made with tailored gene therapy over the last few years, and new treatments are emerging all the time. Your situation is serious, but not without hope."

"I appreciate everything you told me. It's a lot to take in."

"The Institute has a program of psychological and psychiatric counseling to help patients come to terms with their condition. A positive mental outlook can significantly extend the survival timeframe."

"Fight the little suckers, is that it?"

She gave a faint smile. "The brain is a fascinating organ with unrealized potential." She searched his face. "Do you have other questions?"

"A few, but I'd like to do those scans first and see what they say."

"Not a problem." She stood and patted down her trousers. "I'll have someone take you to Radiology."

A nurse injected him with a radiotracer, an antimony colloid solution, she said, and he watched TV for an hour while the tracer traveled through his body. He preferred a magazine or book, but could not have it. He had to remain still as possible, which turned it into a long hour. The PET scan took some thirty minutes, but the SPECT-CT only around twenty, which did not bode well. Afterward, they gave him coffee and he had to wait until the tests were analyzed. Eventually, Amanda Gregory showed up and ushered him into Dr. Dalton's office.

"Please, take a seat, Andrew."

He eased himself onto the edge of the chair, bit his lower lip, and clenched his fists in anticipation.

"Your scans are encouraging, which is good. However, there is some spread into lymph nodes in your left armpit. I identified only a few cells, that's why the scans took so long, but any migration from the tumor center is undesirable."

"I'd say. What's the long-term prognosis, Doctor?"

"The biopsy Dr. Ananankos performed excised significant tissue mass, and the scans did not identify any residual tumor cells, which is excellent. This does not mean there are none present. It is impossible to identify a single malignant cell. I'm hopeful the treatment I prescribed will enable your immune system to eliminate them. It won't be total remission, but your life expectancy will be improved significantly."

"Will this treatment remove the cells in my lymph node?"

"It should. We will run another set of scans in two months. In the meantime, I would encourage you not to expose yourself unnecessarily to strong sunlight. Especially your left arm. No more surfing or swimming…ever. When you do go out, wear suitable protective clothing."

"These tests, did they change my life expectancy prognosis?"

"They're improved, but I'll be in a better position to answer you in two months." She stood and held out her hand. "Reception has your drug pack ready, including renewal scripts, which should last two months. You'll also get an appointment date for your next visit."

Andrew took her hand. "Thanks, Doc. I cannot say you made my day, but I guess it could be much worse."

"If I may, it's important that you don't change your general lifestyle or routine. Try to maintain a positive attitude. If you find yourself in any difficulty, don't hesitate to call me."

"Is it okay if I indulge in a little self-pity for an hour or so?"

Her mouth twitched. "Go right ahead."

He nodded to her and walked out.

Outside, the summer sun still hung high in the sky, although it pushed close to six o'clock. He joined a crowd at the tram stop and hopped onto the first one that came. It did not go to Richmond, but he would catch the right one from Collins Street.

As the tram clattered downtown, he found himself strangely detached and objective. He had his emotional catharsis last night. Like the lovely Dr. Dalton said, he needed to maintain a positive outlook and fight the thing. All very well, but she did not have the tumor. He reminded himself that many melanoma victims survived more than five years…but not ones with polypoid melanoma.

Adriana…

He had hoped to have something going there. Something long and lasting. Regrettably, that can no longer be. In some respects, he found this harder to take than his cancer. They could still be friends, no? For how long, though? A desirable woman like that would get someone else and forget him. Would he want to hang onto a girl if she had terminal cancer? The city skyline had started to gather shadows, and he found himself unable to answer his question.

* * *

First thing the next morning, the Chinese and U.S. navies buzzing around each other in the South China Sea, he went to see Warren, and received the expected sympathetic noises. Nothing else the man could do. At his desk, he opened Outlook and started the day's email war.

His desk phone rang and he picked up. "Andrew Payne."

"It's Regan Price. Can you come over?"

He raised an eyebrow. A call from the executive director and Australasian region general manager not something he could ignore, but not altogether unexpected. Warren probably ratted on him.

"Be there in a minute."

He took the emergency stairs to the sixteenth floor where, in addition to programmers and analysts, accounting, legal, and head of development had their offices. Nora Steel, the general manager's confidential secretary, nodded as he walked by.

"Mr. Price is waiting for you."

He knocked on the plain ceiling-high door and walked in. Price waved and pointed at a chair. Not a tall man, youthful looking despite his forty-three years, promoted from his position as the Asia-Pacific marketing manager a year ago by Mountain View corporate, Price ran the regional area with a firm hand. Andrew always found him approachable and ready to listen, something he appreciated.

"Warren called a minute ago, and I wanted to see you. I'll not add my hollow platitudes to what he said, but I want you to know I'm sorry this happened to you."

"Thanks, Mr. Price. It's not quite the end of the world, but definitely not something I expected."

"Do you need to take time off or anything?"

Andrew shook his head. "They gave me a bagful of pills I must add to my diet, but otherwise, I can pretty much maintain my normal routine."

"With a positive mental attitude, I'm sure."

"That's what I'm told. This won't affect my work or MBA studies."

"Can I ask what is the long term prognosis?"

"Five years. Possibly longer if there is no further spread. I'll need another set of tests in two months, which will clarify my situation."

"I want to tell you that FutureTech will support you in any way we can. If you need anything, anything at all, my door is open."

Touched, Andrew nodded. "Thank you. I appreciate that." Taking this as a dismissal, he stood and walked out.

He decided not to tell his team. They were bound to find out sooner or later through the grapevine, but right now, he only wanted to get back to his desk.

One thing kept the day bright. He had a lunch date with Adriana.

At one, he picked her up and they strode toward Spring Street, jostling among a tide of pedestrians. As usual, traffic heavy along the broad boulevard. A dark cloud cut off the sun. He stopped before the imposing Windsor Hotel colonial façade, eyes running over the display windows and the pricy items inside. Adriana pointed at a crocodile Gucci handbag and grinned.

"I wouldn't mind having one of those."

"When I'm rich and famous," he told her.

"Dupe."

The spacious foyer with its wine-red carpet, tall wood-clad columns, dark tan walls, large chandeliers provided subdued lighting, made him feel like he walked into an eighteenth-century manor. Footsteps muffled by the carpet, they strode down a wide corridor toward a solid wood door with One Eleven embossed above it in white.

The spacious dining hall had enough empty tables not to feel crowded. An undercurrent of conversation made the place feel cozy. A severe-looking woman in a white shirt and red skirt walked up and allowed herself a small smile.

"A reservation for Andrew Payne," he said.

She checked her tablet and extended an arm. "This way, please."

Round tables covered with soft white cloth appeared scattered at random. Their hostess led them to a window table and nodded. Andrew pulled back a heavy broad-backed white chair for Adriana. She smiled at him and sat down. He took his seat and reached for the leather-bound menu.

"I've seen a better selection at a pub," he groused, and Adriana giggled.

"It's the atmosphere, you degenerate."

"Well, now that we're here, we'll sample what they have."

She reached for a finger-thick bread stick stacked in a tall glass and nibbled one end.

"Isn't it awful what's happening in the South China Sea?"

"Right now, I don't want to talk about it."

He wanted to enjoy what might be their last time together, determined to make her laugh and be gay, regardless of what came after.

"All the teeth done?"

"It never ends," she said. "But I *am* allowed to take an occasional lunch."

"Big of them."

"And you? Still gaming?"

"Finished. Today, they started beta testing. If all goes well, it will be released worldwide in May."

She frowned. "It's still February. Why such a delay?"

"The beta test will take three or four days. Then we need to fix any bugs, followed by another round of tests. All that takes time. Then there is advertising, production, and shipping to distributors. The plant in Mountain View does all that. It's quite a logistical operation. If the game doesn't sell, FutureTech could lose upwards of half a million."

"Wow. There is much more to this than I thought."

"A top-of-the-line game might retail for 160 bucks or more, but FutureTech sells it to distributors for around thirty-eight dollars. It must sell a lot of units to cover design, development, administration, salaries, marketing, and everything else to make an acceptable margin."

"I'll never look at a PlayStation game the same way," she declared. "I suppose the game must be compatible with most platforms?"

"That part is easy. The download routines automatically recognize the host hardware."

Their hostess glided to the table. "Ready to order?"

Andrew nodded to Adriana.

"I'll have the roast lamb pie and mineral water," she said.

"For me, the Reuben Club Sandwich," he declared and glanced at Adriana. "Some wine?"

"A chardonnay."

He looked up at their hostess. "Two glasses of chardonnay, please."

"Very good."

Adriana gave him a searching look. "I don't want any wine."

"Believe me, you'll need it," he assured her soberly.

"Mmm. You aren't planning to take advantage of me, are you, Mr. Payne?"

He grinned. "A charming notion, but I wouldn't dare."

They chatted for a while, and their meal and wine came quickly. Adriana eyed her steaming pie covered with a mushroom sauce, fried potato chunks, and assorted vegetables on the side, and picked up her tools.

"Looks good," he told her. "*Bon appetit.*"

"Thanks. That sandwich is large enough to feed four," she pointed out, eyes sparkling.

It did look imposing, filled with pastrami, sauerkraut, pickles, and Swiss cheese.

"A man's meal," he told her, and cut the thing in two. He picked up one half and bit into it. The mustard sauce gave it enough zest without being overwhelming. "I must admit, this is good."

"Better than pub fare?" she teased.

He chuckled. "You got me there. It's better. How's yours?"

"Very nice."

This morning, he took his first round of checkpoint inhibitors. So far, without any side effects. Probably too early for that, the body needing to adjust to the intrusion before it rebelled.

He sipped the icy chardonnay and nodded. Light and crisp without being too dry.

"Relocating to your South Yarra house anytime soon?" Adriana queried.

"I'll be shifting everything and moving in on Saturday. My Richmond lease runs out on Sunday. Dad rented a van and will help with the heavier things. My grandparents left me a fully furnished house with everything in it."

"After being in a cramped apartment, you won't know what to do with all the space there."

"It's a large place," he admitted. "Double-story, four bedrooms, and two bathrooms."

"All that on a small plot?"

"My grandparents built it on a double block. The street is mostly filled with standard terrace houses and tenements." He winced. "Nice house, but a lot of work to keep it clean."

"Poor you."

He grinned. "Not so poor."

She arched her eyebrows. "It must be worth a lot."

"I have no idea, but it set me up for life."

"Mmm." She pointed at him. "How's the arm?"

He felt a surge of tension. He placed most of the uneaten second half of the sandwich on the plate and took a gulp of wine.

Adriana saw the change in his demeanor and paused, knife and fork hovering over the pie.

"What?"

He looked into her eyes. "The pathology test on my mole came back positive. I have polypoid melanoma, Adriana," he said softly.

"Oh, God. This is horrible." Eyes tragic, she stared at him, then picked up her wine glass and took a large swallow. "You were right. I do need this."

He reached for her hand and squeezed. "You don't know how hard this is for me to say. I hoped we might build something more together. Something lasting. I don't know how you feel about it, since we only met. Whatever either of us might feel, it's all gone now."

Her eyes glistened as she fought for control. "I liked being with you, and I want to continue being with you. All this is very sudden, and I told myself not to rush things, but you broke through my defenses and I cannot walk away."

"Adriana, I'm under a death sentence. It just wouldn't work."

"What do you mean?"

"They gave me five years if I'm lucky. If the tumor spreads through my body, I'll have even less. Polypoid melanoma is very aggressive."

"But there are treatments! Chemo, radiation, and drugs."

"Even if they work, it will only delay the inevitable."

She gave a sour chuckle. "So, this is our last meal?"

"It doesn't have to be, but we must be realistic. I'm a walking dead man."

"Five years can be a lifetime," she said gently.

"With you, they could be." He tossed back the last of his wine. "God, I've properly screwed things up for myself, haven't I? Sun, surf, and girls, and I'm paying for it now with interest."

Her soft fingers brushed his cheek. "I won't leave you, no matter what."

He pressed her hand against his face. "I want you, Adriana. More than anything in the world, but not like this. You have your whole life ahead of you. Committing to me will only break your heart. I cannot allow that."

"Don't you think that's up to me to decide?"

"You're reacting emotionally. Once you start thinking logically about this, you'll realize that I'm right."

"Are you telling me to go away?"

"I don't want to, but I must."

"You're a dupe, Mr. Payne," she snapped, eyes flashing fire. With red spots blooming on her cheeks, she stood and hurried toward the exit.

He eyed his empty glass and snorted. "You got that right."

When he got back to the office, work did not interest him at all. After a quick review of the game's user guide, something he had gone over a dozen times, he checked his issues register for outstanding items. No real need as everything looked done, but it kept him from thinking about Adriana. It didn't work.

Here he was, meeting the most wondrous girl in his life, only to see her snatched from him. He glanced at his left arm, and a dark frown clouded his face. Better to have chopped it off when the mole first appeared. Hindsight, such a wonderfully useless tool. It only served to fuel destructive 'if only' scenarios. Maintain a positive mental attitude, Dr. Dalton said.

Doc, you can fold your positive attitude and tuck it.

Adriana had not walked away, he reminded himself. He sent her away because he did not want pity, from her or anybody else. There would be enough of it to cope with, and he so hated sticky family sentiment.

Memory memo to self: Call Mom.

Normally a levelheaded person, totally pragmatic when it

came to her work as an anthropology lecturer at Melbourne University, his mom had an emotional soft underbelly and heaps of empathy for everyone around her. A kiss on a sore thumb *did* make it better, as he and his sister found out. His mom one of those creatures who cared for the whole world. Since she could not when she saw what went on and what people did to each other, it made her dab at her eyes. Dad would then gather her in his arms and comfort her while she had a crying session.

Dad…a tower of wisdom and strength, which Andrew only recently came to recognize and appreciate. If it were not for his father's urging and encouragement, he probably would never have accepted enrolment in the MBA program. Christ, he only got his degree, and more studies held little appeal, regardless of any benefit an MBA would provide later in his career. Fun and surf, that's what he wanted. Bad enough having to hold down a job with FutureTech. The prospect of forty years or so gathering possessions and wealth so he could retire in comfort seemed a silly way to spend a life. He already lived comfortably and didn't pay for any of it.

With 2019 final exams done and his honors degree in the bag, about to turn twenty-two, no more studies—freedom! Dad hosed him down with some very cold reality. Andrew had his degree and the free ride had ended. Time to earn his own way, get a job, or find somewhere to sleep on the street. He never believed his parents would actually throw him out, but when his old man laid down the law, not prepared to bet it would not happen. With some things, his dad had no sense of humor at all.

He valued his father's advice and followed his philosophy on life…most of the time. Still, the prospect of chaining himself to a full-time job came hard, as did the realization his carefree life had ended. Time to become serious, a man.

If Dad were some factory worker or office clerk somewhere, Andrew might have told him to shove it, but his old man was a real somebody. A PhD in Mechanical Engineering, Associate

Professor at RMIT, industrial consultant and amateur astronomer, he knew what he talked about. His dad had not minded his wild behavior through high school and university. Youthful energy needed an outlet, albeit controlled. He and his friends were never bad, hooligans, into drugs, or hung out with genuine morons. Whether he knew it or not, the infusion of morality, ethics, and social norms his parents instilled in him had stuck.

A full-time job or the street. The law had spoken.

What to do? Andrew took the path of least resistance. In February 2020, he took the job offer from FutureTech and immediately found an apartment in Richmond. A compromise, perhaps, but he was free to do whatever he wanted without his parents' stifling, domineering atmosphere, as he saw it. Mom made a scene, wanting her baby at home, but his dad approved. Belana at seventeen, young and rebellious, wanted to move in with him. Dad did not rant or rave. He simply gave *her* a dose of reality.

You can move in with your brother if you want to, he told her. If he lets you. Will he support you, because once you're out of this house, I will not. What about your plans to attend university next year? Will he fund your degree? He'll have his hands full staying alive on a programmer's salary. Belana pouted and sulked, but in the end, she stayed home.

Memories chasing each other, he gave a long sigh.

He dug out his cell and scrolled down the Contacts list. Not sure if Mom lectured, he sent her an SMS.

See you tomorrow night around 7:30.

That meant she did not need to make dinner. Ready to put the phone away, it pinged and he checked the screen.

Fine, dear. Your dad and I are looking forward to it.

She probably thought he wanted to talk about moving out of his apartment. He did, but they would get more than they bargained for. He had no idea how he would break the news of his condition to them. In the end, he decided he would simply blurt it out, not relishing the inevitable emotional scene.

Around five, he powered down the computer, cleaned up his desk, and headed for the elevators with other escapees. It had been a hell of a day…hell of a week.

Outside, dark clouds had the sky boxed in. The city needed rain, but he hoped it would hold off until he got home. A hot, heavy northerly wind stirred the branches. It made no difference to people crowding the sidewalks, or the crawling cars. The gloom made the street and store lighting marginally brighter.

He waited patiently for his tram, most going toward Victoria Parade. His 5:10 came and he climbed aboard. The doors snapped shut and the tram hissed up the street, bell clanging. He stared vacantly at fellow passengers, the passing scenery outside, not seeing anything. Nothing registered. Nothing mattered. He simply went through the motions of being alive. Maintain your routine, Dr. Dalton said, which made him shake his head, bemused.

Don't worry, Doc. I'm not ready to step in front of a bus just yet.

The tram sighed to a stop at Lennox Street and he got off. The wind had picked up and the clouds had a grim brown tinge, camped solid overhead.

She stood under the portico, waiting. Andrew stopped in his tracks and gaped. A cascade of emotions raced through him. For a moment, his mind went blank, unable to cope.

"Adriana…"

Without saying anything, she slid into his arms and her soft lips sought his mouth. He wrapped his arms around her and held her with desperate longing, his world not so gloomy anymore. Confused, uncertain what was going on, he pushed all that aside, not caring. She came to him. Nothing else mattered.

After a sweet moment that wiped away every other kiss he ever had, he pulled back and gazed into her dark olive eyes.

"What are you doing here?"

About to ask how she found him, the question answered itself. She probably looked at his file.

"To see you," she said simply. A chilly gust made her wrap her arms around herself. "Can we talk?"

He tapped in the entry security code. The lock clicked and the glass door slid back. The elevator took them to the third floor, his eyes fixed on her. She stood there not moving, face set in determination.

Inside the comfortable apartment, the building's air-conditioning having to work hard during the last couple of weeks, he closed the door with a backward shove of his hand and turned to face her.

"Do you want to sit down? Can I get you a drink or something?"

She appeared not to hear him, her fingers twisting themselves into a knot.

"I actually don't know why I came," she said breathlessly. "I do, but it's all mixed up. I was angry when I left you. Here you were, someone I thought I might allow myself to get involved with—"

"Adriana—"

She lifted a hand. "Please, let me say this before I lose it totally." She took a deep breath. "The first time I saw you, I felt your desire, figuring it nothing more than hormones. I'm used to getting such looks. You were simply one of many. When you asked me out, I was amused by your directness. Then I saw your eyes. Not a boy, but someone serious who desperately wanted to be treated a man. For a second, I didn't know how to deal with that. Your eyes told me you were different, and I decided to take a chance. Many men have only one thing in mind when chasing a girl, but you wanted more than that. Perhaps for the first time in your life, and I felt flattered."

She bit her lip and gave a small smile. Andrew stood there, not daring to breathe, afraid he would say something stupid and she would flee.

"After our first lunch, I wanted to see more of you, still uncertain if you were a wolf in disguise. I never liked them. I saw the conflict of your emotions not to show yourself as one, because you really were one. Everything you told me about yourself proved it, but with me, you revealed another side of yourself. The serious, mature side. It showed that you cared about me, and I appreciated that. Then today…" She could not go on and dabbed at her eyes.

"Adriana—"

She shook her head. "Don't. Everything you said about your cancer made perfect sense, and I would be a fool to get involved with you." Her glistening eyes locked with his. "But you forgot one thing, Andrew Payne. What I feel cannot be reduced to logic, and life is not a computer program. You did the right thing to push me away, and I respect that act of unselfishness. I could tell you didn't want to, but you did it anyway, and that also made me angry. What I wanted did not appear to matter to you. There are a million sound reasons why we shouldn't be seeing each other, but when put on a scale with love on the other end, the reasons don't matter. I don't know what real love is, or if anyone does, despite stacks of books and poetry on the subject. I don't know if I love you. I hardly know you, but I do know one thing. I don't want you pushing me away. Everyone I know will tell me I'm being a silly girl, but I cannot help how I feel, and it's not pity. There, I've said it."

Andrew listened to her words and a lump in his throat threatened to choke him. He swallowed hard and wrapped her in his arms. His head buried in her hair, he slowly stroked her head.

"I know now how difficult this would have been without you," he mumbled, drinking in her smell. "I'm being selfish for wanting you, Adriana, and I agree about those million reasons. Everybody will say I'm taking advantage of you. Who knows, they might be right. If this is madness, I don't want it to stop. It would be easy for me to say that I love you, but after meeting you, I am not sure I know what that word means either. It is certainly not what I said to all the girls I went out with up to now. All I know, when you walked away today, it left a big, empty hole inside me. A hole that ached to see you back and fill it. For the first time ever, I wanted to care for someone no matter what it cost, and you did that. If it's for five years, five months, or five days, I want to spend them with you."

He pulled back and kissed her forehead.

A fat tear slid down her cheek, but her eyes shone with happiness.

"We're mad, both of us," she whispered.

"Totally," he agreed, and gently touched her lips with his. She moaned and her mouth opened. The kiss transported him into a land of magic he never wanted to leave.

She pulled back and searched his face. "You don't have to tell me you love me. You don't have to tell me anything. Just don't send me away."

"For all the days that are given to us," he promised, and cupped her cheeks between his hands. "For all time."

She sniffed. "That's the wolf talking."

"No, Adriana. That's the real me. You mean more to me than my life, and I find myself a little scared."

"I'm glad to hear you say that, because I am also scared."

He took her hand and kissed her palm. "When you walked off, I wanted to run after you, but I couldn't. I did not want you to stay because you felt sorry for me. What else could you feel? I didn't want that, but I could not dare hope that you felt more, and that you would stay because you did feel more. Then I saw you downstairs and I knew life was worth living again. You gave me that. You gave me back my life." He brushed her hair, and she smiled at him.

"You're a dupe," she said and kissed him hard.

Lightning flickered, setting the shadows jumping, and a rolling rumble walked overhead. Rain smeared the wide window. Adriana winced at the sight.

"I better be going."

"You can stay, you know," he told her softly.

"I think I better before we start something."

"I wouldn't mind," he said and grinned broadly.

She fisted him in the ribs. "Behind that polished façade, I always knew a degenerate wolf waited to pounce."

"I'll drive you home. You'll get soaked to the bone if you step into that crap."

She raised a hand. "No, it's okay. I'll catch a tram to Parliament, then a train to Footscray."

He glanced at the window. "And probably catch pneumonia along the way. Please, let me take you home. It's no trouble, really."

She frowned. "Are you sure? I don't want to impose."

"I'll get the keys."

On the way to the elevator, he turned to her. "Dinner on Saturday?"

She pursed her lips, looked at him, and nodded. "I would like that."

"Great. I'll pick you up at seven."

"What do you have in mind?"

"Surprise."

"Dupe."

Traffic clogged every street, not helped by the driving rain. His wipers swished back and forth at their highest setting, barely managing to keep the windscreen clear. Small torrents raced along the gutters, gurgling into overflowing drains. As suddenly as it came, the deluge stopped. Golden sheets of light broke through the overcast and lit the western sky, making everything sparkle.

"I haven't seen it this bad in a while," Adriana gushed as they hit Dynon Road that led into Footscray.

"These summer downpours can be pretty grim," he agreed.

On their left, two drivers gesticulated at each other, arguing who was responsible for the fender-bender. He figured there would be more than one out there this evening. Regardless of circumstances, the law remained clear. If he rear-ended someone, he paid. In a dispute, the insurance companies sorted it out.

He crossed the Marribyrnong River and Adriana told him to hang a right at Moore Street next to the market. A right at Lynch Street, and they were there. He parked his dark gray Mazda 3 and admired the sprawling brown brick veneer house with its front brick fence. Thick bushes guarded the driveway gate.

"Nice place," he told Adriana.

She leaned toward him and pecked his cheek. "Thanks for the lift. My parents will wonder what happened to me."

"Tell them you were fixing teeth," he quipped.

She laughed, unbuckled her seatbelt, and got out. A blast of cool air came through the door.

He watched her hurry through the small entry gate and pause at the front door. She turned and fluttered her fingers at him. He waved back and put the car into Drive, a satisfied smile plastered across his face.

As he drove toward the city, light rain speckled the windscreen. Regardless how dark or bleak outside, the world shone for him.

* * *

He turned left onto Murray Street, admiring the tall gnarled maples lining the nature strip on both sides, giving the impression he drove through a green tunnel. Low tenements and stately homes built on wide blocks lined the narrow avenue. In the old part of the city, Prahran property values were astronomical. Unless a couple won a lottery, they could only admire the scenery.

Number twenty-six came up and he slowed. The wrought iron gate, supported by two stucco-rendered brick columns, stood open. Dad's large blue Camry blocked the double garage. A two-meter wrought iron trellis rested on a knee-high brick fence running along the sidewalk, broken by tall columns that held the visitor entrance. Trees and broad shrubs in the front yard hid the colonial-style house and broad veranda. Lots of memories in that house, and a few ghosts.

Andrew drove in, wishing he were someplace else.

He pushed the doorbell button and heard hurried footsteps through the chime. Mom opened the solid wood door, beamed, and spread her arms in welcome. He walked into her embrace and held her tight. After an intense moment, he pulled back.

Still trim at forty-five, white slacks and cream T-shirt setting off her perfect English complexion, raven hair outlining a smiling face, she looked radiant.

"And how's my boy?" she demanded, pulling him in.

"You're a knockout, Mom."

She gave him a playful slap on the arm. "Go on. Save it for the girls."

In the spacious lounge, his father mixed drinks at the bar. Thick brown hair, bushy eyebrows, dark eyes, at 173cm, he looked imposing.

"How are you, my boy?" His father held out a tumbler of dark spiced rum. "Your poison."

Mindful of his immunotherapy drugs, he shook his head. "Thanks, Dad, but I'll take a rain check."

His father gave him a hard stare. Andrew did not normally refuse a drink.

"Do you want anything to eat?" his mom queried.

"I'm fine."

"Take the load off," his dad ordered in a heavy voice as he

eased himself onto a dark brown leather sofa facing a crammed ceiling-high bookshelf, TV, and other gadgets. "Quite a storm last night. Any flooding your way?"

"Not much," Andrew said as he sat down, the leather creaking under him. "It freshened the air, though."

"And made today steamy," his dad groused and took a pull of single malt.

Andrew tried it once, but could not stand the heavy aroma and smoky taste. He preferred spiced rum or bourbon. Each to his own, his dad once said.

Mom walked out of the kitchen holding a mug of tea, her favorite drink, and sat in a single-seat leather chair opposite them. The chair not to be touched by anyone, the law he learned from early childhood. It did not stop him and Belana frolick in it, despite an occasional playful smack on the bottom when Mom caught them at it. At night watching TV, talking, or playing a game on the glass-topped coffee table, that was Mom's chair, strictly off limits.

"About tomorrow, son," his dad started. "I'll pick up the van and be at your place around nine. Are you planning to leave anything behind?"

"I won't take the bed, but a second fridge might come in handy. The rest is kitchen stuff and clothing. I'll pack most of it tonight."

"You have enough cartons?"

"Plenty, Dad. Don't worry."

"In that case, it shouldn't take us long to load." His dad took another sip of whiskey. "Your new place has everything there already. Your mother and Belana did a thorough clean last Sunday. Planning to move in this weekend?"

"I'll have to," Andrew said. "My lease runs out on Sunday. By the way, Mom, thanks for the cleanup. I could handle it, you know."

She waved a hand. "Pfui, it wasn't much. Your grandparents

always kept a neat house and we looked after it."

"Where is Belana?" Andrew queried.

"At the movies with two of her friends," his dad said, eyes probing. "You seem preoccupied. Is anything wrong?"

Andrew gave a long exhale and lifted his left arm. No use putting this off. "My mole? I had it cut out last week. No more itching," he added with a wan smile.

"But…" his dad prompted.

"The pathology test came back positive for polypoid melanoma."

His mom dropped her mug and gaped in shock. "My poor baby."

Pale, his dad swallowed the rest of his whiskey. "I think I'll have another," he growled, stood, and strode to the bar. He filled up, took a gulp, and topped up again, then turned. "Melanoma…what's the prognosis? It can't be good."

"I had a PET and SPECT-CT scan on Wednesday at the Lyndon Cancer Institute in Carlton."

"They're the best," his dad agreed.

"My oncologist tells me…five years," he said in a rush.

"Five years…" his mom whispered and broke into sobs. His dad stepped toward her, but she waved her hand and dabbed at her eyes.

Andrew wanted to take her in his arms and comfort her, not much else he could do or say.

"I suppose you're under treatment?" his dad asked.

"A regimen of checkpoint inhibitors. They're making me a little sick in the morning, but there aren't any other side effects. I need to take another set of scans in two months to determine if there is any spread. If there is, it won't be good. At some point, I'll probably need chemo and radiation."

"You appear to be taking it well."

Andrew snorted. "You should have seen me on Tuesday when Dr. Anankos gave me the cheery news, but I'm over it now, mostly. According to my oncologist, I'm supposed to maintain a positive attitude." He chuckled. "What would help is if I swapped places with her."

His dad exhaled loudly. "I'm sorry as hell about all this, son. I would give my life to help you, you know that."

"I know, but there is nothing anyone can do. Shit happens."

"My poor boy," his mom moaned between sobs.

He smiled at her. "Don't worry about me, Mom. I've had a great life, and you and Dad were the best parents I could hope to have, even if I never said it before. Looking back, you *were* great parents. Anyway, it's not the end of the world. New treatments are coming up all the time."

His dad gave him a stern look. "This changes everything, son, and forget about moving. You're coming to live with us. It won't be good for you to be by yourself."

Andrew shook his head. "Remember why I left in the first place? Nothing has changed. Anyway, South Yarra is a stone's throw from here. It's not like I'll die tomorrow."

"Belana will be devastated," his mum mumbled. "She adores you."

"I've got five years, Mom. That's a hell of a long time for things to happen."

"Tomorrow, we'll bring lunch to the house," she declared in a firm voice. "On Sunday, you'll be lunching with us."

"Fine," he said and stood. "I'll see you tomorrow, Dad."

His mom got to her feet and cradled him in her arms, trembling against him, which did not make him feel better. After an endless time, he pulled back and wiped tears off her cheeks.

"It's okay, Mom. It's okay."

He saw that his dad also wanted to hug him. Instead, he stuck out his hand. "Tomorrow," he said gruffly.

Andrew clasped his hand between both of his and held it firmly, trying to swallow a lump in his throat. He turned abruptly and hurried toward the front door before things degenerated into an emotional meltdown.

Shait.

The car whispered to him as he drove up Chapel Street toward Richmond, the traffic moving steadily. He glanced at the clock display: 8:42. Deep shadows cloaked the street, and the city skyline lay wreathed in reds and orange streamers.

With something of a surprise, he found that he actually meant it when he said he had great parents. On reflection, they had given him a lot of slack to do some pretty outrageous things. There were rules not to be broken, and consequences when he crossed the line, but a little discipline tempered with tenderness kept him from being too outrageous. No need to dwell on some of the things he and his friends did out of their sight. It did not bring shame on the family, although it did cost him a sore bottom a few times. Not a case of Dad dispensing high justice and Mom making soothing noises afterward. She had a formidable arm in her own right. When he got a little older and started to understand some things better, words replaced the smack and were more cutting than her palm.

Seeing her broken and distraught, he wished for a way to take away the hurt. There wasn't, but Dad would put her together. Who would put him together? He had seen the anguish in his father's eyes. Everybody said that men are not supposed to cry or show emotion. What a lot of poop.

He *had* seen Dad cry when Belana was born. He remembered seeing him leaking tears bent over Mom, Belana all wrapped up in her arms. Andrew at the time…six? He could not comprehend why all the fuss over a baby. He had a little sister. Big deal. It made him wince the way Mom and Dad clucked over her.

The lights changed to red and he stopped behind a white minivan.

He had great parents, all right, and not too late to tell them that more often.

Memory memo to self: Call Mark and Orwell.

The light turned green and the traffic surged.

He parked in his reserved spot and slowly strode toward the foyer. A neighbor from another apartment walked in from the street and they exchanged shallow pleasantries waiting for the elevator.

He unlocked his place, stepped in, and closed the door with a shove of his foot. His home for a year, he reflected as his gaze drifted across the lounge and open kitchen. A good year. It took him some time getting used to living alone, doing his own chores and cooking, having all those things done for him by Mom, not appreciating what he had. Washing always came easy. Shove the stuff into the machine and let it do its thing. He intensely disliked ironing, especially his business shirts. In a quirky way, he did not mind ironing his pants, but faced with a stack of five shirts depressed him. A slow grin creased his face. Instead of forty years or more of ironing, he only had five—unless he got married, of course. Even then, he would not allow his wife to do everything. It had not meant much then, but he remembered Dad washing, ironing, vacuuming, and doing the dishes as Mom did other things. They both held full-time jobs, and Mom could not do everything. Not if she wanted some personal time for herself. On weekends, Belana also pitched in. Andrew remembered cleaning dishes lots of times, scraping the front and back yard lawn, hauling out the garbage container…and ironing his trousers. He had been doing it since he got his first long pants. Well, perhaps not the first.

He found it useful to have a top floor apartment. Most of the tenants were quiet and sensitive about creating unnecessary noise for others, which could not be avoided with a party going full blast. The thought of people stomping overhead if he had a first or second floor pad made him wince. A top floor place cost him a few bucks extra, but worth it. Penthouse living…

A stack of packing cartons lay at the foot of the TV next to five filled ones. He let out a loud sigh and went to work. Once started, he amazed himself how much clutter he accumulated, tucked into cupboards out of sight. This gave him an opportunity to bin stuff he would never use, including all his T-shirts, which made him sad for a moment.

Memory memo to self: Shop for long-sleeved T-shirts.

Around eleven, sweaty despite the air-con, he finished. Looking around, the place had lost its comfortable lived in feeling, a mere shell. He would leave the single bed and plain sofa for the next tenant, but the small fold-out solid wood breakfast table with matching padded chairs would go. His gramps' breakfast table okay, but heavy and old-fashioned. He would give it to his friends if one wanted it.

After a quick shower, he crawled into bed.

The gauzy curtains swayed gently when the warm breeze puffed against them. An occasional car whispered along the street. It took a long time before sleep claimed him.

* * *

"The fridge empty?" his dad queried, giving the bare lounge a last look.

"Nothing in the freezer, and I packed everything else," Andrew said.

"Are you sure you want to take the thing with you? Your grandparents left you a modern double door unit. What're you going to do with another fridge?"

"It's brand new, Dad. I only had it for a year. I'll stick it in the garage."

"Where it will gather dust and rust. I know you, son. You're a hoarder."

Andrew frowned, eyeing the fridge. Dad had him pegged right. He *was* a hoarder. Stuck in the garage, likely he would never use it.

"I tell you what. I'll take it, but I'll call Mark and Orwell if they want it. If not, I'll give it to the op-shop."

His dad nodded. "Fair enough. Right, let's get it loaded."

After breakfast, Andrew vacuumed and given the place a final clean, including the bathroom, then took some photos. He did not want hassles with the landlord over his bond. With everything loaded into the van, he went back to the apartment and left two keys on the kitchen bench. The lock clicked as he closed the door. End of a life chapter.

His dad already had the Europcar rental going when Andrew drove out with his Mazda 3. With a last look at the apartment block, he set off, making sure his dad followed. Church Street always busy, but flowed steadily. When he crossed the Yarra River, the name changed to Chapel Street. He could never figure out why they did that.

He clicked the voice command button. "Call Mark."

The display screen on his left showed Mark's full name, number, and address. His friend answered after two rings

"Hi, Andrew. What's up?"

"I'm moving to my gramps' place in South Yarra. They have everything there I'll need, and I wondered if you want the fridge from my apartment. There's also a large kitchen table and six chairs. If you don't want them, I'll call Orwell."

"Thanks for thinking of me, but I don't need anything right now."

"Not a problem. High-five."

"Five."

He hung up and called Orwell, not interested either. That made the job easy for him. The op-shop would get the lot.

He turned left into Toorak Road packed with cars going both ways. Two blocks down, a left past Rockley Gardens into the leafy, sleepy, Rockley Street. It had the same tranquil feel where his parents lived: tall established trees on both sides, neat houses, and low upmarket apartment blocks. There would not be any hotrod hooligans doing burnouts in the middle of the night on this street.

He parked at number fifty-eight and deactivated the alarm system using his phone app, then pressed an icon to open the garage. He got out and opened the two-meter iron double gate supported by sandstone columns. Next to the left column stood the visitor entrance gate. A short stone wall made of irregular sandstone blocks extended along the entire frontage, on top of which stood a meter-high steel trellis fence.

He stood back as his dad drove the van in, stopping before the double garage. Andrew left the gate open and walked along the driveway paved with black and brown stone tiles. He paused and looked up at the imposing two-story house built out of yellow/brown sandstone. A broad balcony stretched across the entire top floor, which also served as a portico. Pencil cypress stood tall along both fences. The front lawn looked lush and green, uncluttered by any flowerbeds. His grandparents had the house renovated three years ago, redoing the bathrooms, kitchen, laundry, and getting rid of a downstairs corridor to make the place roomier. Andrew had no intention to change anything.

He knew this house intimately, having spent many happy days here. He created a minor storm whenever he showed up, but his grandparents had not minded. A release from the formal discipline at home. Now, he owned he place, and the realization began to sink in that he'd be living here. He liked going to his mom's parents' house too, but this small mansion topped it.

His dad had the van's back door open and turned. "You going to admire the scenery or help me unload?"

Andrew smiled. "Be right there."

It did not take long to stack all the boxes in the garage. He would unpack later. It took time to unload his kitchen table and chairs, and lugging out the one from the house and loading it into the van. They tied it down and Andrew closed the garage roller door. Inside the kitchen, he opened the fridge and his eyebrows rose. Stacked with fruit, vegetables, eggs, cheese, and sundries, it had something else more immediately useful—beer.

He pulled out two bottles, got the tops open, and handed one to Dad. They clicked bottles and both took a long pull.

"I needed that," his dad said after a long exhale.

"Thanks for stacking the fridge."

"Thank your mom. The freezer compartment is also full. I also stocked up the wine cooler and bar."

"You shouldn't have done that, but thanks."

"I don't suppose you'll be drinking much for a while."

"Not when I'm on medication."

His dad gave him a speculating gaze. "Slept well?"

Andrew shrugged. "Well enough. Memories. You?"

"Your mother and I didn't sleep much. Also memories. You gave both of us quite a shock, you know. It will take a while to accept this."

"Yeah. Me too. Does Belana know?"

"We told her this morning. She was quite upset, as you can imagine. She wanted to rush off and see you and cry all over you. She'll be with your mother bringing lunch."

"Dad, I never told you how much I appreciate all the legwork you did to title your parents' place to me."

"It didn't take much. Our lawyer did it all as part of the probate proceedings. If you ever need someone good, call Reynold Parker. Tompson, Tompson, and Parker is a good firm with a solid reputation."

"And fees," Andrew mused. Someone had to pay rent for their Collins Street address.

"They're not cheap, but you get value," his dad said firmly. "What's more, you can sleep easy knowing they're looking after you. That, my boy, is worth more than any money."

Andrew could not argue with him there.

His dad placed the empty beer bottle on the breakfast bench and patted his stomach.

"I'll take the stuff to the op-shop and return the van."

Andrew walked out with him. Before his dad climbed in, he turned.

"Son…"

"I know, Dad." He embraced his father and held him tight, fighting down a surge of emotion.

The van reversed into the street, and his dad gave a wave before gunning it.

Andrew stood there, then ambled slowly toward his house. "Time for some paid work," he muttered.

He brought in all the boxes through the connecting door in the laundry, which also opened to the back veranda and yard. A ceiling-high glass sliding panel in the lounge led to the backyard. The plot ended some fifteen meters from the veranda against the neighbor's fence. Six pencil cypress broke the view. Along the fence, his grandma kept a veggie garden. He already talked to Mom about it, telling her she could still use it, otherwise, he planned to turn it into a lawn. He wasn't the green thumb type, that's all. She had a nice garden of her own and did not need another, but she said she would teach him to plant some vegetables. Much better than stuff from the supermarket. He would see.

The heaviest boxes were his books. He had enough room for them, but would likely need more bookshelves as his collection grew, having inherited and extensive library. Both his grandparents had been avid readers. Their collection would entertain him during the long winter months, as would their array of DVDs and CDs. The wireless speaker surround system delivered theater-quality sound, complementing the 65" LG LED TV. He moved his TV into the master bedroom. It might come in handy while in bed.

His few kitchen utensils, pots, pans and such, added to things already in the large pantry. He particularly liked the black Chef wall oven/griller/microwave unit with its smoky mirror finish. The black glass induction cooktop also futuristic. To complete

his relocation, he stuffed pillows, sheets, and spare winter com-
forters into cupboards.

He checked his watch: 11:25. A quick shower left him refreshed. According to the weather wall, it hovered around 23C
inside. No need for the air-con yet. Coffee mug in hand—one of
gramps'—he went through the spare bedrooms and bathroom.
Everything looked neat and tidy. Mom and Belana had clearly
gone through the whole house to get it ready for him.

A car whispered down the driveway and he hurried downstairs. His mom and sister got out as he opened the front door.

"Mom...Sis."

Belana gave him 'the look' she used when something went
wrong, and nodded. He hugged his mother and took the cloth
bag from her, his lunch presumably. She shook off her sandals
and slid her feet into slippers arrayed beside the door. His
grandma, determined to keep the hardwood red gum floors pristine, never allowed anyone inside with shoes. When they built the
house in the early sixties, river red gum plentiful and cheap, and
made stunning floors and furniture. These days, the wood had
become scarce and far too expensive for floors.

His mom took one look at her daughter and took the bag
from him. "I'll take this inside."

He nodded and turned to his sister. After a tense moment, he
opened his arms and she flowed into them, trying desperately not
to cry.

"I told myself I wouldn't make a scene," she mumbled into
his shoulder between soft sobs.

He stroked her back, then pulled back, ruffled her short
brown hair and kissed the tip of her nose. Her light green eyes
shone, ready to spill fat tears. She looked good in blue jeans and
a light brown T-shirt.

"It's okay, Bel."

"My God, Andy. This is such an awful thing."

"It made me appreciate what I have."

"When Dad told me, I almost died, wishing it were me."

"You were always strong, Bel, and you must be strong now."

"The thought—"

"Enough of this doom and gloom, I'm not buried yet. Let's go in."

"Do you want to eat?" his mom asked when he walked into the kitchen, holding his sister's hand.

"Put it in the fridge, Mom. I'm not hungry right now."

"Are you taking drugs or anything?" Belana asked, leaning against the breakfast benchtop.

"Pills to suppress cancer cell growth and give my immune system a boost to destroy them."

"No chemo or radiation?"

"I'll see in two months after they run more tests."

His mom glanced quickly around the lounge. "Unpacked everything already?"

"All done. Thanks to you guys, the place is perfect."

"Why don't you come and have dinner with us?" she said. "I haven't seen you in a while, and we can talk afterward."

He gave a sheepish smile. "I can't. I have a date tonight."

Belana's eyes lit and she clapped her hands. "Andy has a date. Andy has a date."

"Who is she?" his mom asked, not exactly enthralled. She had seen some of the girls he used to go out with.

"A dentist at First Teeth. I met her two weeks ago."

"What's she like? I want to know everything," his sister demanded.

"I'll tell you tomorrow at lunch, snoopy nose," he said, and she pouted.

"Spoil sport."

"She was born here, as was her father. His parents are Swedish and her mom is Greek. They live in Footscray, and now you know it all."

"And you love her very much," she added softly, a mischievous glint lighting her eyes.

Andrew jammed on mental brakes as the realization sank in that he did love her.

"I guess I do."

"What's her name?"

"Adriana."

"Nice. I would like to meet her."

"I'll bring her over for lunch or dinner one weekend."

"Come along, dear. We'll leave your brother to finish settling in."

His sister stepped into his embrace and he held her tight. They had always been close, and the thought of losing her churned his insides.

"See you tomorrow. Be good."

"If not, don't get caught, right?" she finished, then kissed his cheek and abruptly strode out.

He gave his mom a hug and watched them drive off. Inside, he blew his nose, opened the fridge, and pulled out two plastic containers. One held noodle soup, and the other a beef stew with chunky potatoes. He put the stew back in and poured the still warm soup into a saucepan, not wanting a heavy meal. He also needed to leave some room for tonight. Thankfully, apart from mild morning nausea, his body had not rebelled yet.

* * *

Andrew pressed the doorbell and it went off with a pleasant *ding-dong*. A few seconds later, the door opened and Adriana stood there. He gave a silent whistle of admiration and her smile widened. In a pale blue shirt and dark green pleated skirt, black pumps, she looked stunning. Not a flighty, giggling girl, but a woman with poise, maturity, and sophistication.

"Wow," he whispered in awe.

"I bet you say that to all the girls," she mused, pleased.

"I used to." He brought his arm from around his back and held out a bouquet of five red roses with a single central white bloom. "For you."

She cooed and sniffed the enticing fragrance. "Thank you, kind sir."

"For you, my lady, anything."

"I'll put these in some water. Back in a second."

When she returned, they headed down the narrow brick path to the street. She closed the small gate and looked up. Patchy clouds drifted eastward, the air perfectly still. Although warm, the low sun did not burn. His long-sleeved T-shirt made sure of that.

"Lovely evening," she gushed.

"With you in it, it's perfect," he said and wrapped her arm around his. "Let's walk."

She glanced at his car. "My mysterious rendezvous?"

"You'll see."

They crossed the street and continued to walk. At the intersection, they turned left onto Nicholson Street. When they reached the Hoa Sen Restaurant, Andrew stopped. Below the cool green neon sign stood a white lotus flower motif with pink tips.

"I hope you like Vietnamese."

"This is my surprise?"

"Hopefully a gastronomic delight," he told her.

"I lived in Footscray all my life, but I've never been to this place."

"We can go somewhere else if you don't like it."

"No, this is fine."

Inside, the place lively and almost full, Asian aromatic scents permeating everything. A petite Vietnamese girl—at least he thought she was Vietnamese—in black trousers and white shirt checked his reservation and led them to a back table. The atmosphere buzzed with animated conversation, many patrons not

Asian. She returned promptly with a large pot of fragrant tea.

Adriana looked approvingly at the colorful décor and nodded. "Cozy."

He poured for her, filled his cup and took a sip without adding sugar. The tea had a pleasant tangy, lemony flavor.

Adriana started checking the menu.

"The idea is to splurge, okay?" he said. "One dish won't cut it. So, go for it."

She chuckled. "Determined to fatten me up?"

"I want you to enjoy something nice. This place has some very good reviews."

"In that case…" She buried herself in the menu, her face getting longer as she turned the pages. "Goodness! This is too much."

"Don't think. If something strikes your fancy, order it," he told her.

Their minder came tablet in hand and smiled. "Ready?"

Nibbling a fingernail, Adriana looked up. "Chicken and sweet corn soup for me, orange duck, and stir-fried barbeque pork with noodles. Some mineral water on the side, please."

"Very good."

"Chicken and mushroom soup," he told her. "Pork and prawn rice paper rolls, chili tiger prawns, and stir-fried spicy chicken. A bottle of Chinese beer as well." A light beer he liked and should not upset his meds.

The hostess nodded, gathered the menus, and ambled off.

He took a sip of tea. "Looking at storefronts, there are a lot of Asians in Footscray."

"Since the 1980s, the Vietnamese and Asian community had pretty much taken over the suburb," Adriana agreed. "Their stores are amazing, and you can get some unbelievable food and spices. The Footscray Market is the same. My Mom and I often shop there. It's always busy, but Saturday mornings are a nightmare. Forget about parking anywhere close."

"Any social discrimination or tension?"

"I haven't seen any. Everybody appears to get along, and the Asians are all very friendly. There are kids doing an occasional night burnout, but it doesn't happen a lot." She gave him a quizzical smile. "Somewhat removed from South Yarra's snobbish atmosphere."

He laughed. "It is somewhat exclusive. Although many people there would not want a Vietnamese neighbor, they enjoy going to their restaurants."

"Old-fashioned ideas are changing, and people are accepting our multicultural mix," Adriana declared. "Did you shift into your new house?"

"This morning. I'm still getting used to all the space…and spare rooms I'll have to clean," he added wryly, and she chuckled.

"I'm sure you'll get used to it."

The soup came and they dug in. By the time they finished, the first course arrived. He pointed at the rice paper rolls.

"These are to share. I had some at a Prahran eatery, and I'm curious to try these."

Adriana forked a roll, dipped it into a bowl of sweet chili sauce, and took a bite.

"Pork, yum."

"Glad you like it." He bit into a prawn one and raised an eyebrow. "Tasty."

Adriana put in some serious work into her orange duck, and he fatally dented his tiger prawns. After a pull of mild beer, he nodded.

"This is really good."

"I must bring my parents here," Adriana agreed.

"Did you tell them…about me?"

"They know. Dad isn't too happy that I'm going out with you, but Mom is very sympathetic and understanding. What about yours?"

"I gave them the cheery news last night. Mom didn't take it

well."

"And your sister?"

"She is all broken up about it, but Belana is young, and death doesn't mean much to her yet. Like I told them, five years is a long way off."

"How do you feel?"

He shook his head. "No problems. A bit of morning nausea from the pills, that's all."

"I didn't mean that," she said, her eyes studying him.

He laid down his knife and fork. "It's tough having to face my mortality at twenty-four. At our age, we think we'll live forever. Yet, in a curious way, that hasn't changed."

"What do you mean?"

"I haven't changed. Not really, and neither has my outlook on life. I still feel there is nothing I cannot do. I'm very aware what's in store for me, but that's something intellectual and in the future. The emotional shock has mostly worn off. Last night, I realized that we're all living identical lives. We plan and work for tomorrow, but there is no guarantee that we will wake up tomorrow. Anything can happen to jerk that rug from under us. My situation is somewhat different because I know when that rug will go. That still doesn't mean I won't break my neck falling down the stairs before then."

She looked thoughtful, then took a sip of mineral water.

"I didn't think of it like that, but you're right. We don't know what's in store for us, especially with China and America facing off. Live your life to the fullest every day and rejoice when you see another dawn. Some poet said that."

"Glad did I live and gladly die. Lay me down with a will," he quoted. "Robert Louis Stevenson."

Her eyebrows climbed. "Are you into poetry?"

"Not particularly, but this phrase stuck in my head from somewhere. Apt, I figure."

"And when you live those glad days, can I share them?"

He reached for her hand and squeezed. "They'll be glad days if you're in them."

"I will be," she said softly.

Her barbeque pork arrived and broke the spell. She eyed the succulent dish. "I don't think there is any room left for this."

He took a bite of his spicy chicken and waved a hand. "Keep loading. It will go down."

"Around my waist," she quipped and laughed.

Pushing remains around their plate, both had enough.

"Dessert?" he asked her. "They have a very nice almond cake."

She shook her head. "Almonds and I don't exactly agree."

"Allergic?"

"Well, not actually, but every time I nibble on some, my body goes into revolution mode."

"Fine, no dessert."

He paid the bill and they strolled out, where night had claimed it all. Colorful neon signs glared bright, traffic noises seemed unnaturally loud, and people were everywhere. He took Adriana's hand in his and they walked slowly up Nicholson Street, not saying anything, content to enjoy a moment of togetherness. In front of her house, he unlocked his car and swung an arm at the passenger side.

"Want to go for a short ride?"

"What do you have in mind?"

"Another surprise."

"Dupe."

"It's only 8:30. Come on. It'll be something different."

"Mmm." She bit her lip, then nodded. "Okay."

Happy, he climbed in and started the engine. When she buckled up, he pulled away from the curb. Motoring along Footscray Road, the city before them stood bathed in light, the tall towers like Christmas trees. He drove across the Yarra, a short stint along the West Gate Freeway, and took the St. Kilda Road exit.

Brightly lit, the wide boulevard teemed with cars. He neared the Shrine of Remembrance and parked.

Adriana climbed out and looked around. "This is my surprise?"

"It gets better," he assured her and pointed at the Shrine.

"Is that where we're going?" she queried in a skeptical voice, not sure she liked the idea.

"Trust me."

They walked up a steep grassy slope until they hit a broad stone-paved walkway that led to the Shrine, bright under yellow floodlights. The imposing structure looked massive, the stone colonnades reminding him of Greek temples. They passed the eternal flame and mounted the steps to the first landing. They were not alone. Others strolled about admiring the views.

At the top landing, he turned and pointed. Adriana gasped when she took in Melbourne's glitter, car lights crawling like white and red fireflies.

"Wow," she managed in an awed whisper.

He sat on the steps and tugged her hand. After a moment, she sat beside him, her eyes roaming over the spread vista.

"It's magical," she breathed and rested her head on his shoulder.

"Not a bad view is it," he replied softly.

The night warm without a breath of wind, he soaked in the vista. Adriana at his side, he felt content. She stirred and he looked at her.

"Thank you," she whispered. "You're surprisingly sensitive, you know. Not at all what I expected."

"You thought I'm merely another one of those muscled surfers, all gonads and no brain?" he teased, and she smiled.

"When I first saw you, yes. Tall, good-looking, but still a boy. I couldn't have been more wrong, and I'm glad I found you, Andrew Payne."

He leaned toward her and brushed her soft lips with his. Her arms went around his neck and they kissed. After a very satisfying moment, he pulled back and stroked her platinum hair.

"You are the most wondrous thing that has ever happened in my life," he told her seriously, and their lips found each other again.

She sighed and stared at the city. "I never realized Melbourne could be so beautiful."

"I used to come here a lot as a kid. Only during the day. I wondered around the park and the Botanic Gardens, pretending I'm exploring in a deep jungle. I would take a tram from my parents' place and lose myself. Or I walked down to the Yarra and followed the river."

"Weren't your parents worried, wandering around alone?"

"Don't talk to strangers, and don't get into any car, that's all they'd say."

"They obviously trusted you to be responsible."

"Looking back, they did. Although at the time, I thought it a bunch of nonsense. Who would hurt me?"

Silence held them in its embrace as they gazed at the city.

Adriana stirred and stood. "This is lovely, but I need to get back."

"Care for a coffee and pastry somewhere?"

"Thanks, but I'm still getting over my dinner. I won't eat for a week."

He stood and took her hand. "In case I forget to tell you, thank you."

"For what?"

"For being you. For going out with me. For caring."

Her eyebrows arched. "If I didn't know better, I'd say the wolf inside you is preparing to pounce."

"And what a tasty meal you'd make."

"Dupe."

Hand in hand, they descended the steps.

Chapter Three

Dr. Gail Dalton cleared her throat. Andrew bit his lip and immediately prepared himself for bad news. He learned to read the signs and wondered if she knew she did it.

"I have your test results. They're not encouraging."

He steeled himself. "In what way?"

"Despite the immunotherapy treatment, your tumor has metastasized into several lymph nodes on the left side of your neck and both arms. There is also some invasion into your liver and left lung. This is disappointing, as I hoped for a better result."

Disappointing hardly the word he would use. Over the last two months, he had gotten used to his condition, and reconciled himself to a curtailed life. It had been difficult and he sank into mild depression a few times, but he pulled through. Things had settled into a comfortable routine, and his parents and sister no longer clucked over him every time he showed up. He and his friends continued to go out, and his work went on. His relationship with Adriana had blossomed, and she had become a very important part of his life. Without her, he might not have made it. He even considered asking her to marry him, not altogether certain he could make such an important life-changing step.

"I also hoped for better news. What's next?"

"I'll book you in for an immediate axillary dissection of affected lymph nodes and liver. Following surgery, you will undergo aggressive chemotherapy and radiation treatment for a period of two weeks. You'll be at the Institute during this time. I don't like using chemo, but it should destroy any residual tumor cells with minimal side effects. I'll also change your checkpoint inhibitors regimen and include interleukin-2, as the current treatment has not been successful, something the Institute is looking at very closely to determine why. At end of two weeks, you'll need another set of scans."

She would operate tomorrow? The seventh of May his birthday, and his mom made plans.

"Is there *any* good news here?"

"I'm afraid not. Your PET and SPECT scans identified cancer cells in most of your organs, but the groups are too small for surgical removal. About chemo…when individual polypoid melanoma cells metastasize, there is a significant time lag before onset of rapid angiogenesis, or division."

"Because of this, it might not be effective. Is that what you're saying?"

"Correct. However, your immune system is already primed with checkpoint inhibitors, and the new regimen should be able to identify and target any remaining cancer cell groups." Dr. Dalton locked her fingers and her eyes probed into him. "You need to know, although these procedures will significantly retard further spread—"

"The long-term prognosis isn't favorable," he finished for her. Mouth dry, heart palpitating, he gazed at the ashes of his life. "How long do I have?"

"Twelve months, perhaps fourteen."

He felt the shock squeeze his stomach and he grunted from the almost physical blow. His mind went into overdrive in an attempt to process the inflow of information, raging emotions, and conflicting thoughts. He stared Death in the face and saw it grin. It came for him, and his body chilled.

He did not want to die! Stevenson's 'Lay me down with a will' a load of nostalgic poop. A nice sentiment for someone pushing ninety, not twenty-four! Hardly fair, and felt he'd been cheated.

He wrapped his arms around his chest and shivered violently.

Dr. Dalton immediately reached into her desk drawer, pulled

out a small brown bottle, and removed two red pills.

"Take them. It's a sedative and will help counter the shock."

He took the offered pills, gulped them down, and winced at the bitter taste. Perhaps a psychosomatic effect, but within a few seconds, he started to feel better and color returned to his face.

"Wow. That worked fast."

"I am sorry. I don't know what else I can say."

"Thanks, Doc, but don't worry about me. I know you did everything possible. I simply drew the short straw."

"I haven't given up on you yet."

He gave a wan smile. "I hope this new round of treatments will do some good."

"I would strongly recommend that you take some psychological counseling to help you manage your condition."

"Keep a positive mental outlook no matter what, right?"

Her mouth twitched. "It might seem that it has not helped you so far, but your quality of life is determined by your mental attitude. Sliding into a depressive state will seriously affect your survival."

"I haven't lost it yet, Doc. I'll simply make some lifestyle adjustments." He took a deep breath. "Once I'm out of here, what then?"

"You'll be able to resume your normal routine. Debilitating effects will only appear in the final stages of the disease, and you will require hospitalization and palliative care. In the meantime, I want to take scans every three weeks to make any necessary adjustments to your treatment."

He looked at her. Her voice and attitude firm and clinical, and he initially considered it insensitive, but he had seen a glint of pain in her eyes when she pronounced his sentence. It clearly hurt that she could not help him, that she could not make this go away. How many other patients sat here before him, hearing their death knell? What did she do to make *her* pain go away?

Don't feel and survive, probably her professional mantra.

He had gotten a raw deal, but hers would keep going long after they buried him.

She cleared her throat. "Be here at seven. Don't take any food or liquids, other than water, after six this evening. No liquids in the morning."

"How long will the operation take?"

"Up to three hours. We must excise several lymph nodes and your liver, which will be done using minimum invasive endoscopy. Recuperation should be fairly rapid, and your liver will regenerate quickly. You will feel some post-operative discomfort, particularly under your armpits and neck, but that will subside within two days."

"Will you be performing the surgery?"

"I'll be your lead surgeon." She stood and held out her hand. "I'll take care of you, Andrew."

"Uh, tomorrow is my twenty-fourth birthday. Can we postpone this until Sunday?"

She gave a faint smile. "I doubt one day will make much difference…and happy birthday."

"Yeah, there's a lot to celebrate." He rose, shook hands, and walked out.

Outside, a cool breeze ruffled his hair. May would soon herald in the final autumn days. Dark clouds had settled over the city for what looked an extended stay, although no forecast rain. He did not trust the weather guys. Despite all their satellites and computer models, if they opened a window to see what the weather actually did, it would help make their navel gazing more accurate.

The pills Dr. Dalton gave him were still working well enough for him to feel his normal, cynical self. Once they wore off, what then? No liquids, he reminded himself. A small amber one, perhaps? Two?

As he waited for the tram, he dug out his cell and pressed a Contacts icon. His mom answered after two rings.

"Hi, Andrew. Nice to hear from you, dear. What's up?"

"I'm dying to sample one of your fabulous dinners, Mom, but I must contain myself and go without. If you guys are free tonight, I would like to pop over around eight."

"Fine. We'll see you then."

"Bye," he said and cut contact.

This latest development would send her into another round of grieving. It would also hit Belana hard. If only he could spare them that pain.

He gazed at the phone, shook his head, and pressed another icon. The conversation with Warren Kant short and to the point without any sticky sentiment. The poor man couldn't say much except wish him luck. The next call much harder to make and made his heart flutter. If only he could turn back time and undo some things.

"First Teeth, Penny speaking. How may I help you?"

"This is Andrew Payne. Is Dr. Teller available?"

"She finished with a patient. Let me check."

"Andrew?" Adriana queried a minute later.

"I need to see you."

"Where are you? The Institute?"

"I just left. I'm waiting for a tram."

"What happened?"

"I'll fill you in when we meet."

"It's bad, isn't it? I can tell from your voice."

"See you in ten," he said gruffly and hung up. This would likely break her heart, and would not do much for his either.

Life had turned into one long crappy deal, and the fates had heaped it on him generously.

The tram sighed to a stop and he hopped on. He got off at Collins Street and crossed to the sidewalk. Adriana already waited outside, face grim. A brown leather bag hung from her left shoulder, something he got for her in March. Not Gucci, but close enough. He took her in his arms and held her, feeling her tremble. She pulled back and he smiled.

"Hello, gorgeous."

"What's going on?"

He pointed at one of the green steel benches the local council had installed along the sidewalk.

"Let's sit."

Hands clasped in her lap, her eyes threatened to spill. She watched him and waited.

"I don't quite know how to say this, so I'll blurt it out. My melanoma has spread and I need surgery to remove several lymph nodes and cut out part of my liver."

"Oh, God." Her lips trembled as she fought for control. Then the tears came. He reached for her and she sobbed quietly against his shoulder. After a moment, she leaned back and dabbed at her eyes.

"You'll be well afterward? Tell me you will."

"I'm afraid not, my sweet. Those five years we hoped for? Well, I now have a year at best."

She moaned and sagged against him, shoulders heaving uncontrollably. It took some time before she composed herself. She sniffed, took a deep breath, and looked at him with determination.

"Remember what you said once? Five years, five months, or five days? We may not have those five years, but we still have one."

"Adriana—"

"You want to send me away? Logic didn't work last time, and it won't now."

Something hot broke inside him and burned. His eyes stung and he tried to say something, but the words would not come. Throat tight, he swallowed hard.

"I don't deserve you," he managed to choke out.

Her face cleared, radiating warmth. "I know, but I'll keep you on probation anyway," she declared, then turned serious. "This must have been hard for you the first time, and it'll be even harder now. I can tell. You need me, and I want to be there for you."

He crushed her against him. "I'm being selfish, but I do need you, desperately."

She looked at him. "Let's go to your place. You need some physiotherapy, Mr. Payne. Doctor's orders."

He had seen that look before and learned not to fight it when she made up her mind about something. Right then, he did not want to change her mind.

"Your patients…"

"You're my patient now." She stood and tugged at his arm. "Our tram is coming."

"A taxi will be quicker," he told her firmly and raised his arm. She did not protest.

* * *

Adriana shifted and snuggled closer, head resting on his shoulder. Her fingernails marched across his chest, and a mischievous smile played across her face. His right hand moved slowly down her side and thigh, marveling at the silky smoothness of her skin. A woman's skin lived to be stroked, loved, and admired. Men only had thick hides.

When the taxi dropped them off, he paid the driver and followed Adriana through the small visitor gate to the front door. Inside, he almost forgot to switch off the security system in his rush to take her upstairs. Once in the bedroom, they did not hurry. He had all the time in the world to love and cherish this enchanting woman who stole his heart. She walked up to him and began to unbutton his shirt, her green orbs smoldered fire.

Standing there, both naked, he lifted her chin and gently kissed her. She tugged him toward the bed and took charge with restrained ferocity. Time stopped. She lay in his arms and he felt complete and content. Nothing could be more fulfilling if he died there and then. He did not and was glad, because he hoped there would be more moments like this.

After a brief rest, she straddled him.

Finally satisfied, they held each other, not saying anything. Among the room's shadows, he lay there and stroked her.

"How come you're so muscular?" she murmured, fingers marching across his chest.

"Genes, I guess. Plus a bit of sun and surf," he added playfully.

"Your father is also a strong man."

"You should have seen my gramps. At sixty-five, he could pick up a ten-kilo bag with one hand. As a kid, I felt that hand more than once."

She giggled. "You've been a bad boy, eh?"

"Not at all. Getting into minor mischief like other kids. He never hit me hard, just enough to sting. I know that many child behaviorists are saying never to hit a child, and the permanent trauma that can leave, but I don't subscribe to that theory. I pushed my limits to see how far I could go, and accepted the subsequent reprisal. Scolding didn't matter much then. Once I got older, that's when words started to mean something." He looked at her. "Did your parents ever smack you?"

"My mom did, but I always knew why. It hurt my pride more than my bottom."

"And what an exquisite bottom it is."

She fisted him lightly in the ribs. "Dupe, and randy old goat."

"Not that old, and everything still works."

"And I'm glad it does," she whispered and nuzzled his cheek, her breath sweet.

"Remember the first time we went to dinner at my parents' place? You were so nervous and fidgety."

"You were no different," she countered. "You thought my

dad would flatten you."

He chuckled. "His initial scowl did intimidate me a little, but after a couple of drinks and we started to talk, he turned out to be an okay guy."

"Next to you, he is my favorite man. Your mom is a doll, though."

"One of a kind, all right. You know, we should bring our families together for a grand dinner, and we'll have it here. The dining room table is huge and can easily hold all of us. I'll cook," he said and grinned at her. "You're welcome to land a hand."

"Sounds good. Can we do it soon?"

"Before I—"

"I didn't mean it like that, you degenerate."

He laughed. "I know. Just yanking your chain, my gorgeous."

"Not funny."

"Talk to your parents and text me a date."

"Getting back to your father. All those credentials, and an amateur astronomer."

"A very wise man, although it took me some time to appreciate it."

She palmed his face and turned it to face her. "You'll be all right, won't you? I mean, living by yourself—"

"I'll be fine. The initial shock has worn off, and one year has become another number. There are some things I'll have to do sooner than planned, but otherwise, nothing has changed."

"I could move in with you, you know."

"Your parents wouldn't approve, and I don't want to cause such a problem for you."

"I only care about you."

"I would love having you here, but it's better if you don't. If things had not changed...Say! Let's go away somewhere. In July, perhaps. Melbourne gets pretty miserable then, and it would be fun being somewhere warm and sunny. We could go to Darwin—"

Adriana winced. "Too steamy."

"Or Perth. I've been there once. A really terrific place. Still warm in July and not humid at all. We could take long walks along the beach—"

"No surfing or swimming. Isn't that what Dr. Dalton said?"

"I won't go into the water, and I'll cover myself. Anyway, what difference does it make now?"

She sniffed and looked like she would cry. He cursed himself for being a jerk.

"I'm sorry. I shouldn't have said that."

Her eyes bored into him. "Do you want to go away?"

"I wouldn't mind. If you could, that is. I don't know how busy you are at First Teeth."

"There's no problem taking a couple of weeks off."

"I don't want to push you into anything," he added hastily. "Think about it."

"Nothing to think about. What about your job?"

"I can take time off anytime I want. I thought about resigning, but I like what I do. My home project is keeping me busy, but not that busy."

"What are you working on?"

"I'm almost finished testing my 3D rendering sets macros, and I'll use them to create a new VR flight simulator game pro-totype."

"How will it differ from what's out there now?"

"Current games provide an external mockup and a simple view of an aircraft's cockpit, operated using a hand-controller, a gaming console, or standard keyboard. That cannot be avoided…yet. In my game, a person will sit in a chair and the VR headset will project a totally realistic cockpit and steering column. He would need to correctly operate the thrust levers and all other instruments to fly the aircraft. It'll be the next best thing to being in a real one, and it will *feel* real."

"You sound pretty excited about it."

"VR is the future for heaps of applications," he said eagerly, "and I have ideas you wouldn't believe. I'll talk to my lawyer to patent the 3D sets, and once my prototype is ready, I'll run it past FutureTech. I'm sure they'll be interested."

For several moments, neither said anything. Caught up in his dream, he had forgotten that his clock now ran on fast-forward. He might not be able to do everything he wanted in the time left, but if he could talk FutureTech into recognizing the quantum leap in game design his rendering sets would give them, they could become the dominant player in the VR world. He would be satisfied with that.

Adriana kissed his cheek and slid out of bed. "I need to get going."

He watched her dress, then got up and slipped on a black silk kimono with a yellow dragon at the back. He did not want her to leave, but understood why she had to. At the foot of the bed, he retrieved his jacket, pulled out his phone and held it up.

"I'll call Uber to take you home. Unless you want to go back to the city?"

She glanced at her wristwatch. "At four-thirty?"

He made the booking and walked her down the stairs.

"Thanks for everything," he whispered and stared into her eyes.

She gave him a tight hug.

When the Uber cab pulled up, she gave him a tight hug and hurried toward it. She did not look at him when the cab drove off. No need, her eyes already told him everything.

The front door made a hollow bang when it closed. He could read so much into that, but not in the mood to philosophize.

In the kitchen, he opened the fridge. The stuff in the freezer would last, but all the perishable things needed to go, including the veal stew leftover he made yesterday. Living alone, he learned quickly how to take care of himself. He spooned enough into a small saucepan for dinner, poured the rest into a large Ziploc bag and stuffed it in the freezer, then cleaned out the fruit and veggies container. In the garage, he dumped the garbage bag into the disposal bin. The council collected rubbish on Wednesdays, too early to wheel out the bin tonight, a Friday. It would also be a clear 'nobody at home' beacon, and he'd be in hospital next week.

Memory memo to self: Ask Dad to take out the bin on Tuesday night.

In the laundry, he checked the washing basket. Shirts and socks mostly. He shoved the stuff into the washing machine, added powder, set the cycle, and let it rip. While the thing ruminated, he went upstairs to pack a bag with everything he would need for the two weeks at the Institute. His laptop and a couple of books prominent among them. With his birthday party tomorrow night, he did not want to be rushed.

At five, a bowl of warm stew on his lap, he turned on the TV and switched to YouTube. Trawling through the selections, he came across an old 1960s Dave Allen show. For no reason he could think of, he clicked on it. The comedian not bad, and some of his jokes made him smile, as did the sketches. Stew finished, he strode into the kitchen and cleaned up.

At 7:50, he gave a long sigh and ambled into the garage, not looking forward to what would happen next. He drove out, set security, and headed toward Toorak Road. It only took some six minutes to reach his parents' place. He parked in their driveway, set his mouth, walked to the front door, and pressed the bell button.

Hurried footsteps came from inside and the door opened. Belana grinned broadly and hugged him.

"Hi, Andy! Glad you could make it."

He followed her in, feeling like a man walking to the gallows. *Shait.*

* * *

A cute little nurse showed Andrew into a private room. Her

short black hair framed a radiant round face and penetrating azure eyes. Tight white trousers outlined an attractive form. She pointed at a folded gown on the bed.

"Please disrobe and put that on. Keep your underwear and socks. It gets cold in the operating theater," she added with a conspiratorial grin.

He regarded the flimsy garment with distaste. If the operation did not kill him, the pneumonia would.

"Thank you…"

"Despina. I'll be looking after you during the day shift, Mr. Payne." She nodded and briskly walked out.

Everybody so efficient, he mused. At least they gave him a private room. He knew the Institute was primarily a research facility, not a hospital. According to their website blurb, referrals were redirected to proper hospitals like the Peter MacCallum Cancer Center, a public facility. Dr. Dalton must like him to keep him at the Institute. Perhaps she only considered him as another challenging case and material for her next paper.

The west-facing room had a large window with an unspectacular view of rooftops and buildings. At least he would get lots of afternoon sunlight. A large castor-mounted bed stood tucked against the corner. Apart from the TV screwed to the wall, a clothes cupboard, a round table, and three visitor chairs, the room otherwise bare. Definitely not a place to camp for an extended stay. He wondered about the food, having heard uninspiring stories.

He unpacked his bag and changed. The short gown left him feeling foolish and exposed. About to sit down, a knock on the door and a grim orderly pushed in a wheelchair.

"Please sit down and I'll take you to the operating theater."

No sense of humor, Andrew decided. Given where he worked, best to leave humor at home. He eased himself into the chair and enjoyed the ride. The elevator took them to the fourth floor without seeing anyone else about. The orderly pushed open a wide double door and rolled him into a decidedly cool theater. Two nurses in light blue gowns and masks fussed over the instruments tray. A male doctor stood beside a woman studying a large screen. The woman turned.

"How are you, Andrew?" Dr. Dalton asked pleasantly and walked toward him.

"Want to swap places?" he queried hopefully, and saw her smile behind her mask.

"Next time around, okay?" A glance at the orderly, and he made a hasty retreat.

He did not need help to get onto the operating table. One of the nurses covered him with a warm white blanket, which he appreciated.

She leaned toward him. "Please remove your gown."

He sat up, undid the thing, placed it at his feet, and lay back. A shiver rippled through him as a shot of anxiety made him want to leap up and run from this place.

Hands across her chest, Dr. Dalton bent over him. "These are simple procedures. Although it may not seem that way to you. Try and relax."

He nodded, not trusting himself to speak. A fine image he made, trembling like a kid.

She looked at one of the nurses and nodded. The nurse placed a black rubber mask over his face and told him to breathe deeply. He started…

A tunnel of light expanded rapidly, and he blinked and opened his eyes. Just like that, he came awake, aware of everything around him. It happened the same way when he had his tonsils out. No drowsiness or lethargy, although he heard people react differently. He turned his head and winced as mild pain pulled at the left side of his neck. He felt a little uncomfortable with pads under his armpits. A catheter on his left wrist connected him to a drip bag.

Despina beamed a ray of sunshine at him. "Good morning.

Did you sleep well?"

Obviously not morning and likely one of her nurse/patient lines.

"No dreams," he croaked, his throat very dry.

She held a glass of pink liquid to him and he sucked through a glass straw, feeling overwhelmingly thirsty.

"Thanks, I needed that."

"How do you feel? Any nausea or pain?"

"All good," he told her and meant it. Whatever happens next, the messy part now over, unless his lovely doctor felt like doing more carving.

"You probably feel hungry, and I'll bring something later. Drink as much as you can, okay? Dr. Dalton will be along shortly." She hit him with another smile and walked out.

Not long afterward, his favorite doctor strode in. She stopped beside the bed and looked at him.

"The operation was very successful, and I don't expect any complications. We'll start radiation and chemo first thing tomorrow, which will allow your body to recover from the operating trauma." She glanced at the drip. "I already started the immunotherapy regimen. If you experience any degree of unusual discomfort, buzz a nurse. I'll be back this evening to check on you."

"Thanks, Doc. I'm sorry what I said about swapping places. No one deserves what I have."

She smiled. "That's okay. Rest and I'll see you later."

The door closed after her and he turned his head to stare out the window. High in the sky, the sun cast a pool of light into the center of the room. After a while, his gaze became fixated on the featureless ceiling and his eyes closed.

"Andrew," a melodious voice called urgently, and someone shook him.

Whatever he dreamt vanished and he opened his eyes to see an angel hovering over him.

"Despina…"

"Time for lunch," she said brightly and helped him sit up. She shoved a spare pillow behind his back, which helped. The pain in his neck and arms only a mild throb.

"I'm not hungry," he mumbled, wanting to recapture the faded dream.

"You must eat something, or I'll feed you through a tube."

"I see you have a sense of humor, but you try that, and I might not be the one with a tube down the throat," he countered sourly. "Go away."

She ignored him, swung a broad wooden tray across his lap and wheeled the food cart closer to the bed. He eyed the tubs of yogurt and fruit salad she placed on the tray with indifference. A piece of crumbed something, surrounded by peas and rice, did not look very appetizing.

"You be a good boy now and eat," Despina ordered. "You don't want me to get into trouble with Dr. Dalton, do you?"

"What can she do? Make you scrub the floors?"

Her eyebrows rose. "You don't know? She's a very strict disciplinarian. All the nurses and resident researchers walk softly when she's around."

Not the picture he had in his mind of the lovely doctor, but he had only seen her twice, not counting this morning. Resigned to the inevitable, he sighed.

"Okay, I'll behave."

"Good," she said and wheeled the meal wagon out the door.

He drank some water, then started on the fruit. Once his stomach accepted the invasion, his appetite got the better of him, but he only managed to eat half the crumbed chicken. The rice had a nice flavor. He mashed in the peas and set to work. Finished, he pushed the tray to one side and drank more water.

Full, he let out a loud exhale and wriggled down into the bed. He tried to get rid of the extra pillow, but his right arm protested when he lifted it. Tempted to buzz someone, he decided not to bother with trivia, feeling comfortable enough. Without willing it, his eyes closed.

After what seemed only a minute, he heard the door open and came instantly awake. His dad stood there looking serious, his mom and Belana hovering beside him. Andrew grinned, pleased to see them, although he had pretty much ruined his birthday party. At least he allowed himself to indulge, not certain when he could have rum or whiskey again.

"Hi, guys. Welcome to my new pad."

Belana rushed to his side and planted a kiss on his cheek. "How's the invalid?" she bubbled.

"So so," he said, wiggling his palm from side to side.

His mom walked in, stared at him for a moment, churning emotions clear on her face, and tried a small smile. She gave him a tender hug and kissed his forehead.

"My poor baby."

He never liked being called her baby, poor or otherwise, and told her so repeatedly, but what his mom did not want to hear, she ignored. One of life's things he learned to put up with.

"I'm okay, Mom."

His father glanced at the drip bag and the bandages around his neck. "Are you comfortable? Any pain?"

"A little uncomfortable, especially my arms, but that should go away in a day or so. That's what my doctor tells me anyway."

Belana pointed at the drip. "Is that chemo? Will you lose your hair and stuff?"

He grinned. "Immunotherapy drugs, snoopy nose. Chemo and radiation start tomorrow, and for your information, I'll not lose my hair. The treatment will not last that long."

"Will it make you sick?" she added.

"I don't know. I'll find out, I suppose."

"Did you have anything to eat?" his mother asked, concerned.

He glanced to his right, but the meal tray lay folded against the bed. Someone clearly cleaned up while he napped.

"I had lunch."

"I can bring you a Big Mac or a pizza, if you want," Belana declared brightly, and he laughed.

"I doubt that's something I'm allowed to eat. Not a bad idea, though."

After some pleasant, but inconsequential chatter, he got more hugs and they left, promising to visit tomorrow. He told his mom she shouldn't, but she did not appear to hear him. A worrying type able to soothe away troubles and pain, she could not do anything for his troubles, and that clearly upset her.

Nobody could do anything for him. Not even Dr. Dalton. She would do the necessary thing, but Death did not need to hurry. It had a certain customer.

He had plenty of time to acquaint himself with death. The initial shock when Dr. Ananankos told him he had melanoma slammed him hard and he realized he might die, but still something far off. He mostly felt rage at the unfairness of it all. Why him? Even his five-year sentence did not seem real. Death happened to somebody else, the oldies. At twenty-four, five years seemed an eternity, but he only had twelve months now. Yesterday, faced another type of eternity…and was terrified.

After a tearful session with his parents on Friday night, his birthday party last night not a happy occasion, his mom sobbing inconsolably, Belana grim, he drove home. His comfortable, spacious new home now a chamber of echoes for his thoughts. Suddenly, he did not want to be alone with those thoughts. When he finally crawled into bed and switched off the lights, Death came out of darkness and looked at him with its many faces conjured from his imagination. Some were benign and angelic. Others were crawling horrors. He wondered if any were real.

As he stared into blackness, what surprised him, he did not actually fear dying. It would be like falling sleep, except he would not wake. He feared what might come after, if an after existed at all. Would he burn an eternity in some fiery cauldron, an amusement for the demons? Did hell actually exist, or merely an invention of priests to keep the faithful in line?

Not religious, his parents were also firm atheists. They taught him right from wrong, and instilled ethics and morals necessary to survive in a complex social environment. Would a vengeful god punish him because he did not believe? If a creator existed, he could not accept that such a being would inflict an eternity of damnation for wrongs committed in someone's short lifetime, regardless how evil those wrongs might be. It seemed all out of proportion. Andrew could not believe in such a harsh god. Easier to believe in priests promising hellfire if parishioners did not yield to their authority without question.

Whatever the truth might be, he would find out soon enough.

It took a long time before night embraced him and he slept.

Around five, according to his cell, Despina wheeled in his dinner, casting rays of light and cheer with her smiles and mere presence. He did not know how she did that, glad to bask in her warmth. If it were not for Adriana…

As he picked at the food, he wondered about her. She had not called or visited. Probably busy with patients. He glanced at the cell beside the laptop on the bedside cabinet. Should he call her? Later, he decided. He finished his fruit salad and pushed back the tray.

At six, he heard a knock and the door opened. Adriana peered in and hurried to his side. He opened his arms, ignoring the twinge, and she leaned over him. His hungry lips found her and everything faded into irrelevancy. She pulled back and brushed his cheek with feathery fingers.

"Adriana…" He wanted to drag her into bed, never letting go. Something of his desire must have shown, for she gave him an amused smile.

"I know what you're thinking, you randy old goat."

"Bet you don't," he teased, his heart filled with joy.

"I do, and I want to, but what if a nurse walked in? I'd die."

"I would tell her to get out and close the door after her."

She laughed, a tinkle of running water, and pulled a chair close to the bed. He reached for her hand and squeezed.

"I'm so glad you're here," he said.

"I wanted to call, but I had one of those impossible days. I haven't even had time for lunch. Just coffee and tea."

"I had one of those days myself," he assured her.

"I can see that. All those bandages…"

"To keep me warm."

"Dupe. Everything went well?"

"Dr. Dalton seemed pleased, so I guess things are humming." She glanced at the drip bottle. "Chemo?"

"Immunotherapy drugs. Chemo and radiation tomorrow."

"How are you coping?"

"I would rather not be here." He shrugged. "What can I say?"

"As long as you're alive, there is hope," she told him sternly.

He sighed. "I don't know. Nothing I read has given me hope."

"Did Dr. Dalton talk to you about experimental treatments that might help you?"

"Not yet, but I suspect she'll get around to it. I figure she wants to try the proven methods first, I guess. I'll talk to her about it." He glanced at his laptop. "I'll read up and see what I can uncover. Nothing much else to do around here."

Her eyes filled and she sniffed. He brushed her cheek.

"I'm not done yet, you know."

"I only wish I could swap places with you," she gushed.

A wave of tenderness swept through him. "Even if you could, I wouldn't let you. You're my flower and I want you to bloom for me. If I know that you're out there, it will keep me alive."

She leaned against him and he cradled her in his arms, murmuring soothing words.

She pulled back and dabbed at her eyes. "You tell Dr. Dalton that one year isn't enough time to do everything we want. Hear me? Tell her to pull her finger out and do something about it or

I'll scratch her eyes out."

He grinned, liking the idea, and seeing Dalton's expression.
"I'll do that."

They chatted for a while, then she left and took the sunshine away, promising to bring it back. He looked forward to it.

Around seven, Dr. Dalton came to check on him. After some routine questions, and advising him what would happen tomorrow, she left.

Not in the mood to watch TV or play with his laptop, he managed to do his bathroom routine and settled himself under the covers. When he closed his eyes and darkness took him, he welcomed it with a smile.

* * *

Andrew waited for the heavy glass doors to slide apart, strode to the steps landing, and stopped. An elderly couple on the sidewalk glanced at him, and slowly ambled along. Two faces among a tide of forgettable others. Carry-on bag in hand, he gazed at the bustle along Victoria Parade. Cars always multiplied on a Friday, and this one no exception. A fresh southerly tugged at his hair—he had not lost it—and he silently thanked his mom for bringing one of his sweaters.

Bunched dark clouds obscured most of the sky, but they were not harbingers of rain. That's what the weather presenter said on this morning's news. The situation between China and the U.S. had eased, with China agreeing to dismantle a number of bases on several artificial islands it created in the South China Sea. Confronted with a determined American administration to enforce the 2016 Permanent Court of Arbitration ruling that China had no historical rights based on the nine-dash line, Beijing appeared reluctant to force the issue, at least for the time being.

Pushing end of May already, he reflected. Cold, rain, and wind. Nothing to write home about. Not yet winter, but almost there, it set a miserable stage for what he could expect. May can have some gorgeous, sunny, still days to remind people the sun had not actually packed up and gone somewhere else. He treasured those days, having learned that every day must be valued. There would not be all that many left for him.

Funny how life worked. Some people drifted all their lives through a predictable, unvarying pattern, and then everything ended. What they achieved and experienced during those humdrum years merely to exist hardly important. Motes on the river of life. It did not mean anything. His mote may be battered somewhat by eddies and fast currents, but he felt that in his twenty-four years, in some respects, he lived a lifetime. Intense, and not without some rewards. Not enough time to enjoy them? His years were now compressed into months, but he would pack into them decades of living.

Chained to a bed for two weeks, glaring at drips from a bag that never left his side, hammers for his eyes, feeling weary, used and ancient as the chemo drugs worked him over and radiation zapped through his insides, probably creating more cancerous cells along the way, he had lots of time on his hands to think. There should be a daily quota on thinking, he reflected. Better not to think and have peace. Has anyone really achieved such a thing? Did those Hindu fakirs or fuckers actually reach nirvana by gazing at their belly button? Or perhaps the Buddhists. Hell of a way to spend a day, he figured. Empty the mind and encompass the cosmos, right? It must be a damn small cosmos.

In his bed, the drip tube an inseparable companion, he spent his time thinking, among other things, but those were mundane body housekeeping chores. His parents visited regularly, as did Adriana. His eyes softened as her angelic face floated before him. Mark and Orwell came a couple of times to talk over the good old days, and hashed unabashed over his grim future. They never had a dying friend, and the clinical aspects fascinated them. A few laughs and they disappeared into the amorphous mass of other dust motes. They could not do anything for him except wish him luck. Nobody offered to swap places. Would he? Probably not. Each had enough problems managing their life to worry about someone burning his at both ends.

What did all that thinking get him? Acceptance, a release from self-pity, a measure of inner peace, and a lot of soul-searching, if he had the right word for someone who did not believe in that stuff. Pulling out all his inner drawers and seeing what lay hidden in them might be more appropriate. It might have been better to leave some closed, but like Pandora's Box, once opened, there were no U-turns. Besides, he had not lived long enough to do anything mean and nasty to anyone. Some of the pranks he pulled on Belana caused his conscience a twinge, sorry for the pain he caused her, but she usually got even using verbal sabotage with Mom, which ended with a scolding for him, and when younger, a warmed rear end.

The one thing he figured thinking had done for him, he grew up a whole lot. That happens when a year is compressed into a day and he got to shake the hand of Death. At least it happened to him. He lost his innocence, and the stars in his eyes were now merely pinpricks into faded dreams. First came the unfair phase, then helpless anger, moody retrospection, then a bit of enlightenment when he realized he still had many pieces in the jigsaw of his life to put together. He would simply have to assemble them faster.

No use bitching about things he could not change. Once he came to accept that brutal reality, he developed a much more positive mental attitude. Dr. Dalton had recognized his inner struggle and eventual resolution, and approved. His regret, and a sharp one, the years he hoped to have with Adriana could never be. Five years, five months, five days…It took him two weeks of serious deliberation to realize how profound those words were— until the outside world stepped in. She could never be his in total union. Both their worlds forbade such a thing. Well, not exactly forbade, but severely frowned upon as stupid on his part, selfish, and unreasonable. They lived in a social matrix and had to obey its laws, willingly or otherwise.

He accepted the stark fact that even if they could be together, he would never bind her into something formal, not for one lousy year, regardless of his five months, five days sentiment. It simply would not be fair to put her through the inevitable anguish she would face to satisfy his selfish desire. She would suffer enough as it is. They would share what time he had left for as long as she wanted to, and he would gladly pick up any pieces of love she cared to throw his way. It would have to do, and she would need to accept what he could give her. The last thing he wanted is see her pine for him. A dewy white rose, she would find someone else to share the abundance of her love. That is how the great wheel turned. At least that is what he thought.

His Mom and Dad? They would mourn, but the pain would eventually diminish, if not the memory. He read that it always did. The body protecting itself from self-annihilation. They raised him to be responsible, and that had to be enough. A shitty deal that they would end up burying him when he expected the reverse, but they'd get over it.

An Uber cab waited at the curb, and Andrew descended the steps to the sidewalk. He got in and the driver merged into the flowing traffic, knowing already where to go.

Adriana wanted to meet him and take him home. In the end, she settled for dinner tomorrow. Dinner tonight at Mom's place. Anyway, he needed to get domestic and return to his house routine, and some shopping more than likely. Thankfully, tomorrow a Saturday, he had two days to get everything sorted out, which his mom had probably done already. He found that he actually looked forward to Monday and getting back to work, whatever that might be. Did Warren have something for him, or would FutureTech keep him there out of pity? He gave a lopsided grin.

There would be no pity once they saw his flight simulator proto-type. He had not spent two weeks simply staring at the ceiling. A wireless connection gave him access to his home server, and he applied himself tirelessly. The laptop not VR, but that's all he had to work with. The evening nurse sometimes had to snatch it off him. The wheels at Tompson, Tompson, and Parker were already rolling to patent his 3D rendering sets.

Eat your heart out Microsoft and Google.

Developing his macros at home, he scrupulously avoided us-ing FutureTech's proprietary editing software, making do with an off-the-shelf toolkit. This complicated his work somewhat, but also protected him from potentially having his patent application rendered invalid.

He glanced at the carry-on bag beside him loaded with immu-notherapy pills that were now part of his permanent diet. It might be worth taking them merely to eke out another day or week. Perhaps not, but if he did not, Dr. Dalton would know and give him a tough time. Possibly even force-feed them to him through a drip. He smiled at the thought. His lovely doctor had come to see him every day, dispensing encouragement and nodding ap-proval at his progress.

The chemo shock worked, but did little for his internal dispo-sition. There were days when he wondered how many times he could throw up. Then came the numbing fatigue and pain in his knees and ankles. By comparison, the ache in his neck, arms, and side where Dalton carved out his liver, were mere distractions. Sympathetic to his discomfort, she insisted it had to be done. Once he placed himself in her clutches, he had no further say in what happened to him. He could have walked out and nobody would stop him, but he valued the days this treatment would give him.

Yesterday, she ran an intense set of PET and SPECT scans and seemed satisfied. No more chemo or radiation, she told him. His lymphatic system, lung, and liver were clear. Cancerous cells were still present in his body, but the blockers should keep those in check—for a while. Once they mobilized and got going again…

Her long-term prognosis? Still a year…maybe. Nothing could stop his cancer from metastasizing through every organ, slowly shutting them down. He should feel fine for the next nine months or so, then the cumulative disruption to his organs would start to become apparent. He stopped her there, not wanting to know. He had researched that part himself and knew what to expect.

In three weeks, another set of scans.

At least his health insurance covered what must be an enormous bill. The bastards tried some fast maneuvering, denying part of his claim based on non-disclosure of his condition, a load of poop, of course, but Reynold Parker appears to have sorted them out, because Andrew had not received anymore negative emails. A person pays premiums for years, but when it comes to making a claim, the microscope comes out looking for loopholes in the fine print.

After two weeks staring out a window, it felt good seeing the open city again. The same, yet different. He now looked at it with new eyes. The version of himself who thought only of sun, surf, and girls now truly gone. Well, he still thought of girls, but only one filled his life now. In an indescribable way, he felt if his connection with Adriana broke, he would bleed.

Had he changed so much, or his drug-doped mind talking? It did not matter what caused the transformation. The new him was here.

* * *

The bell rang and he heard hurried footsteps inside. His mom stared at him for a moment, then spread her arms and embraced him.

"My poor baby. Home at last."

His dad stood in the doorway and nodded. "Son."

Andrew pulled back. "It's good to see you guys. And how are you, Dad?" he said and held out his hand.

"Fine," he answered soberly as they shook.

Andrew smiled at his mom. "I love you desperately, but don't call me your poor baby or boy anymore, okay? We're done with that."

His mom blanched. After a moment of scrutiny, she nodded. "Welcome home," she said in a strained voice.

Did she think she had lost him? Birds leave their nest, and he left his some time ago. A lifetime ago.

Belana ran out, squealed, and threw herself at him. "Oh, Andy! I missed you." She planted a kiss on his cheek, then frowned. "You've lost weight. They forgot to feed you over there?"

"It's the chemo, sis. Throws everything out of whack."

"You're still taking that stuff?"

He shook his head. "All done."

"Good. We'll put some meat on those bones. Right, Mom?"

His mother smiled faintly. "Absolutely, my dear. Okay, inside, everybody. I'm getting chilled."

Belana took his hand and dragged him in. She planted him on the couch and snuggled close, one arm wrapped around his.

"Tell me everything. How is it?"

His dad walked over from the bar and held out a tall glass. "I know you're not allowed to drink, but this is a non-alcoholic mixer. Try it."

Andrew took a sip and raised his eyebrows in appreciation. "Not bad. You must give me the recipe."

His mom sat in 'the seat', studying him. "You *have* lost some weight, dear. Or is that also too endearing?"

"Aw, Mom. Don't be like that."

His dad shook his head at her. Belana noted the undercurrent of momentary tension and tugged at his arm.

"You were telling us about your stay."

"Okay, overall. They had this drip connected to me 24/7, which became a nuisance after a while."

"I saw it."

"I had to watch myself when I moved to make sure I didn't pull the tube from the catheter. I had radiation and immunotherapy in the morning. In the afternoon, a nurse switched bottles and started me on chemo."

"That saucy little one?"

He grinned. "Despina. She took care of me during the day. In the evening, I had a grumpy older nurse who took a blood sample. After a while, the inside of my elbows looked like a pin cushion."

"Did chemo make you sick? I asked when we visited, but you wouldn't say."

He winced at the memory and Belana laughed.

"It made you spew?"

"Every day. I didn't like that part. It also made my knees and ankles ache. Really not that bad, and the nurses gave me stuff for the pain."

She touched the scar on his neck. "Is that where they took out the lymph nodes?"

"That's right. Under my arms as well. The scars should fade after a while."

"Is it still sore?" his mom asked.

He shook his head. "Not anymore, but I won't be doing any hard exercise for a while."

"No sun and surf?" Belana smiled mischievously.

He looked at her. "Not ever."

She sobered instantly as the import of his words hit her, and the realization that he was dying.

Sensing that things might get emotional, his mom slapped her lap and stood.

"Dinner time. Help me with the soup, Belana."

His dad led him into the dining room with everything laid out formally. As usual, Mom went all out, he mused as he sat down.

"What are your plans, son?"

"Back to work on Monday and pick up the pieces. There are bills to pay," he said with a grin.

Belana carried in the soup tureen and sat it on the table. His mom placed a glass bowl of croutons beside it.

"Dig in."

His dad looked at him and tilted his head at the soup. "Son…"

Andrew smiled, filled his dish, and passed the ladle to Mom. He tried the thick vegetable soup, but could hardly taste anything. A shame, as he enjoyed her cooing. Probably the chemo, he figured.

"This is great, Mom," he said to please her, automatically adding ground pepper. For him, a dish without pepper not fit for human consumption. Mom tried to cure him out of this habit, but he had an iron-clad defense. Why have it on the table if not meant to be used?

"Thank you, dear. I'm glad you like it."

"We had Adriana over for lunch last Sunday," Belana gushed.

Andrew looked at her. "I didn't know that."

"I like her."

"Your mom and I are very impressed with her," his dad confided.

"A sensible girl," his mom agreed. "She came to visit you?"

"Almost every evening, and sometimes during lunch. It doesn't take long by tram from Collins Street to the Institute."

"Are you going to marry her?" his sister demanded, eyes sparkling.

"Belana!" His dad scowled at her, but it did not faze her at all.

"Only asking."

"I would love to, sis, but the way things are…"

His mom pointed at his dish. "You're not eating much," she

said, tactfully steering the conversation from an awkward subject.

"It will take a few days for my appetite to come back fully."

A succulent lamb roast followed the soup. He took a small piece, a wedge of pumpkin, some potato cubes, with a mixed salad on the side.

"By the way, Mom. Thanks for stocking up the fridge."

"We had to do some shopping for ourselves last night and got a few things for you. I knew you would need milk and bread."

"You got me more than that."

"Are you all settled in?" she asked.

"I did some washing this afternoon, but I had nothing else to do." He cocked an eye at her. "Your doing?"

"Belana and I did a light dusting last Saturday."

"Thanks, guys."

"Pfui, it wasn't much," Belana said. "Now you owe me."

"What's in store for tomorrow?" his dad asked.

"Nothing too strenuous. I'll work on my flight simulator prototype, and probably take a light nap in the afternoon. All the chemo and stuff has made me tired." He turned to his sister. "And I'm going out with Adriana in the evening. Just so you know."

She rolled her eyes. "A romantic outing. How thrilling."

"I talked to Reynold Parker about your patent application," his dad put in. "He is intrigued with the concept. One of his office gofers had to do some digging to make sure you were not infringing on another patent, but you're in the clear. That's quite something you did, son."

"Thanks, Dad. I hope FutureTech will take it on board. It's only a prototype game, and it'll take a bit more development to turn it into a commercial product, but my rendering sets will speed that up a lot."

"Will they take it? From what you told me before, this could make all their existing games obsolete."

"Not obsolete, perhaps, as they can be reworked using my

sets, but it should give their corporate office a lot to think about. If they're not interested, there are other VR development companies around, which I'm sure FutureTech will be aware of. I created those macros on my own time and they have no claim over them."

"You would license your sets to them?"

Andrew nodded and smiled. "They won't be getting them for free, that's for sure. Mr. Parker already made useful suggestions how I should handle this, and he registered Usque Vision for me to minimize my tax liability. If I handled everything under my own name, the tax department would clip me at the top marginal rate of forty-five percent. Working through my company, I'll only pay thirty percent."

"Smart move. You have something very valuable, and if you're not careful, the corporates out there will steal it from you."

"I appreciate what you're saying, and I'll be careful."

His mom waved a hand. "Computer games, rendering sets, let's talk about something else." She turned to her son. "Eat. What you had so far would feed a bird."

Belana leaned toward him. "There's cheesecake for you later," she teased, knowing it was his favorite.

"Sounds good."

He managed a few spoons of the delicious cake topped with blueberries, chased down with freshly brewed coffee, and had enough, feeling weary. His mom saw this and told him to go straight to bed. He did not argue with her.

When he got home, feet dragging, feeling like someone had beaten him up, he crawled into bed and everything went black.

* * *

He woke refreshed to a clear, still day. As he shifted in bed, he felt something wrong. This occupied his mind for a few seconds before he recognized the faint smell of antiseptic. No monitor beside him tracing wiggly lines, and no drip tube. He really got to hate that catheter. The spot on his wrist where they stuck it into him still tender and red, but at least they took the thing away. He expected Despina to walk in at any moment pushing the meal wagon. No more sunny smiles. He would miss her and those smiles.

A shower washed away his lethargy and he dressed. The first thing he did as always, was switch on the ABC news. While it droned in the background, he made himself a cup of instant coffee and fried a single egg, then prepared a slice of toast. Beside the coffee mug, he arranged four pills. Looking at them, he marveled at the science that lay behind them. Capsules of life, literally. Organic chemistry, such an infernally complex thing. The human body truly a wondrous piece of machinery.

Morning chores done, he went to the local Coles supermarket for some shopping. His mom had not gotten everything he needed, but he did not mind. She got the essentials. For lunch, he planned to have a little rice and some fried beef cubes. The general light weariness he felt probably something that would stay with him always, but long walks and exercise should build up his stamina and make him feel better. That's what Dr. Dalton told him. Determined not to waste a great morning, he decided a stroll through the Rockley Gardens just what the doctor ordered.

After lunch, he took a refreshing nap. Later, a coffee mug at his side, he walked into a spare bedroom he used as his workshop, and powered up the server and computer.

He logged into the FutureTech system and checked his emails, not intending to take any action, curious to see what happened while he loafed. A lot of CC stuff, and one from Warren that said *Tank War* release sold well. He took the news with indifference and logged off. The game not his problem anymore.

A gulp of coffee and he started third-level testing of his prototype. Around four, tired of the thing, he switched off and went downstairs, mindful of his seven o'clock rendezvous with Adriana. He had a booking at the La Mariett, a French restaurant not far from the Southern Cross railway hub on Spencer Street. When he made it on Thursday, he felt confident in his fitness. Given what happened last night at his parents' place, that confidence somewhat exaggerated. This morning, he looked at himself in the full-length mirror, and a stranger stared back. His once muscular, trim body had wasted more than a little. Something needed to be done to pad things out. Whatever happened this evening, he wanted to see Adriana somewhere other than from a hospital bed.

Around six, he took another shower, slipped into heavy black pants, a light blue raw silk shirt, and brown jacket made of lightweight calf leather. He glanced at himself in the mirror and nodded.

"Cool."

It would do.

Around 6:20 according to his Rado, he heard a car pull up in the driveway, and wondered who it could be. He did not expect his friends; they would meet next Saturday. Mom and Bel? Possible, but they knew he'd be going out. He shrugged and went down the stairs.

He opened the front door and stood rooted. Adriana smiled broadly at his goggling expression.

"What…" He found himself stuck for words.

She dropped the heavy bag she held and stepped toward him. Her arms went around his neck and her sweet mouth locked with his. After an eternity of time, she pulled back.

"Surprise."

In dark blue trousers and cream turtleneck, she looked gorgeous.

"I was about to head out to pick you up," he finally managed.

"And I saved you the trouble," she said brightly, then frowned. "You don't seem pleased to see me."

"Stunned, but very pleased. Why are you here? Not that I mind, of course," he added hastily.

"To be with you. What else?"

"But—"

"Trust me. This will be better than any old restaurant." She gave him an admiring look. "Dressed to kill, I see."

He picked up the bulky bag. "Come on in."

In the kitchen, he placed the bag on the breakfast bench, one of those insulated things designed to keep stuff hot. He sniffed at the contents and removed four round plastic containers.

"Chinese takeaway," she declared and pointed at the bag. "Chopsticks are inside."

He took them out and helped carry the containers to the breakfast table. She sat down and started to open them.

"Sweet-and-sour pork, Singapore noodles, special fried rice, and chili prawns."

"Would you like anything to drink?" he asked, one hand on the fridge handle.

"Mineral water, if you have it. If not, orange juice will do."

He had several bottles of mineral water, knowing she liked it. He poured for her and placed the bottle and glass at her elbow, then took some pineapple juice for himself.

"We'll need a couple of plates," she told him. "And a spoon."

Mouth set in concentration, she spooned a bit of everything onto her plate. He also liked the idea of having a little of each serving. He lifted his glass of juice.

"To a wonderful surprise."

A smile lit her face and she touched her glass to his. "To my walking wounded."

He tried the Singapore noodles and nodded. "These are great."

"I picked them up at a place in Footscray. Their stuff is yum."

"It certainly is," he agreed, helping himself to some sweet-and-sour pork.

"You're not mad at me for spoiling your plans?"

"Mad? I'm delighted to see you. I simply didn't expect you here."

She placed the chopsticks on her plate. "You came out of a hospital yesterday after two weeks in bed, having horrible stuff done to you. I figured a long evening might be a bit much this soon."

He sighed. "I hate to say it, but you could be right. Those two weeks took more out of me than I realized." He reached for her hand and squeezed. "Having you here is better than any chemo."

"What did Dr. Dalton say?"

"The chemo and radiation did their thing, and I must keep up my diet of checkpoint inhibitors. Apart from that, I still have my twelve months. Perhaps a little more now. At least I hope so."

She frowned. "I don't get it. If chemo is so effective, shouldn't you be in remission or something?"

"It doesn't work that way. Chemo and radiation don't kill every cancerous cell. It removes rapidly dividing cells, but individual melanoma cells can lay dormant for a while before they start dividing again. Chemo chemicals only work while they remain in the body, which means constant replenishment. Once treatment is stopped, the cancer cells start to grow again and metastasize. The inhibitors will keep them in check, but it's a delaying tactic only."

"Will you need chemo again?"

"Probably. Dr. Dalton didn't say. I'll know more in three weeks after my next set of scans."

She sniffed, took a deep breath to compose herself, and picked at her food. He did not have much of an appetite left either.

"How about some coffee?" he suggested.

"Can I have some tea instead?"

"What would you like? There's Earl Gray, chamomile, and a fruit mix."

"Earl Gray would be fine."

He got the water boiling and she brought the plates to the sink. Not wanting the food to go off, he spooned the leftovers into a steel bowl, slapped on cling wrap, and shoved it into the fridge. He made tea for both of them and carried the mugs to the table.

"Milk and sugar?"

"Just sugar, please," she said.

After a satisfying sip, she sighed and looked around. "It must be nice having a whole house to yourself."

He smiled. "I've gotten used to it."

"I have a small room to myself, but little privacy. With Mom and Dad around, I cannot do some things I would like." She gave him a sidewise glance and grinned. "I could if I moved in with you."

"You can have two rooms if you want, and everything else you see." He searched her eyes. "Nothing has changed, Adriana."

"Not even if we were married?"

A curious pain squeezed his chest. He swallowed hard and took a sip of tea.

"I want that more than anything, but we can't."

After a while, she gave a small smile. "I want a fantasy, a dream come true, and I might have it for a while, but when I eventually wake up, that's all it would be, a dream. Wouldn't it?"

Emotions warred inside him, and he did not know what to do. Those million reasons she mentioned? Still there, and more. What would his parents say if she moved in with him? What would hers? What would others say? Fence gossip, titters, with a flavor of scandal. Would it matter? Did he give a damn? Nobody's business how he and Adriana lived their lives. Five months, five days…a century…If it were only five minutes, he wanted them to be with her.

"When can you move in?"

She gasped and went white. "But…but…"

He brought her hand to his lips and kissed it. "I'm mad, and scared. I don't want to steal these moments from you, and I'm being selfish in the extreme, but if this is what you want to make you happy, then I'll be happy." He looked deeply into her eyes. "I love you, Adriana Teller."

Her eyes sparkled, ready to spill. Then they did spill, and the tears ran down her cheeks. She sniffed and let them run, then stood up, hurried around the table and sat on his lap, hands tight around his neck. He winced at the stab of pain, but forgot everything as her mouth found him. Still holding him, she silently wept.

Totally at peace, Andrew held her, not saying anything. This felt right and good.

She pulled back, brushed her face, and her eyes bored into him with an intensity of fire. Without saying anything, she stood and tugged at his arm. Not letting go, she led him up the stairs to his bedroom. She slowly removed his clothing, then proceeded to disrobe.

They did not make love, but simply held each other. Her head on his shoulder, one arm across his chest, he felt content. He ran his hand down her silky side, then pulled her against him. If this is what her dream looked like, he would gladly share it with her.

After a time, he did not know how long, she stirred and looked at him.

"What made you change your mind?" she whispered, perhaps afraid if she spoke loudly, the dream would shatter.

"That fantasy you mentioned? I know it well, because it's also my fantasy. Then it hit me. Why settle for a fantasy when we can have the real thing?"

She giggled. "You know, of course, in a fantasy, the prince and his princess always live happily ever after."

"Then we better make sure this remains a fantasy."

Her fingers marched across his chest. "We'll wake up sometimes, you know."

"Not for a long time, I hope."

"If only it could be forever."

"If we believe strongly enough, it will be forever."

"I didn't know you were so romantic," she murmured.

"I had two weeks of solitude where I pried open every part of myself to see what made me tick. Looking back on my carefree days, there were things about myself and things I did, which I didn't like. I'm only twenty-four, and still a kid at heart in some respects. Responsibilities, job, career, family, those were things others did. I wanted my life of sun, surf, and girls to continue. The fates had other ideas. I had my fun and it's time to settle the bill."

She lifted her head and looked at him. "You've changed, and you know? I like this new you much better. Perhaps you're ready to commit after all."

"Faced with my mortality, I grew old in those two weeks."

"Matured, I would say. No longer the smooth surfer who asked me out."

He smiled. "I've never been nervous about asking a girl out. With you, I had the flutters. I still don't know why you said yes."

"Because I saw in you a glimpse of this new self of yours you didn't know you had," she said simply. "Despite the nerves, you had the courage to ask."

He kissed her forehead. "And I am so glad I did."

Her hand slipped down his stomach and grasped him. A moment later, she rolled on top of him and took him in.

Chapter Four

Andrew rolled the F/A-18 Super Hornet, still inverted, and pulled the stick back, diving the fighter into a half loop Split-S. The maneuver depleted his energy, enabling him to line up with a group of tanks laagered in a ravine. He pickled off a CBU-97 cluster munitions laser-guided bomb and sent the Hornet vertical, tracers streaming after him.

He heard a thump and immediately pulled off his tethered VR headset. Warren Kant lay sprawled on the floor, gasping for breath. Heads popped over bullpen dividers to check the goings-on. Warren staggered to his feet and slumped into a gray ergonomic chair, sweat glistening on his forehead.

"Christ!" After a couple of deep breaths, he straightened his tie and stared at Andrew. "I thought you were going to crash us into those tanks."

Andrew smiled, pleased with the demonstration. "I wanted to lose speed and not overshoot the target."

"God, I've never seen anything like it. I almost puked. I might do that anyway." Warren stared at his headset as though seeing it for the first time, then looked up. "You developed this on your own using a commercially available toolkit?"

"That's right."

His boss stared at him, wondering if he lied.

"Regan has to see this. Can you set this up in the conference room?"

"No problem. I'll log on to my server from one of the computers in there."

"Do it!" Warren ordered and rushed off.

Andrew had everything set up when Warren pushed open the

door, followed by the skeptical general manager.

"Warren tells me you have something sensational to show me."

"Please put on your headset, sir, and we'll get started. I'll operate the game, so you won't need tracking gloves. I also suggest you sit down."

Regan Price smiled indulgently and complied.

Andrew put on his headset and gloves, and a full 3D menu screen hung in front of him. He selected in-flight mode and the room around them disappeared. He sat in a Super Hornet cockpit, right hand on the stick, facing fully laid out instrument panels, the thunder of engines howling in his ears. His aircraft fast approached a black dot, which expanded into a twin-tailed fighter. He pulled the Hornet into a high yo-yo to stop him from overshooting as the Mig-29 Fulcrum made a sharp turn to starboard in an attempt to get a missile lock. The sky wheeled above them as the Hornet thundered up in afterburner. Andrew flipped the Hornet onto its back and dove. The Mig-29 had turned full circle, having lost sight of its pursuer. He centered the targeting reticle on the enemy and got an immediate warbling tone from the AIM-9X Sidewinder radar-guided missile. He squeezed the trigger and the missile whooshed off the rail with an initial tail of white flame, which quickly faded. The Mig-29 jinked and headed for the deck, but it could not avoid the supersonic missile boring in on him at Mach 2.5. Triggered by its proximity sensor, it detonated and the Mig came apart in a spectacular fireball.

He stopped the game and pulled off his headset.

Price slowly removed his, looking shaken, breathing deeply. He stood up somewhat uncertainly and reached for the glass pitcher of water on the table. Two large gulps settled him and he sat down.

"Jesus…" he managed to mumble. He took another swallow of water and placed the glass down. "Warren tells me you developed this?"

"That's right," Andrew said. "I created a set of 3D rendering macros that simulate in real time backgrounds, motion, and interaction scenarios that look totally real."

"Yes, I saw. Absolutely remarkable. I thought I was actually in the cockpit. Tell me. How did you achieve such realism?"

"Let me say that my rendering sets employ a variation of fractal geometry. I cannot be more specific for obvious reasons."

Price and Warren exchanged glances. "Did you patent this process?"

"Applications for an Australian, U.S., and world patent were made and registered."

"Your rendering sets will make all existing games look like cheap cartoons, including ours," Price said. "I suspect I know why you showed this to me, but I want to hear it from you."

"I'm prepared to sell this prototype to FutureTech for thirty-five thousand through my company, Usque Vision. It still needs work to turn it into a proper commercial game, including additional background scenarios and tactical fighter maneuvers. To run this game will require a high-end computer, a tethered headset equipped with an eye and head-motion sensor, and augmented reality." The AR feature allows the wearer to see the normal view before the game is activated. Connected to a powerful gaming computer, a tethered headset provided a richer visual experience compared to standalone sets equipped with internal processors.

"Thirty-five thousand doesn't sound much for something like this."

"There is something else I want, a two percent royalty of the wholesale price for every unit FutureTech sells, payable to Usque Vision." Given that some popular games sell well over seven hundred thousand units annually, the two percent return would add up. "I will also retain all intellectual property. If FutureTech wants to retrofit its existing games and develop new ones based on my rendering sets, I'll give you an exclusive development license through my company for an annual fee of two hundred thousand dollars."

At a cost of a new game, he offered FutureTech a bargain.

Price looked thoughtful. "I see. I suppose your macros will have a key integrity checker?"

"Yes, sir. A developer key and a user key, based on the license key. The macros will be black boxes, offering programmers a standard industry-compatible rendering palette and motion options similar to what FutureTech uses now. Developers cannot access the macro's internal code, which is encrypted. Any attempt to breach the encryption will scramble the code."

"You seem to have thought of everything," Price suggested.

Andrew smiled. "I learned a few things at RMIT, and your games employ a similar concept to prevent hacking."

"What if a third party wants us to develop something for them?"

"My license won't stop you from doing that, but you cannot sub-license my macros."

He did not spell that one out. Allowing anyone else access to his macros, FutureTech would lose its competitive advantage, and Andrew could open himself to pirating. Suppression always better than taking costly legal action against a company for breach of license.

"I'll raise this with our corporate office for any agreement to your proposal."

"I understand, Mr. Price. If you like, my law firm will email you a sample contract."

Price gave a mirthless grin. "You *have* thought of everything. Just out of curiosity, if headquarters turns you down?"

Andrew shrugged. "No hard feelings. What I'm offering, it's a seller's market, sir."

"I'm certain FutureTech will be able to accommodate you, and I'm not insensitive to the competitive advantage we would gain by using your rendering sets. As of now, you're a senior analyst with a salary of $165,000. I shall notify Accounting."

Andrew was taken aback somewhat, not expecting such a quick response, but understood why Price did it. FutureTech did not want to lose what he had to a competitor.

"I would make you a project manager, but I think even you would agree that you lack the necessary experience. Once you complete your MBA, I'll review your position," Price said, then immediately winced in contrition. "I'm sorry. That's insensitive of me."

Andrew lifted his hand. "It's okay."

"Given your, ah, condition, there is something I must ask, and please don't misunderstand me. If FutureTech enters into an agreement, we must have the right to access the macros code once you…" Price did not quite know how to finish.

"Of course. That item is covered in the contract." Andrew leaned forward and stared at the general manager. "There is another provision in the contract, sir. Any work I do on games designed by FutureTech, but developed using my rendering sets, FutureTech will retain all intellectual property rights."

"That is standard industry practice," Price acknowledged.

"However, any game or application I design, whether on my own time at home, or at FutureTech premises, I retain IP. If FutureTech likes what I come up with, I'll sell it to you at a mutually agreed price. If the game or application is developed into a marketable product, I'll retain two percent of every unit sold."

Price sat up and his face clouded. "When you work here, Mr. Payne, whatever you create belongs to FutureTech. If you develop a prototype of something at home, we'll talk."

"I have ideas for a number of possible gaming and commercial VR applications, sir. They could be very valuable revenue earners for FutureTech. However, given my medical condition, it'll be impossible for me to develop a prototype for each idea in the time I'm expected to live, even if I worked 24/7. It will not matter to me if FutureTech does not wish to enter into this agreement. I will simply withhold my ideas and work on whatever project I'm assigned."

Price scowled, then burst into laughter. "You're a scoundrel, Andrew."

"Yes, sir."

"I see that your MBA course hasn't been wasted on you," the general manager murmured, perhaps wondering what FutureTech had created.

Andrew felt no grudge against Price. The general manager simply looked after FutureTech's interests, as would the corporate office.

"I must confess, sir, this has not been all my idea."

"Your law firm? They also created Usque Vision for you?"

"Yes, sir."

"They clearly know what they're doing. You must realize, our legal department will scrutinize your contract to safeguard ourselves."

"I understand completely. There is no fine print in my contract, Mr. Price."

The general manager smiled and stood. "You've blown me out of my seat with your demo, and you have my support. This will turn the VR gaming world on its head, and I'll make sure that FutureTech rides its competition into the dust. If you can email me your contract, I'll forward it to corporate." He extended his hand. "Well done."

Andrew shook hands, a broad smile on his face. "Thank you, sir. I look forward to a productive relationship, and thank you for the promotion."

"FutureTech looks after its own," Price said briskly and pointed a finger at him and Warren. "This is strictly confidential, understand? If this were to leak out, we could have a bull run on our stock, and the last thing I want are charges of insider trading from the regulators," he said and quickly walked out, undoubtedly a lot on his mind.

As Price closed the door after him, Andrew gave a small sigh at having one of his plans ruined. Once he got his $35,000, he intended buying FutureTech stock, but understood why he could not. There would be an opportunity later.

"And I thought I knew everything about VR," Warren said and shook his head. "How in *hell* did you come to develop these 3D sets?"

"An assignment I did during my final year at RMIT gave me the idea," Andrew told him. "I developed some code on my home PC to test the concept, and it went from there."

"Damndest thing I ever saw. I would not have believed it possible without using something like a Cray supercomputer. Of course you know, once we start rolling out games based on your macros, sooner or later, our competition will come up with something similar."

"Probably, but not for a while, and not without violating my patent."

Warren placed an arm on Andrew's shoulder and steered him toward the door. "Let me buy you a cup of coffee and we'll talk."

Andrew did not mind the coffee, but if his boss thought to pump him, he would not get much change for his efforts. He may be young and still naïve about many things, but not *that* naïve. His MBA course opened his eyes into the workings of the corporate world—the white, the gray, and the black. He also owed a huge thanks to Reynold Parker, without whose guidance, he might not have fared so well.

"Give me a moment, will you please? I want to send Mr. Price the sample contract."

Warren nodded. "Of course. See me when you're done."

Andrew watched him leave, and dug out his cell. He managed to get Parker right away and gave him an update. Parker said he would send Price the contract and take care of all negotiations with FutureTech, with Andrew's full participation, naturally.

He finished at his usual time and hurried down to catch his tram. June 18 a special day—Belana's eighteenth birthday. It would be a modest affair, as Bel planned an outing with her friends for a proper blowout. It also meant that she could now drive a car, as she already had her probationary license. Another young and immortal driver thrust into the unfeeling jaws of traffic and idiots. He still thought of her as a little kid in a ponytail, the family's whirlwind. Definitely no longer a girl, his Bel a grown young woman with all the complications that had already surfaced for her parents. Their problem, he decided. His problem? Make sure he got the special German Black Forest Gateau from the Prahran cake shop, her absolute favorite, and bring it over at seven. If anything went wrong, his name would be mud forever, long after he was no longer around. He rang the shop around two to make sure they had everything ready.

Since his discharge from the Institute, his recovery amazed the stern Dr. Dalton and everybody else. He had filled out and felt his normal vigorous self. The round of scans on Monday showed no additional spread, which made Dr. Dalton smile faintly. Having Adriana live with him set his heart singing and made his footsteps light. His parents and her folks surprised him by wishing them both luck and happiness. They all preferred a formal union, but nobody said anything negative to them. What transpired in the background, he did not give a damn. Deliriously happy, and Adriana positively shone. They had lunch together almost every day, except when one of them had work commitments. He did not mind. Life glowed and he basked in its warmth, relishing every golden moment. He would not have swapped it for anything. What good were years when discontent and ongoing arguments clouded the days?

He found being together had little to do with intimacy, which he and Adriana enjoyed unreservedly, playing some weird erotic fantasies. What bound them were the quiet moments they shared in front of the TV, listening to music with a book in hand, or him watching her tend the garden as he sipped a light beer, sprawled in a chair on the back veranda. He relished moments of searching conversation, probing every and any subject, hotly debating opposing points of view, getting to understand and discover each other as complex individuals, that made him complete.

She used to do some things he found irritating, like leaving her hairbrush on the vanity unit full of hair, or forgetting to flush strands of hair from the sink after a shower. It took a while before she learned not to walk into the house in her street spikes, but these were minor quirks. She did not like that he used to leave an open tube of toothpaste lying around after him, or piling only a couple of dishes into the washer, instead of giving it a full load. Both had adjusted and things were humming.

They were yet to have a genuine argument. About what, he could not imagine. Something that would probably come out of nowhere, hiding some deeper disquiet. Invariably, as the months wore on and his condition began to deteriorate, he figured an argument or two might ensue. Then again, perhaps not. They were open with each other, and learned early to discuss an irritant or disagreement, rather than see it fester and develop into something more serious. That came with trust after a period of initial shyness as they adjusted to living together. He could no longer do some crazy things he used to, but he adjusted. When something awkward came up, a hug or a quick kiss made it all better.

He remembered wistfully the first time Adriana played her violin for him, a rendition of *Trumpet Voluntary*, one of his favorite Baroque pieces. She did not force the melody, but the intensity made the hairs on his arms stand as he clearly heard the trumpets in his head. Sheer magic, and when she finished, he looked at her in amazement and wonder at this talent of hers.

When he got home, he immediately hopped into his car and drove to the cake shop. Luckily, they were open until eight-thirty, evening customers relishing the tempting spread. The critical job done, he showered and changed. Around 6:15, Adriana showed up and had a quick shower. They went home together whenever possible, but her work sometimes held her back, as did his. When a tooth had a problem, it had to be attended to, regardless of the time. It did not happen often, though. First Teeth an upmarket dentistry with mostly professional clients who looked after themselves. Still, even a lawyer could get a toothache without a prior appointment.

Adriana looked sharp in a deep green skirt and light brown alpaca sweater. The black pearl earrings she got from her father on her eighteenth birthday complemented her platinum hair. A touch of dark lipstick drew attention to her face and olive eyes. In simple black corduroy pants and jacket, Andrew looked presentable enough.

He reversed the car onto the street and they were off. In her lap, Adriana held their presents. She would not tell him the contents of the little red box. He got even by not telling her what he had in his flat one. She promptly stuck the tip of her tongue at him.

Overcast, the heavy cloud layer reflected the city lights. Traffic thick, but moved steadily. Thankfully, he only had a short trip to his parents' place.

He drove through the open gate and parked behind his old man's Camry. A fresh breeze tugged at his jacket, and they hurried for the front door. Adriana handled the presents and he carried the cake box. His mom embraced them and ushered them into the brightly lit dining room, decorated with balloons and a purple 'Happy 18th Birthday' tinsel stuck to the wall. His mom relieved him of the cake box as his dad emerged, two bottles of beer in one hand, a tall mix in another.

"How are you, son...Adriana?" He held out a low-alcohol bottle to Andrew, and the mix to Adriana. They all clicked glasses and sipped.

"This is nice, Markus," Adriana commented.

From the first, his dad insisted that Mr. Payne was far too formal. It made him feel like an old professor. His mom demanded that she call her Ethel.

Andrew heard stomping feet coming down the stairs and an energetic bundle wrapped her arms around him.

"Hi, big brother. Looking sharp tonight." Belana untangled herself and gave Adriana a warm hug. "You simply must tell me how you do that, Adri," she gushed.

"Tell you what?"

"How you manage to always look so stunning."

Adriana grinned and held out the little box. "For you, darling."

"Wow." Belana immediately tore off the wrapper and cooed at the white rectangular box. "I always wanted one of these expensive perfumes, but Mom would never get one for me." She uncapped the box, took out the frosted bottle, and unscrewed the top. She took a sniff and sighed with pleasure. "Heaven," she murmured and tilted the bottle against her index finger. A little dab behind the ears and she preened. "Fit to kill," she declared happily and gave Adriana another hug. "Thank you, my sister."

Adriana offered her the flat box wrapped in black paper. "From him," she said with a tilt of her head.

Belana grinned at Andrew and made a mess of the wrapping to reveal a red satin box. Eyes glowing, she slowly opened it and gasped at the gold necklace studded with red garnet and matching earrings. Without saying anything, she walked into his arms and planted a kiss on his mouth.

"Thank you, dear brother," she whispered, eyes misty. She shoved the box into his hand, took out the earrings and inserted them, then glanced at the box. "Would you mind?"

Grinning, he clipped the necklace around her slim neck.

"Knock 'em dead, princess."

His mom nodded approvingly. "Nice," she said and strode into the kitchen. A moment later, she emerged with the cake on a glass stand. Belana stared at it, then looked at Andrew.

"Tell me it's not."

"Black Forest," he assured her, and she clasped her hands, face radiant.

"The best."

Mom and dad fixed candles around the edge and lit them. In the middle in white lettering, it had 'Happy 18th birthday, Belana'. His dad turned down the rheostat to dim the dining room lights.

"Happy birthday to you," he started, and everybody pitched in with enthusiasm.

With a sniff and a dab at her eyes, Belana blew out the candles in one go, and everybody cheered and clapped. She picked up the carving knife and held it above the cake while Andrew and his dad snapped shots with their cellphones. She got busy and cut a slice for everybody, revealing layers of sweet cheese, dark pastry, and cherries. Andrew did not need prompting to get stuck into his delicious piece.

A car horn blared and Belana looked stricken. "I don't know how to thank you, guys," she gushed, "but—"

"Enjoy yourself, dear," her mother assured her and gave her a peck on the cheek. "Don't forget your coat. It's cold outside."

Belana rushed to the door, grabbed a short beige coat off the wall rack, and vanished, slamming the door after her. He glanced at Adriana and shrugged. His sis still an irrepressible whirlwind. His dad brightened the lights and extended his arm toward the lounge.

"Now that our terror has gone, let's get comfortable."

"There's some lasagna if you like, dears," his mom said. "With Belana out with her friends, we're not having a formal party."

"Lasagna is fine, Mom," he told her.

"Do you need a hand, Ethel?" Adriana offered.

"You can help lay out the dishes."

Andrew sat opposite his dad. "How are things at RMIT?"

"Lecturing undergrads and some master's classes. Not too busy. It gives me time to research a paper I'm writing."

"About what?"

"How to calculate safety parameters for various construction materials used in high-rise buildings. Many architectural firms still use dated tables and take safety and integrity shortcuts to satisfy builders' budgets. The building goes up, and a year later, sometimes sooner, the thing develops cracks, some serious. This leaves owner-occupiers who bought off the plan with enormous costs to rectify the defects, including lengthy litigation. In the meantime, builders hide behind weasely contracts and building inspectors who rubber-stamp self-inspections."

"Like Boeing doing its own certifications," Andrew growled.

"Exactly. The 737-MAX scandal almost crippled them in a drive for short-term profits."

"Well, Dad, you certainly picked an interesting topic."

Adriana laid out the plates and cutlery, and his mom placed a large glass baking tray onto a cork pad. With everybody seated, his dad served himself a generous slab of lasagna.

Andrew took a bite and nodded. "This is great, Mom," he told her, and she smiled.

"Thank you." She gave him a speculative look. "I'm glad to see you filled out."

"I feel great," he said and glanced at Adriana. "You can blame her cooking for that."

"Dupe," she declared promptly, and his mom laughed.

"It's good to see you two so happy."

"Seriously, though, I do some cooking as well."

His dad cleared his throat. "Did you demonstrate your prototype to FutureTech yet?"

"As a matter of fact, I have. This morning. I definitely wowed them."

"What did Regan Price say about the contract?"

"He sent it to our corporate office to pick over. I don't think he liked the two percent royalty I want, but he figured Future-Tech got the better of the deal, seeing I won't be around all that long to collect it." He chuckled. "I would have liked to see his face when he got to the clause where it says the two percent is payable to my estate in perpetuity as long as the game is sold or until it's withdrawn."

His dad grinned. "I told you Tompson, Tompson, and Parker were a top outfit."

"And I'm glad you did. Mr. Parker was terrific. There is one other thing. Price promoted me to senior systems analyst."

Adriana glared at him. "Well, you could have told me!"

"I didn't have a chance. We were busy getting ourselves ready to come here. Anyway, we'll celebrate when we get home," he said, and she fisted his shoulder.

"Congratulations, dear. You deserve it." His mother smiled warmly.

"Thanks, Mom."

"When do you expect a response?" his dad asked.

"Probably on Tuesday. Their legal weenies will likely pick over every clause to see if they can sweeten the deal for themselves. I already made it clear to Regan, if FutureTech baulks, I walk."

"Why Tuesday?" Adriana asked.

"Time zones," he said. "America is one day behind."

"They're one day behind in many ways," his mom observed darkly, and his dad laughed.

"What you're giving them is a competition killer, son. They would be silly to knock you back."

"That is in effect what Regan said, and probably why I got the promotion."

"Enough, already!" his mother declared. "Contracts, competition, corporate shenanigans…Let's talk about something else."

"The weather?" Andrew offered brightly.

"I'll give you weather on your bottom," she suggested darkly and everybody laughed.

* * *

"This is ABC Breakfast, September 1, 2021. Good morning to all viewers, this is Michael Rowland. For those joining us, here are the main points.

"The Chinese Belt and Road Initiative effectively collapsed when the World Bank and the IMF made what were virtually interest-free loans to South American, African, and several Pacific island nations to bail them out of untenable debt traps designed to expand Chinese influence and control."

Andrew wished he could say they did it out of altruism instead of open political maneuvering by the West to limit Chinese aggressive expansion. The bankrupt policy of past American administrations to improve the standard of living for ordinary Chinese through open trade in the hope it would soften the Communist Party's authoritarian regime exposed for the failure it was.

"FutureTech, a leading U.S. developer of interactive virtual reality games, announced the release of Fighter Combat, *based on a revolutionary new image rendering concept, which promises to take VR games to an unprecedented level of reality. Here is a preview of what gamers can expect."*

"Andrew! Come here, quick. It's about your game," Adriana cried from the lounge.

He leaned over the breakfast bench and peered at the TV. Not 3D, but the density and realism of a fighter in pursuit of its quarry palpable. Everyone seeing this might as well be looking at the real thing, and not a game.

It took him and four developers three long, sometimes frustrating, weeks to turn his prototype into a fully tested commercial product. When the lead programmer first saw it, she simply stood there and gaped in disbelief. The others could not hide their enthusiasm to get stuck into it.

Seeing the thing on TV raised goosebumps all over. Overwhelming pride flushed through him, knowing his work caused a major industry shift, whose tentacles would grow and generate yet unrealized opportunities.

FutureTech had mobilized the might of the entire corporation and every regional office in a retrofit program of their most popular games. Reprogramming one game would take two to three weeks, followed by a rigorous testing regimen, culminating in a beta run, which ordinarily took about a week. Fortunately, the games had existing test harnesses used during initial development, which would greatly speed up the verification process. Moreover, the games came with no preexisting bugs. In December, FutureTech planned to release everything, which should make all gamers go nuts. His game an industry teaser designed to confound the competition.

He recalled the meeting with Regan Price on June 25 with a degree of nostalgic fondness and satisfaction. Without any preliminaries, the general manager slid two documents across the table.

"Your contract. Signed by headquarters without amendment. Tompson, Tompson, and Parker has validated an electronic copy. I understand you received an email from them to that effect."

"That's right," Andrew said, pulled a pen from his pocket, and signed both copies. He pushed one toward Price.

The general manager stood and stuck out his hand. "Congratulations, Mr. Payne."

"Thank you, sir."

"Just Regan. You and I will be seeing a lot of each other, and I look forward to your next surprise."

Andrew shook hands and smiled. "You won't be disappointed...Regan."

He returned to his desk buoyed.

To think it happened only a couple of months ago.

He blinked when the simulation ended and the presenter launched into other news items.

Basking in a warm glow, enjoying the look of adoration in

Adriana's eyes, he recalled another such look when he and his family, and her parents, pulled a surprise birthday party for her. It really came as a surprise and he pretended not to know that July 24 was her birthday—he called her mother to find out.

Belana floored her by giving her a large case wrapped in heavy purple cloth, a joint present from everybody, and Adriana pulled out a full-size Spruce Stradi violin. Crying happy tears, she hugged everyone, and he got a big kiss. Later that evening, he got more than that. It added a month to his life seeing her bright and bubbly for days afterward, not counting several emotional moments listening to her play for him.

He shook off the memory as she walked up to him and flowed into his arms. "You made it," she gushed and kissed him tenderly, then pulled back and brushed his cheek. "I'm so proud of you, I could burst."

"Thanks, sweetie. With so many people in the loop, I thought this would leak, but FutureTech managed to keep a lid on it."

"What about the bits on social media about the pending launch?"

"Marketing teasers designed to generate anticipation."

Memory memo to self: Buy FutureTech shares.

He would do that after his session with Dr. Dalton. He wanted to get some before, but understood why he could not. No legal impediment existed to stop him now.

Not paying much attention to the TV, he and Adriana finished breakfast. Around 7:30, she put on a heavy coat and shouldered a bag.

"Good luck with the scans!" A flutter of fingers and she was gone, leaving him to clean up. He did not mind, his appointment at the Institute not until nine.

He cleaned up everything and stacked the stuff onto the drying tray, the house suddenly feeling empty and dead without her in it. He shook off the moment of introspection, made himself another cup of coffee and walked into the lounge to watch the news. After a sip, he placed the mug on the coffee table and absently scratched an itch on his left forearm.

Warren already knew he would not be in until after lunch. The retrofit of the game in Andrew's work basket progressed well, and his team was fully familiar with the 3D macros and how to use them. Another week and the thing should be ready for the beta guys. A complicated hack-and-slash Viking invasion game with several interactive scenarios. Upgrading background animation and characters took exacting work. Regan came to look at it once, shook his head, and walked off.

Around 8:15, Andrew rugged up and walked to Chapel Street to catch a tram that would take him all the way to Victoria Parade. He needed to catch another one that went into the city, but he would make it in plenty of time.

Melbourne had weathered a particularly cold and wet winter, and they were now officially in spring. That is what the calendar said, but September could be patchy and delivered an odd surprise from time to time. This morning, it delivered a pleasant one, with clear skies and crisp air. Cold, but not the numbing chill of winter, and he walked with a satisfied grin on his face.

His last set of scans did not show any major spread, although a slight buildup of cancerous cell groups in his lymphatic system, lungs, and liver, which, according to Dr. Dalton, may need another chemo session, but not until October or November. Otherwise, he felt good. Even she commented positively on his condition. She would do that anyway to maintain his morale, but he had come to know her well enough to tell that she genuinely cared and worried about him. Not only him, but probably all her patients. Her veneer of detached professionalism a reminder and shield not to get too close, because sooner or later, she would lose all of them.

Don't feel and survive.

The tram came to a stop not far from the Institute. He tapped his Myki card and got off. Traffic streamed in unbroken lines on both sides of the boulevard, and the sidewalks were full. By ten, everything would thin out as workers settled into another day.

Amanda Gregory met him on the first floor and took him down to Radiology. An old customer, he knew everybody there. After a boring hour waiting for the radiotracer to work its way through his body, he said 'Hi' to a technician who led him to the PET scanner room. Half an hour or so later, he had the SPECT-CT scan, and took the elevator to the first floor to wait for the results.

Amanda ushered him into Dr. Dalton's office and closed the door after her.

"Good morning, Andrew. Is everything well?"

"Humming, Doc. FutureTech has released my game!"

"I saw something about that this morning. I must confess, I don't appreciate the excitement."

"Today is a dawn on a new VR world!" he told her, bubbling with enthusiasm. "The possibilities are endless, although it will take some time to realize them. The important thing is, the doors are open, and there's no going back."

"Well, I wish you luck. Now, how have you been feeling? Any nausea or joint discomfort?"

"No nausea, but there's persistent morning lethargy and fatigue, which subsides during the day, but it's always there."

She nodded. "The side effects of your blockers."

"My knees and ankles hurt sometimes, but my regimen of long walks and general exercises keeps it manageable, and I rarely take any painkillers."

"How is your appetite?"

"Mostly good, but there are days when I don't feel like eating anything," he said and absently scratched his forearm. Dalton saw this and pointed a finger at him.

"How long have you been doing that?"

"Doing what?"

"Scratching your arm."

He expressed genuine surprise. "I wasn't aware I did it."

"Well, you did." She cleared her throat, and he tensed.

Here it comes.

"Your condition has not deteriorated significantly in the three weeks since your last set of scans. However, this morning's tests show additional spread and buildup of cell groups in several organs, bones, and the lymphatic system…including your forearm, the original tumor site. I'm recommending another session of chemotherapy."

Chemo…he did not like the sound of that.

"Will I need to come here for that?"

"You'll be able to administer the five-day treatment orally."

Better than being all wired up again, he mused, but still not good.

"What about side effects? The first session knocked me around quite a bit, and it took most of a month before I recovered."

"You might experience some nausea and diarrhea, but little else. There is an increased risk of infection because of damage chemo will cause to your immune system."

"What if I don't have chemo? The blockers I'm taking are supposed to boost my immune system, but chemo will knock it out."

Dr. Dalton frowned and rubbed her chin. "The objective is to eradicate as many cancerous cells as possible. Despite the side effects, the end result will be more positive."

He looked hard at her. "That's not all, is it?"

She pursed her lips and gave a soft sigh. "When you walked out of here in May, I told you that you had twelve months or so. Since then, you responded well to treatment. Surprisingly well. However, this morning's tests indicate a potentially aggressive return of your cancer. Infection of your bones will over time release excessive calcium and begin to interfere with your brain and heart. The body has mechanisms to counter this, but given that your other organs are also under attack will strain your body's ability to cope. My prognosis that you might live until next May must be revised down."

Tense, he clenched his fists. "To what?"

"Six months, perhaps a little more."

"Six months? But I thought with chemo—"

"Without the chemo, you would have even less. You must understand, once your immune system reaches saturation, its ability to fight the cancer will deteriorate rapidly. By next February, you will likely need permanent palliative care."

Shaken, he wished for a stiff drink…several, and damn the medication. He always knew it was only a matter of time, but he had adjusted to having nine more months at least, not six, and perhaps not even that.

"There are no other treatments that might help?"

"I can try some targeted genotherapy to supplement the checkpoint inhibitors regimen, but I cannot guarantee any improvement in the long-term prognosis." She leaned forward and her eyes bored into him. "Cancer cells have metastasized throughout your body, and your immune system is slowly succumbing to the attack. The blockers are helping it cope, but there is nothing I know that could lead to remission."

"Not even experimental drugs?"

"Research into various treatments is being carried out by a number of biotech companies around the world, but it'll be several years before anything becomes available for general use. I'm sorry to have to tell you this."

He gave a wan smile and nodded. "Don't worry about it, Doc. I know I'm living on borrowed time. I didn't expect it would run out this quickly." His turn to clear his throat. "When will I start to feel real bad?"

"You'll progressively begin to experience loss of energy, as well as general fatigue, but this will not be pronounced until December or so. Your appetite will also start to decline by then.

Debilitating effects are likely to appear in February, and you'll require hospitalization."

"At the Institute?"

"Normally, we transfer patients to a hospital such as the Peter MacCallum Cancer Center, which is especially equipped to handle such cases. However, the Institute is a research facility, and progression of your condition is an ongoing study that has yielded a lot of useful data. Please excuse me if I sound overly clinical."

He waved a hand. "That's all right. I knew I'm a guinea pig."

"We'll do everything possible to extend your lifespan and quality of life, even if this entails application of experimental treatments."

"I don't have anything to lose, Doc."

She stood and held out her hand. "I look forward to seeing you in three weeks."

* * *

Outside, he looked up at a clear sky, took a deep breath, and exhaled slowly.

Borrowed time, a very amusing phrase. Amusing because he would not need to pay it back, which he found droll in the extreme.

As he waited for the tram, he took stock of his situation. Okay, instead of nine months, he had six. An inconvenience, but basically, nothing had changed. He would live each day to its fullest and cherish every moment given him. Those jigsaw pieces? He simply had to assemble them much faster. Even if he did not manage to put all of them together, he would leave a discernable picture.

Should he tell Adriana and his parents? Nothing would be gained, except cause needless grief. He would tell them about the chemo, but nothing else.

His FutureTech plans? Lots of companies had already developed most action game scenarios in numerous variations, and he could not think of anything genuinely original. Producing a variant on an existing theme would wear off quickly, as gamers sought something new. Space, ground and naval warfare, terrorism and crime themes, historical twists, fantasies, safari hunts, all were saturated.

What he considered still largely virgin territory were commercial and industrial applications. He had ideas, but FutureTech's business lay in VR game development. He needed to change that mindset. In the meantime, he would give them one more game, *Hunter*. Whether he liked it or not, humans had an insatiable drive to hunt large land game and sea monsters. Society frowned on real shooting safaris, but that did not mean brave bwanas could not indulge their fantasies in a VR world, and he would give them more realism than they bargained for. Playing his game would be better than the real thing. The skeletal prototype he worked on at home looked promising, but needed at least another month of development before he would show it to Warren.

He checked his Rado: 12:16, and dragged out the cell.

"First Teeth, Penny speaking. How may I help you?"

"Hi, Penny. This is Andrew. Can you tell me if Dr. Teller is available, please?"

"Hi, Andrew. Let me check...she said she'll call you in ten minutes or so."

"Thanks, Penny."

"You're welcome."

Instead of taking a tram, he walked to Collins Street. The exercise would do him good and clear his head. He reached the Parliament underground station and his cell went off.

"Hi, gorgeous," he said warmly when he saw her icon.

"Sorry, Andrew. I would love to have lunch with you, but I'm all tied up."

"Not a problem. I'll see you after work. Will you be able to leave around five or so?"

"I can't tell right now. I'll call you. How did the scans go?"

"I must take chemo for a week."

"Will you have to go to the Institute for treatment?"

"Just more pills."

"That's it?"

"Everything is okay, Adriana. Truly."

"I can cancel a patient and we can meet."

"Don't worry about it. We'll talk later."

"You're not keeping anything back, are you?"

"I'm an open book, sweetie. Take care," he said and hung up.

Andrew knew he wasn't much good to anybody the rest of the day. His heart and mind were simply not with it, focused on navel gazing. Intellectually, he knew exactly what went on inside him. Since the initial diagnosis by Dr. Ananankos, he studied and became somewhat of an expert on melanomas, cancers in general, human physiology, intricacies of the immune system, and general research into immunological diseases.

To know all was to forgive all, someone said. Perhaps, but tell it to a cancer cell, it kept right on dividing. To any cancer, the *all* meant total conquest without quarter. No negotiation possible. Against mechanisms perfected over a billion years of adaptive evolution, man's weapons were still spears and bows and arrows.

Score one for intellectual understanding, which did squat to add a few more months to his life.

He felt sorry for himself, and that about summed it up.

Maintain a positive outlook, he kept telling himself. What good did it do when Dr. Dalton kept cutting his string of life.

Like his dad said more than once when working on a piece of wood, 'I keep cutting and cutting, and it's still too short'.

For Andrew, whichever way he cut it, he still found life too short.

Around 4:30, Adriana called, saying she had to work back, which meant he went home alone. In a crowded tram, a crowded street, crowded city, he felt alone.

Six months…Not fair!

He did not want to die when the world held so much promise. Screw the fates, every one of them. Screw life and the shitty deal it dished out, and screw all those who would live to be hundred and not accomplish anything.

Shait in spades.

When he walked through his front door into the lounge, he threw the package of pills Amanda gave him in the general direction of the breakfast bench and strode to the bar cabinet. He pulled out a half-full bottle of black spiced rum and poured a generous measure into a crystal tumbler. He sniffed the fragrant aroma and the alcohol smell, and lifted the tumbler in a salute.

"To our noble selves. There are damn few of us left."

About to toss back the liquor, he paused.

What good would it do to get himself stoned? It would wash away your bout of self-pity, his inner self sneered. Drink up! To hell with it all. He stared at the tumbler, then gave a long sigh and poured the rum back into the bottle. He made one concession to his inner self. He sniffed the cork before driving it in with a slap of his palm.

Unaccountably, he felt better, and the weight he felt pressing on his shoulders tumbled off. He still felt a little abused at the practical joke the fates were enjoying at his expense, and gave them the finger. They have not beaten him yet.

Upstairs, he changed into jeans and sweater, and trundled down into the kitchen. He did not know when Adriana would show up, and he wanted to have dinner waiting for her. He opened the fridge and pulled out a saucepan of leftover beef casserole, and decided to cook some rice to go with it. While the casserole warmed, he rinsed two handfuls of rice and boiled the water. He added a touch of olive oil and stock powder, and added the rice. He left it to simmer for three minutes, slapped on the lid, and switched off the element. The residual heat would cook the thing.

The front door opened and Adriana walked in.

"Brr, it's getting chilly out there," she declared and hung her coat. She walked into the kitchen and sniffed at the pots. "You are useful to have around, Mr. Payne."

He grinned, planted a kiss on her cheek, grabbed her around the waist, and swung her around to her protesting squeals.

"Hey! Why the happy smile?"

"Because, my gorgeous girl, you brought joy and sunshine into my humdrum existence, and I love you."

She looked at him and frowned. "Have you been drinking?"

He lifted his right hand. "I merely sniffed the cork."

"Mmm. Okay, what's going on?"

"Nothing. Celebrating the start of my new chemo program. I thought that deserved some cork sniffing."

"Dupe." She lifted the lid off the small saucepan. "The rice is done."

"In that case, you take your sweet self upstairs and change while I get everything set. Would you like some wine or anything?"

"No thanks. Just mineral water." With a dubious sidewise glance at him, she headed for the stairs.

Andrew pursued the last bit of rice and sauce with a piece of crusty bread and popped it into his mouth, satisfied. A simple meal, yet wholesome. He made tea for both of them and they sipped. Warm mug held between his hands, he tilted his head.

"Did you know that your eyes change color in response to your mood?" he mused.

"How can eyes change color?" she countered. "They are what they are."

He wagged a finger. "Nope. When you are thoughtful, they're deep green. When you're gay and sparkling, they light up."

"What are they now?"

"Somewhere in between."

"Okay, out with it."

"Out with what?"

"I saw that bag of pills on the bench."

"Dr. Dalton figured I might like a change of flavors."

"You're not having chemo because she wants you to try new flavors."

He took a sip of tea and placed the mug down with a click. "No, she didn't. There is some spread."

"And?"

"And that's it."

"Don't treat me like a child. I know what chemo means and what it does. I also studied up. What's the prognosis?"

He shrugged. "Too early to tell, but she'll know more in a couple of months."

Her eyes bored into his soul and he felt that all his lies lay exposed.

"Will the pills make you sick?"

"A little. They learned a lot about my body chemistry from liters of blood they took out of me, and tailored the least effect treatment."

She sighed and her shoulders slumped. "I get used to living with you, then every three weeks, you have your scans and I dread that our fantasy bubble will burst and you'll be gone. I look at that bag of pills and realize that our fantasy is slowly developing cracks, and there is nothing I can do about it. I know that one day you'll tell me that we only have a month. I've been preparing myself for that day, but I fear I'll fall apart when it eventually does come, and it will. That's my constant terror." She sniffed and hurriedly took a sip.

He reached for her hand and gently squeezed. "I can never thank you enough for being with me, sharing my pain, but we also shared love and joy. Those joys might be numbered, but they're eternal because you made them eternal. For me, each day is a lifetime, and with every new dawn, I greet it as a bonus. I couldn't wish for more."

"I don't know if you can tell how much you've changed," she whispered, eyes glistening.

"If I have, it was because of you. Will you play for me, my lotus flower?"

"Let's go upstairs," she said with resolve and stood.

Chapter Five

"Despina! My favorite girl. You don't know how I missed you," he told her forlornly.

"Pooh. Save it for Adriana." She wheeled in the meal wagon and began unloading.

Andrew had no real appetite these days. Not good, but the drip made sure he would not expire. He could still attend to his bathroom chores unassisted, but Francis or another orderly nevertheless hovered close by in case he should stumble. The way things were going, apart from having to pee, he did not need a toilet. Shortly, they would probably wrap him in a man-size nappy and hook him to a urine bag. The thought mortified him.

He had been wasting away for two weeks, and nothing from Broca Genetics. Well, he gambled on a long shot anyway. Time slowly slipped away from him and he did not notice. Sometimes, he would take a bite of something—they were feeding him strained baby mush these days—close his eyes, only to find it already evening when he woke. He did not hurt, not much. Must be the drugs they fed him, or his body had decided to close the books.

The pureed chicken and vegetable stuff tasted like cardboard. Everything tasted like cardboard, and his sense of smell had almost gone. His thin hand shook a little as he tried to spoon stuff out of the glass jar. He swallowed the mush and drank some apple juice, something he could taste a little.

"The nurses still running a pool on me?" he queried.

"And growing," the little nurse said brightly. Her sunny smile and effervescent disposition no longer cheered him up. "I've got ten bucks on you that you'll pull through. There is quite a pool, and I want to collect. So you better not disappoint me, Mr. Payne."

"Andrew," he mumbled, which she ignored as always.

She glanced at the door, and hurriedly placed a small dish on the feeding tray.

"Gelato. I thought you might like it."

"Outstanding!" he hooted, delighted. He had not had a decent ice cream in…he could not remember. "I'll marry you if you agree to bring me ice cream every day," he announced.

Despina gave a merry giggle. "What you're thinking would get both of us in trouble with my husband."

"It would be worth it," he cackled.

"I'll tell Adriana that you're propositioning me. She'll tear the drip tube out of your hand."

"I wish somebody would." He had a couple of teaspoons of ice cream and leaned back against the pillows.

"You've got to eat, Mr. Payne!" Despina looked stricken.

"Let me rest for a minute, and I'll finish it." Both of them knew he never would.

"Buzz if you need anything." She fluttered her fingers at him and wheeled out the wagon.

"I've been buzzing, but nobody is at the other end," he mused and glanced at the electronic clock. It said 12:42, March 19, 2022 in glaring amber. Like it made a difference.

He slid farther down the bed and closed his eyes. It disturbed him that he no longer thought about tomorrow or next week, nor even about today. He always seemed to drift into his yesterdays. The stuff he Googled said this was a common symptom with terminal patients and the very elderly. If he did not have tomorrows, at least he had his past to gnaw on.

By December, he could no longer hide his condition from Adriana. He still showed up for work, but found he could not concentrate for the hours required to do something productive. He sold them *Hunter* for $40,000, glad to be rid of the thing. On

Friday, December 10, he tendered his resignation and walked out. Normally, he should give them four weeks notice, but he decided FutureTech can sue him. No farewell party or a useless 'sorry to see you go' present. He simply handed Price the letter, shook hands, and left. End of chapter.

His year ended on one positive thing—two really. He earned his MBA. Perhaps a symbolic achievement, but he worked hard for the thing. If nothing else, it gave him intellectual satisfaction knowing he completed it. FutureTech released nine revamped VR games based on his 3D macros, amid a lot of publicity and fanfare, and the market went crazy. From what he saw on TV, there were lengthy queues around department stores and other outlets, gamers salivating to get their hands on them.

He could not get over the wondrous mystery how the stock market worked. When FutureTech released his *Fighter Combat* game in September, the share price jumped from its initial value of $5.32 to $7.16 within three hours. Two days later, the price had climbed to $11.17. He saw a bubble forming, decided to speculate, and purchased 10,000 shares. It did not quite clean him out, but it left a substantial dent in his savings. After a week, the stock climbed to $38.18, and he cashed in. Four days later, the bubble burst and the stock plunged to $14.25, a much more reasonable level, but still a healthy appreciation from its starting value.

He got Tompson, Tompson, and Parker to create a trust for Belana using most of the money. It would fund her degree and give her a leg up when entering the workforce. Creating a will turned out not as easy as he imagined, but Parker made the process painless. Adriana would get a shock, and he wished he could be there to see the look on her face. His parents approved his decision without reservation, which made him sigh with relief. Giving away a house to someone he had known for less than a year a big step, but he could not think of anyone more worthy.

She would have all the room she wanted to play her violin without causing a disturbance. The downside, he would not be there to share it with her.

In January, his *Fighter Combat* royalty netted him over $287,000. With the $200,000 license fee, it added nicely to his bank balance. He immediately purchased 20,000 FutureTech shares. They would not do him much good in a pine box, but it would leave a nice legacy for Adriana. He also urged Dad to invest in the company, and told his friends to do the same thing.

He took long walks, exercised as much as his body could stand, read a lot, and listened to music. Adriana wanted to take leave and be with him, but he was not that far gone yet. She fretted and worried and loved him, and that kept him going. Fortunately, his parents and Bel were not around all the time clucking with sympathy. When they did visit, his mom always cried, which made him feel bad. She even called him 'My poor baby' a couple of times, but he saw little point arguing over it. Bel did not know how to handle it. She watched him slowly waste away, helpless to do anything. In a grim way, it enabled her to gradually adjust to the idea that she would lose him. When that day came, it would not be such a shock.

Adriana also adjusted, and it tore her up. He wanted to send her away to spare her this pain, but as a fleeting thought. She would only slide into depression worrying about him. At his side, both comforted each other. Anyway, he was selfish enough to want her with him, and it helped maintain his positive outlook that Dr. Dalton kept drumming into him.

They spent Christmas day at his house. Adriana's parents were Catholic, although it had ceased to mean anything for most followers a long time ago. Habit, that's all. The supermarkets and department stores loved it, though. December a money-making machine, especially the frantic last two days when crowds flooded the stores looking for that last-minute present, anything to get the thing done.

He got Adriana a nice case of accessories for her violin, and Mrs. Teller received a large bouquet of dried Australian flowers. At least they would last a while. Mr. Teller nodded in appreciation at the forty-year-old bottle of port, his favorite drink according to Adriana. What could he give his parents when they had every-thing? A bottle of very old cognac for his dad, a gold bracelet for mom…and keys to a new Hyundai in the driveway for Bel. He provided the money, and Dad did all the legwork. Belana stood there stunned, unable to believe it, then hugged him and cried.

He and Adriana did not decorate a Christmas tree, but nobody seemed to mind. It turned into one of the nicest family gatherings he'd had. A visit by Mark and Orwell the next day closed the festivities.

2022 rolled in with a subdued lunch at his parents' place. His once powerful body looked shrunken, and his knees grated when he walked. Feeling unutterably weary all the time perhaps the worst. He only wanted to sit and not be bothered. He tried to maintain a cheerful disposition, and on most days, made it. Then one morning in mid-February, he could not get out of bed, and Adriana rang the Institute.

* * *

He heard the door open and blinked. Dr. Dalton strode in, followed by a nurse he had not seen before.

"Good afternoon, Andrew," she said, pulled up a chair, and sat down.

The nurse walked to the drip bag and changed it with a smaller one containing pale yellow liquid.

"Hi, Doc." He tilted his head at the drip. "What's that? A different combination of blockers?"

"This is a solution of stimulants for fixed macrophages that reside inside all organs. We received the packages two hours ago."

"So, Broca Genetics has managed to develop a treatment after all."

The nurse took out a large needle filled with something darker yellow, stuck it into the drip tube input slot, and pressed the plunger. He felt a cool rush spread through his arm. The nurse nodded and walked out.

"The injection contains the modified macrophages." Dr. Dalton cleared her throat and rubbed her chin. "You must understand, this treatment is highly experimental without any guarantees. Broca has worked 24/7 to reengineer your immunosurveillance macrophages, tailored specifically for your melanoma, and there's enough serum for four days. They're working on a more potent variant, and will make further modifications from blood samples we'll send them."

"They've been busy," he said.

"Keep in mind that Broca and I are laboring under a tremendous handicap. Their primate test subjects underwent months of rigorous controlled treatment. With you, we don't have that luxury. We don't know the appropriate dosage to give you that will generate the maximum response, or the frequency when it should be administered. We don't have any methodology to guide us."

"Does this mean you're discontinuing the checkpoint inhibitors?"

"They may interfere with your natural macrophages. For the next two days, I'll give you the maximum dosage recommended by Broca, administered three times a day. A blood sample will be extracted an hour after each application. On the third day, we'll run PET and SPECT-CT scans to evaluate your condition."

"What were the changes made to the macrophages?"

"As per the article you read, they modified them to block attempts by your cancer cells to switch off the eat-me receptor. They also enhanced the automatic switchback to the cell-repair state, giving the macrophages a quicker response. An added receptor now binds with T-cells to enhance your immune system's ability to identify and destroy cancer cells. The modified macrophages will trigger a faster than normal reaction."

"All that sounds good."

"It's positive."

He bit his lip. "But…"

"Given the advanced state of metastasis, even if there is a degree of improvement, you must accept that it might not be enough to stop or reverse the cancer. At best, you might gain some extra time."

He reached out and touched her arm, the first time he ever showed her any sign of affection.

"Dr. Dalton, even if this doesn't help me, I'm grateful to you and Broca. I honestly didn't expect anything in such a short time. I reconciled myself to my condition some time back, and I'm not afraid to face death." He ventured a faint smile. "We even became somewhat close friends."

She pursed her lips and her eyes glistened, clearly touched. Then the facade snapped into place, and she cleared her throat.

"I'm pleased that you hold such an attitude. Even at this late stage, emotional stability and mental strength can greatly influence your body's response."

"This treatment, will there be any side effects?"

"Broca Genetics don't anticipate any, as your body will be using its own macrophages, but they're unable to say categorically. Their test primates could not articulate a pain response. However, Broca told me they didn't exhibit physical discomfort or emotional stress. They're keen to get your input."

"Well, it's the least I can do. By the way, I'm not sure my health insurance will cover this. They've already given me a hard time over my stay here."

Dr. Dalton raised an eyebrow. "You couldn't know, of course, but Broca Genetics is paying for everything. You're potentially saving them millions in clinical trials by agreeing to this treatment."

He chuckled. "I always knew they were exemplary humanitarians."

She stood and patted his shoulder. "We haven't lost the fight yet."

He watched her walk out, then tilted his head at the drip bag, wondering what the little suckers were up to.

It made no difference to him how the treatment went. A normal bag of blockers goo, or this newfangled thing. Either way, he had about two weeks, perhaps not even that. How much can his macrophages realistically do in that time?

As Dr. Dalton promised, an hour later, Despina walked in and took ten CCs from inside his left elbow. He did not look forward to these jabs—three times a day—expecting his elbows to look like pin cushions again.

He made himself comfortable and watched the drip bag. After a while, his eyes closed.

Around five-thirty, Adriana showed up, smiling and chipper.

"Hi. How's my favorite patient? By the way, you look like crap." She walked to the bed and gave him a peck on the mouth.

"Thanks. I needed that tender piece of encouragement," he said.

"Don't mention it. I would do it for anybody." She pointed at the drip bag. "What's that? A diet version?"

He smiled, her presence lifting the veils of doom. "That, my sweet, is the latest thing in targeted immunotherapy, and I provided all the raw materials."

Her eyebrows climbed. "Broca Genetics came through?"

"I barely finished lunch when Dr. Dalton showed up and had me hooked up. Neat, don't you think?"

"When will you know if it's doing anything?"

"I'm having scans done on Monday. Hopefully, they'll show some improvement."

"How long will you be on this stuff?" Realizing what she said, she blushed. "Sorry. I didn't mean it like that."

"That's okay. I guess they'll keep feeding me until the garbage truck comes to collect me, or I walk out of here on my own. Don't take any bets either way."

Her eyes regarded him. "Is that possible, you walking out of here?"

He shrugged. "Highly unlikely. The cancer has spread too far. I might get some extra time for good behavior if I'm lucky."

"I'll pray for you harder."

"I thought you didn't believe in that stuff."

"I don't, exactly, but I was raised a Catholic, and it took time to shake off that conditioning. I guess the good points are still there. Anyway, it can't hurt."

"I guess not."

"How are you generally?"

"About the same since you asked me that question yesterday."

"Dupe."

"Like you said. I look and feel like crap. No chasing you up the stairs anymore in this worn out chassis."

Sunshine lit her face and made the room bright.

"What about you?" he asked.

"There is always the next patient. Dr. Hendrix gave me some useful pointers how to manage my stress levels. Sometimes, I feel so sorry for what some of my patients are going through."

Stay detached and survive, he reflected.

He inclined his head at the window, the sun high in the sky. "What's it like outside?"

"Warm and very pleasant." She looked wistful. "We can go for a walk along the beach, even take a swim. Or we can simply stare at the sea and let the water lap at our feet."

"Sounds good. Let me put on my pants and we're out of here."

She sighed. "If only we could. We never did take that trip to Perth last year, or anywhere else."

"Yeah. Perhaps one day we will."

"The fantasy has ended, and we're back in the real world."

"Hey, a fairy might touch me with her wand and we could have our fantasy back."

She cocked an eye at him. "You told me once the fates can screw themselves."

He winced. "Well, about that…I didn't actually mean it."

She laughed. "You're hopeless. Do you need anything?"

"The one thing I need, they won't let me have."

Adriana stood and hugged him. "Your princess is waiting in her tower for you to rescue her," she whispered, and tenderly brushed his cheek.

"I'll tell my groom to ready my trusty steed, and I'll be right over."

She glanced at the drip bag and glared. "And you do your thing or I'll pour you down the sink."

"That's my girl."

The door closed after her and the room appeared darker.

He gave a deep sigh, locked his fingers behind his head, and looked for cracks in the ceiling. Since there were none, this made it a challenge.

Shortly afterward, the stern Mrs. Courtney came to inject another round into the drip tube, and later helped herself to what looked like a liter of blood. Everything done professionally with cool detachment. Just once before they swept him away with the rest of the garbage, he wanted to see her smile.

He had a better chance going to the Moon.

Around seven-thirty, his parents came. Bel could not make it, a hot date. Mom worried about her. Dad worried about her, and Bel kept on doing her thing, oblivious to the anxiety she caused every time some young man took her out. Well, no other way existed to earn experience points. His Belana usually a sensible girl and fussy about the people she associated with. There were always strangers, he used to tell her. Like hunky bronze gods who preyed on innocent damsels, she would retort with a smirk, and

Andrew realized it was true. Exactly what he and his friends used to do.

Talk about what goes around…

They chatted for a while and Mom kept her composure, something he appreciated. He hated her sob sessions, which only made him depressed. He could see his dad had talked to her about this.

When they left, he drank some pineapple juice, snuggled under the blankets, and watched Netflix.

He did not remember falling asleep.

The next day, more of the same; drip, needle, blood extractions. Adriana kept him company after lunch, and then she too left. Visit tomorrow, she said.

Monday came and Francis wheeled him down to Radiology. This time, he beat the system by having the radiotracer squirted into him in his room where he waited in comfort.

Almost lunchtime by the time Dr. Dalton showed up. She pulled up a chair and eased herself on it. Noting her puzzled expression, Andrew could not wait any longer.

"I haven't gone anywhere, Doc."

Her mouth twitched. "Organizing my thoughts. Your scans are very encouraging and show a measurable reduction in stray cancer cells, especially in your lungs and liver. Several nodules in your lymphatic system also lost mass."

"But…"

"This is an exceptional result after only two days of treatment. However, the rate of shrinkage needs to increase substantially to affect the eventual outcome. Your body and bones are filled with cancer, as is your stomach, which accounts for your poor appetite. We may have to resort to direct infusion of nutrients."

"What you're telling me, the operation was successful, but the patient died."

"Not at all. There are still two days of serum left, and I intend to restart the drip right after lunch instead of waiting for tomorrow. I will increase your injection dosage at the same time, as you showed no adverse symptoms. We're also receiving another batch on Wednesday." She studied him. "Have you felt any changes?"

"Now that you mention it, the pain has gone down, and my knees don't ache so much."

"Mmm. It could be merely a psychosomatic reaction. I'll discontinue the painkillers, and then we'll know." She stood and rubbed her chin.

"Just curious, Doc. How do they ship my blood to Broca? A commercial flight?"

"They chartered a Gulfstream executive jet. San Francisco to Honolulu, then Melbourne. Same for the return trip."

"Wow. They don't waste time, do they?"

"Like I told you before. This trial is saving them millions. I'll see you tomorrow."

After Francis came to clean up the lunch stuff, Despina breezed into the room and gave him an extra-large squirt into the drip tube. She beamed and sauntered out, carriage swaying. In the evening, another large helping and a change of drip bag.

Not daring to hope, but nevertheless encouraged by Dr. Dalton's news, he slept well.

On Friday, after another round of scans, something happened that worried him a little. Despina gave him the injection, but before she could record it in her tablet, the fire alarm went off and she rushed out. A couple of minutes later, flushed and looking flustered, she announced they had a false alarm. She picked up the needle and looked at her instrument tray.

"Forgot the serum," she gushed and hurried out.

He craned his neck and stared at the empty serum vial next to the plastic blood container. She had obviously not seen it. A minute later, she came back and filled the needle.

"Despina—"

"One moment. This won't take a sec," she mumbled, shot the serum into him, and placed the needle on the tray. "What is it?"

"You gave me the injection before the alarm went off," he told her gently.

She went pale. "Are you sure?"

He pointed at the empty vial.

"Oh, God." Her lower lip quivered, and she looked ready to cry. She ran out and banged the door after her.

Some ten minutes later, Dr. Dalton walked in and dragged up a chair.

"What happened to Despina?" he asked calmly, afraid she had been disciplined. "It wasn't her fault."

"She is justifiably upset at what could have turned into a serious breach of protocol. In this case, there were extenuating circumstances, but that's not an excuse. Don't worry. She will not face dismissal. The effect of the extra dose is unknown, but should be benign. Now, about your scans.

"There is a measurable reduction in the cancer cell population and shrinkage of group masses. This is extremely encouraging, and frankly, unexpected. Broca Genetics seems to have made a genuine breakthrough. How is your pain threshold?"

"A little twinge here and there, otherwise good. I also feel less fatigued."

"Your skin tone shows some improvement. I am particularly pleased to see that tumor groups in your stomach lining and large bowel almost completely eliminated. This should improve your appetite, which will have a positive effect on the ability of your immune system to target cancer cells. Broca has sent us a new batch of serum, and I'll start you on that immediately with four doses a day."

"And the long-term prognosis?"

"It's still too early to tell, Andrew. You probably gained an extra week at most." She stood and smiled at him. "Rest and we'll take care of you."

* * *

The following Wednesday, Andrew woke to a drizzly morning. He could not tell if it was cold, not from the air-conditioned room, but it did not look pleasant. Definitely not pedestrian weather. Then again, it had to rain sometimes.

He lifted himself up and leaned back against the wall, hands locked behind his head. Energy flowed through him in waves. He felt restless with a desire to jump off the bed and run and run. According to the bathroom scales, he gained two kilos. Not much, and he still looked like a walking skeleton, but a gain. Better than see it go the other way.

His vision sharp and clear, he thought he could hear the granddaddy longlegs scampering across the wall. He could not, but outside traffic noises came through distinctly, and he could not recall hearing them before. He lifted his arms and stared at the firm skin, its color almost normal from its anemic white. A small pinch, it snapped back with what he imagined an almost audible plop. Hunger gnawed at his insides, and he wanted to sink his teeth into a thick juicy steak smothered in mushroom sauce, baked potatoes and veggies on the side, and a large serving of salad. A glass of heavy shiraz to go with it made his mouth water. Enough of the strained baby slop they were giving him.

He tossed back the blankets and padded into the bathroom. Chores done, he shaved, reminding himself to recharge the shaver. A dab of Nivea balm, and he nodded with satisfaction. The face in the mirror stared at him with a pixie gleam in the hazel eyes. His cheeks did not sag and had filled out. Still not the bronzed hunk that made girls flutter their eyelashes at him, but a start. He nodded with approval seeing his hair had regained some color.

As he stared at himself, he wondered if he dared hope. The Broca treatment obviously had an effect, but too little too late? Could the battle be won after ten short days? Perhaps not, but he gained a reprieve of sorts, and death would have to wait a while longer. A month or two? He was pretty far gone when the treatment started. Even a month able to see an open sky, walk along the beach with Adriana, listen to her play for him, lough freely, feel rain fall on him, would be worth it. He would not mind going then. Well, he would, but perhaps with a little of that 'Lay me down with a will' sentiment.

To hold Adriana one last time and slowly dance with her…

After a quick shower, he scrambled back into bed, eager for breakfast.

Around 7:30, Despina walked in with the meal wagon. "How do you feel today, Mr. Payne?" she chirped brightly, back to her normal bubbling self. Last Friday, he worried that she would suffer professionally because of the dosage mishap, but it appeared all went well.

"Terrific, and hungry."

"That's lovely, and you're looking much better." She swung the wooden tray across his lap and began to lay out the jars. He immediately lifted his hand.

"Hold it right there, my dear. You can take that baby mush and feed it to somebody else. What I need is man food! So, pack up this stuff and bring me something I can sink my teeth into."

She looked uncertain. "I don't know if I can do that. Your chart calls for a specific diet."

"Then tell whoever set up this chart to eat this himself. Now scat."

A frown creased her face. "Are you all right, Mr. Payne?"

"I feel great, and dying to eat something solid."

"Mmm. I'll have to check on this." She removed the jars and rolled out the wagon, still wearing a frown.

Some fifteen minutes later, another nurse came and injected him with a radiotracer, which meant no breakfast, and that made him grumpy. Dr. Dalton did not have to wait for his cancer to kill him. He would starve to death first. An hour later, Francis came in with a wheelchair and took him down to Radiology. Back in his room, his stomach began to protest earnestly at this inhumane treatment.

Despina strode in, smiled, and started to lay out his belated breakfast: a fried egg, two small sausages, potato cubes, and a slice of toast. She also placed a small steel carafe of coffee on the tray.

He rubbed his hands. "Now, this is more like it."

Despina grinned. "I checked with Dr. Dalton, and she said you're back on a normal diet."

"She did, eh? Did anyone tell you that you're a doll?"

"All the time, Mr. Payne. All the time."

He looked exasperated. "Can't you call me Andrew just once?"

"Okay…Andrew. I must go now. Enjoy your breakfast."

She breezed out and he poured himself some orange juice. The flavor mesmerized him, and he helped himself to another glass, then tucked into the egg, not believing how good it tasted. Everything tasted great! When he finished, he wanted to lick the plate clean, wishing for more, but his stomach said it had enough to work on for the moment. He gave a long sigh, swung out the tray, and sagged against the pillow feeling totally content for the first time in…a while anyway.

He finished brushing his teeth and took a pee. Tucking himself into bed, a knock came and Dr. Dalton walked in.

"Good morning. I'm told you're feeling particularly well today," she observed and pulled up a chair.

"Ready to jump tall buildings, Doc."

"Well, perhaps not for a while." She glanced at the breakfast tray. "I see you have your appetite back. This is extremely encouraging."

"I forgot how good a fried egg and sausages tasted. Hell, everything tastes good. I feel a current of energy surging through me, and my mind is running like a dynamo. I want to jump and prance with joy. What's going on, Doc? This isn't some terminal reaction before the body cashes in, is it?"

"Hardly." She clasped her hands together and hesitated. "I don't know quite how to say this…"

"I can take it. I've been waiting for this moment for some time now," he said softly. Strangely, he did not feel disappointed or sad, accepting what he knew would eventuate.

Her eyebrows arched in surprise. "You misunderstand. Your scans didn't find any trace of cancer cells. You appear to be in total remission."

"What?"

"You're recovering. Still weak, and your body mass is way down, but we'll hold you here for another week until you regain some weight. You'll undergo a rehab program of exercises to build sufficient stamina so you can look after yourself. If everything goes well, I might release you on Saturday, April 9."

He tilted his head. "This isn't some April fools gag, is it?"

"I am being perfectly serious. You're recovering. This is an unprecedented medical event. With your permission, I would like to write a paper on you. Your anonymity will be protected."

He would actually live? The shock hit him and he couldn't say anything. At any moment, he expected to wake from what had only been a pleasant dream. A surge of emotion made him swallow hard and his eyes stung.

"Ah, shit," he mumbled and sniffed. He reached for the box of tissues beside the electronic clock, plucked out two and blew his nose. After a loud exhale, he gave a wan smile. "Sorry about that," he mumbled.

"I'm delighted for you. Not many of them leave this room walking." She cleared her throat, cool and collected. "I will maintain your treatment for another two days. Next Tuesday, we'll carry out a final set of scans to confirm my diagnosis. I also want to run another set two weeks after your release." She stood and smoothed down her skirt. "I shall see you this evening."

"Dr. Dalton?"

She turned, hand on the door handle. "Yes?"

"Thank you," he said, voice thick with emotion. "About that paper? Go for it."

She nodded and walked out.

Shait.

He groped for the phone, scrolled down the Contacts list, and pressed an icon.

"First Teeth, Penny speaking. How can I help you?"

"Hi, Penny. This is Andrew Payne. Can you please ask Dr. Teller to call me at her earliest convenience?"

"Of course."

"Thank you. Bye." He hung up and pressed another icon.

"Andrew! This is a pleasant surprise, dear," his mom gushed. "How are you?"

"You won't believe this, Mom, but I'm in remission! The treatment worked."

She gasped, and he heard a sob. "You're in remission?"

"Dr. Dalton is keeping me here to fatten me up, but I might be released on April 9."

"Oh, this is such wonderful news. I cannot believe it."

She cried, and his own tears welled. "Let Dad know, will you?"

"Of course. We'll visit as soon as we can."

"Love you, Mom."

"Bye, dear."

He reached for more tissues and blew his nose. Hell!

The cell trilled and he smiled when he saw the caller's icon. "Hi, gorgeous."

"Penny told me you called. Is everything all right?"

"Remember that fantasy we had?"

"Fantasy? What are you talking about?"

"We can have it now, my sweet, and it will last forever. I'm going to be okay. The cancer is gone."

"Oh, my God! Tell me you're not joking."

"It's gone," he said gently.

"Don't go anywhere! I'll be right over."

"No need to rush. I'll be here all day."

"Ten minutes!" she declared and hung up, but not before he heard a happy squeal.

When his Adriana makes up her mind about something, like a force of nature, best to simply hang on and enjoy the ride. A broad smile on his face, he pressed the buzzer. Despina walked in after several minutes and he spread his arms.

"Will you let me hug you?"

She looked at him suspiciously. "What's up?"

"I'm in remission. It looks like you'll be collecting that pool after all."

She cried out and walked into his arms. He kissed her cheek and brushed back a lock of hair.

"You were swell, and you helped me through the tough parts."

Her smile lit her face and she dabbed at her eyes. "You should see some I deal with." She straightened and pulled down her uniform. "How long will you be here?"

"If I'm a good boy, Dr. Dalton might let me go in a weeks' time."

"Oh, this is wonderful. I've got to tell the others."

"Can I have some more coffee, please, and another cup? No, tea! Adriana is coming, and she prefers tea."

"Does she know?"

"I just called her."

"I'm sure she is bursting with joy."

Despina rushed out and he shook his head. Another whirlwind.

It did not take ten minutes. More like twenty before Adriana burst into the room. Without saying anything, she flung herself at him and sobbed. It took a while for her to calm down. He did not feel too steady himself.

She lifted her head, eyes swimming in happy tears, and kissed him. "Oh, Andrew. I hoped and prayed, but I never dared imagine that my dream would actually come true."

"Neither did I, my sweetie. That walk along the beach? It looks like we'll manage that after all."

"Anything! Anywhere!" She sniffed and stroked his face. "You still look like crap, you know," she declared. They both laughed hysterically as all the pent-up emotion, tension, and anxiety finally dissolved.

He squeezed her against him, never wanting to let go.

* * *

Andrew swept his gaze around the room, his home for the last seven weeks, feelings mixed. He was not sorry to leave. Too many unpleasant indelible memories he never wanted to experience again. On the other hand, he never expected to walk out either.

A smile tugged at the corner of his mouth as he looked fondly at his formidable doctor. How does one repay someone for saving his life? Too bad nobody from Broca Genetics could share this moment. He sent Dr. Ivone Masters a personal email expressing his heartfelt thanks and appreciation for everything they had done for him. Expecting a formal, clinical response, her warm reply surprised him. They were truly all nice people behind those professional masks.

He stuck out his hand. "Dr. Dalton, a simple thank you cannot fully express what I feel for what your tireless efforts have done for me."

Her mouth twitched as they shook hands. "You haven't seen the last of me yet."

He certainly would not. For the next six months, he'll undergo regular scans, and Broca wanted blood and tissue samples for ongoing analysis. The inside of his elbows twitched at the prospect, recovering from abuse they received to date. Pin cushions.

"I trust it will not be for an extended stay."

"Good luck."

He turned to Despina and gave her a firm hug. "Your sunshine helped me more than you can know. It's time now that you cast that sunshine on someone else."

She smiled and her arms went around him. "I'll miss you, but not that much that I want to see you here again."

He nodded and turned. "Mrs. Courtney, thank you for everything."

Her small grin did not crack her face as he expected.

He picked up his carry-on bag, glanced at Adriana, and walked out, his strides strong and filled with purpose.

You can stick it, Death.

A week of strenuous rehab, a regimen of some very uncomfortable exercises, a full diet, restored a lot of his normal weight and condition. A few more kilos would do it. He could not believe the repair factor his body exhibited. All the nurses expressed surprise at his rapid recovery. Whatever Broca made for him had performed beyond all expectations. Not only his physiological recovery that amazed him and everyone else, but how he felt inside.

He fancied if he touched an appliance, it would start without being plugged in. He tried it once with his shaver. It did not work, of course, but it did not diminish the feeling of raw power coursing through him. He also felt incredibly strong, able to lift barbells he used to strain over at his peak. The sense of unlimited energy made him feel that he could run forever. All his senses were sharper, but Dr. Dalton assured him it was a normal post-trauma reaction. Perhaps, but he still believed his treatment had improved him somehow, including a heightened IQ. He tested himself using Googled quizzes. Not clinically definitive, but his mind buzzed with ideas, and seemed to grasp concepts faster. It simply felt giddying.

As he waited for the elevator, he wanted to raise his arms and jump for joy. Adriana gave him a whimsical smile.

"Happy thoughts?"

"If only you knew, sweetie."

He had a better part of Sunday to insert himself back into a normal life. Dinner at his parents' place should prove memorable, if his mother did not descend into hysterics. Totally different from her calm and detached professional persona at the university. He decided she could get emotional all she wanted. Nothing would spoil the euphoria he felt being well again.

Outside, not much traffic along Victoria Parade. April greeted him with warm sunshine and clear skies. Not a breath of wind stirred. Adriana led him to her dark green Corolla and he dumped his carry-on onto the back seat. He buckled in beside her and she looked at him.

"Ready?"

"Let her rip, gorgeous. Andrew Payne is back, world."

She laughed. "Dupe." Her face became serious. "Thank you for giving me back my fantasy," she whispered, eyes sparkling with feeling.

He leaned toward her and gave her a light kiss. "You kept me alive, Adriana. Broca may have healed my body, but you kept me going when the nights became dark, as were some of my days. Then you came to visit and life became bright again. I would not have made it without you."

She brushed his cheek. "I have you back. That's all that counts."

As she drove through the city, neither said much. Hand on her thigh, comforted by the connection, he gazed at the city he never expected to see again. In some subtle way, it looked the same, yet different. He decided the city had not changed. He changed. How that change would manifest itself something he looked forward to seeing.

Neither Dr. Dalton nor Broca Genetics could tell him if his

recovery was permanent and he could look forward to a normal lifespan, or something transitory that would see his cancer rear its head again. Hence, the ongoing scans and blood tests. He did not worry about it. Five years…five months…five days, he once said. He would use whatever time he had and make it count.

"What are you thinking?" Adriana said, waiting for the light to change.

"How lucky I am to have you, and how selfish I've been."

"Selfish?"

"Even before I got benched, feeling sorry for myself because I felt cheated out of a life I never expected to end, I only thought how this affected me. I knew you were taking it hard, watching me waste away, and it must have been tough, I kept thinking how you helped me through this without getting anything back in return. I didn't ask how I could help you deal with your own emotions and trauma, and I'm sorry for that. If you give me another chance, I'll try and make it up to you."

The lights changed and she headed past the Arts Center and up St. Kilda Road. After a moment of silence, she glanced at him.

"Despite everything, you kept loving me, and that gave me strength to cope. I didn't need anything else. I know that you wanted to send me away more than once to spare me watching you suffer, but you didn't. I know I helped you, and I would have done more if I could. You may think you were selfish, but so was I. I wanted to hold onto every moment I could with you, and you let me do that. Our fantasy is back and there'll be lots more time for both of us."

When she pulled into their driveway, he got out and stared at his house…their house. He nodded and dragged out his light carry-on. She opened the front door, switched off the alarm, and turned to face him. A small smile played across her face and she walked into his arms.

"Welcome home."

When the kiss ended, he exhaled loudly. "Wow. If I knew it

would be like this, I'd have come back sooner."

"Do you want to rest? Eat anything?"

He pulled her against him and stared into her eyes. "There is only one thing I want to eat, gorgeous," he growled, burning with a different type of hunger.

"In that case, I better feed you," she murmured, eyes bright.

She did. Afterward, he rested content in her arms. A soft purr of satisfaction came from somewhere deep in her throat as her fingernails marched playfully across his chest.

"My bronzed hunk."

"Not bronzed anymore," he countered. "Maybe not ever again. If I dare go out without a long-sleeved shirt, every part of me plastered with sunblock, Dr. Dalton will put me in solitary."

She giggled. "Is she really that terrible?"

"Behind her formidable façade lies a very caring person. I was lucky to have her as my doctor."

"She is very pretty."

He smiled. "Jealous?"

"I saw how you looked at her."

"She is a beautiful woman, but I only have eyes for you, and I always will."

She sighed and snuggled closer. "You'd better, or I'll scratch them out."

He wanted to tickle her, but refrained. He did it once and got a shock. Helpless with laughter, she managed to free herself and slapped him. It surprised the hell out of him. He apologized, and she apologized, blushing furiously, the reconciliation satisfying for both. She did not mind his hands wandering over her, but no funny stuff.

His hands did roam over her as they showered, and he helped wash her back…and front.

After a simple lunch, they had to leave room for what would undoubtedly be a sumptuous dinner—lunch next Sunday with her folks—she wrapped her arms around him as they sat on the couch listening to easy music coming from the surround system, mugs of tea on the coffee table. Not normally a tea drinker, he got to like it and alternated.

"You want to go to work tomorrow?" Adriana asked, a finger tracing the outline of his chin.

"What am I going to do at home? I feel grand. Not a hundred percent perhaps, but good enough for FutureTech. I spoke to Regan Price on Thursday and he gave me my old job back. Why wouldn't he? I'm his ideas man. They've got bright-eyed geniuses always tossing around new things, but I've got angles they might have missed. Anyway, they can always say no if they don't like what I come up with."

"And you have a bright idea now, I can tell."

He looked at her, anxious to share his vision.

"The *Fighter Combat* game? I used that as a testbed for a grander scheme. How do you think commercial and military pilots get trained?"

"Taking lessons like anybody else, I suppose. They also use flight simulators, I think."

"You're darn right they use flight simulators, and the more complex an aircraft, there is a need for a correspondingly complex training simulator. Those things can run to twenty million or more, and all major airlines have them, or send pilots to one of the manufacturers for training. Now imagine a virtual simulator that replaces existing mechanical boxes."

She thought about it for a second and sat up. "Is it possible? I mean, an airliner has a cockpit full of instruments and switches and stuff. Can all that be programmed?"

"You played my *Fighter Combat* game. How did it feel?"

"I thought I flew the real thing. It took me a few goes to get the hang of all those controls, but it felt real."

"Imagine if I created a totally real B737 cockpit, with all the instrument visuals, switches, and mechanical controls. A pilot would strap himself into a seat—he would fall out if he didn't—

slip on his sensor gloves and a full motion headset—"

"And he or she would see themselves in a real cockpit," she mused, beginning to see what he was getting at.

"Damn right, and he would carry out every procedure to fly the aircraft as in a mechanical trainer. All the instrumentation and selectable visual displays must provide authentic feedback, including motion reactions, but that's easy to program. It would take some time, but it can be done. For all intents and purposes, he would be flying a real aircraft against a realistic background."

Her eyes lit and her mouth formed a large O. "A trainer on a DVD," she breathed in wonder.

"Well, it wouldn't be on a DVD, but you get the idea. I could give aircraft manufacturers and airlines trainers for a fraction of what they're paying now, and pilots would be able to get all the regulatory certifications. The other advantage of having a VR simulator, aircraft upgrades could be programmed in a jiffy. Once the design architecture is worked out, the concept can be used to create flight simulators for all major commercial and military aircraft. FutureTech would be sitting on a mountain of gold."

"But they're a games developer."

"And I'll give them a real world game they have never seen before. I'm surprised that nobody has thought of this. No, that's not true. Somebody must have thought of it, but the technology didn't exist to realize it. My 3D rendering sets makes this now possible."

She turned away for a moment.

"What is it?" he asked gently.

"It's a wonderful concept…"

"But…"

"Just thinking how many people will lose their jobs when existing trainer companies fold because of your invention."

"I thought about that, and people *will* lose jobs, and some will never work again, but I can't sit on this because of that. I've got to do this, you understand?"

She sighed and snuggled closer. "I know. There's always a price to pay when something new comes along," she murmured. After a moment, she sat up, eyes round. "There is something you could do that won't cost anyone their job!"

"What's that?"

"You could build an application to train dentists!"

He stared at her, startled by the concept.

"When I studied for my degree," she gushed, "we trained using plastic skulls and teeth. We were not allowed to work on real patients until the final year, and then under strict supervision. Understandably enough. A slip of the drill or cutter, and I could do a lot of damage. With a VR trainer mimicking a real patient through all possible procedures, students would benefit enormously and build confidence. You cannot image how nerve-racking it is to handle a real patient who has put their trust into your hands."

"That's a great idea, sweetie. It really is. What's more, I'll have you as a subject matter expert while building it."

She smiled. "After the flight simulator, right?"

He looked sheepish. "Well…"

"Never mind. I understand."

He wagged a finger. "I won't forget, though. You have me fired up with the idea, you know."

"And I'll make sure you don't forget," she declared and settled into his arms. "We're going to have fun, you and I."

"What we had a few minutes ago wasn't fun enough?" he teased, and she fisted his ribs.

"Dupe, and randy old goat."

He lay back, Adriana a warm bundle at his side, and he sighed with contentment, not wanting anything else.

Chapter Six

Adriana wrapped her arm around his, and they strolled along the sleepy tree-lined street lit by tall light poles toward the bustling, noisy Toorak Road. Although relatively warm, the evening had a fresh bite when the gentle southerly stirred the leaves.

Andrew wore a thick sleeveless black sweater and navy pants. In dark olive trousers and cream turtleneck, Adriana looked smart and fashionable without being formal. Only a Saturday night dinner, no need to dress up. Did he make a mistake not picking something more formal? Too late now.

They turned into Toorak Road and entered a new world. Trams clattered along the tracks, cars streamed past like beads on a string, and sidewalks were full of people ambling along, perusing store displays, or checking restaurants offering a range of local and international cuisine to satisfy the most discerning connoisseur. From a quick takeaway, a fish and chips shop, pizzas, to the refined and elegant.

Farther down the street, a police siren wailed after a miscreant, or simply in a hurry. An ordinary driver goes three kilometers over the speed limit, and a blue light would flash behind him in seconds. Many cops openly flaunted the road rules. After all, who would book them? The police also handled speed camera records, Andrew reminded himself. He once received a ticket on this very road following a cop driving fifty in a sixty zone. He overtook, momentarily going over the speed limit, and the cop immediately flashed his lights. The crusty sergeant showed no interest in Andrew's reason for violating the speed limit and issued him a ticket. He refused to pay and received a summons for a court appearance. Ordinarily, fighting a traffic infringement not worth the hassle, but he felt wronged. The magistrate heard the evidence and invited Andrew to plead his case. When the reason behind the fine surfaced, the magistrate glared at the sergeant in disgust, dismissed the case, and awarded costs to Victoria Police. He got off, but the bastards refused to cancel one demerit point off his license. When he told Reynold Parker, the lawyer offered to take this further, but Andrew declined. It simply did not pay to start a war over it.

He stopped before a large plate glass window and pointed at the painted sign. Adriana looked up.

"Caffe Giordino? Our pit stop?"

"We're here," he declared. "Shall we?"

He opened the heavy glass door and waited for her to get in, and were immediately assaulted by animated conversation and smells of Italian food. An attractive brunette in a white shirt and black pants confirmed his reservation and led them to a back corner table. He specified this when making the booking. A crowded restaurant did not bother him, but he wanted a semblance of privacy for what he had in mind tonight.

The small square table covered by a heavy cream cloth, a lit candle resting in a red jar, and the warm atmosphere, made for a cozy ambiance. Some places he visited had a decidedly cool feel, regardless of décor and the clientele. This restaurant exuded friendliness and informality. He had been here before and always liked it.

He poured water into Adriana's glass and had some himself. Taking a sip, she looked around with approval.

"Comfy," she said and picked up the menu.

The waitress came wearing a standard customer smile. "Would you like anything to drink?"

"Mineral water for me, please," Adriana said.

"A bottle of chilled Luigi Cavalli Lambrusco," Andrew told her. She nodded and strode off.

"Busy week?" Adriana asked.

"Catching up with the latest at work," he said, picked up a finger bread stick and crunched on it. "FutureTech canned all pipeline projects to make them compatible with my macros. This will delay some rollouts, but it will be worth it. Since the December release, the bottom has pretty much fallen out from under all other formats. Old games are still selling, as are some of Future-Tech's, but players who can afford high-end computers have flocked to the new format. My two games are also selling well. With royalties and license fee, I took out an option to purchase more of their shares. The way business is going for them, it's a sound investment."

"I'm not into these things, but I think my dad may have listened to your advice. Did you speak to your boss about the flight trainer?"

He shook his head. "It'll take me a week or two to research the B737 cockpit layout, and two months or so of programming to develop a basic prototype. I won't have anything to show him until July at the earliest. I could tell him what I'm planning and work on it at the office, but I want something tangible to show him. A demonstration is the best way to convince FutureTech to go commercial."

"What are you working on now?"

"Storyboarding a Mars mission and building a habitat, with some aliens thrown in for flavor."

She chuckled. "Little green men?"

"Not little or green, or naked," he added. "It amuses me no end to see aliens in movies and social media posts portrayed naked with bulging heads and large black eyes. If people need to dress, I suspect aliens need pants as well. What about you?"

"Also busy," she said. "It never ends. I spoke to Dr. Hendrix about the VR training simulator, and he seemed excited. There is nothing on the market now remotely like it."

"We'll work on it," he promised.

The waitress came with her tablet and hit them with another

smile. "Ready to order?"

Adriana looked at her. "I'll have the crayfish. For dessert, the Tiramisu."

"Can we have some bruschetta to start?" he said. "For the main, the saltimbocca. A Tiramisu for me as well."

"Very good." She tapped quickly into the tablet, nodded, and walked off.

Adriana gave a sheepish smile. "Every time I see Tiramisu on a menu, I'm done. I simply love it."

"That's why I got it too," he said.

Almost immediately, the waitress brought the bruschetta and the wine. He poured half a glass for both of them and took a sip. Nice and chilled, which enhanced the flavor. Adriana tried hers and nodded.

"Not bad."

He picked up the chargrilled bread topped with chopped to-matoes, herbs, and olive oil, and took a bite.

"This is also not bad."

Adriana helped herself to one. "Fresh tomatoes. I had one once where they were positively sagging. Ugh."

He chuckled at her expression.

"How does it feel to be working again?" she asked between bites.

"A little strange for the first two days, but the sight of familiar people and surroundings helped me settle in quickly. It's only been a week, but I feel like I never left."

"I know," she said. "I felt the same way after I took some time off. A week later, I wanted more leave."

He laughed. "I know the feeling. It's like I never had a break."

"Seriously, you should develop the dentist simulator. It would make an invaluable training tool."

"I will, count on it. You could help me by digging up proce-dural material."

"There's lots of stuff from my course. I can also get you shots of our clinic and treatment rooms. I'll have to get permission from Dr. Hendrix for that, but I'm sure he won't mind, provided you don't use anything that could identify us."

"You got it."

Shortly, the main course arrived, and Adriana looked at her crayfish smothered with fried onion rings, cherry tomatoes, and strips of raw ham, with a gleam in her eyes, ready to get started. His large portion of veal stuffed with prosciutto and fried sausage looked and smelled inviting.

He lifted his glass, and she touched it with hers.

"To what we're about to receive, may we be eternally grateful," he intoned seriously, and she laughed.

"Dupe."

He peered at her from time to time as he ate, marveling at the transformation since his return from the Institute. Always trying to cheer him up when she visited, an undercurrent of gloom and helplessness nevertheless hovered about her. Now, she glowed with happiness, and he basked in her glow, ridiculously pleased.

He felt stronger every day, and his body slowly regained trim and hardness. An incredible recovery in such a short time. After considering it might be too soon, Adriana agreed to accompany him on his morning runs. He simply had to release the energy bubbling inside him. During the week, they lunched together three times, and managed to go home twice. Once home, he did little things for her to express his love and thanks for being with him. In bed, they talked, sometimes long into the night. She played her violin a couple of times, and he got all chocked up. He would hold her in his arms as she slept, content. They would wake up in the small hours, make tea or coffee, and talk some more. It did not seem to matter that they were both short on sleep. They always greeted a new day energized.

He tried some of her crayfish, and he shared his veal. Done, they dug into the Tiramisu with undisguised gusto, Adriana grinning insanely between bites, and he laughed. They were both crazy. That was all there was to it. A delicately sweet cappuccino topped off a great meal. Sensing the time had come, he took a long breath to still a tremor of nervousness, and pulled out a little black box from his pocket. Adriana saw it and froze, eyes alive. He opened the box and took out a gold ring with a glittering rectangular sapphire.

"Adriana, I loved you from the moment I saw you. I loved you when you stood by me through the black days. If possible, I love you even more now. What we have may be a fantasy, but if it is, I don't want it to end, and I want to share it with you for all time. Will you marry me and make it last for all time?"

Eyes bright, her radiant smile melted his heart.

"You're a dupe, Andrew Payne. I thought you would never ask."

He reached for her hand and slipped on the ring, fighting back a surge of emotion. She leaned toward him and her sweet lips melted against his.

"For all time," she whispered.

A couple at the next table beamed at them and clapped enthusiastically. He smiled and nodded.

Adriana splayed her fingers and gazed at the ring. After a moment, she looked at him. "How did you know that I don't like diamonds?"

"I didn't. Little things, I suppose. A word here and there told me that you might like something else. I couldn't be sure, as diamonds are the expected thing."

"I like this much better," she declared firmly, and her eyes turned deep green. "Let's go home."

* * *

Andrew could not believe the things that needed doing even for a simple wedding.

His lovely bride-to-be insisted on something modest. He did

not want a large gaggle either. Apart from his two friends and immediate family, there were not many on his side he wanted to invite. Even so, the final tally came to fifty-eight people.

Actually, he did not have much to do, since parents from both sides organized the whole thing. As expected, everybody expressed delight when he announced the engagement, his mom looking exceptionally radiant. As one of the bridesmaids, Belana could not contain herself. He asked Mark Sanders to be his best man, and Orwell Young his gofer and general helper.

When Mark saw Adriana's maid of honor for the first time, the girl working at the North Melbourne clinic, Andrew could see sparks fly between them. Petite, slim, raven hair that fell halfway down her back, black eyes that glinted with humor, Susan Chee looked like a walking Chinese jade doll. Hard-bitten, a confirmed bachelor, Mark could not take his eyes off her, suddenly awkward, not at all in character. She saw his confusion and, according to Adriana, derived much amusement. Andrew liked Susan immediately, and hoped the two would hit it off. She would be good for his friend. That only left Orwell to sort out.

Adriana's parents booked the wedding at the St. Francis of Assisi Catholic church in Footscray, something that pleased Adriana's mom, and his dad organized the reception at the Crown Tower on Southbank in the city. Andrew did not know what went on at Adriana's hen night, perhaps a good thing, and his buck's party did not involve anything wild, like being tossed off the St. Kilda Beach pier.

It all came together in a sudden rush on Saturday, June 11. Andrew stood before the altar, Mark beside him. The church organ began to play Richard Strauss' *Also sprach Zarathustra*, which made his arms prickle with goosebumps. Adriana slowly walked down the aisle, her father beside her to give her away, an angel in her bridal gown. A small tiara held her veil, but it could not hide her radiance. She stopped beside him and hit him with an intimate smile. If he died on the spot, he could not be happier.

"I do," Adriana said in a clear voice, and he slipped on the wedding band.

The parish priest closed his book, smiled, and nodded. "You may kiss the bride."

Andrew lifted her veil, gazed deeply into her enchanting green orbs, and gently kissed her. When he pulled back, her eyes told him this was not the end.

Then came the signing of the register and marriage certificate, photo shoots, and he finally led his bride down the aisle. Outside the church, both were showered with confetti. He felt relief when he got into the white stretch limousine, embraced his brand new wife, and kissed her properly.

"Hello, Mrs. Payne."

"Hello, Mr. Payne."

Looking at each other, they burst out laughing.

The limo took them to Treasury Gardens for a formal photo shoot, which took a better party of an hour. Although cool, they were fortunate to have a clear, sunny day. The business done, Adriana glad to get into the warm limo, they were driven to the Crown Casino tower for the reception. At two in the morning, the party finally broke up. Totally exhausted, they were happy to have Mark drive them home. After a shower, the bed felt wonderful, and they could relax after a hectic, but satisfying day.

Adriana's head in the crook of his arm, one hand holding him tight, he slowly stroked her back.

"You know something?"

"What?"

"This is our wedding day, but I don't feel any different. Should I?"

"You should...if we were newlyweds and this was our first night together. We're not, because I married you the day I moved in with you."

He turned his head to look at her, but could not see anything in the darkness.

"You're right. That's when we had our true wedding day. Still, I ought to feel something."

"You don't feel anything because you're an insensitive, degenerate lug."

"Insensitive degenerate?" He grabbed her and squeezed until she squealed, her fists pounding his chest. He let go and she lay on top of him, kissing his cheeks and forehead until their lips met. She gave a contented sigh and rested her head against him. After a while, she rolled away and her breathing slowed.

Cradled in warm darkness, Andrew held his wife, waiting for the night to take him.

The next afternoon, a QANTAS flight took them to Darwin for ten days of incomparable ecstasy and sightseeing.

They took a day trip to Kakadu, and a half-day boat tour to Adelaide River where the guide dangled bait on a pole to entice crocodiles to jump out of the water for it. They rested for a day at their Palms City Resort hotel, right on the Esplanade, a block away from the Bicentennial Park and the Crocosaurus Cove, where they got to see more crocks.

Adriana enjoyed Katherine Gorge and the Litchfield National Park. She had never seen the real outback, and neither had he. Both loved the dry interior heat, a far cry from Melbourne's cloying cold.

They spent lazy evenings walking hand in hand, watching red sunsets and painted skies. Darwin a small city and everything laid out within easy walking distance. When not touring, they explored curio shops and indulged in exotic cuisine. For the first time in her life, Adriana saw Aborigines everywhere. Sadly, seeing a few slumped beside a supermarket, staring vacantly at nothing, a bottle at their side, momentarily spoiled their enjoyment. The clash of cultures sounded loud there.

Then it ended, and they had to return to the real world.

The airport cab dropped them off at their house, and Andrew shivered, still in his summer gear. Light rain blurred outlines. He ran to the front door and sighed with relief when he stepped into the warm interior, the automatic heating system at work. Adriana made to walk in, and he put up his hand. Without saying anything, he picked her up and carried her in.

"I haven't had a chance to do this before, Mrs. Payne."

"Dupe," she murmured into his ear.

She hugged his neck and her soft lips found him. Suddenly, it became much warmer.

* * *

The port engine fire alarm display blinked red, accompanied by urgent beeping. Andrew stabbed the button to shut off the noise and pulled back the left thrust lever. The engine spooled down to a stop. Immediately, the starboard engine pushed the B737-MAX to port and the aircraft sagged into a steep bank. The sky outside wheeled left and down, showing the suburban sprawl around Inglewood in the western approach to LA International. The control yoke in his hand began to shake in warning.

"Stall...Stall...Stall," a female voice announced urgently. "Power...Power...Power."

"Port flaps! Full," he commanded. This would give the left wing more lift and keep it up. Warren reached with his left hand and selected forty degrees of flap. The simulation showed him in a blue uniform with three stripes of a senor flight officer.

Andrew turned the yoke to the right to counter the bank and pulled back slightly. He stepped on the right rudder pedal and pushed the right thrust lever forward a bit, adding power, which leveled the aircraft and turned it to starboard, back on course.

"LAX tower, this is flight DL375, declaring an inflight emergency. Requesting permission for immediate landing," Warren called out.

"DL375, you are cleared for immediate landing. Runway 24L. Twenty-one knots crosswind, gusting west to east. Traffic at your three o'clock. Airbus A350. Distance, two miles."

"DL375, roger."

Andrew lined up with the outer parallel runway, the approach strobe lights a welcome sight. High cirrostratus clouds wound through a murky sky. LAX International lay spread before him in a profusion of runways, taxiways, and terminal spokes filled with parked and moving aircraft.

"Starboard flaps," he called out.

Warren selected thirty-five degrees. "Gear down and locked," he added.

Andrew checked the three green lights and nodded. He cut power and pushed the yoke forward, the LED displays showing the artificial horizon and glide path, the screens replicated on the copilot's side. He corrected a slight port drift with the rudder pedal, and the runway came rushing toward him. The B737 came down with a scrape of tires and a simulated jolt. He immediately engaged half reverse thrust, holding the yoke firmly to prevent the aircraft from skewing port induced by the right engine. A few seconds later, it stopped and he flipped switches to cut power.

Everything looked and felt very real, but lacked the jolt of an actual landing. He could simulate the six degrees of freedom a body could move through while in flight, but nothing existed to replicate the physical sensations—yet. He had ideas about that.

He nodded to Warren and took off his headset and controller gloves, and found himself back in the conference room.

Regan Price dragged off his headset, eyes glazed, breathing heavily. He wiped sweat off his brow with an unsteady hand.

"Jesus Christ! I thought we bought it when the thing went into a stall. I almost fell out of my seat." He exhaled loudly and grimaced. "I think I wet my pants. I never imagined something like that could be possible."

Andrew smiled at the reaction, somewhat pleased. He had run multiple simulations with Adriana acting as pilot and copilot, and the realism always left her shaken. She actually came to like the non-event takeoffs, landings, and routine instrument checks. The emergency scenarios made her gasp for breath. Both had a lot of fun playing the simulator.

"To evaluate this properly, Regan," he said," I suggest you get a real airline pilot to try it."

Price stared at him. "Are you kidding? We show something like this to a commercial pilot, it'll be page one news an hour after he walks out of here. This remains under wraps until I've had a chance to brief corporate. Is that clear?" He gave a soft sigh. "You probably gave this some thought and have a plan. Spill it."

Andrew took a deep breath. His proposal may flounder for business reasons, but his MBA studies gave him a firm handle how to prepare for these things. Reynold Parker's coaching also helped.

"From what I've read, it's estimated that by 2025, the world commercial and military flight simulator market will be on the order of eight billion."

Price stared at him. "Eight billion?"

Andrew could see dollar signs in the general manager's eyes, and sympathized. He looked at a staggering sum. World travel on the rise again and would keep rising as countries and airlines opened new destinations.

"There are some eighty-two companies directly and indirectly involved in building flight simulator trainers," he continued, "of which twelve are the most influential. You're looking at the likes of CAE, Airbus, Boeing, Raytheon, and TE Flight, among others. By end of 2020, there were approximately 1,700 simulators of various types installed around the world. With the commercial market recovery post-COVID-19, this number should expand substantially. I submit, if FutureTech rolls out virtual reality trainers, it could become a dominant player in the marketplace."

"In the same way your 3D rendering macros made us in VR games," Price mused. "What will it take to finish developing your prototype?"

"The software needs to be made fully FAA and EASA certificate ready," Andrew told him. "That's something I cannot do as I lack the necessary technical expertise. However, I feel that eight weeks of development, followed by two weeks of testing, will turn the prototype into an adequate marketing demo. Once the simulator is ready, I suggest FutureTech engage someone like TE Flight Corp to complete development and conduct final certification testing and marketing. If FutureTech can bring in TE, or somebody like them on board, you'll be in a position to distribute trainer simulators for a whole range of commercial and military aircraft. They're an industry leader and know how to do these things."

"Why TE Flight? Why not somebody like Boeing or Raytheon?"

"I feel Boeing would want to preference their own aircraft, while Raytheon is primarily a military supplier. In my view, FutureTech should aim to provide simulators for all major aircraft types and manufacturers to maximize return on investment. Before the collapse of passenger services during 2020, CAE, Inc. was the largest manufacturer of commercial and military flight trainers, with 73% of the world market. Early in 2021, TE Flight, a company based in California, mounted a hostile takeover, and now controls CAE."

"Go on," Price prompted.

"A conventional mechanical trainer can cost anywhere from ten to twenty million. Most of that cost is absorbed interfacing with real time movement mechanical jacks. A VR simulator won't have that overhead, and I believe we could sell one for about a million. Corporate marketing, and whomever you choose to partner with, can work out the optimal numbers."

Andrew looked hard at the general manager. "Right now, flight simulators are only built for large airliners and the military, which ignores the enormous marketplace represented by small jets and propeller aircraft. This is primarily due to cost considerations. I believe FutureTech should enter that market. It would take time to develop simulators for some of the more popular aircraft, but we've got a captive market," he added with a smile.

Price looked thoughtful. "Getting into the military space would require security clearances. Why not let TE Flight use your macros to convert existing trainers?"

"That would be a simple solution, I agree, but with a nil gain to FutureTech."

"We would demand a royalty for every trainer they sell."

"And that's all you'd have. By doing the development, you'll be expanding our skill base, grow the company, and establish a broader market footprint."

"If we go with TE, they might insist on doing the work themselves for proprietary and security reasons."

Andrew shrugged. "They're not the only flight trainer developer out there, Mr. Price."

"And what do you want for this?"

"Twenty thousand FutureTech shares, and a three percent royalty for every trainer sold or used by TE for internal training purposes—if you go with TE—payable to my company, Usque Vision."

At the current share price, this came to $563,000. In Andrew's opinion, a reasonable demand for what he offered FutureTech. He could have asked for more, but the deal sweetener lay in the royalty, something Price understood.

In July, his royalty came from sale of *Fighter Combat* and *Hunter* games, over $657,000. Adriana could not believe it, somewhat staggered by the sum. He immediately purchased 24,000 FutureTech shares and made a call option to purchase 12,000 within twelve months at the current market price. An unbelievable change of fortune since April. A fairy must have touched him after all.

He considered buying into Broca Genetics, but decided to

stick with a company he knew and understood. For the time be-ing anyway.

"Twenty thousand, eh? I'll run this past our corporate office and get back to you. Can I demonstrate this for them?"

"If they have a pilot able to run the simulator, I'll give you restricted access to my home server. However, no one sees this without a signed nondisclosure confidentiality agreement."

Price nodded. "I suppose you filed a patent for this thing?"

"Already registered."

Price stood and made for the door, then turned. "Warren will assign another project leader to take over your existing work. You and your team are now full-time on the flight trainer project. He'll get their nondisclosure signatures for you."

Andrew slowly rose. "Thanks for your vote of confidence, Regan. I'm happy to start work, but I trust you'll understand why I cannot upload the software to FutureTech's system until I have a signed agreement from corporate."

Price's mouth twitched. "You have a prepared contract?"

"Of course."

"Send it to me," he ordered and shook his head. "I still cannot believe what I've seen," he growled and strode out.

Downstairs, Andrew fixed himself a mug of coffee and went to his desk. In the kitchenette, some of his coworkers wanted to know what went on in the conference room. Demonstrating a new game, he told them, and left it at that. It would all come out in due course, provided FutureTech came on board, which he felt certain they would. Well, almost certain. They were a VR games developer, and doing very well using his 3D macros. Cor-porate might not be too keen to change a business model that worked. He felt a high degree of confidence they would, for one simple reason—money. What he put on the table for them had the potential to make them an absurd amount, provided they were willing to meet his price.

He wanted payment in shares to minimize his company's tax

liability, and to maintain a growing dividend return from his port-folio, having assigned his stock to Usque Vision. The popularity of his two games assured healthy sales for at least twelve months, which would fuel option purchases of more stock. That in turn would generate more dividend and more purchases in an escalat-ing progression. Sale of his games were bound to flatten as other FutureTech releases begin to take over. By then, he hoped his flight simulator would start generating revenue. With Adriana's dentist project in the pipeline, he had little interest developing new games.

Memory memo to self: Call Parker to send Price the contract.

His ongoing scans showed no traces of cancer, and he felt full of energy and drive. He spent a lot of his free moments develop-ing the prototype simulator. Although busy, he made sure to make time for him and Adriana. Something his dad warned him not to neglect. It would have been all too easy to bury himself in his home office full time, a certain path to marital disaster. He *wanted* to spend as much time as possible with her, and he did it by getting her involved with his simulator project. After a hesitant beginning, she came to enjoy her sessions piloting a B737-MAX. He also kept his promise to make himself familiar with all aspects of dentistry, and came to have a deep respect for Adriana's skill and valuable input. By end of the year, he told her, he would start to prototype the application.

Since his recovery, he found that he read faster and retained most of it. He sampled his grandparents' extensive library and delved into topics he never considered before: geopolitical eco-nomics, philosophy, science and technology. At times, his mind whirled in a cauldron of possibilities he struggled to absorb. He kept a notebook in his desk drawer to jot them down before new images swamped him.

What was happening to him? What had those macrophages done to him? Would he shine like a supernova, only to fade into nothingness? He stared at death and lived, but what had he become now? Would he pay a price down the track for his vigorous health? More than once, he lay awake long into the night…thinking, wondering.

As long as he had Adriana, he would cope.

He may have changed, but the world around him had not stood still either. On July 30, a joint NASA/SpaceX ship landed on the Moon for the first time since the Apollo project. Lots of talk to establish a permanent base and mine abundant rare earth minerals to break the Chinese monopoly. There were also valuable metals to be had in abundance, such as titanium, aluminum, and manganese. Sending pre-refined shipments to Earth would be easy…downhill all the way into Earth's deep gravity well. But first, they had to get there and set up complete product manufacturing. However, that was more complex than it sounded, as producers relied on numerous supply chains not available on the Moon.

Although a Monday, Andrew decided to go all out and celebrate a possible deal with FutureTech. Happy as a kid with a new toy to take apart, he waited impatiently for Adriana to come from work. They managed to go home together two or three times a week, but work commitments did not make that possible all the time. He wanted to wine and dine her at an expensive restaurant, and share with her a successful demonstration. When she walked through the door around 6:30, he saw the fatigue on her face and his plan died stillborn. Instead, they had a quiet candlelight dinner against a background of soft music. He made *gluhwein*, which filled the kitchen and lounge with the scent of cloves and cinnamon, and made both of them a little giggly. They followed dinner with a leisurely spa bath, and their cares dissolved in soapy bubbles. In bed, he held her until her breathing slowed and she slept.

After two weeks gnawing his fingernails, he walked to work on a gloomy September 5 morning. A chilly southerly drove misty rain across the city, and pedestrians hurried to get to wherever they were going. Sixteen degrees, not bad for that time of year, but the chill factor made it decidedly unpleasant outside.

He hardly had time to make himself a mug of tea and open Outlook to check emails, when Price called, wanting to see him. He took the elevator up and walked into the general manager's office. After being invited to sit down, he waited, hands on lap.

Price cleared his throat, which made Andrew remember how Dr. Dalton delivered bad news.

"Corporate has reviewed your flight simulator proposal very carefully, taking into account many commercial variables," Price began heavily. "As you pointed out, FutureTech is a VR games developer, and that's a business we understand. Venturing into the aviation sector is unknown territory fraught with risk. However, by partnering with experts in the field as you suggested, the board feels the risks can be mitigated, and I concur." Price cleared his throat again. "Rather than a share settlement you asked for, they were willing to make a one-time offer of $650,000 for your simulator, and FutureTech retains IP rights."

When Andrew heard this proposal from Reynold Parker, he told him that FutureTech should read his existing contract. He did not mind haggling over the price, but not the IP rights.

"As you know, Tompson, Tompson, and Parker, rejected this, and I have a new offer, which I understand you discussed with Mr. Parker. Twenty thousand shares, but only a two percent royalty, and you retain all IP," Price said and slid papers across the desk.

Andrew *had* discussed this with Parker, who urged him to accept, something he wanted to do anyway. The three percent claim had been an opening gambit only.

"Your law firm has validated the agreement," Price added.

Without saying anything, Andrew pulled out his pen and signed both copies, keeping one for himself. He looked up and smiled at Price's nonplussed expression.

"We have a deal, Regan," he said and stuck out his hand.

They shook and Price chuckled. "For a minute there, I thought the two percent would be a deal breaker."

"I could have made it so," Andrew said. "A twenty thousand dollar royalty on one million is small change. However, development and launch of the simulator represents a considerable investment for FutureTech, not only for the B737-MAX prototype, but for other aircraft types you may choose to handle. Some of that cost will be shared by your industry partner, but it's still a very large expense item on the company's balance sheet without an immediate return. Ordinarily, I shouldn't be concerned about stuff like that, but I feel we have more than an employee/employer relationship here."

"We do, and I'm pleased to hear you say that, Andrew," Price said. "However promising, this project faces a major risk before we realize any return at all."

"The software might not get Level D certification from the FAA or EASA?"

"Although your simulator is very realistic, it lacks actual physical motion feedback. The regulators may downgrade it for that reason."

"The board must have considered this a minimal risk, or you would not have offered me a contract. If I may, who did the evaluation?"

"One of our corporate pilots. According to the Managing Director, she couldn't stop raving about it."

Andrew smiled. "Did you select a business partner yet?"

"TE Flight Corporation is shortlisted. We invited them for a demonstration on December 14. This should give you and your team enough time to complete the prototype."

"It might not be," Andrew pointed out, and Price waved a hand.

"It should be sufficient. You'll make the presentation at our headquarters in Mountain View, followed by a visit to the TE

Flight Los Angeles facility at Long Beach. I trust you can make yourself available?"

Broca Genetics had their labs in Sunnyvale, not far from Mountain View. It would give him an opportunity to visit Dr. Ivone Masters, and personally thank her for saving his life.

"With a day at Disneyland?" Andrew queried with a smile, and Price laughed.

"You're a scoundrel, but we'll give you more than a day. Show your wife the sights. Remember, this will only be a demo to solicit an expression of interest. If TE wants to come on board, we'll talk more."

Andrew turned serious. "FutureTech must realize that TE, or any other flight simulator manufacturer, may reject this outright, as it means making their existing products obsolete."

"We considered that, of course. However, VR trainers will only make the mechanical component obsolete. The fundamental business model should not be affected. I'm sure TE will appreciate the enormous cost saving represented by a VR trainer, compared to ten or twenty million versions they now produce, and the resulting savings to airlines. I doubt their board will reject our proposal. If they do, we can approach other parties. VR is the future, and not only in flight simulators. By the way, your twenty thousand shares will be transferred to Usque Vision within the next two or three days."

"Thanks, I appreciate that."

"Now that we have a signed agreement, I'll ask Warren to assign your existing work to someone else. Anticipating your agreement, he already has nondisclosure confidentiality documents from Sandra Perkins and Thomas Anderson. Copies will be mailed to your law firm. We will provide you with a dedicated server as your development and testbed, access restricted to you and your team."

Andrew stood and nodded. "In that case, I better get started."

"One more thing. As of now, you're a project manager with a

salary of $180,000."

"Thank you, Regan. I appreciate the confidence and support you showed me."

He did not mind the promotion, but suspected an ulterior motive behind it. FutureTech may not want a mere systems analyst making a critical presentation to crusty TE Flight execs. Then again, he might be overly cynical.

Price waved a hand. "Get out of here."

Outside the office, Andrew pumped his fist. "Yes!"

At his desk, he pulled out his cell, scrolled down the Contacts list, and pressed a call icon.

"Hi, honey," Adriana replied immediately. "What's up?"

"I'm not catching you at a bad time?"

"Having a tea break. My next patient needs a root canal, which will keep me occupied for an hour or so. I'm still good for lunch, though."

"Great. I want to share some news. FutureTech signed a contract to develop my flight simulator."

He heard a happy squeal. "That's marvelous! I'm so thrilled for you."

"I'm somewhat pleased myself. We'll talk more at lunch. Love you."

"See you then. Love you too."

He hung up and smiled. With a glance at the cold mug of tea, he got up and made his way to the kitchenette. On the way back, he stopped at the bullpen where his team lived.

"Guys, can we meet in the conference room in ten minutes? There's something I want to show you."

Sandra and Thomas exchanged glances. Everyone on the floor knew of his mysterious shuffling back and forth to Price's office, but Warren had not said anything.

"A new project?" Sandra asked brightly.

"In ten minutes," Andrew told her.

* * *

Dr. Dalton cleared her throat, and Andrew tensed. The first thought that flashed through his mind, his cancer had hit back. He bit his lip and waited.

"Your scans are clear, which is excellent. From now on, I think a set of tests every three months should be sufficient. However, there is a development. During your personal research, did you read anything about telomeres?"

Vastly relieved, he gave a loud exhale. "For a minute there, Doc…"

Her mouth twitched. "You're perfectly healthy, amazingly so. That's why I want to talk about telomeres."

"Well, I do know something about them."

"Tell me what you know. It will help me explain what has happened."

"From what I understand, each chromosome is capped by a loop of nucleotide sequences. During every cell division, one set of telomere sequences is truncated. When enough of these are removed, the cell blocks further division, which induces aging and eventual cell death."

Dr. Dalton nodded. "Somewhat simplistic, but accurate enough. There is a lot of ongoing research into techniques to repair telomere sequences and restore the loop to its original length. This has extended the lifespan in experimental animals, and helped overcome several types of cancers. Cell division is not a perfect process, and repetition results in cumulative errors. After approximately fifty to seventy divisions, the cell produces a toxin to stop further mitosis, which between 24 and 48 hours, depending on cell type, leads to apoptosis—cell death. This is a vital mechanism to prevent spread of cells with damaged DNA, which is essentially cancer. Dead cells are usually eliminated by the body's macrophages. Not all cells are removed, though, the process manifesting itself as collective aging. However, in some organisms such as sponges, corals, and lobsters, senescent cells—old cells—undergo conversion to an immunogenetic phenotype that enables the immune system to eliminate them, and prevents the onset of normal aging. This process also slows down the epigenetic clock, but does not reset it. Otherwise, we'd have organisms that are effectively immortal. The term epigenetic clock is a misnomer, as there are several regulatory DNA mechanisms that control aging."

It took a few moments for Andrew to digest this, but remained confused.

"Are you saying that Broca's treatment has enabled my immune system to eliminate cells that stopped dividing, and that's what is keeping me healthy?"

"That's right, but it has done more than that. It appears to have also reset your epigenetic clock."

"Which means…"

"Your body is effectively living in year one."

He stared at her, thoughts racing. "Wow."

Year one…it's like his first twenty-five years never happened. He could easily live to a hundred! The things he could do…

"Just because your body appears able to eliminate all senescent cells, does not mean you'll not age," Dr. Dalton added. "It simply means that you've been given an extended lifespan."

"How…how did this happen?"

"Broca are not certain, and their experiments failed to replicate the result in trial patients. Their immune system eliminated dead cells, but it has not slowed or reset their epigenetic clock. In your case, numerous factors may have contributed to the eventual outcome: dosage, frequency, the condition of your immune system, the effect of checkpoint inhibitors left in your body. Many things."

"What about the extra dose Despina administered?"

"Although a possible contributing factor, we simply don't know."

"Do they have *any* idea how this happened?"

"They believe the more potent second batch of reengineered immunosurveillance macrophages, designed to block your cancer cells from deactivating the eat-me switch, is responsible. With the added receptor that binds with T-cells to mobilize your immune system, blood and tissue analysis shows that these modifications may have worked too well."

"What do you mean? These macrophages killed my cancer."

"Indeed, but they did more than that. Once the macrophages removed identified cancer cells, they reverted to their normal cell-repair state."

Understanding dawned and he gaped at her. "They restored the telomere loops in damaged cells."

"In *all* cells, Andrew. This process also somehow reset your epigenetic clock. Your cells are not immortal, as experiments show they still undergo apoptosis. Broca Genetics reengineered your macrophages by bypassing many clinical steps in order to produce something that would arrest your cancer within a very short timeframe they had available. It is therefore not surprising the results did not turn out entirely as expected.

"The Institute has worked closely with Broca on this, and our work supports their findings. The exact mechanism how your macrophages affected your cure is not entirely clear, and we were not able to replicate this with macrophages from other patients. They even tried injecting your macrophages into one patient, but he immediately exhibited a skin rash, nausea, and breathing difficulty equivalent to an anaphylactic shock. His immune system recognized your macrophages as an allergen and sought to eliminate them. Another patient did not exhibit any response at all. Given the complex biological mechanisms that control aging, I'm not surprised that we weren't able to replicate your condition."

Something occurred to him and he sat up in alarm. "Are macrophages present in seminal fluid?"

Her eyes grew large. "They certainly are, and I see what you're getting at. Has she exhibited any reaction?"

He found this somewhat embarrassing. "Well, a few days after our first time, she did say she felt a little feverish."

"Mmm. Interesting. Nothing else afterward?"

"She didn't mention anything."

"It might be an idea to bring her in for a blood sample."

"Is it possible my macrophages might be active in her body?"

"Bring her in and we'll run some tests." She pulled at her chin. "About your condition…"

If he indeed infected Adriana, would his macrophages reset her epigenetic clock? He would have to talk to her.

"Andrew…"

"Sorry. What were you saying?"

"Your condition."

"You're telling me I'm living in year one. Okay, I accept that. That won't change my life."

"It could change the lives of many others. You represent a medical puzzle, one which the Institute and Broca are keen to solve. If we can repeat this process, we could potentially offer everybody a prolonged and healthy lifespan."

"I see what you're getting at, but it's perhaps not such a good thing, Doc. Evolution has given us a fixed lifespan for a very good reason. Superficially, an extended lifespan sounds like a great idea, but there are serious social issues to consider. Given the current rate of population growth, with corresponding problems providing food, shelter, and productive employment for everyone, a hundred-year lifespan could quickly lead to mass starvation and war."

She nodded. "These are definitely issues to consider, I agree, but I suggest the benefits far outweigh any risks."

"There is something else," he said slowly. "Would this treatment be available to all, or restricted to a select few? That's how tyrannies are created."

Dr. Dalton sighed. "You're being needlessly dramatic, Andrew."

"I don't think so. You told me that Broca already has an effective treatment to cure a number of cancers using reengineered macrophages. What do they want? An immortality pill?"

"They seek to expand the breadth of human knowledge, just as I am. All knowledge has a duality, which people sometimes used to further their own ends. This should not stop us from advancing. We learned much from history and gained sufficient wisdom to apply knowledge for the benefit of mankind, not its destruction."

"And you're being idealistic, Doc, when all evidence to date demonstrates the illusion of your position."

Her mouth twitched. "You have reason to be skeptical. However, debating this does not address my immediate problem."

"Which is?"

"Broca Genetics has invited you to attend their Silicon Valley facility for three months of extensive testing and observation. They're prepared to give you substantial compensation for your cooperation, with all expenses included. I would urge you to consider this carefully."

He goggled at her, then laughed. "There's nothing to consider. I'm not interested. I have a wife, and both of us have careers. I'm not prepared to do anything to risk that. If Broca or the Institute want samples of my blood and tissue, I'm happy to give it to you, but I won't turn myself into one of their experimental animals."

"I expected this reaction, although I consider it somewhat selfish."

"Selfish? I must say, I'm surprised to hear you say that."

"Why should you be surprised? Your body holds the key to eliminate most human diseases. Isn't this worth some personal sacrifice?"

"I consider staring death in the face and living through it enough of a sacrifice."

"There may be a way for all of us to get what we want."

"I'm listening."

"The Lyndon Cancer Institute is one of the largest research centers of its type in Australia, perhaps the largest in the southern hemisphere. We have extensive facilities that made significant contributions to treatment of many cancers. I already suggested to Broca Genetics that we pool our resources. If you agree, the Institute could support their efforts without you having to go anywhere. We could research your condition from here."

"I'm already bleeding for the cause, Doc."

"We need more. We need internal body tissue samples."

Andrew stood and looked at her, hugely disappointed. Instead of a caring human being who hid her feelings behind a façade of professionalism, she actually remained hard and insensitive. To her, people were merely test subjects in a quest of some lofty goal. He had not expected this.

Something else struck him. "This isn't about saving humanity at all, is it? This is about you. The woman who found the immortality pill."

"Don't be ridiculous! You're a walking biological anomaly, which Broca and I want to solve. That's all."

"I'm sorry, Dr. Dalton. I'm prepared to donate blood and skin tissue, but I won't consent to a biopsy."

Outside the Institute building, Andrew squinted at the glare and slipped on his shades. He soaked in the ambient summer heat and shook his head, wishing he could take off his shirt and bare his body to the sun. Dr. Dalton reminded him more than once to resist such temptation, pointing out that overexposure caused all his previous problems. A hell of a way to start December, he reflected.

Dalton…and he once wanted to date her.

Heavy traffic flowed both ways along Victoria Parade. A tram clanged its bell and stopped at the pickup point. Somewhere down the boulevard, a cop siren wailed. Nobody glanced his way from the sidewalk, absorbed in their little world, like he was absorbed in his.

He descended the steps, paused on the sidewalk, and merged with others pursuing their destinations. A glance at his watch showed 11:51. Plenty of time for a leisurely stroll to Collins Street. A tram would get him there too quickly, and he had some thinking to do. Last year, when his future looked bleak, he recalled telling the fates to screw themselves. If telling them off got him a new life, perhaps he should do it more often. On reflection, he figured it might be better not to push his luck.

Year one...

What exactly did that mean? A promise? A possibility at best. That proverbial cement truck could still collect him at any time, which would be kind of stiff for someone who might live to a hundred. When Dr. Dalton said that his tailored macrophages repaired every cell, logically, that must also include his neurons, although those things were unlike any other cell. That had to account for his increased IQ and mental sharpness. He never mentioned this to her, and could not come up with a sound reason why he had not. Whenever tempted to do so, some inner compulsion told him to shut his trap. It would definitely lead to more poking and prodding, and he had enough of that.

Tossing it around, he came to a simple realization. If his macrophages were regularly removing his body's trash in order to keep him humming, he thanked the fates, ignoring their twisted sense of humor. His steps lighter and his world brighter, he began to whistle. This earned him an odd look from more than one passerby.

Screw you, Death.

Adriana already waited outside her building when he rounded the corner. His face split in a broad grin, he gave her a tight hug and kissed her. She pulled back and smiled.

"Did you win Lotto or something?"

He took her hand in his and they headed toward Collins Place.

"Better than that, my gorgeous. Your loving husband is now a hundred-year man."

She frowned. "What do you mean?"

"The special macrophages I have swimming in me? According to my favorite doctor, they somehow reset my epigenetic clock to zero. For my body, this is year one."

"And you're acting like a baby too," she quipped, and he laughed.

"Don't you get it?"

"I know what an epigenetic clock is, but reset to zero?"

"That's right."

"How?"

"Nobody has a solid idea. Broca invited me to visit with them and become one of their experimental specimens. I told Dr. Dalton they can shove it. I prefer being right here with you."

"Dupe, but a romantic one." She frowned. "Does this mean you won't grow old?"

"Not at all. It simply means I have twenty-five years of catching up to do before I start to age again."

"Mmm."

He gave himself a mental kick in the ass for that remark. He would remain young while she grew old, and no woman liked that. That's what he read anyway. Then again, he could not keep something like this from her. If it became an issue somewhere down the line, they would simply have to handle it.

She gave him a sidewise glance, a mischievous glint in her eyes.

"Can they reset *my* epigenetic clock?"

"They might."

She stopped and looked at him. "What do you mean?"

"Dr. Dalton wants you to come to the Institute for a blood sample."

"Why?"

"Well, I may have infected you when we, ah, made love."

She stared at him. "Wow."

"You did mention you had a fever a few days later."

"Nothing, a sniffle."

He smiled at her. "If you want to know if your epigenetic clock has been reset, have yourself tested."

She fisted him in the ribs. "Dupe."

They resumed their walk.

"Then I'll be living in year one too, won't I?" she said after a while.

Hah!

They strolled into Peroni's, the upper and lower ground floors packed with lunch goers. The covered plaza kept out direct sunlight, and the twin tower structures made the atmosphere relatively cool.

Adriana ordered a veal parmigiana and a mixed salad with her fruit mineral water. He asked for a baked trout, stir-fried vegetables, and a light ale. These days, he did not drink much spirits. More than a year of abstinence had cut his craving. The restaurant buzzed with animated conversation, but their back corner table provided an illusion of privacy.

"Looking forward to our trip?" he asked casually, not wanting to talk about his epigenetic clock, or any other clock.

"I cannot believe we're leaving on Sunday," she gushed.

"And all of it business class," he added with a smile. The fourteen-hour non-stop QANTAS flight from Melbourne to San Francisco would be a drag, but the comfortable B787 Dreamliner should make the trip more endurable.

The actual presentation would not be until Wednesday U.S. time. They would arrive in San Francisco in mid-afternoon on Sunday, which would give them two days to get over any jetlag and see some of the sights. This was, after all, a business trip, and FutureTech were more than generous giving them the extra time.

"That means I better get everything packed by Saturday," she added.

"Remember, put on the bed whatever you plan to take, then pack half," he told her. "We can always buy stuff over there if we need to. San Francisco can get cold in December, so take something warm, but LA shouldn't be too bad."

Her eyes became dreamy. "San Francisco…I always wanted to see the Golden Gate Bridge, Muir Woods, and gorge myself at the Fisherman's Wharf."

"This will be your chance."

"I can't wait to see Disneyland, Hollywood, and Beverly Hills."

"Once I finish with TE Flight, we'll have three whole days in LA all to ourselves, my sweet."

Their attendant brought their meals and drinks, and they dug in. He cut a slice of trout and forked it onto her plate, and she gave him a piece of parma.

The hour passed all too quickly. On the main ground floor, he gave her a peck on the cheek and watched her melt into the crowd. He gave a satisfied sigh and headed for the ANZ tower. Today, they would not be able to go home together. As he waited for the elevator, he mulled over what to prepare for dinner. Champagne on the side, perhaps? Perhaps not. It might serve as a pointed reminder that he would stay young while she grew old. He did not need that hang-up right now.

In bed that night, she said something that melted his heart and made him love her even more.

"Andrew, you don't have to worry that I'll resent you staying young," she whispered. "As long as I'm with you, I'll also stay young."

He pulled her close and held her. "And you'll always be beautiful to me, through all our years."

* * *

The cab turned into a broad driveway and whispered along a

stone-paved road surrounded by manicured lawns sprinkled with shrubs and tall trees. It all looked neat and impressive. They stopped in front of a modern, glass-clad, six-story square building. Andrew paid the cabby and watched it drive off.

He invited Adriana to accompany him, but she preferred to wander around San Francisco and perhaps do some shopping. More interesting than hanging around FutureTech's canteen the whole day, she said.

A pleasant sixteen—sixty Fahrenheit, they called it here—high clouds smeared the sky, he had an impression he visited a landscaped resort than a high-tech industrial zone. Lots of powerful companies and startups crowded Mountain View and Silicon Valley in general. An address here meant they were comers.

He twitched his tie into place and ascended two steps toward reflective glass panels that guarded the entrance. They slid away with a soft hiss as he approached. The spacious foyer with its deep green stone floor and light green walls felt cool and formal. A uniformed security guard looked up from his round desk and waited.

"Andrew Payne to see Mr. Sergey Nelson."

The guard checked his computer. "Can I have some ID, sir?"

Andrew handed him his FutureTech pass.

"Sixth floor," the guard said, holding out the ID and visitor badge. "Please keep that pinned on at all times."

Andrew nodded and headed for a bank of two elevators.

The open plan sixth floor had lots of light from unbroken window panels. Workstations lay scattered randomly, with tall plants providing a semblance of privacy. Nobody looked at him as he walked in. He could only see three offices at one side. He approached the reception desk and a nice girl with an olive complexion smiled and stood.

"Mr. Nelson will see you right away, Mr. Payne. Please come with me."

She led him to the corner office and knocked. A muffled

'Come in' sounded inside and she opened the door.

"Mr. Payne, sir."

"Thanks, Juana."

Sergey Nelson smiled broadly and heaved up his five-foot-seven frame from behind a large, dark wooden desk crowded with papers, a multifunction phone station, flat computer screen and keyboard. His pale blue eyes shone with intelligence. Completely bald, which somehow made him look young despite his forty-three years, he exuded a friendliness to which Andrew warmed instantly. The FutureTech co-founder, chairman of the board, and managing director, dressed in an open T-shirt, did not look like an owner of a multimillion-dollar company.

"Welcome to FutureTech, Andrew. I looked forward to meeting the man who earthquaked the VR gaming industry," Nelson boomed in a surprisingly deep voice.

Andrew shook hands and smiled. "It's a pleasure, sir."

"Call me Sergey. We're very informal here." Nelson walked toward three comfortable-looking soft chairs surrounding a glass-topped coffee table loaded with a steel carafe, cups, and sundries. "Please, take a seat."

Andrew settled in and crossed his legs.

"I trust you and your wife are enjoying San Francisco?"

"We had a great time, and the weather remained kind to us. A little fresh, but we were prepared."

"It's summer Down Under, right? Care for some coffee?"

"Thanks, I wouldn't mind."

Nelson poured for both of them, added cream and sugar to his, and sipped.

"Regan has filled me in on your history, Andrew, and your remarkable recovery. By the way, Broca Genetics is a stone's throw from here."

"I know. I went to see them before coming here. I thought chemistry was test tubes and Bunsen burners, not banks of computers and gene splicers."

Nelson laughed. "We moved on, as has FutureTech, largely thanks to you. I tell you, when I saw *Fighter Combat*, it left me totally floored. It made all our existing games look like crayon drawings. Our competitors are still scrambling around figuring how to catch up, which does my heart good.

"Several major U.S. and European film studios knocked on our door to license your 3D rendering macros. Regan Price will talk to you about that. Then you dropped your flight simulator on me. When I saw the demonstration, I couldn't believe it."

Andrew chuckled and sipped the excellent mild coffee, completely at ease with Nelson.

"I was not certain FutureTech would be willing to run with it."

Nelson lost his genial look and turned serious. "Some on my board lacked vision and were reluctant to change our business model to venture into shark-infested waters. There are risks, but as you pointed out to Regan, we can mitigate them. That's why TE Flight is keen to see what we have." He glanced at his watch. "They'll be here at ten-thirty and we'll glad-hand. You'll then do the demo. We'll chat over lunch and handle any questions. The system is set up and your Melbourne team made sure there won't be any hang-ups."

"How many TE Flight people are coming?"

"Three. The CEO, a CAE lady who is their head of trainer development, and a pilot with military and civilian experience. You ran the demo for me last week and I like it. A takeoff, landing, some maneuvers, and cockpit procedures should be enough for now. If they decide to come on board, we'll discuss details."

"Sounds good," Andrew said.

"If TE wants something more, can your simulator handle it?"

Andrew grinned. "Like a crash?"

Nelson laughed. "Perhaps not that, or we'll all crash."

"Actually, Sergey, I would like the TE pilot to run through whatever he wants."

Nelson frowned. "Is that wise?"

"We all invested a lot of time and money on this project. If we cannot make a good impression now, we might as well pack it up."

"You're right. It's no use tiptoeing around this. Okay, go for it." Nelson walked to his desk and pressed a glowing button on his phone station.

"Yes, sir?"

"Juana, please have Manny come to my office."

"Yes, sir."

Nelson sat down and picked up his cup. "Emmanuel Dela Torres, my co-founding partner and CFO, is keen to meet you. A pure numbers man, he lacks corporate vision, but he keeps me and this company firmly on the ground. You'll like him."

A knock on the door and a skeletal man, olive complexion, and a healthy crop of dark hair, strode in. He smiled, showing an upper front gold tooth, and stuck out his hand. Andrew liked him on sight.

"Mr. Payne?"

He stood and they shook hands. "Just Andrew."

"You can call me Manny. Everybody else does. Money Manny behind my back." Torres laughed at the joke, sat down, and poured himself coffee. He turned to Nelson. "You didn't tell him?"

"Tell him what?" Nelson countered.

"How much all this is going to cost us?"

"For Chrissake, Manny. It's not like we're short a couple of million. Keep in mind that Andrew is the one who's earning them for us."

Torres lifted his palm. "Only asking."

A knock on the door and Juana peered in. "The TE people are here," she said and closed the door.

Nelson slapped his knees and stood. "Right. Let's go to the conference room and wait for them."

Tastefully paneled with light wood boards, thick navy blue carpet, the long wooden table loaded with plates, coffee carafes on warmers, and cakes, left little room for anything else. One wall taken up by a mosaic of four large TV screens. Arrayed in front of it were six soft chairs. On each lay a high-end Trans Vis VR tethered headset connected to a USB distribution panel. Two had sensor control gloves. Only the pilot and copilot would need them. Everyone else would be a passive observer.

Andrew walked to the first chair, picked up the headset and put it on, glad to see the simulator menu up. He pulled off the headset and nodded to Nelson, who smiled in acknowledgment.

A knock on the door and Juana ushered in three individuals. A youngish man wearing a blond crewcut, clear gray eyes, perhaps in his late thirties, looked friendly. Andrew took him to be the pilot. The older man, silver hair framed a stern face, held himself with reserve. The African-American woman beside him took everything in with a penetrating glance. They were the ones Andrew had to convince.

Nelson made the introductions, and handshakes were returned all around. He waited for everyone to take a seat, a cup of coffee in front of them, and swept his gaze around the table.

"I want to thank you all for coming, and I trust you'll find the following demonstration interesting. We already discussed the advantages and disadvantages of a VR trainer simulator. Your presence here tells me the advantages far outweigh the disadvantages. I would now like to hand you over to Andrew, who managed the development."

Andrew took a deep breath and stood. "Thank you, Mr. Nelson. Mrs. Talbot, gentlemen, for the purpose of this demonstration, Mr. Burton can act as pilot. I'll be his copilot. All flight modes are available to him for trial."

The TE people exchanged quick glances.

Andrew pointed at the soft chairs. "Please take your seats and

put on your headset. Mr. Burton might indulge in some unortho-
dox maneuvers, so it's okay if you hold onto the hand rests."

Everyone cracked a smile, and some of the stiff formality
evaporated. Garry Burton clearly knew his way around a VR system as he pulled on the sensor gloves and headset without fuss.
Andrew sat down, put on his gear, and looked at him.

"What do you want to do first?"

"A takeoff."

Andrew reached with his index finger, touched the 'On
ground' menu bar and was instantly transported onto a B737-
MAX flight deck. He thought he heard a sharp inhale form someone. Around them lay a real-life view of LA International terminal spokes, parked and moving aircraft. Muffled engine noises
came through the headset. He fancied he could smell avgas in the
air.

He saw Burton look at him, nod, and with economical move-
ments touched overhead switches to start both engines.

"Starting one and two," he said calmly.

The LED displays correctly showed buildup of thrust and status condition.

"Ready to push back," Burton ordered quietly.

"Flight AA246, pushback, please," Andrew spoke into his
simulated mike, and the background shifted to show the aircraft
pulling away from the air bridge.

When the push truck disengaged, Burton spun up the engines,
released the brakes, and the aircraft began to move toward the
taxiway.

"Flaps," Burton said.

Andrew set the flaps lever to forty degrees. "Tower, this is
AA246, rolling," he added.

"AA246. Proceed to runway 25L for immediate takeoff."

"AA246, roger."

Andrew had another aircraft in front of them waiting for takeoff. It started rolling, engines thundering, and climbed gracefully

into the sky. Burton positioned the aircraft at start of the runway and braked.

"Tower, AA246, ready for takeoff," Andrew said.

"AA246, cleared for departure."

Burton pushed forward both thrust levers and the engines spooled up to a roar. He released brakes and the B737 began to move, picking up speed rapidly.

"V1," Andrew called out. This represented a refusal point beyond which the flight cannot be safely aborted. They were committed.

"VR," he said when the indicator showed 130 knots, or 150 miles per hour. "Rotate."

Burton pulled back the column and the B737 soared smoothly into the air, the expanse of LAX opening below them like a postcard.

"Retract gear and flaps," Burton ordered.

The winding sound of retracting flaps came through clearly in the headset.

Andrew relaxed a little. So far, everything had gone smoothly. He reached with his finger and touched a blue box on the bottom right corner of the virtual image. The menu overlay came up and he selected 'Starboard engine failure'.

Immediately, a bang sounded from the right engine and the fire alarm began to blink, accompanied by loud beeping. The aircraft shuddered, but continued to fly level. Burton pulled back the right thrust lever and pressed the fire extinguisher button. Andrew contacted the tower and issued a PAN-PAN emergency request for immediate landing.

The runway came into sight and Burton lined up without any side to side wobble. The aircraft seemed to float, then gently touched down with only a mild jolt audio effect. Clearly, he had done this more than once. Not bothering with reverse thrust, he allowed the aircraft to lose speed, then braked to a stop. Andrew immediately cut power to the engine.

Burton slowly turned his head and looked at him. Without saying anything, he pulled off his headset and sensor gloves. Andrew blinked when he found himself again in the real world. The elderly TE exec and Mrs. Talbot took off their headset and looked at each other.

With everybody seated around the conference table, the coffee carafes were passed around.

Talbot, head of TE trainer development, took a long sip and turned to Andrew.

"Mr. Payne, you developed this simulator?" she asked softly.

"With a lot of support from FutureTech."

"And you're not a pilot?"

"I had to bone up, ma'am."

"Very impressive." Talbot looked at Burton. "Garry?"

"I thought I actually flew the thing. The external view came through absolutely lifelike, as were the audio effects and cockpit layout."

"Yes, we saw," she added.

"The software needs rigorous testing for procedural compliance, and Andrew seems to have the switchology covered. I think we're onto something." Burton took a sip of coffee, then his eyes turned wide and he pointed a finger at Andrew. "It just hit me. *You* are the one who created *Fighter Combat*?"

Andrew smiled. "I used it as a testbed for the simulator."

"My son pestered me to get it, and I bought the thing as a Christmas present. I had to get a new headset and control gloves, but when I tried the thing, I believed I had an F/A-18 strapped on." Burton chuckled. "I had to fight my son to see who would play with it. I'm not surprised that you were willing to tackle something complex as an actual trainer."

The atmosphere immediately became warmer and everybody relaxed.

Talbot looked at Nelson. "He's been bending our ear about that game ever since he got it, telling us he wanted to meet the person who invented it, certain he was a pilot," she said, then cleared her throat. "Garry, can we integrate our software with this thing?"

Burton immediately shook his head. "Andrew's graphics are too advanced for that, Mary. We can use our procedure flows to validate the simulator responses, but that's about all. Keep in mind that a lot of our software is used to control jack motion interfaces. Eliminating that need is our savings window."

"Do you want to go through more simulations?" Andrew asked.

"Definitely. This thing is an evolutionary leap."

Looking pleased, Nelson stood. "I'm delighted that you found the trainer interesting. However, I suggest we adjourn for lunch. Afterward, Mr. Burton can have his fun."

When everybody filed out, Nelson motioned to Andrew to stay. Alone, the FutureTech founder stuck out his hand.

"Congratulations. I think you wowed them. Extremely well done."

Late in the afternoon, the shadows already lengthening, the cab took Andrew back to San Francisco. Burton and he ran two more simulator scenarios while the execs from both companies discussed a possible partnership.

Tired but satisfied, he watched traffic stream along Bayside Freeway. He had a lot to talk about with Adriana. Tomorrow morning, they had a flight to Los Angeles to see the TE complex. Their Canadian CAE subsidiary still produced the majority of trainers, but TE now set policy on how they did business. He looked forward to seeing a real live aircraft training simulator.

Then, the part Adriana looked forward to, three days of sight-seeing.

Chapter Seven

Andrew saw himself sitting in the reclined dentist chair, and looked at his wife's eyes through tinted glasses protecting him from the glare of the overhead lamp. Clad in a light green surgical gown, a white mask covering most of her face, drill in her right hand, hair covered by a gauzy cap, she still looked angelic.

Everything a treatment room should have lay there: a stand that supported the x-ray head, instruments tray, and an adjustable overhead lamp. On his left, another stand held a suction attachment, a water spigot, and a rinse cup to wash his mouth once the dentist was through butchering it. He even had a live Chanel 7 feed in the ceiling TV, complete with subtitles. That took some tricky coding to achieve, but it added to the realism. The walls were covered with anatomical images of heads and teeth in various states of disaster. He used Belana as a model for the attending nurse.

When he discussed the initial application parameters with Adriana, she envisaged a realistic treatment room, but with a passive manikin patient. If she wanted realism, he told her, the patient also must be real, either as a responsive 3D image, but preferably, an actual person. That way, she would get real-life feedback how a patient felt during a procedure. Students could alternate being patients and dentists.

"Open wide," Adriana said and brought down the drill.

He heard the whir of the bit, and the nurse applied suction.

"Ouch!" he cried out in mock pain and pulled away his head.

Adriana laughed. "Don't be a baby."

He removed the headset and instantly found himself back in

his home work office. She took off her headset, a broad smile on her face.

"I think we're ready," she said softly.

He embraced her and held her for several long seconds.

"You did it, gorgeous. You did it."

"I still cannot believe how realistic everything is. All it needs is tactile feedback and it *would* be real."

"Mark and I are already working on that. He's modifying a standard Trans Vis headset to send impulses to the brain and induce genuine physiological responses from all senses."

She stared at him. "Is that possible?"

"We're not looking to set up a brain-chip interface, which would require surgery. A lot of research has been done with brain-computer interfaces, but most of it is with chip implants. What Mark now has is bulky and cumbersome, but all we need is a proof of concept device. Our problem is that bone is semi-conductive, and conductivity varies with direction of the applied voltage, which means bleed and attenuation of signal. We've been experimenting with different voltage frequencies, amplitudes, and waveforms to stimulate various brain areas. We cannot affect only the cortex, as many functions are controlled from deep within the brain."

"How do you know all…ah, Mark has experimented on you?"

Andrew shrugged. "Someone had to do it."

"Isn't this dangerous? You could have your neurons burned out."

"Not likely. We're dealing with micro-voltages and amps, and there are surge protectors everywhere."

"Have you gotten anywhere with this?"

"Well, I had some encouraging responses. Part of the problem is generating an electrical stimulus in real time based on visual cues generated by the VR headset. It requires complicated coding and chews up a lot of computing power, but we'll get there. Reynold Parker has already applied for a patent. Once Mark has it working properly, we'll demonstrate it to FutureTech and get Trans Vis or some other major headset manufacturer involved to create something more user-friendly."

"If you could do it, it would be something. How long before you'll have it ready?"

"Hard to say. Mid-July maybe. In the meantime, we'll push on with the dental trainer. Tomorrow, I'll talk to Price and arrange a demo. He's been dying to look at it. You can be the doctor if you want to, and can fit the demo into your schedule."

Adriana blanched. "Me?"

"Treat him as another patient with a hole to fill. He's a great guy and easy to talk to. You have nothing to worry about." He shut down the computer and server, stood up and stretched his arms. "Enough for the day, let's go to bed."

After a quick shower, they snuggled under the doona in the cold bedroom. Even when he lived with his parents, Andrew never had his bedroom heated, preferring an open window and fresh air. Mouth and nose sticking out from under the cover did the job. Crawling into bed felt a little uncomfortable at first, especially when Adriana wrapped her cold feet around his legs. Once both were nice and toasty, they did not have to cling to each other. They still did, liking the closeness and emotional comfort touching provided.

"We must invite Mark and Susan over for dinner sometime," she murmured against his shoulder. "We haven't had them here since their wedding in January. I can't believe it's already May."

"Step outside and you'll believe it," he said.

His longtime best friend married…and he had never seen Mark happier. Smart, down to earth, always cheerful, Susan provided his friend an anchor, curbing his overflowing adventurism, a good thing. With Orwell, the three of them still had an occasional night out, but these days, mostly with wives in tow, and Andrew liked it that way, keen to share everything with Adriana. What went on when she and Susan were alone, perhaps best left as a mystery.

"Your friend Orwell must feel left out somewhat these days," she added.

"He'll be all right. We don't do some of the things we used to, but we still go out regularly."

Her fingers explored his throat and chin. "Do you miss it? Sun and surf?"

"I used to at first. I wouldn't mind an occasional beach outing and swim, but I can't risk it. I might be in remission, but having melanoma once could make me more susceptible despite all those macrophages looking after me. Besides, I'd hate to have you drilling into me if I looked at anyone else."

She chuckled and prodded him in the ribs. "Dupe. You can look, but no touching. I know what men are like and there is no changing them."

"There is only one woman I want to look at and touch, my sweet, and you know it."

She slid an arm across his chest and sighed. "I'm all yours, and always will be. Even if I'm not living in year one."

She had herself tested after their trip to the States. His macrophages were present in her blood and appeared active, but her epigenetic clock remained unaffected. Well, if they kept her healthy, it wasn't such a bad thing.

"I cannot believe SpaceX made two follow-up Moon missions. I guess they're serious about setting up a base there."

"It's about time we did something with that place," he agreed. "Relying on NASA and its moribund bureaucracy would never have gotten us there."

"I always wondered why NASA never made return Moon missions after the Apollo project."

"They're saying it's too costly, but they spent hundreds of millions sending rovers to Mars. Go figure."

"How's your work on the B787 simulator?"

"Another week or so and we'll be ready for beta testing. TE

Flight helped us a lot. With all the operational processes mapped out, we didn't need to research anything. Still, a B787 is a complex aircraft, and there is a lot to code for."

"Why don't you and FutureTech let TE code some of it?"

"If we gave TE access to my macros, they wouldn't need us anymore. This way, FutureTech provides the value-add, we retain IP and grow our business. With development for several aircraft types in the pipeline, FutureTech has created a new division and hired dozens VR analysts and programmers. Pretty soon, they'll need a new building," Andrew added.

"Has Boeing seen the B737 simulator?"

"They sure have, and are salivating to get it certified."

"Will the FAA do it? You told me they raised reservations because it doesn't have actual physical motion."

"What the VR graphics provide is almost as good," he said. "It will take a few months for the FAA and the European EASA to go through it, but I feel the simulator will eventually get certified. Boeing is a key economic power in the U.S., and they have a lot of influence inside the FAA and Congress, perhaps too much, as the MAX scandal revealed."

"You urged TE Flight to get EASA certification. I bet they're now glad they did."

"TE was reluctant at first to seek simultaneous certification, but Airbus is a major industry player, and TE would needlessly alienate them by denying access to what is shaping to be the future in pilot training."

"My husband, responsible for two industrial revolutions," she murmured.

"And my darling wife will be responsible for another one once the dentist trainer hits the market."

"This full-sensor headset you and Mark are working on. It will turn the entertainment industry on its head."

"It will make an impact, all right, and not only in entertainment."

She looked at him, eyes searching.

"I sense a 'but' here," he mused.

"It's a fantastic thing, don't get me wrong, but did you consider the downside?"

"You mean, someone could invent a game so real, a user may prefer to stay in it rather than face what might be a dull or unhappy life? Become a VR addict?"

"Something like that."

"Believe me, I thought about it, and it will probably happen. Everything has a duality, a dark side, and there is nothing we can do about it because it's something in us. We use things against each other, and we use people against each other. I'd like to think that one day, we might stop."

After a while, her breathing slowed. He shifted to his side to face her, and her arm instinctively pulled him against her.

All the money in the world could not make up for what he felt right then.

* * *

"Dr. Payne, a genuine pleasure," Price gushed warmly, holding Adriana's hand in both of his.

"Thank you, sir. And it's just Adriana."

"And you can call me Regan," he said and extended an arm toward the conference table. "Care for some tea?"

"Thank you, I would like some."

They made themselves comfortable and Regan poured for her, then took coffee for himself. Andrew also helped himself to coffee.

"When your husband told me what you had in mind," Price said, "you had me intrigued, as was Sergey Nelson. Frankly, the idea never occurred to us. We were all hardened games developers before venturing into the VR world, and not used to thinking outside the box. Since Andrew rejoined us last year, we were forced to learn, and we have a number of bright people at corporate looking at possibilities." He took a sip of coffee. "How do you want to run your demonstration?"

"I'll start with a simple teeth cleaning procedure, and follow it up with a filling, with you as the patient. Normally, these procedures would run to around half an hour, but I'll shorten it to five minutes. The simulator will create a real treatment room, and every procedure will be done as though you were actually getting your teeth cleaned and had a filling. I could run the demo with you as a passive observer, but Andrew felt you would get a better perspective if you acted as a patient."

"I understand." Price pushed back his chair and stood. "All, right. Let's do it, and then we'll talk."

Andrew put on his headset and sensor gloves, acting as Adriana's assistant. Transported into a treatment room, Adriana invited Price to sit down. The teeth cleaning part went relatively quickly. She then took an x-ray of Price's left side where the tooth supposedly had a cavity, applied anesthetic, drilled out the infected area, and packed it. Price went through the motion of rinsing his mouth, and they were done. He took off his headset and gloves and exhaled.

"I hope you filled the right tooth," he quipped with a wry smile.

Adriana grinned. "If you will kindly go to reception, they'll fix your bill."

"I'm sure they will," he said dryly, walked to his chair, and poured himself more coffee. "No need to convince me further, either of you. You gave me an astonishing demonstration. I'm sold, and I'm sure so will the board. This is an untapped business opportunity, and FutureTech will be at the forefront." He took a sip and looked at Andrew. "I went through the sample contract you sent me. Another twenty thousand shares and a two percent royalty. I think Sergey Nelson will go for it."

"Thanks, Regan."

"You said the app is ready for beta testing?"

"It is, but as you already guessed, our test team isn't qualified to handle something like this. Not in its entirety."

"I'm aware of that. What do you have in mind?"

"Dr. Hendrix at First Teeth has looked at the application and agreed to test all procedures a student aiming for a dental technician or a full dentist degree will need, to a graduate professional seeking to upgrade his skills. Our test team will handle everything else."

"Send me Dr. Hendrix's details and I'll talk to him," Price said and looked at Adriana. "I suppose there is a certification process involved for something like this?"

She nodded. "The Australian Dental Council is responsible for administration of all dental practitioners, education, and training programs. However, you will first need to obtain approval from the Dental Board of Australia. They're responsible for developing standards, codes of practice, and guidelines. No university or institution will use this package without these approvals. To make the trainer available worldwide, FutureTech would need to obtain certification from relevant authorities."

"You two have done your homework. I'll get things moving here, and corporate can handle the rest." Price pursed his lips. "Sergey Nelson will want a demo. Adriana, can I call on you to handle this?"

"I don't mind. I would require a day's notice to clear my patient schedule."

"Certainly," Price said and stood. "Thank you again. Dr. Payne. This has been enlightening to say the least."

"A pleasure, sir."

"Andrew? Can you see me after lunch? Say around two o'clock? I want to discuss some things with you."

"Not a problem."

Downstairs, Andrew gave Adriana a hug. "I'll call you when I finish with Dr. Dalton. Perhaps we can go home together."

"I might be running late. My afternoon is pretty full."

"I'll call you anyway and we'll see." He gave her a peck on the mouth. "You were great with Price, my sweet."

She hit him with a radiant smile. "Thanks." She glanced at her watch. "I've got to run. See you tonight."

He watched her hurry up Collins Street, nodded, and started walking toward the elevators, oblivious to the noise and throng around him. The demonstration may have impressed Price, but Andrew worked for a salary and had a B787 project to run.

After a salad roll and a mug of tea for lunch, he checked outstanding issues with his team and went to see the general manager.

"I'll come straight to the point, Andrew," Price said. "Future-Tech considers you a valuable resource we're not utilizing fully. Frankly, you're wasted working on flight simulators. That's nuts and bolts stuff more suited to professional project managers like Warren Kant. Your MBA has given you a level of business acumen and judgment unusual in someone your age. We want to apply that talent in a broader context. What I would like you to do, and Sergey Nelson agrees, is work full-time prototyping new ideas you might come up with. Ordinarily, anything an employee creates on company time belongs to us. However, we have a special contract with you that guarantees your IP. Nelson doesn't mind, because what you produced for us more than offsets any financial payout your contract requires. Your dental trainer promises to be another considerable revenue earner."

"I must thank you for the support you gave me, Regan," Andrew said. His MBA gave him a sound business grounding, and his heightened IQ helped, but Reynold Parker's advice went a long way to sharpen his skills. "FutureTech legal could have made things difficult for me over the IP clause."

Price laughed. "According to Nelson, they did, but he quashed them. You're the goose who lays golden eggs, and you don't serve one of those for dinner."

Andrew smiled. Price did not say it, and he did not need to. If the managing director insisted on strict legality, Andrew would have walked, taking his golden eggs with him. Nelson was right to remind Emmanuel Dela Torres where the bulk of company's revenue came from.

"What do you want me to do?" he asked.

"Warren will assign another project manager to take over the B787 work, and I would like you to concentrate on getting the dental trainer fully tested. I need a firm completion estimate in order to approach the Dental Board and the Dental Council."

"Can I keep Sandra and Thomas? We work well together."

"I noticed. Go ahead, they're yours."

"Thanks."

Price inclined his head. "Do you have anything new in the pipeline?"

"As a matter of fact, I do."

"And…"

"I recently purchased an accounting package to manage Usque Vision's finances and my investments. It does the job, but it's tedious to use. I know something about basic and management accounting from my MBA course, but even so, it took me a while to familiarize myself with all the package's procedures."

Price raised a finger. "Don't tell me. You want to build a VR version?"

"Not exactly. There are hundreds of nuts and bolts packages out there for small and large businesses. What I have in mind is a voice-controlled management interface that would extract data from an established package. Any package. Imagine if I could ask it to show me last month's balance sheet, ledger, profit and loss, or anything else, and see the information displayed for me graphically. Information, not data."

"Information?"

"You look at financial statements all the time. There are some on your desk. What do you see?"

"Printouts of figures most of the time."

"Exactly. Those figures may interest an accountant, but what you want is information on what those figures and numbers mean. You want to see expense and profit projections, market analyses, sales warnings, all done in multi-graphical form. Something you can grasp and understand at a glance on which to make decisions. That's what I want to build."

Price looked thoughtful. "You're right. I spend too much time massaging numbers to get what I want. What you're proposing would save executives everywhere a lot of valuable time. It would be complicated to deliver, though."

"It would take time to build data extraction interfaces," Andrew admitted. "The graphical representation isn't all that difficult. I tried a few things at home. I would need a qualified management accountant for some things. I could use the company's system as a testbed, with corporate's permission, of course."

"I'll look into it." Price smiled. "I suppose you already took out a patent for this?"

"And registered," Andrew said. Without a patent application, he would be relinquishing all intellectual property rights to FutureTech. "There's something else I'm working on, and before you ask, I already applied for a patent."

"Another app?"

"My friend and I are developing a full-sensor interface headset." Andrew quickly outlined what he and Mark were doing. "There won't be a need for new connectors either. It will use a standard HDMI cable." Price gaped at him, visibly stunned by the enormity of the concept.

"How close are you to a proof of concept device?"

"Two months perhaps. Hard to say. Mark has a full-time job and is newly married. There are not all that many free hours he can devote to this."

"No, I suppose not. Most of our games would require retrofitting," Price reflected, then sat up. "This would mean retrofitting the flight simulator program as well."

"And the dentist trainer," Andrew added. "I don't see it as a problem. Once the prototype headset is ready, FutureTech needs to bring on board somebody like Trans Vis to perfect the gear and make it user-friendly. I don't see anything coming on the market for two years or so."

"Would your friend consider working for us to finish the prototype?"

"I don't think so, but I can ask. He has a career path where he works now. Once the prototype is done, there would be nothing for him to do at FutureTech. We're not an engineering company."

"Fair enough. Only a thought. Wait till I tell Sergey about this." Price shook his head. "You certainly came up with something huge here. We'll talk more about all this tomorrow."

At 3:15, Andrew took a tram to the Institute. Amanda Gregory accompanied him to Radiology where they gave him a shot of radiotracer. A boring hour later, he had the scans, which went relatively quickly, something he appreciated. A quick scan meant no new problems. Upstairs, Amanda took him to Dr. Dalton's office.

"How are you, Andrew?" she queried pleasantly, straightening papers on her desk, looking cool and detached as always.

No clearing of throat, he observed. A good sign.

"Not too bad, thanks. Waiting for spring."

"It has been a rather cold autumn so far," she agreed indifferently. "Your scans are clear. However, if you don't mind, I would like to continue with them every three months."

"Not a problem."

She crossed her arms. "Broca Genetics and the Institute appreciate the ongoing contribution you made to our research by giving us blood and tissue samples. We still don't know how your epigenetic clock became reset, something all of us are looking at closely, but there is an additional development.”

“A breakthrough in your research?”

“In a manner of speaking, but it’s specific to you.”

“In what way?”

“Broca believes, and I concur, your epigenetic clock is not only reset, it’s frozen.”

Andrew frowned. “I don’t understand.”

“You’re not only living in year one, but our findings suggest that this condition might be permanent.”

“Are you saying I won’t age at all? This is impossible.”

“So was the resetting of your epigenetic clock. Your reengineered macrophages were clearly responsible, but we don’t understand the mechanism used to achieve this state, and we definitely don’t understand how your epigenetic clock became frozen.”

“How do you know it’s frozen?”

“Experiments on your tissues, which we have now used up.”

“I still don’t fully understand what you mean that my epigenetic clock is frozen. Are you telling me that my cells have become immortal, like corals and those sponges we talked about?”

“Frankly, Andrew, I don’t know. It’s far too early to tell with any degree of certainty. We’ll keep monitoring your physiological condition. In five years or so, we might be in a better position to know. In the meantime, I’m pleased to see you fully recovered.” She raised a finger. “You may be in remission, but remember—”

“I know; no more sun and surf. You keep telling me.”

“Given this development, Broca has renewed their offer for you to go to their Sunnyvale facility.”

Andrew immediately shook his head. “We already discussed that, Doc, and my position has not changed.”

She appeared not to hear him. “To make a definitive assessment of your condition, we need tissue samples from several parts of your body. The two extractions you provided prior to your treatment were simply not enough."

"I'm afraid that's all you're going to get. I don't mind giving you blood and skin scrapings, but no more biopsies, and definitely nothing from my liver, lungs, or anywhere else."

"This is very important research, Andrew. Something that has enormous ramifications for all mankind, and you're the only person in a position to help us."

"I'm already helping you. I simply don't want to become a lab specimen."

Dr. Dalton pursed her lips. "One week, that's all I'm asking. You'll be staying at the Institute."

"I can never repay what you and Broca has done for me, and I do understand what this research means, but I'm a person, not an experimental subject. I regret if this is a source of disappointment, but that's how it is."

Her mouth firmed into a scowl. "Don't you realize what is at stake here?"

"Broca's drive for an immortality pill. Perhaps your drive as well. I don't care. I won't submit to being an experimental subject."

"Very well. I guess we'll keep working with what you're prepared to give us." She stood and stuck out her hand. "I'll see you in three months."

He shook her hand without enthusiasm, a little angry that she kept pushing her single-minded position, disregarding his wants as a person. *Screw her!*

Despite a stiff, cold westerly, he decided to walk to Collins Street. His overcoat kept out the wind and made him sufficiently comfortable. He glanced at his watch: 5:16. He pulled out his cell and called First Teeth. Penny told him that Adriana would not be finished until six or so. Might as well take a tram home, he decided.

His epigenetic clock is frozen?

He tried to get his head around what all that meant, but could not. It was too enormous to grasp. He had to let this sink in and allow his mind to work through the possibilities. Intellectually, he understood what Dr. Dalton told him—he might be immortal. The emotional impact still to hit. Should he tell Adriana? He sensed that she already had an issue with his year one thing. How would she react if he landed this new bombshell on her? She might accept it in the short term, but as the years rolled by and he stayed young while she aged, this could become a serious problem in their relationship.

He always had that cement truck, he mused.

Damned whatever he did.

Chewing it over, he decided not to tell Adriana anything…not for a few years. Would his conscience let him sit on this for that long? What if she kept something like this from *him* and he found out years later? How would he react?

Soft rain began to fall as he waited for the tram, which topped off his day.

Shait.

The tram clanged its bell, stopped, and the doors snapped open. People jostled on board, anxious to get out of the weather and into their warm home. Overcrowded, pressed elbow to elbow, Andrew grabbed a steel stanchion, not even considering looking for a free seat. A vast change from 2020 when only a handful of adventurous individuals took a tram. He was one of them, with mask and latex gloves. To take his car into the middle of the city every day would be very expensive madness. For those who did not want to use public transport had to put up with a twice-daily highway gridlock.

The driver sounded the bell and the tram surged from the stop.

He got off at Toorak Road and walked quickly toward the Rockley Gardens. A light rain still fell, visible as slanting lines under the street lamps, and he had no umbrella. This morning, he decided not to take even a pocket one, believing the weather forecast. A hardened, cynical Melbournian, he should have known better than to believe the Bureau. They were very good telling everybody that spring would come in three months, but could not tell if it would rain in the evening. One of life's enduring mysteries.

Grateful to be home, he sighed with relief when warm air enveloped him as he opened the front door, the automatic heating timer doing its job. He hung his damp overcoat on a hook beside the door and reset the alarm. Upstairs, he changed into something casual and wandered down to check the fridge. Four lamb cutlets left over from last night, and some potato salad. It would do, not in the mood to cook, but he decided a hot soup would be in order, and Adriana liked soup.

Once the finely diced onions, carrots, and parsnip were browned, he added water, powdered stock, and let the stuff simmer. A few minutes later, he threw in a handful of thin noodles. On impulse, he walked to the bar cabinet, took out a half-bottle of shiraz and poured some into a crystal goblet, a set he inherited from his grandparents. He sniffed appreciatively and took a sip. Full-bodied and mellow, just the way he liked it. Some time back, his dad took time to educate him how to grade and appreciate various wines and spirits. Up to then, as long as it went down, he and his two friends did not much differentiate between wine types.

The soup done, he switched off the element and had a taste. A touch more salt and the thing was ready. Living alone in his Richmond apartment, he had to learn the art of cooking quickly. Not all his culinary experiments panned out as the cookery books made out, but in the end, he turned into a fair chef.

He took his glass to the couch and switched on the TV to watch the six o'clock news. At six-thirty, he changed to the SBS channel to get some world coverage, and topped up his glass. The presenter droned on, Andrew not really listening or paying attention. Something to fill the lounge with background noise.

With time on his hands, mind freewheeling, the emotional impact of what Dr. Dalton told him finally hit. He might be immortal. Everybody wanted that, didn't they? There were endless historical quests to find the fabled fountain of youth, and when they could not find it, enterprising scammers peddled potions and elixirs to the gullible. If everybody wanted to live forever, why did he find himself in the dumps? It took no time to figure that one out. After all, he had a heightened IQ and could add two and two. One and one in this case.

Adriana...

Around 6:45, the front door opened and she shook water off a large umbrella before stepping in.

"I want to move somewhere warm," she declared with feeling.

He walked up to her, smiled, and hugged her. "A warm house is the best I can do, I'm afraid. Here, let me have your coat." He hung it beside his and followed her into the kitchen. She sniffed the soup and smiled.

"That was thoughtful of you. I think there is still stuff left over from last night."

"I know. I checked. Let's get into the soup and worry about the rest later. Want a glass of wine?"

She glanced at the goblet on the coffee table. "Making sure it hasn't gone off?"

"It hasn't," he assured her and switched off the TV.

"I wouldn't mind a bit. It's miserable out there."

She busied herself with plates and cutlery, and brought the soup pot to the table. She waited for him to fill her glass, picked it up, and raised it in a salute.

"Home sweet home. Be it ever so humble. Not that it is, mind you," she added hastily.

He chuckled and touched her glass. The crystal sang with clear purity.

"To our humble home."

Both took a sip and ladled some soup.

"Ah, I needed that," she said after trying it.

He felt the soup warm his belly and the warmth spread through him. The reheated cutlets and potato salad finished a good meal. Adriana went upstairs to change, and he poured himself some cognac. It seemed the night for it. He sat on the couch and waited for her to come down. She fixed herself tea and sat beside him.

"Why the long face?" she asked, studying him. "Bad day at work?"

"No, far from it. Price took me off the B787 project to work full-time on the dentist trainer. I also told him about the sensor helmet Mark and I are working on. That got him excited."

"So, if it's not work, it must be something else. You've been moody and withdrawn all evening. It's Dr. Dalton, isn't it?" She sat up in alarm. "You're not having a relapse, are you?"

He grinned and shook his head. "I'm fine. That's the problem. I'm too fine."

"What do you mean?"

A sip of cognac did not help settle him. Still not too late, he reminded himself. Damn it all, he would not be able to look her in the face if he did not tell her, or look at himself in the mirror. They shared everything and trusted each other not to keep secrets, the important ones anyway. Holding this back would betray that trust, something more damaging than revealing his condition.

"I was tempted not to tell you because I'm scared how you might react," he said in a rush.

"Tell me what?"

"My epigenetic clock? It's not only reset, but according to Dr. Dalton, it's frozen."

Her eyes turned dark green. "Frozen? Does that mean you won't age…ever?"

"She doesn't know, but I had to tell you. I couldn't hold this from you."

"Silly man. You wanted to spare me the shock that you might live for a very long time and always stay young while I started to wrinkle and sag?"

"Something like that."

She slid close to him and her arms went around his neck.

"You're a dupe, Andrew Payne," she whispered and brushed his cheek. "You don't get it, do you?"

"Get what?"

"We're all living in year one, day one. Every morning is a new day, with no promise that we'll see the night. It doesn't make any difference to me how long you might live. That's only a possibility. Whatever days I have left, as long as I can spend them with you, I will also live forever." She leaned toward him and her lips found him.

Overcome with emotion, he blinked the sting out of his eyes and held her tight against him.

"I love you so much, Adriana," he whispered into her hair. "What's more, I don't deserve you."

"Well, you got me anyway. So you'll simply have to make do."

"I was so afraid I might lose you over this, I went out of my mind."

She smiled. "You're so smart in many ways, but also ignorant. You were afraid of losing me, when all the time, I was the one afraid of losing you."

"What?"

"In ten, twenty years, when I start to show my age and you'll still look like a twenty-five-year-old, your eyes will start to roam, looking for someone younger, fresher."

He gaped at her in shock. "Never!"

"Don't make promises you might not be able to keep."

He cupped her cheeks between his hands. "I will never leave you. You saved me when I thought I had it, wanting nothing but my love. You have it, and you'll have it for all time. Remember what the priest said, 'For as long as both of you shall live.' When

I heard those words, they sent a shiver down my spine. I took those words literally." He kissed her lightly. "For as long as both of us shall live," he whispered. She melted against him and he kissed her hard.

Later, she played for him.

* * *

"Good morning, gorgeous," he whispered as her eyes fluttered open. "Is there anything I can do for you on this cold and wet day?"

"Stay in bed and keep me warm," she mumbled sleepily.

He wrapped his right arm around her. "How's that?"

"Mmm. Nice. I think I'll keep you until spring."

"And then?"

"Trade you in for a young hunk."

"What about all my biceps and triceps and things?"

"Same old thing," she muttered. "A change is as good as a holiday, so they say," she purred contentedly.

"In that case, I'll turn myself into a cuddly tub of fat."

"You tried that once, and it all melted off."

Testing the dental trainer, he lost control of his diet for a while and gained a couple of unwanted kilos. Too much chair parade. He did not like it and went on an exercise binge. Within two weeks, all the excess fat disappeared faster than he expected. It appeared that his internal body image did not allow him to deviate for any length of time.

"You want a boy-toy?"

She giggled. "I already have one." She raised her head and looked out the window at a gray sky, swaying branches, and driving drizzle. "Can we skip June and go straight to October?"

"I'll send an email to somebody," he said as he opened the bedside cabinet and hauled out a flat blue velvet case. "For you. Happy anniversary, Adriana, my wife."

She sat up, eyes round. He opened the case and she gasped.

"You wonderful man, you," she whispered, and gingerly ran a finger over the gold necklace holding a dozen emeralds. In the center of the box lay matching pair of earrings. She sniffed, looked at him, and her soft lips merged with his. She pulled back and smiled. "Thank you."

For his birthday last month, she got him an emerald ring set on a gold band. It took a week or so for him to get used to wearing it, and now liked it. The ring reminded him of her eyes.

He removed the necklace and clipped it around her throat. She touched it with splayed fingers, her eyes sparkling like the green stones, sighed, and rested her head on his chest.

"I think I'll keep you until next June. I'm curious to see what you'll come up with then."

"Deal."

They held each other for a while not saying anything. Nothing needed saying. He had a wife he loved unreservedly, a promising career, moderate wealth, the respect of his friends and colleagues, he did not need anything else.

"What are we going to do today?" Adriana mused at length. "I want to stay in bed forever."

"That might get somewhat inconvenient after a while," he pointed out.

"Dupe. You know what I mean."

"Well, we can have breakfast in bed and watch movies."

"I'm not hungry, and I don't want to watch a movie."

"Fine. We'll fossilize, then."

"Is Price really leaving?"

"At end of the month, Daniel Cheong becomes the new Australasian general manager."

"And Price is taking over the European region?"

"That's the poop."

"He's been a good friend to you."

"I liked working with him. I don't know about Cheong. Supposed to be a tough operator, and did a lot to expand the Asian market. I'll have to wait and see how things go."

"And if they don't go?"

"Then he'll go, or I will. Simple."

She propped herself on one elbow and looked at him. "You have the power to get rid of a senior general manager?"

He laughed. "Hardly. I'm very much a junior project manager."

"A rich junior project manager," she added.

Adriana was right. He had done very well for himself.

When his end of year royalties came through, he immediately purchased additional FutureTech shares, and took out a call option for more. His net worth now over five million.

"What I do have is influence with Sergey Nelson. At least I hope I have. Without my 3D rendering macros, FutureTech would still be an also-ran games developer. I gave them an unbeatable competitive advantage, and Nelson knows it. Once TE Flight gets the B737-MAX trainer certified, and your dentist package is approved, FutureTech will be raking it in. They won't do anything silly to disrupt that."

"How are you and Mark doing with the sensor device?"

"We're testing it with my *Fighter Combat* game. I'll have to get a seat with a four-point harness, it's that realistic."

"I wouldn't mind trying it on the B737 simulator," she said. "A simple takeoff and landing won't need a harness."

"You're on."

"Don't forget."

He took a deep breath and threw off the doona. Adriana gave a squeal and hastily wrapped the cover around her.

"Time for breakfast," he declared. "What would you like?"

"What's on the menu?"

"Let's see. French toast, plain toast, no toast, eggs any way you like, juice, or nothing. A mug of tea, perhaps?"

"Mmm. I think I better make breakfast before I starve."

"Want to use the bathroom first?"

"Go ahead. I'll snuggle in here for a while longer, then break-fast."

He threw a pillow at her and headed for the bathroom.

"Don't forget it's lunch at my parents' place," she called out.

"And we're having dinner at the Vue de Monde tonight," he reminded her.

She made a face. "I forgot about that. After my mom's lunch, I'll be bloated. Would you mind terribly if we went there some other time? I would prefer a quiet candlelight dinner with only the two of us," she said and smiled. "And there'll be a special dessert afterward."

"Deal!" he hooted with delight.

* * *

Apart from being Monday, July 3 rolled into simply another day having to go to work. Andrew and Adriana walked to Chapel Street and took a tram to the city. Although fresh, only nine degrees C, the clear morning made a pleasant change from the blustery weather the week before. Two days of sunshine before another cold front came in, the man said.

They got off at Collins Street and were submerged into a rolling sea of people and cars. Andrew kissed his wife and watched her walk briskly toward the First Teeth building. He turned and headed for Collins Place.

He made himself comfortable in his bullpen cubicle and powered up the computer. Outlook had the usual cascade of emails to go over. Fortified with a mug of coffee, he opened the first item. He had a status meeting at ten with Sandra and Thomas on the dentist trainer. The issues register only had three items to clear up, which meant he could give the app to the beta test team.

Dr. Hendrix had validated all the procedures and provided valuable feedback. Two weeks at most, and the app would be ready for formal demonstration to the Dental Board and the Dental Council. Sergey Nelson had already approached the American Dental Association and the European Society of Cosmetic Dentistry, keen to get the app approved and inserted into colleges and teaching institutions. Andrew looked forward to finishing it, anxious to start serious work on the VR accounting interface.

By nine, Outlook messages cleared and replies made where necessary, he got himself a fresh cup of coffee. He managed a couple of sips when his desk phone went off.

"Good morning, Regan," he said, reading the caller ID.

"Hi, Andrew. Can you come up, please?"

"Of course. Be there in a minute."

He took the stairs to the sixteenth floor, nodded to Nora, and strode quickly toward the general manager's office. He knocked on the door and walked in. Price smiled, rose out of his cloth soft chair, and swept an arm at his guest sitting beside the coffee table.

"Andrew, I want you to meet Daniel Cheong, the new Australasian general manager and executive director."

Andrew walked toward the coffee table and extended his hand. "A pleasure to meet you, sir."

Judging by Cheong's sour look, the pleasure not shared. The short man dressed in a dark gray suit slowly stood and they briefly shook hands.

"I heard a lot about you, Mr. Payne," Cheong said, his voice cool and formal.

"I hope it's been favorable," he replied, not sure where he stood with him.

"Well, that's it for me," Price said and stuck out his hand. "I wanted to say goodbye personally, Andrew. You've made several outstanding contributions to FutureTech, and I trust you'll continue doing so. Call me any time if I can help with anything."

"Thank you, Mr. Price. I enjoyed working with you."

"Good luck, Daniel," Price said and walked out.

Andrew genuinely regretted seeing him go, but taking over Europe meant a major step up the corporate ladder. All the managers and staff gave him a farewell lunch on Friday, which ran longer than the customary one hour, but no one seemed to notice or care. Price definitely did not. He thanked everybody for their support and hard work, and looked forward to a warm London, which raised a few laughs. The most junior VR programmer walked up to him and held out a shoe-size box with the latest iPhone. Price already had an Apple, but over six years old, he needed an upgrade. Clearly touched by the gift, he kissed the programmer on the cheek, which made her blush.

Andrew would miss him.

He turned and made for the door.

"A moment, Mr. Payne," Cheong called out sharply, walked to what was now his desk, and sat down. He did not invite Andrew to sit in one of the visitor chairs.

"Yes, sir?"

"Mr. Price and I discussed the unique arrangement you have with FutureTech. Frankly, I find it irregular in the extreme. I brought up the issue with corporate legal, and I believe we can redress the imbalance."

"Redress in what way?"

"There is not much we can do regarding your intellectual property claims because they're protected by your patents. However, legal feels the two percent royalty might be untenable. I am advised the two payments of twenty thousand shares, a ridiculous amount, caps FutureTech's liability. All sales are controlled from our Mountain View headquarters, a U.S. registered company. You're an Australian employee, and there may be a legal precedent that bars you from any royalty entitlement."

"Mr. Cheong, my contracts were vetted by corporate legal and signed without amendment. My royalty entitlement derives from the license I granted FutureTech to use my 3D rendering macros.

Such an agreement has precedents without number."

"That's not exactly true, but I will not debate this. I want to advise you that steps are being taken to annul the royalty clause in all your agreements. Your proposed VR management accounting interface has merit, but FutureTech will provide a contract for its development, not you. As a valued employee, your ingenuity and efforts will be rewarded with a once-off bonus without further liability to the company. This will also apply to the full-sensor device you're developing."

Andrew stared at the little man with distaste, wondering how he came to his position with such predatory tactics. Because of them? Did Dela Torres have anything to do with this? It had the smell of a numbers deal. Perhaps Cheong saw before him a young man who could be intimidated. He would be disappointed.

"FutureTech signed those contracts for a sound commercial reason. You now want to exploit my work for a throwaway gift and expect me to walk away happy? I regret, sir, it doesn't work that way."

"That's how it will work from now on," Cheong said sharply. "Another thing. Mr. Price allowed you to use company's resources for prototyping without violation of your IP claim. That stops as of this moment. What you design on company time belongs to us. The law is clear on that, regardless of any contractual or verbal agreement you may have entered into."

"Very well. As there is no contract in place between me and FutureTech for development of the VR accounting interface or the sensor helmet, I will not offer one to this company."

"By discussing these projects with Mr. Price, they belong to us."

Andrew shook his head. "No, sir. I registered patents for both applications, which protects my IP. You have no claim on them."

"We shall see, young man. Corporate legal will be in touch with your law firm."

"If you insist on taking this course of action as a condition of my employment, I resign, effective immediately. I will also with-draw FutureTech's license to use my 3D rendering macros. You'll get formal notification from my lawyer."

Cheong slowly stood and planted his hands on the desk. "You're not in any position to do that."

Andrew smiled without warmth. "Did you read the license agreement?"

"I looked closely at all your contracts."

"Allow me to refresh your memory regarding Clause 17C. It basically says that either party can terminate the agreement at any time with a notarized letter. On termination, the license granted to FutureTech to use my 3D rendering macros lapses, and all work in progress that uses these macros must cease forthwith. This shall not apply to products developed using my macros al-ready available for sale. I think there is also something there about litigation for damages if FutureTech contravenes this clause."

Reynolds Parker wrote the license agreement most carefully to protect Andrew's IP, mindful of possible changes in Future Tech management or policy. Without the license, FutureTech would only have games already available for sale, and games de-veloped using old software. More importantly, the VR flight sim-ulator program would be effectively dead, as no version was yet available for sale. Andrew figured that TE Flight Corporation would not be pleased. The new general manager had not thought this through, or received some very bad advice. It did not matter. He would make his own deal with TE and another VR games developer.

"Clean out your desk, Mr. Payne, and remove yourself from these premises within the hour," Cheong grated.

Andrew nodded and walked out, feeling surprisingly calm. If this represented a new face of FutureTech, he wanted no part of it. If anything, he felt huge disillusionment.

At his desk, he typed his resignation and sent the email to

Cheong, with a CC to Sergey Nelson.

He strode to the kitchenette and made himself a mug of tea, figuring Cheong would not begrudge him that. He could bill him if he did. He went to the stationery room and snagged a carton. Nothing much to pack; a framed picture of Adriana, an electronic clock, and a notebook he used to jot down possible projects and stuff for the VR accounting interface. Warren Kant leaned over the divider.

"What are you doing?"

"Packing up."

"I can see that, but why?"

"I've quit," Andrew told him, and Warren gaped.

"What happened?"

"A disagreement with the new general manager."

His cell trilled and his eyebrows climbed when he saw the caller ID.

"Good afternoon, Mr. Nelson."

"I read your email and I couldn't believe my eyes. What the hell is going on, Andrew?"

"Sir, can you hold on for a minute?" He hurried into the storeroom. "Sorry about that. I wanted somewhere private."

"Okay, talk to me."

"I'm under the impression Mr. Cheong acted with your full knowledge and approval, sir."

"I don't know what you're talking about."

"Mr. Cheong has advice from corporate legal suggesting that my royalty claim is without foundation, and he is taking steps to annul that part of all our agreements. I'm no longer permitted to use company resources to prototype any new idea at the risk of invalidating my IP claim. He also maintains that discussions I had with Mr. Price regarding the VR management accounting interface and the full-sensor helmet has effectively transferred all IP rights to FutureTech regardless of my patents. I could not accept his claims and I resigned. I then told him I'm revoking the license agreement with FutureTech to use my 3D macros."

"Jesus Christ! Tell me you're joking."

"I have one hour to clean out my desk and leave the building."

"Shit! Andrew, I don't know anything about this. My lead council and I discussed your contract and license agreement clauses when the matter first came up, and he raised several concerns, but I overruled him. If Cheong is seeking to undermine me, he's doing it without my knowledge or approval. Did you take any formal action regarding the license?"

"Not yet."

"Can you give me an hour to sort this out before you do anything final?"

"I look forward to hearing from you, sir."

"For heaven's sake! You used to call me Sergey."

"I wasn't sure where I stood…Sergey."

"An hour, okay?" Nelson said and hung up.

Andrew returned to his desk, found the tea cold, and made himself a fresh round. A glance at his watch showed almost ten. He gave a sigh and headed for the stairs. Sandra and Thomas were already in the conference room.

"The meeting is off, guys," he told them.

"What's going on?" Sandra asked.

"It might only be postponed. I'll fill you in later."

When they left, both giving him full of questions stares, he pulled back one of the comfortable cloth-covered chairs and sat down to wait, his mind churning.

He believed that Nelson knew nothing. He simply did not operate that way. The managing director must be painfully aware what it meant to FutureTech if Andrew revoked the development license. The whole company might very well fold. What he did not understand, why did Cheong take such a hardnosed stand? He *had* to see it would not work. In his opinion, whoever at corporate legal advised him was a total asshole.

Andrew sat in the chair and gazed out the window.

After almost forty minutes, his cell trilled.

"Are you okay to talk?" Nelson asked.

"Go ahead."

"I finished a conversation with Cheong, then fired his butt. I then told my chief counsel to fire the legal twitch who provided that asinine advice. Price will hang around for a few days until I appoint a new general manager. Believe me, Andrew, I have no intention of challenging our agreements, or any new ones you might come up with. I can only apologize for this incident and hope you'll continue with FutureTech. Are we good?"

"I'm ready to get back to work," Andrew said, vastly relieved.

"Excellent. You're a very valuable resource, for reasons both of us understand, something that Cheong clearly did not. To show my appreciation and further our relationship, I'm going to do something unprecedented. You currently hold 79,000 Future-Tech shares, which demonstrates your commitment to this company's future. As of this moment, you're an executive director, not an employee. Consult with the local general manager, but you set your own program of work using whatever resources you need, and you only report to me. You'll attend board meetings via a video link and vote on resolutions. Legal will issue all relevant notices, but that's paperwork. A special stockholders meeting will ratify your appointment, but you're a director when I say you are. I'll send Tompson, Tompson, and Parker your remuneration package details. If you have an issue with anything, pick up the phone and call. Are we clear?"

Andrew gaped, not believing the speed with which Nelson handled things, or his offer.

He took a deep breath. "I accept, Sergey, with thanks."

"Next time, call before you resign, okay?"

Andrew chuckled. "I'll do that."

He heard a cheerful laugh and the connection cut.

Stunned, bemused, he walked out of the conference room. Cheong appeared, holding a slim valise, and stopped. He shot

Andrew a stern stare and stomped toward the elevators. Nora Steel gave Andrew a puzzled look. He shrugged and headed for the stairs.

A fresh mug of coffee at his elbow, he rescheduled his meeting with Sandra and Thomas for two o'clock. Now that he still had a job, he had to earn his keep, wondering about the package Nelson would send him. No longer on a salary opened windows into legitimate tax minimization options. Something to discuss with Parker.

He took a sip, sat back, and sighed.

The idea of being his own boss felt strange, yet exhilarating. He now had a say in setting FutureTech policy, tactical and strategic direction. Perhaps only a small voice, but a voice nonetheless. A voice other directors would have to listen to, and he had ideas. In his view, the company needed to establish a wider market footprint and shed the image of a VR games developer if it wanted to be taken seriously. The managing director must have considered all this already. Still…

Gradually, he became aware of an undercurrent of talk around the floor. He stood and peered over the dividers. People huddled in small groups engaged in lively conversation. Warren walked into his cubicle, eyes bright.

"Did you hear the latest?"

"Hear what?"

"Nora said that Cheong got booted, and Regan is coming back." The senior project manager gave him a speculative look. "This morning, you went up to see Cheong, then you told me you've quit, but you're still here. Then you have a chat with Mr. Nelson and Cheong is gone. If I had a suspicious nature, I'd say all those things were connected."

Andrew smiled. "It's a good thing you don't have a suspicious nature."

"Come on! They didn't find me in a shopping cart. What gives?"

"I simply pointed out to the Managing Director that he needed me more than he needed Cheong."

"I see. Is there anyone else you've taken a dislike to around here?"

"The list is lengthy."

Warren shook his head and walked off.

The rumor mill grinding in overdrive, Andrew got more than one curious stare. He opened the dentist work program issues register, but it still said the same thing it said this morning. His heart and mind were not on work.

He leaned back and sipped his coffee.

Some ten minutes later, a red flag email popped in his Inbox, addressed to all FutureTech employees. He clicked on it and began to read. Juana Medina, Nelson's confidential secretary, announced the departure of Daniel Cheong, with the usual blurb of thanks for his years of loyal service to the company, and the temporary reinstatement of Regan Price as the interim Australasian general manager.

The next paragraph made him wince.

The managing director was pleased to announce the appointment of Mr. Andrew Payne, project manager at the Australian Melbourne office, as a FutureTech executive director with immediate effect.

He closed the email, knowing what would happen next, but unable to avoid it.

Warren rushed into his cubicle, a broad grin on his face, and pumped his hand.

"Congratulations…sir."

Andrew stood and slapped his friend on the back. "You say 'sir' once more and you're fired."

Holding hands, they both laughed.

Others on the floor came to offer their congratulations. Sandra and Thomas showed up, uncertain how to approach a company director. He made it easy for them.

"Nothing has changed, guys. I'm still Andrew, and there's a testing program to finish. Don't forget, status meeting at two. Go away now."

They smiled, relieved, and walked off talking to each other.

He sat down and looked at Outlook. Another red flag email from Juana, personal for him. He clicked on a lengthy message and groaned. An attachment showed him dates and times of all board meetings. Thankfully, not many. The executive directors who acted as regional general managers ran their areas well. What interested him were login details to a director's eyes only server. Juana suggested that he log on and immediately reset his password. The directory, she said, contained past meeting minutes, outstanding issues, pipeline projects, short/medium/long-term strategies, sales figures from around the world, projections, problem areas, and a raft of information a director needed to know in order to help set policy and take action when regional general managers were found wanting.

His shoulders sagged, realizing that being a director meant more than relaxing in a plush office, but he already knew that. He recalled the maxim that said, 'When the gods want to punish us, they grant us our wishes.' Poetic justice, he figured.

His phone rang and he picked up. "Yes, Nora?"

"Congratulations, Mr. Payne. Would you be able to come up for a few minutes? The others on the floor would like to extend their best wishes, and I want to discuss an arrangement for an office."

"Thanks, Nora, but I'm happy where I am. I might be a director, but I still have a job to do, and my team is on this floor.

"But, sir—"

"No buts, and it's still Andrew, okay?"

"If I may…Andrew. You'll often get important calls and conduct video link meetings. You cannot discuss confidential matters from your workstation. You need an office."

Chastised, he sighed, realizing she was right. No longer one of the boys, but someone trusted to handle privileged information competitors would pay a lot to gain.

"Do what is necessary."

"I think Mr. Simmond's office should suffice temporarily. You'll be able to move in tomorrow morning."

Simmond, the head legal weenie who, Andrew thought, did not rate an office at all, as corporate handled all heavy legal stuff. Perhaps Nora kicked him out because of it.

"Fine. I'll be right up," he said and hung up.

An office?

Tempted to call Adriana and share the news, he refrained. He would see her at lunch anyway. Instead, he logged into the corporate server, changed his password, and started reading through the last board minutes. The most significant item, a worldwide recruitment drive to cope with the number of VR flight simulator projects for civilian and military aircraft. CAE had not wasted any time approaching manufacturers. His eyebrows climbed when he saw the projected cost, more than eighteen million. What opened his eyes were sales and earnings figures: $184 million and some change for the June quarter. It did not surprise him the company offered an annual dividend yield of 17.2%.

Out of curiosity, he took a peek at the June 2022 quarter: $56 million. Still respectable for old format games, but those earnings came from twenty-nine games, not the twelve that used his 3D macros. The trend clear. Gamers were jumping into FutureTech products, and the old format doomed to wither, as were developers who used it.

He gave a wry grin when he saw several meeting entries rejecting requests from Microsoft, Google, and Apple to license his 3D macros. Even if FutureTech wanted to enter into such an agreement, it could not grant a license, as the macros were not theirs to give away. Whatever plans the big guys had on the drawing boards, they can junk them until they developed something equivalent, which he figured might take a very long time. His patent covered a lot of ground in application of fractal geometry sets.

Suffer…

Those monsters needed cutting down a notch or two.

At 12:20, he powered down, snagged his overcoat, and headed for the elevators. Several colleagues waiting for one going down nodded politely, which made him uncomfortable, not used to the aura that surrounded a senior exec or director. He still felt the same person, wasn't he? When the elevator doors opened and everybody waited for him to get in first, he realized he was not the same anymore, at least not on the outside. It made him want to laugh.

He approached the First Teeth building and saw Adriana step out, hugging her beige overcoat. Patchy clouds filled the sky, and feeble sunlight made no attempt to warm things up. At least the wind had eased, which made the bracing air bearable.

"Hi, sweetie." He opened his arms and hugged her.

"Well, hi yourself. You're looking particularly cheerful," she observed.

"I am, because I'm no longer a wage slave. I've sold out to the establishment. For your information, Mrs. Payne, I'm now a freshly minted FutureTech director. How about that?"

She looked round eyed. "A director? How did that happen?"

"Mr. Cheong and I had a difference of opinion. I won and he has joined the ranks of the unemployed."

She slipped an arm around his and pressed herself against him. "I'm so proud of you, I could burst."

They turned left into Spring Street and merged with the flow of pedestrians and lunch seekers.

"And I'm getting an office. Would you believe it?"

"I guess you'll need an office to mess with the secretary," she quipped, eyes sparkling.

"Mess with the secretary? You're mean, did you know that?"

"Sharpening my claws, dear one."

"Relax, already. There is only one girl your loving husband wants to mess with, and you know it."

"Good."

They walked in silence for a while.

"I guess your bit of good news needs sharing with some of mine," she said slowly.

"And what would that be?"

"Well…you're going to be a daddy."

He froze in his tracks and stared at her.

She nodded. "I had a test this morning."

He gathered her in his arms and held her. "I couldn't be happier, my sweet," he murmured and gently kissed her.

A father…He would be a father, when not long ago, he was making out his will.

As he stood there, he vowed never to question the fates again.

He needed to ask Dr. Dalton one thing. Since he infected Adriana with his macrophages, would they infect the baby?

Chapter Eight

Overhead, a white sun bore down on the Okavango mean-dering streams and grassy plains. Six large elephants shel-tered beneath two enormous baobab trees. The air felt thick with heat, and had a heavy, earthy smell. Deep silence held the land in its grip.

Sloan took a long breath, wiped sweat off his brow, and drank deeply from the canteen. He lifted the powerful Remington Mag-num rifle, flipped off the safety, and squinted through the tele-scopic sight. The sharp crack sent birds squawking into the air in alarm. Several gazelles and antelope bound from the tall grass and raced across the meadow toward a stand of acacia. A bull ele-phant raised his trunk and trumpeted a bellow of agony, and slowly toppled to the ground, making the earth tremble. The oth-ers pounded away in panic. The acrid stink of burnt powder lin-gered in the air.

A fish eagle soared majestically overhead.

Gradually, silence returned to the Okavango.

Without saying anything, Sloan dropped the rifle, reached up and removed his sensor helmet. Disoriented for a moment when he found himself back in the conference room, he placed the hel-met on the table and reached for the pitcher of water. He downed the glass in four large gulps.

"Christ almighty," he muttered and patted his forehead with a tissue.

Andrew had watched the simulation through a normal VR headset. Not an all-senses experience, but he knew how Sloan felt, having run the thing before with Mark. He had not forgotten Adriana's warning about the potential misuse and abuse of full-sensor games or applications. When he thought about it, the solution turned out relatively simple to implement. Since his software-induced brain responses, he simply suppressed stimulus levels to the pain and pleasure centers. Good enough for now, but he accepted the unpalatable fact that someone in the future would develop products to deliberately excite maximum responses, which would then create a new breed of addicts. That's how the shitty world worked. However, he did not intend to spoil this moment with thoughts of doom, or moralize on human behavior.

Displayed in the four wall screens video link, sitting in his office, Sergey Nelson looked pale. "Shit…"

Andrew winked at Mark. "I think they like it."

"I should hope so." His friend smiled and helped himself to some coffee. Trim, black hair combed straight back, he took a sip and leaned against the chair.

Sloan shook his head as though emerging from a powerful dream, which in a sense, he had.

"Like it? You guys created a revolution, you know that," Nelson declared. "Not only in VR games and how movies are made, but for stacks of industrial applications as well. Whatever you two want for this thing, it's yours."

He and Mark had worked hard for the last two months to get the sensor helmet and interfacing software working properly. It still needed tweaking, and the bulky helmet made much smaller, but that meant engineering. The important thing, it all worked.

For the demo, he wanted to use the B737 simulator, but Mark convinced him that his *Hunter* game would generate greater emotional impact. He was right.

"Thirty thousand shares and two percent of every sale…for both of us. In addition, an immediate payment of one million for Mark."

Nelson banged the table with his palm. "Done! Send me the contract."

"Thanks, Sergey."

"Wait till Money Manny sees this. He'll crap himself." His face became serious. "What do you propose as the next step?"

"You and I already discussed this. The first thing is to make the sensor helmet much more user-friendly. I think we need to bring in Trans Vis or some other major VR headset supplier for that. They have the necessary engineering expertise."

"Agreed. I'll get things moving from here."

"I understand TE Flight will get Level D FAA and EASA certification next month," Andrew said.

"That's right. Boeing and Airbus already put in orders for 120 B737-MAX and A321 simulators each at $1.3 million a pop," Nelson confirmed.

This would net Andrew $6.24 million. Not a bad return at all. A soon as the money came through, he intended to purchase additional FutureTech shares. With twenty thousand FutureTech shares he got in May for the VR management accounting interface, and a call option purchase in July, he held 169,000 shares, which would generate a very handsome dividend every six months, enabling him to purchase more shares.

"I know what you're going to say," Nelson went on. "We need to show TE what we've got and retrofit all our simulators. I'll need a hundred more analysts and developers."

"Get yourself a new building," Andrew told him with a grin.

"I'll have to."

"Seriously, I wouldn't rush into this, Sergey. The full-sensor software works, but needs refining. That will take me a month or so to do, and three weeks at least to familiarize my team how to code the response interfaces, document everything, and set up testing harnesses. Once everything is ready, I'll need to develop a formal training package for your coders. Keep in mind; apart from the helmet I sent you, there's only one other down here. We can code some things without them, but we need helmets for testing, and they won't be available for some time if we wait on a supplier."

"I've already given that some thought, Andrew. Polish your software and get the documentation and training program done. Use whatever resources you need. Got that, Keith?"

The new Australasian general manager nodded. "Not a problem."

"I would like to raise this new development with TE," Nelson said, "but I have reservations. What do you think, Andrew?"

"You're the managing director, Sergey, and it's your call. My advice would be to hold off for a while. They already have their hands full rolling out the VR trainers and sounding off other customers. Telling them what's coming would needlessly disrupt their sales and training programs."

"I agree."

"Once the sensor interfaces are perfected, there's still a fair amount of work to upgrade the B737 and the A321 simulators before I would be comfortable having them demonstrated. I also want to upgrade the dentist trainer package and finish prototyping the management accounting interface."

"Your problem. Handle it," Nelson said and looked at Mark. "As you've gathered, Mr. Sanders, lack of sensor helmets is our bottleneck. What would it take to build another one?"

"Three weeks if I don't stop to sleep, and around forty thousand dollars for parts. With the two I already built, a new one should go much faster."

"I know you've been working on this in your free time, and I hate to load this on you. Would you be prepared to build us another helmet?"

"I'll talk to my boss if I can get three weeks off without pay. It'll take me a couple of weeks to wrap up my current work before I can start anything."

"Mr. Sanders, anything you could do would be of enormous help."

Mark grinned. "I gathered that."

"I'm prepared to offer you another million for this." Nelson smiled, which made him look very young. "Plus a hundred thousand for all expenses. Consider it a bribe."

Mark laughed. "You have a deal, Mr. Nelson."

"Thank you, and it's Sergey, okay?" He turned to Sloan. "Keith, can you arrange an immediate transfer for him?"

"I'll get it done right away."

"Mark, it's been a genuine pleasure. I regret that FutureTech is not a good career fit for you, as we need people of your vision and caliber."

"Thanks, Sergey. I must admit, when Andrew first approached me to work on this, I thought he'd flipped. I wasn't at all sure the thing was even technically feasible."

"I believe it. He's a driven man. Thank you for taking the time to demonstrate this for us."

Keith Sloan stood and extended an arm toward the door. "I'll take you to Accounting, Mark."

Andrew waved at his friend. "Talk to you later," he said and made to stand up.

"Can you hold on for a minute?" Nelson asked.

"What's up?" Andrew topped up his coffee.

"You and your friend have blown me away, and you've taken FutureTech another quantum leap into tomorrow. When you initially canvassed the idea, I thought you had some minor software tweaking in mind to give the illusion of real movement and tactile feel, but when you said full-sensor, you actually meant it. I thought I was actually in Okavango. I could feel the heat on my skin and smell the grass. When that gun went off, I nearly fell out of my chair. I still can't believe the realism. This is better than going all the way to Africa."

"The engineering interfaces took some work to accommodate different responses," Andrew admitted, "but Mark deserves the credit for that. You should have seen our test jury-rig. A Medusa's head of wires."

"It's too bad that we can't use him." Nelson frowned. "Is this thing safe? I don't want to face lawsuits down the track because someone claimed we burned out his brain."

"We had that aspect researched and tested thoroughly. We're safe, but somebody may launch a lawsuit down the track anyway."

"Probably. There's always someone out there who wants something for nothing. It might be an idea to get CalTech and Johns Hopkins proof it for us. I'll look into it. Anyway, that's not why I wanted to talk to you. At the last month's board meeting, you proposed that FutureTech approach General Dynamics Electric Boat Division to build them a VR trainer for their *Virginia*-class attack subs. With flight simulators and the dentist trainer programs, I felt we had enough on our plate."

"There *are* sound business reasons why Money Manny didn't embrace the idea," Andrew pointed out.

"At the time, I agreed with him. However, after considering your suggestion more closely, I came to change my mind. I believe your proposal is exactly what FutureTech needs to establish a solid marketplace footprint as a visionary company worthy of our name. At the next board meeting, I'll announce that we open talks with General Dynamics for an expression of interest. This might take a while, as there are security issues, but they might be more receptive when we tell them we already hold Department of Defense security clearance for our work with TE Flight on military fighter trainers."

"It might be a difficult sell to the board, Sergey."

"We'll see what happens. Your throwaway remark about needing another building might not be far off the mark either."

Andrew grinned. "There's plenty of space for another building where you're now."

"When we relocated from downtown San Francisco to Mountain View, I did it with this very possibility in mind. I didn't count on expanding this quickly. Then again, I never figured on having someone like you joining us either. Anyway, I wanted to give you a heads-up about the submarine thing."

"There's something else I'd like to raise at the next meeting, Sergey."

"What's that?"

"That we approach major manufacturers to build pilotless fighters."

Nelson looked puzzled. "They're already doing it with drones."

"Drones have their uses, but they're slow and not contact combat rated. From what I've read, somebody like Lockheed Martin could build a much more capable fighter, but for one thing…G tolerance. Even with g-suits, most pilots black out at six Gs. Now, you strap him into a comfy chair equipped with my full-sensor control system, he won't worry about pulling Gs. Not only that, the aircraft wouldn't need all that instrumentation, controls, and life-support systems clutter. If the defense forces think this would degrade pilot skills, they're wrong. Pilots would need even greater skills to operate such aircraft at maximum rated performance. There is something else to consider. Such aircraft would save lives. If one crashes or is destroyed in combat, it's only hardware. The pilot can link himself to another one and he's off. If you want to take this one step further, the concept can be applied equally well to helicopters, tanks, or any other front line self-propelled vehicle."

"Warfare reduced to a VR arcade game," Nelson muttered. "I'm not sure I like that."

"Dealing out remote death is already here," Andrew pointed out.

"Not at the level you're proposing." Nelson snorted and shook his head. "When you dream up something, you certainly don't think small. I'll have to think about this."

"This is worth doing, Sergey."

Nelson tilted his head, a quizzical smile making his eyes sparkle. "If I don't, you'll run with this on your own, is that it?"

Andrew chuckled. "The thought *had* crossed my mind, but I would never do it."

"Just kidding. All right, leave it with me. By the way, how's your wife?"

"Everything is good so far. Thanks for asking."

"You'll like being a dad. Not for the first six months or so, perhaps, but that'll pass."

Andrew laughed. "I can't wait."

"I've got to go. Talk to you later," Nelson said and switched off the video link.

Despite some morning sickness, Adriana was ecstatic about her pregnancy. Although they could test for gender now, both agreed to wait a few months. His mom and her mom had her firmly in hand on things she should not do. Andrew would be there to help and support Adriana in whatever way she needed. He did not know what else he could do.

He stared at the dark screens for a moment, then glanced out the window. September still shaking off winter's hold, but the noticeably warmer and longer days made the world a brighter place—at least his corner of it.

He walked out of the conference room, sensor helmet under one arm, and headed for his office. Nora hurried toward him.

"A Mr. Falzon is waiting to see you."

"Who's he?"

"Some executive from the States."

Andrew scowled. Competitors called him all the time offering deals, not in the mood to listen to another sales pitch. He could make millions licensing his 3D macros at the cost of compromising his relationship with FutureTech, something he did not want to do.

Nora handed him a laminated business card.

Byrne Falzon
Chief Executive Officer
Evagen, Inc.

In small font below was a phone number, email, and a Phoenix address, which made him rise his eyebrows. This guy flew all the way from the States to see him without a phone call or introductory email? The man might be a competitor, but his curiosity peaked.

"Give me five minutes, then show him in," he said.

Nora nodded and walked toward the neatly dressed man sitting in a visitor chair.

Andrew strode into his office and Googled Evagen, Inc. Only one entry came up from the U.S. corporate names register, the company not listed on the stock exchange. This made him frown and bite his lower lip. If Evagen was a competitor, they were short on advertising. A nutcase with a grudge? The man he saw outside did not strike him as a nutcase, but how could he tell?

A knock on his door and Nora stepped to one side. "Mr. Falzon."

"Thank you, Nora." Andrew stood and gave his visitor a quick scrutiny. Of average height, dressed in a dark gray suit and maroon tie, pale features, he looked unimposing. Andrew stepped away from his desk and stuck out a hand.

"Welcome to FutureTech, Mr. Falzon."

The Evagen CEO smiled, his grip hard and dry. "Thank you for giving me a few moments of your time," he said in a deep voice.

Andrew extended his arm at soft chairs surrounding a black marble-topped coffee table. "Make yourself comfortable. Can I get you something? Coffee or soft drink?"

"I'm fine, thank you."

Andrew sat down, crossed his legs, and studied his visitor. Falzon returned the gaze without looking away.

"I must admit, you've got me intrigued. All this way from the States without even a hello."

"If you will allow me to explain, Mr. Payne, you'll understand the reason for my circumspect visit."

"Just Andrew, if you don't mind."

"Thank you…Andrew. Please call me Byrne." Falzon paused, apparently gathering his thoughts. "Before this goes any further, let me assure you that I don't represent a competitor or a government agency."

"The thought had crossed my mind."

"You also established that we don't have a public footprint, and it's for a very good reason."

"That's what got me curious."

Falzon leaned forward slightly. "Can I rely on your total discretion on what I have to say? If certain parties or the government discovered what we developed, we would be severely compromised. Before you ask the obvious, our work is perfectly legal."

"You can speak freely, Byrne," Andrew told him seriously.

"You have a remarkable record of achievements, Andrew. I know that you invented a unique set of 3D macros that made FutureTech a leader in VR games, and your flight simulators are poised to do the same thing in that market. This is where Evagen needs your expertise."

"You want us to build a flight simulator for a secret aircraft?"

"Well, it's not an aircraft in the normal sense. What we need is a flight control system that uses your full-sensor interface."

Andrew sat up. "How did you find out about that?"

"We researched you and FutureTech extensively. I apologize if this sounds alarming, but you'll understand better after I explain what we have."

"Okay, you want a VR flight control system. For what?"

"A gravitomagnetic vehicle," Falzon said simply.

Andrew gaped at him, images of Podkletnov's electrogravitic

lift disks sprang immediately to mind. The concept theoretically feasible from what he read. NASA, DARPA, and lots of large companies around the world had spent millions researching the subject without achieving a workable breakthrough…as far as the public knew. There were lots of rumors and conspiracy theories about strange aircraft tested at the secret Nevada Groom Lake facility. He had not heard or read anything about gravitomagnetic vehicles, though. It looked like his visitor might be a nutcase after all. Before he could say anything, Falzon raised his hand.

"I know what you're thinking, but let me assure you, I'm serious. If you give me a moment, I can prove that Evagen has a prototype gravitomagnetic vehicle." He pulled out a Blu-ray mini case out of his jacket and held it out. "Once we're done, take a look at this, and then I ask that you destroy it."

Andrew took the case, stared at it for a second, and placed it on the coffee table.

"Let's say I accept your startling claim. If you've actually built such a ship, I can understand why you wouldn't want premature disclosure. I also understand what this means for the general aerospace industry. They'll be out of business, hundreds of thousands will lose their jobs, airports as we know them will disappear, and you'll probably set off the biggest stock market crash since the COVID crisis. Add to this the geopolitical and military dimension, this could be disaster."

Listening to himself, he felt somewhat startled by his words. Two years ago, global politics, economics, military goings-on were merely interesting sidelines. He followed local and international news, but never analyzed what he heard and saw, something to fill time. Since his remarkable cure, his world view and understanding had expanded enormously, which made him wonder if all smart people shared this characteristic.

"You can appreciate, then, the need for total secrecy until we're ready to reveal our development publicly," Falzon said. "If you think about it, things will not be as dire as you paint. I don't deny that vehicles based on our propulsion system will cause major industrial and social disruption at many levels, and cars and aircraft as we know them will become obsolete, but not for a long time. However, the potential is there to build a whole new family of different vehicles, private, commercial, and passenger. They'll have to be designed and produced from new plants. This will require engineers and a skilled workforce to assemble them. Instead of layoffs, aerospace and auto industries will need more people than ever. With a positive spin, we'll be creating a bull market, not a slump, and the possibilities don't end there." Falzon gave a slow smile. "You see, a GM vehicle isn't confined to atmospheric flight."

Andrew stared, startled by the possibilities. "It can travel in space?"

"Our group made an engineering breakthrough five months ago and we used the testbed vehicle to achieve low-Earth orbit." Falzon's mouth twitched in a small smile. "We had to hurry down as the ship lacked the necessary life-support system for proper spaceflight. However, not every vehicle needs to have that capability. There are engineering and life-support considerations for airless flight."

Andrew shook his head and gave a long exhale. What Evagen had would create a transport revolution, but the invention also harbored a dark side.

"You *have* considered the military potential for such a craft?"

"Of course, and that's why we didn't partner with NASA, DARPA, or companies like Lockheed Martin. They would want it kept secret, least of all because it would interfere with their work on electrogravitic vehicles. Evagen will make the technology available to all. You can understand why."

Andrew did understand. A country with a fleet of military gravitomagnetic ships would create a serious geopolitical power imbalance.

"You'll give away the design?"

Falzon smiled. "We're not *that* altruistic. We'll license the drive hardware, but Evagen will provide BIOS-like chips for every vehicle without which the drive cannot operate."

"The U.S. government might stop you doing this."

"If they attempt to do so, Evagen will post the design on the Internet."

"You have a manufacturing plant in Phoenix?"

"It's a research and assembly facility. We make room-temperature superconductor components for the drive, but we custom source structural and circuit board modules. We're not planning to compete with major auto or aerospace industries who're already set up for large volume manufacture."

"And the reason you're here, you want me to design a flight control simulator for your craft?"

"You misunderstand, Andrew. We want an actual control system installable in every vehicle type. All manual controls require procedures and training to execute, and pilots need to keep a constant eye on instrumentation. A GM craft is far easier to operate than an aerodynamic aircraft, but there is more to running a commercial-grade vehicle than merely telling it where to go.

"What we want is an interactive graphical system with a semi-autonomous capability that almost anyone can operate using voice commands through your VR helmet without the need to develop a sophisticated and expensive AI pilot. The system needs to display to the pilot only those things that threaten the safety of the ship without the usual instrumentation distractions. It must *tell* the pilot what is going on and what action to take, rather than merely flash a light and sound a warning. Collision avoidance, as an example, must be automatic. Your sensor interface can do that. The first step is to build a proof of concept. Then we'll look how to create a configurable production version."

Andrew mulled it over, the idea not far off his proposal to Sergey Nelson for pilotless fighters. An idea now dead, as were all existing military aircraft concepts. Existing concepts, yes, but he saw no reason why a remote flight control system cannot be applied to gravitomagnetic fighters, and there would be such things.

Closer to home, Evagen's vehicle represented a serious long-term disruption to FutureTech's flight simulator program. All crap flowed downhill, and the little guy at the bottom always got it all.

"Let's put aside how the thing works for the moment," he said.

"The DVD will explain that in general terms."

"Can you tell me something about Evagen?"

"Terrance Maceroy founded Evagen in 2017 by luring away some of the brightest scientists and engineers from several universities, NASA, and a number of aerospace manufacturers, civilian and military. He set up a research facility in Phoenix and gave them an almost unlimited budget to pursue their vision."

"Pardon me, but I never heard of Maceroy," Andrew said.

"He's a multibillionaire who made his fortune during the 1990s dot com bubble and invested heavily in Apple and Microsoft. He sold out before the Global Financial Crisis hit, then bought back in, tripling his fortune."

Andrew rubbed his chin. "Before I decide to do anything, I would require a demonstration."

"And we would require a demonstration of your sensor helmet."

"That's reasonable. Mind you, the helmet is also a prototype, and won't be ready for market release for at least a year."

"And neither will our ship, not for general manufacture anyway. If FutureTech is prepared to consider creating a control system, I can arrange a demo flight this evening."

Andrew stared at the man, and the realization hit him. "You came here in your ship?"

Falzon chuckled. "Somewhat faster than taking a commercial flight both ways. We'll be at the Fawkner Park cricket oval at ten this evening and wait five minutes." He stood and extended a hand. "It has been a pleasure, Mr. Payne."

Andrew shook his hand and sighed. "You know, I feel a little sorry for SpaceX. Elon Musk has come a long way to revive the American space industry."

"He can continue doing so far more cheaply using GM vehicles than wasteful rockets."

"I suppose. You've given me a lot to think about, Byrne," Andrew said and escorted his visitor toward the elevators.

"I look forward to seeing you later tonight." Falzon nodded when the elevator doors opened, and walked in.

Back at his desk, Andrew stared at the Blu-ray disk, shook his head, and inserted it into the computer. The theoretical principle behind the vehicle simple enough, first proposed in 1913 by the French mathematician Elie Cartan. While working on his unified field theory, Einstein later confirmed the possibility of spinning counter-gravitational fields. Only a theory, as technology did not exist at the time to test it. Evagen apparently did by inducing a strong magnetic field in an electro-magneto toroidal device using an impulsive electric current through superconducting coils embedded in a dielectric material to generate a fast rotating co-gravitational vortex that produced selective motion. They also used the field to power the vehicle's systems.

The presentation did not provide equations that underpinned the theoretical basis behind the Evagen vehicle, which he understood readily enough. What convinced him beyond doubt were movie clips of the craft in flight. He supposed they could be faked, as computer animation can fake just about anything these days—he ought to know—but he doubted that Byrne Falzon would come all the way from the States to show him a fake flying disk.

Anyway, he would find out tonight.

Something occurred to him, which the Evagen CEO did not mention, perhaps deliberately. Their power source could also act as fixed bed generators to feed an electricity grid. The enormity of this potential left him gaping. Limitless power for all…The transport industry would not be the only ones affected.

He extracted the DVD and gently tapped it against the edge of his desk, deep in thought…then broke it.

Sorely tempted to call Nelson, he decided not to. Although the managing director had a need to know, telling him now would break trust with Falzon. The Evagen CEO would probably understand, but that trust would be eroded. He did not want a potentially profitable partnership aborted by an indiscretion. He would talk to Nelson after the demo—if the thing existed—and let him do a thorough background check into Evagen and its people before committing the company to anything.

Too excited and distracted, he found it difficult to concentrate on his work, which made the day unbearably long. At 5:30, he wrapped up and hurried down to meet Adriana. She already waited in the open plaza when he stepped out of the elevator. He walked toward her and gave her a quick kiss.

"How was your day?" she asked. "Did Nelson and Sloan like the presentation?"

"They were floored, my gorgeous, and your enterprising husband got a very nice deal for us."

She snuggled close and wrapped an arm around his waist. "I'm glad it went well." She peered at him. "What is it?"

"What's what?"

"You appear distracted. A new project?"

They lived together long enough to read each other's moods and feelings. He did not want to hide anything from her, but this time, he had to.

"It's a new project, but I can't talk about it right now, sweetie."

She smiled. "It's okay. I won't pry…much," she added with a mischievous gleam in her eyes.

They caught the 5:40 tram that went up Chapel Street and

squeezed into the crowded car, tapping the Myki card against the sensor pad. They got off when it stopped at Toorak Road, and walked slowly toward the Rockley Gardens, her arm wrapped around his. The sun already down and dusk had taken over. The good thing about spring, they no longer went to work or came home in the dark. In October when daylight saving started, their mornings would be dark again, but only for a few weeks.

Conversation flowed back and forth over a dinner of stir-fried seafood and a mixed salad, complemented by a crisp Riesling.

"Some good news," he told her. "Sloan received certification for the dental training program."

"The Dental Board and the Dental Council?"

"Both. He got Nora to send emails to all Australasian universities and dental teaching institutions inviting expressions of interest. We're hoping some of them will include the trainer in their 2024 schoolyear curriculum."

"That's terrific!" she gushed with undisguised enthusiasm.

"Nelson told me he's well advanced with the American Dental Association. He's preparing a worldwide advertising campaign to push the app. It'll cost a fortune, but worth it in the end. All other regional general managers are also seeking certification."

"What're you going to sell it for?"

"I don't have final figures from Money Manny, but we're looking at twenty thousand U.S. for an annual five-user license, and fifty for a teaching institution with unlimited users."

"That doesn't sound much."

"That's a hundred million a year if we license two thousand institutions, and there are thousands of private practitioners out there as well. It isn't much compared to revenues we get from game sales, but some things are worth more than money. On top of that, the initial purchase price will be around twelve hundred dollars."

"That's a lot," she observed.

"Not really. A university will have a single copy on a server to which students will log on. If the package is loaded on a sufficiently powerful standalone PC, that will count as a sale."

At 9:30, Andrew rang Uber and arranged a pickup. Adriana ribbed him about a secret rendezvous with Nora, and he laughed. At 9:40, the cab tooted from the street. He gave his wife a quick kiss, grabbed a jacket, and hurried out.

Fawkner Park only a few blocks from Rockley Street, and he had the driver drop him off at the South Yarra Primary School situated next to the dark, deserted grounds. He walked over the cut grass toward the cricket oval and waited. The sound of traffic along Punt Road seemed unnaturally loud. At ten precisely, he saw a black shape descend quietly to hover above the pitch.

Round, stubby, the craft did not look anything like saucers in movies or UFO documentaries. There were no windows. It had a makeshift look of work in progress. A hatch opened, spilling a rectangle of weak light, and Andrew ran toward it. Falzon extended a hand and helped him in.

"Welcome to tomorrow, Andrew," he said with a grin, shut the hatch, stood behind a young woman seated in the left of three seats positioned before a cluttered control panel, and extended an arm. "Make yourself comfortable."

Andrew felt the floor shift slightly, then nothing. He slowly walked to the right seat and gingerly sat down. A deep hum permeated the air, accompanied by a faint electric smell. The interior and the deck looked like polished aluminum, but he could not be sure. The flat central panel had a crude array of switches, dials, two radar displays, and a large screen showing blackness.

The woman turned her clear penetrating eyes on him and smiled. Short blond hair framed a face used to command.

"I'm Masina, the bus driver," she said and offered her hand.

Andrew shook it. "Pleased to meet you. When are we going up?"

"We're already up and hovering at ten thousand feet," she replied and pointed at a small vertical bar showing altitude beside the artificial horizon ball.

"I didn't feel anything," Andrew said.

"If you did, Mr. Payne, we'd be in trouble. This craft generates a co-gravitational field that makes it go, which also cancels inertial effects. I'll show you." She moved the handgrip control and the artificial horizon ball shifted left. In the screen, Melbourne's lit sprawl lay spread exactly how it would look from an airliner.

"Wow."

Falzon smiled at his reaction. "That's what I said when I first went up," he said and inclined his head at the control panel. "This thing is a jury-rig testbed, but it works. The full prototype model under construction will have better streamlined and organized controls, but you can see why we want a VR control interface."

"If this ship can move so fast, does it generate a sonic boom?"

"The co-gravitational field repels air molecules rather than compressing them, which conventional aircraft do, and we fly through what is in effect a low pressure tunnel," Masina explained.

"Mmm. Tell me, Byrne. With all the zipping around you've done, didn't air traffic control or somebody get excited when they saw you pop up on their screens?"

"They certainly did, but we moved too fast for them to do anything about it. Another unconfirmed UFO sighting. We're most vulnerable during takeoffs and landings from our Phoenix facility. We don't dare do too many atmospheric tests, as over time, the nearby Luke Air Force Base is likely to triangulate our location."

"How did you manage to hide what you're doing?"

"We didn't, exactly. The FBI looked in on us once. While they're in the hangar, we attached four large fans to this testbed vehicle and the prototype to make it look like we're working on new types of fan-driven air cars. We actually do have an air car mockup in the hangar in case we need to move our GM vehicles in a hurry," Falzon added with a wry grin.

Andrew chuckled, tickled by the ingenuity of the idea. "You expect a raid?"

"That, I'm afraid, is an ever-present possibility. If the government found out what we're doing, they would probably confiscate everything in the name of national security and make us disappear."

Andrew bit his lip and nodded, forced to agree. It did not say much for American democracy and freedom.

"Tell me. If this ship generates an intense co-gravitational field, how can you operate your radar?"

"Perceptive question," Masina said. "The field *does* distort electromagnetic radiation, but it's a torus, which means the central part of the craft isn't affected. That's where most of our radio, optical, and radar gear is mounted. The torus also largely dictates the shape of the craft."

"If this thing is potentially space-capable, how far can it actually fly?"

"Theoretically, as long as the vehicle is within a magnetic field, it can fly anywhere. The Earth's magnetosphere extends well beyond the Moon, and the entire Solar System is enclosed within the sun's field. We're still to test the field strengths the farther we move from Earth to see if it can generate enough power to sustain flight," she added wryly.

Andrew grinned. "That should prove interesting."

"Is there anything else you would like to see?" Falzon asked.

"Can we go higher? Say, a hundred kilometers? I always want to see for myself if Earth is actually round."

Masina laughed, flipped several switches, and shifted the handgrip. Some five minutes later, she tilted the craft. In the screen, Earth lay in darkness broken by clusters of city glitter. In the east, the Pacific had a faint phosphorescent glow. Andrew sat and watched his world suddenly shrink. Goosebumps crawled up his arms.

"It struck me the same way when I saw it like that," Falzon

said gently, his eyes reflecting understanding.

"I am officially impressed," Andrew said slowly. "If you can see me tomorrow at nine, I'll demonstrate my helmet."

Falzon gave a wry smile. "I think I'll be able to manage that."

"Do you mind if I clue in our managing director?"

The Evagen CEO reached behind him and held out a small case. "Use this for all future communication with us, and anything relating to Evagen with Mr. Nelson. It's an encrypted Nokia flip phone. It allows you to make and receive calls and nothing else. Instructions how to use it are inside. A courier will deliver one to Mr. Nelson."

"Won't this raise NSA's eyebrows, including our Signals Directorate?"

"Probably, but they won't be able to do anything about it. The phone has military-grade software using a 256-bit random key that changes every second. The exchange with the switching system's authentication center provides connection, but the encryption chip inhibits recording the event and passing it to the billing module. NSA or anyone else trying to crack the conversation will have our call numbers, but won't know where the call is made from or who received it. Something one of our engineers borrowed from Lockheed Martin," Falzon added with a small smile. "NSA's computers are likely to assume it's a genuine military call and leave it at that."

"Sounds good," Andrew said and shifted in his seat. "This morning, Byrne, you didn't told me everything."

"What did I leave out?"

"That your power generation principle can be applied for commercial use."

Falzon and Masina exchanged glances. "An astute observation," he said, "and quite accurate. An induced alternating magnetic field in a superconductor will generate current. However, we're not about to give Earth free power. Creating a lanthanum-based room-temperature superconductor is very expensive, as

China controls most rare earths. Forced into a humiliating withdrawal from some islands they occupied in the South China Sea, they're not about to sell the West any of their rare earths. We're hoping to source commercially required supplies by mining the Moon and the asteroids, but that will take time."

"Vested interests would kill to keep what you have under wraps."

"They certainly would. You can now understand the need for total secrecy until we go public."

"There is one thing I must know, Byrne. How did you find out about my full-sensor project?"

"Nothing dramatic, I'm afraid. A lot of detective work and accumulation of small facts. Your friend Mark Sanders gave it away. An electronics expert and your frequent meetings with him were telling. We had one of our operatives check out his work shed," Falzon said and looked contrite. "Somewhat unethical on our part, but given the circumstances, I hope it will not prejudice you against us."

"I understand, but I don't like how you do business."

"I can only apologize again, and we placed ourselves at great risk revealing this craft and the technology behind it to you. We're still at risk should you choose to expose us. Mr. Maceroy almost did not contact you at all."

"What convinced him to do it?"

"Your work and the vision behind it."

Andrew dropped it, but reminded himself to warn Mark that he is compromised, and should get a monitored security system and a safe in his work shed. He would also take steps to beef up security of FutureTech's server room, especially his own server.

When the ship brought him down, Andrew shook hands with Masina and the Evagen CEO, and watched the remarkable craft rise straight up without any sound. With a lot on his mind, he decided to walk home. Gravitomagnetic ships…it hardly seemed real. Then again, only a matter of time before somebody else applied engineering to theory. Falzon had put a positive spin on their breakthrough, but Andrew suspected things might not be so rosy when the megacorps and governments got involved.

Even if Evagen did not set off a market panic, would existing FAA and EASA regulations cover craft capable of random non-ballistic flight? How would they confine them to flight corridors? International skies were already highway gridlocks. Adding hundreds of thousands passenger-carrying flying saucers into the mix, would make any air controller go pale. When he considered private air cars and crazy things people already did on roads, a city full of flying machines presented a genuine danger for those walking the streets.

He began to appreciate the magnitude of Falzon's request, and the enormous social, industrial, economic, and political impact of Evagen's craft. To sidestep the social problem, he needed to design a flight control system smarter than a potential idiot using it. Operating limits must be built-in to ensure individual user and general public safety. Order from day one to eliminate chaos. He bit his lip. Doable and a perfect opportunity to explore remote piloting, at least for passenger craft. Then again, perhaps not. People would inevitably have second thoughts traveling somewhere while the pilot sat snug and safe on the ground. How much skill would a pilot need to operate a craft not subject to normal aerodynamic vagaries? Masina used a simple handgrip, so the thing must be easy to run. A commercial craft must also be easy to run, with hack-proof protocols to prevent direct or remote hijacking.

Hip deep in existing projects, the foremost being the sensor helmet, a new flight system would swamp him and he could not create a team to handle it. The security risks were obvious.

Evagen had not opened a Pandora's Box of problems, but an entire shipping container!

Adriana lay fast asleep when he walked into the bedroom. He

showered and slipped into bed beside her. She mumbled something, rolled against him, and slid an arm across his chest.

He clasped his hands behind his head and stared into impenetrable darkness.

Still asleep when he woke, showered, and went downstairs to make himself a quick breakfast of scrambled eggs mixed with a finely diced tomato. Instead of catching a tram into the city, he called an Uber cab to pick him up. When he stepped out of the house, a crimson eastern sky promised a fine day. He breathed deeply, the crisp air filling him with energy.

It must have been late when he finally slept, his mind too revved up to relax. Despite being minus on sleep, he felt eager to tackle the new day. There were no problems, someone said, only solutions. Evagen probably worked through the problems that nagged him last night. If they did not—they were a bunch of scientists and engineers, after all—he had a whole list that needed ticking off.

The cab dropped him off at Collins Place. Even at 7:30, traffic crowded the street, and the plaza had a sprinkling of customers tucking into breakfast or nursing a cappuccino. He strode quickly toward the ANZ tower and waited for an elevator to come down. When one gave a soft *ting*, he got in, pressed his FutureTech pass against the sensor, and touched the sixteenth floor button. Without the pass, the elevator did not go anywhere. This sometimes presented a problem for staff who forgot their pass, and Nora received more than one sheepish morning call requesting a temp. One thing he did when he became director, he blocked access to the 15th and 16th floor from the emergency stairwell. No point controlling elevators when anybody could walk in from the stairs, he argued. This sometimes created an inconvenience for the staff, but he did not want to compromise the competitive nature of FutureTech's work. Industrial espionage a thriving industry.

He snagged a mug of coffee from the kitchenette, settled himself in his office, and flipped open the small Nokia phone. He typed in Nelson's number and saved it in the Contacts list with Falzon's. After a deep breath, he tapped the call icon. Nelson answered after two rings.

"Andrew, I've been chewing my fingernails for the last two hours ever since Juana gave me this damn phone from Evagen," the managing director groused sourly. "I never heard of them, and why a secure phone? Talk to me."

"Are you alone?" Andrew asked.

"Talk!"

"You're not going to believe this," Andrew said and summarized yesterday's events. He heard breathing at the other end and nothing else.

"You're shitting me, right?" Nelson said at length, and Andrew chuckled.

"Call Falzon and ask him for a ride."

"Believe me, I'll do that, and I'll have a serious talk with Maceroy. I know him. You said they're in Phoenix?"

"That's right."

"Out in the desert, eh? And you're going to demonstrate your sensor helmet to Falzon? Is that wise?"

"After the flight I had, I don't see how we can avoid doing that. We *could* if we don't want any part of this. Your call."

"Are you kidding? I want to jump into this with both feet. I share your concerns, though, and I hope Evagen has a working plan, but this is a ground floor opportunity of a century."

"Sergey, if I were you, I would invest heavily. Evagen is not a listed company and FutureTech won't be contravening any insider trading regulations."

"Are *you* going to invest in Evagen?"

"As soon as my proceeds from TE Flight simulator sales comes through."

"Which, by the way, will dry up as soon as Evagen goes public. They won't like us much."

"Not necessarily. Flight simulators will be around for a while."

"You're right. Anyway, I want to talk to this Maceroy guy first before making any decision. In the meantime, this flight control system they want you to build, it'll take a while to design. I don't want this to impact existing schedules, Andrew."

"It won't, and is something I'll raise with Falzon this morning. It *will* require a visit or two to their Phoenix facility for consultation."

"At least the trips won't take long if they fly you there," Nelson said and laughed. "What do you have in mind businesswise?"

"Thirty thousand shares and two percent of the wholesale flight system cost for every vehicle type sold. We'll need something that can be configured for any vehicle. Creating a new system for every type would be a nightmare. You can work out FutureTech's margin with Mr. Maceroy."

The return would not come in for some time, but considering the market potential, Andrew could be looking at an income stream of millions every six months. FutureTech would not do too badly out of the deal either. Once Evagen became a listed company, another thing to discuss with Falzon, their stock price would go orbital.

"You got it," Nelson said. "Send me the contract. You know, this will scuttle development of autonomous cars, trucks, buses, and fan-driven air cars. It also sinks your proposal for pilotless fighters."

"Perhaps not. Think laterally and apply the concept to GM fighters."

"Mmm. I recall a Chinese curse on an enemy. May you live in interesting times, or something like that. Evagen will definitely give all of us an interesting time. Call me when you finish with Mr. Falzon, no matter what the hour."

"This is strictly between the two of us and Dela Torres for now, Sergey."

"Don't worry, I understand. Talk to you later," Nelson said and hung up.

* * *

Andrew finished the pumpkin soup and Adriana brought a pan of pork medallions with thinly sliced potatoes, everything swimming in thick gravy. He helped himself to two slices, added salad into a glass bowl, and began to eat, keen to get into his study and work on the full-sensor interface. He left Falzon speechless running through the B737 simulation, although not fully converted. Evagen would discuss business arrangements with Nelson and develop a work plan. Mark called late in the day saying he got three weeks off starting in October, all great news. Things were humming.

Adriana put down her knife and fork. "Andrew…"

"What is it? A hard day at work?"

"Not mine. Yours."

He looked at her in surprise. "Mine?"

"We need to talk."

"About what?"

"About you and me."

She had his full attention. "I'm not sure I understand."

"That's been clear to me for a while," she said. "Yesterday, I felt happy that we managed to go home together for a change. We haven't done that for a week or so, and we're not lunching like we used to."

"We're both working, Adriana."

"That's the problem. This morning, you left early and came home late, and you're starting to do this more often. When you're here, you're spending a lot of time upstairs playing with your computer. We don't talk much or do anything together anymore. I know you're busy and have commitments, but in your drive to conquer the world, you're leaving me behind." Her eyes glistened, swimming in tears ready to spill. Miserable, dejected, she looked at him as though he were a stranger.

Genuinely shocked, he felt his face drain in consternation. He *had* been spending a lot of his free time upstairs, and his week-ends had become extensions of his working week. He allowed it to become all-consuming and all-important. The last lunch they had…he could not remember when. Last week sometime, or the week before?

He slowly strangled the most important thing in his life without realizing he actually did it. Worse, his dad warned him about this.

Shait.

He stood, walked around the table, and knelt before her.

"You're right. You're right about everything, and I'm sorry," he choked out. "And I thought I knew better. Can you forgive me?"

She sniffed. "My dad used to work all the time. Long hours, often on Saturdays. We didn't have much, and he wanted to provide for us. He did provide for us. We had a house, car, all the things we always wanted, but somewhere along the way, we lost what made us a family. As I went through primary school, I felt something missing, but I couldn't tell what. All I knew, when I needed my father, he wasn't there.

"Mom and Dad argued a lot, and that made me even more depressed. After one particularly nasty shouting match, Mom left for two days. I stood in the living room doorway and watched them, not totally understanding what went on, but unhappy seeing them tear each other up. When she left, I asked Dad if Mommy would ever come back. I remember how he looked at me, totally surprised, then lost it. He gathered me in his arms and cried. I never saw him cry before, and it made me cry. Mom did come back, and Dad stopped working those long hours and Saturdays. We played games in the evening, went out on weekends, and they didn't argue anymore." Adriana gave a small smile as tears trickled down her cheeks. "I thought you and I had everything, a fantasy," she whispered brokenly, "and I couldn't be happier. Then you started doing the same thing my dad did and I feared my world would crumble."

He stood and gathered her in his arms. She clung to him and silently cried. He swallowed something hard, not feeling too steady either. After a while, he pulled back, brushed her cheeks, and kissed away the wetness.

"I *am* a dupe, Adriana," he whispered. "And I'm sorry for everything. I won't be your dad all over again. I promise. We can't always lunch together, or go home together, but I'll try whenever possible. No more weekends locked in my study with a helmet on my head. You mean more to me than anything, and I would set fire to my computer rather than see you unhappy." He looked deep into her enchanting eyes. "Tell me how to make things better and I'll do it."

"I want a husband, not a director."

"I'll give you both," he said, and she smiled. Her eyes turned dark, and her lips brushed his, lingering, sensuous. He squeezed her against him and kissed her hard.

Did he come that close to losing her?

"Let's go away!" he told her, suddenly excited. "We never went to Perth or anywhere last year. Tell me where you want to go and we'll recapture our fantasy. Anywhere!"

She searched his face. "You mean it? What about your projects?"

"FutureTech won't collapse if I take some time off, and I'm sure First Teeth won't either. I'll buy it if necessary."

She laughed, delighted with the idea. "You wouldn't really?"

"Why not? I've got—we've got—the money."

"Seriously, do you want to go away somewhere?"

"If you can leave your patients for a couple of weeks, I'll get Nora book the tickets tomorrow."

Her eyes sparkled. "Maybe you'd prefer going with her?"

"Oh, that's droll, but you're the only woman in my life, my sweet, and always will be."

"I wouldn't mind going someplace quiet. Fiji, maybe. We

could be lazy on the beach, take walks in the jungle, mix with the locals…"

"Done!"

She shook her head. "It's a nice dream, but you can't. Your melanoma…"

"I'll take precautions," he told her. "What's more, some quality beach time will be good for both of us."

"It would for me," she murmured and brushed his face. "I didn't mean to unburden myself on you like this, but I feared I lost you. The thought terrified me."

He cradled her head against his chest. "I'm glad you opened my eyes. What astounds me is how slowly, insidiously, my work took over, and I was blind not to see it." He cupped her cheeks between his hands and stared into her eyes. "I'm sorry. Never again."

She wrapped her arms around his neck and sighed with contentment. "I'll hold you to that."

"Can I do anything for you tonight?"

A wry smile made her look demure. "Well…"

He took her hand in his and led her toward the stairs.

Chapter Nine

"What did Nelson say when you told him?" Adriana asked between mouthfuls of caviar hors d'oeuvres. The Florentino a little pricy, but provided extraordinary food delivered by superb service, and Andrew could afford it. They liked to sample the exotic, but often preferred simple, tasty meals at Collins Place. Wealth had not made him snobbish.

"His language rather colorful," he said, and Adriana tittered. "He needs me, especially now, and accused me of running out on him. I told him you needed me more, and I needed you, which is far more important than my job. In the end, he gave in. He had no choice. If I quit, we could live like pampered royalty for the rest of our lives, and FutureTech would turn into just another games developer. Anyway, it's only for ten days. So, on Friday, my sweet, we're off to Fiji's tropical paradise. You've got a day to pack everything. It's an exclusive resort, so you better take some formal evening gowns."

Her eyes became dreamy. "Fiji…sun, warm ocean, corals, palms…" She gave a long sigh, and hugged him.

He cocked an eyebrow. "Pack a bikini. I've never seen you in one."

Her laugh a tinkle of running water. "Randy old goat. I'll check my wardrobe to see if I need to buy anything."

"Whatever you want. On Friday morning, we're off."

"I'm so excited, I wish we were going right now," she declared, bubbling with anticipation.

The waiter brought their delicately browned quail with baked potato cubes, everything smothered in rich gravy, and a mixed salad. He topped up their glasses with a fine Chablis and quietly withdrew.

Andrew looked forward to some private time with Adriana. They had not had a real break since January, and he felt ready for a break. Ready to clear his head and rearrange his focus. He wanted to change the world as Adriana said, but with her in it as an integral part. Success, achievement, wealth, did not mean a thing if he could not share it with her. She was his first and only priority, and he would see to it that she remained so for all time.

Nelson may have bitched about his little holiday, but Nora gave him her full approval, wishing she could go with them. Come Christmas, he would see to it that she got a salary increase and a hefty bonus. She earned it. Unassuming, always deferential, she made the top floor hum. If someone had a problem, she would fix it with a smile. Invaluable, he silently thanked Price for finding her.

The next day, he sorted out a few work things with his team and Sloan, and went home around four. He also called Mark and told him he'd be away. His friend asked if he had room in the suitcase for a body, and Andrew laughed. 'Make your own arrangements with Susan,' he told him. Adriana showed up in a taxi soon afterward with a new handbag and several large shopping bags from exclusive boutique stores. She hugged him and unwrapped four elegant cocktail dresses. He looked forward to seeing her wear them. When he asked what she had in the small package from Witchery, she smiled coyly and told him it would be a surprise.

He also had a surprise, and presented her a black satin box. She drew a sharp breath and splayed her fingers across her chest. He slowly opened the box and she stared at a platinum chain necklace with a single rectangular 15mm ruby and matching earrings. Her eyes softened and she kissed him.

"Thank you," she whispered tenderly.

"In case I ever forget," he said gruffly. The greater the guilt, the greater the gift, he read somewhere. Certainly true in his case.

They had a quiet dinner of homemade hamburgers stuffed with sweet-and-sour pickles, tomato slices, fried onion rings, and cheese, accompanied by a mellow Barossa Valley cabernet sauvignon. After cleaning up, they luxuriated in the en suite spa, champagne flutes at the elbow. Soapsuds flew everywhere as they fooled around, laughed, and life laughed with them.

They often used to take baths together. That changed to an occasional shower, then nothing. Acting like kids, reveling in each other's togetherness, Andrew could not believe he had been so stupid to give it all up for work as a substitute.

They dried each other with soft towels, Adriana yelping when he dabbed at places he should not have, and carried the champagne bucket into the bedroom. Snuggled under the doona, her head in the crook of his arm, they talked softly. They had not visited her parents in a while, and he promised they would after Fiji.

His wife in his arms, loving her unreservedly, nothing had changed between them, and he thanked the fates for giving her to him.

An Uber cab picked them up at six on a crisp, clear morning. It threaded its way along Kings Way and the driver took the Tullamarine Freeway on-ramp that went to Melbourne Airport. Most people simply called it Tulla Airport, but everybody knew what it meant.

With business class tickets—Fiji Airways did not have first class for short hauls—they checked in their small suitcases without having to queue in the economy line. Nora had printed boarding passes for him, but the check-in attendant gave them formal cards. With some forty minutes to kill, they went through passport control and strolled among glittering duty-free shops.

Despite being early, the terminal had a lot of people going somewhere or arriving. An occasional announcement blared departure of such and such a flight, and directed all passengers make their way to the boarding gate. A couple of times an exasperated voice called for latecomers, the aircraft ready to depart.

Andrew and Adriana looked at each other and shook their heads. Some people were simply dumb or simply inconsiderate. Perhaps both.

Finally, a call came to board their flight. The modern Airbus A350 had a faint tropical smell, probably his imagination. The business class section had large seats appointed in light gray leather. They stowed their carry-on bags and slipped into the central row sixteen seats, which thankfully had lots of legroom to accommodate his length. An attractive attendant brought them hot face towels and a glass of white wine. He nodded to her and raised his to Adriana. They touched glasses and smiled at each other like children who had pulled off a piece of successful mischief.

They pushed back the aircraft a few minutes early. It made its way along the taxiway while a boring safety presentation droned in the background. It turned onto the active runway and paused. Andrew pictured what went on in the cockpit as though he were there. The pilot applied full thrust and the A350 rushed down the runway.

The four-hour 45-minute flight to Nadi went quickly. A sumptuous breakfast around 8:40 filled some of the time. They chatted about the things they would do and see. When the captain announced they started their descent, he automatically glanced at his Rado and set it for local time. The A350 came in smoothly and touched down with a gentle scrape of tires.

Once through the mercifully quick passport check, they collected their luggage and strolled into the busy arrivals terminal. Despite the air-conditioning, he immediately felt a wave of heat and light humidity. A smiling brown Fijian holding up a card with

Payne on it led them to an open six-passenger cart and drove them to the Pacific Island Air helicopter pad. The young pilot packed away their suitcases and made sure his charges were strapped in before starting the Eurocopter's twin engines.

The fifteen-minute flight to VOMO Island took them over pristine azure waters dotted with small islands. Adriana cooed with delight at the enchanting scenery. Although warm, around 28C, the sun did not burn, but the pilot warned them to take care, the mild temperature very deceptive.

Their destination loomed before them, with the craggy little Vomo Lailai island close by. Thick palm groves hid beachfront villas and cabins farther in. With a five-kilometer circumference, VOMO not a large island. At one end, Mt. Vomo reached into a deep blue sky.

Two Fijians quietly removed their baggage and led them to the administration building, where smiling girls in brown *jaba* dresses put rings of flowers around their necks and gave them tall glasses of fruit punch with little blue umbrellas stuck in the middle. Once they checked in, a Fijian in a white *sulu* kilt showed them to the cart and drove them to their hideaway tucked at the edge of the resort. He stopped at a massive yellow stone house and carried in the luggage. Small surf lapped against white sand. Adriana gazed longingly at the placid ocean and gave Andrew a happy hug, then pointed at the house in disbelief.

"This is ours?"

"Yep. Four bedrooms, lounge, kitchen, and a private swimming pool all to ourselves."

"Are we sharing with somebody?"

"It's all ours, my sweet."

"Oh, my God. You're insane, but I love it." She ran up dark stone steps and disappeared inside.

The Fijian porter emerged and Andrew gave him twenty dollars in local currency. The man smiled broadly, nodded, and clambered into his cart.

The grand foyer opened into a large lounge. At the other end, a long pool with beach chairs beckoned to be used. With half of it covered, he would worry about getting burned. He found Adriana in the modern kitchen rummaging through the fully stocked refrigerator. He walked to the bar and gazed at bottles of various spirits and wines stacked in the cooler. The management clearly intended that they enjoy their stay.

"Want anything to drink?"

"I want to see the bedroom," she declared and headed toward the master suite. She gaped at the king bed, and poked her head into the bathroom. "You're not going to believe this. There's a spa here large enough to swim in."

She padded past the pool and gazed at the open beach a dozen meters beyond. A light, warm afternoon breeze washed scented air over them. She turned and looked at him.

"Want to go for a stroll?"

"Let's make ourselves comfortable first," he said, eyeing the vista.

They unpacked quickly and he slipped into lightweight trousers and a white shirt. Adriana emerged from the bathroom and his eyes popped. The tasteful black bikini set off her shapely long legs and narrow waist. She rolled her hips and leaned against the doorframe.

"Hi, Mister," she husked in a deep voice. "I haven't seen you around here before."

"You will from now on," he growled and reached for her. She laughed and slammed the door in his face. He sighed and applied sunblock to his face. When she emerged, she had a filmy green thing wrapped around her waist, and wore a shirt and a broad hat.

Hand in hand, his bare feet enjoying the feel of clean, soft sand, they walked toward the water. She dropped her gear, waded in up to her thighs, turned, and waved him in. He stirred warm water with his arms and stopped beside her. She grinned widely and pushed him.

"Hey!"

Arms flailing, he fell with a splash. Spluttering, he jumped up and sprang at her. She squealed when he picked her up and threw her. She landed with a plop and launched herself at him. After some robust frolicking, she slowly began to swim out, her strokes slow and powerful. He sat on the sand and watched until her head almost vanished. When she returned, she sprawled on the warm sand and purred contently. He stretched beside her and listened to the softly slapping waves.

That night, they had cocktails at The Rocks Bar and watched a fat sun paint the evening sky with orange and red streaks. They dined at The Reef Restaurant, Adriana stunning in a low cut dark green dress, the ruby necklace and earrings caused more than one female guest to glance at her, as did several men. Later, in bed, they held each other without saying anything.

Over the next three days, Andrew basked in a glow of peace and contentment with a woman he adored. They walked the entire five kilometers around the island and climbed Mt. Vomo to gaze at nearby atolls and the azure sea. They snorkeled among unbelievable coral and colorful fish, swam far into the ocean, took long strolls early in the morning, and followed the sunset in the evening. The resort provided whatever service they wanted, and they enjoyed superb meals by the beach, delivered by smiling native men.

On Tuesday, they spent half a day exploring the rugged Vomo Lailai, the resort providing hampers of food and cold drinks. They had little isle all to themselves. Surrounded by paradise, Andrew figured Robinson Crusoe never had it this good.

On Wednesday evening, the VOMO beachfront lit with burning torches, the resort guests were treated to a cocktail party and a Lovo feast of native foods cooked in the sand. Afterward, local men and women entertained them with traditional Meke dances.

Early on Thursday, a helicopter took them back to Nadi. They explored the Garden of the Sleeping Giant, had a scenic helicopter flight over the islands, visited the Fiji Cultural Village, and had a sumptuous late lunch at the marina Boatshed Restaurant. Afterward, they strolled along Main Street, peeking into souvenir and curio shops, the street crowded with locals and tourists. Late in the afternoon, the helicopter took them back to the resort.

Adriana was made for the sea, and she spent long hours in it. On one of their swims, a pod of inquisitive dolphins peered at them, circled a few times, and disappeared. Adriana loved the fruits of the sea, slurping large oysters with a sparkle in her eyes, crunched lobster legs, fingers smeared with butter sauce. She laughed gaily, a little girl living a fantasy. A fantasy Andrew shared. She tanned easily, and he never tired exploring her wondrous body. She would stretch out on a beach towel, glistening with sunscreen, and soak in the sun while he watched her beneath a shaded palm, a tall drink in hand, gulls soaring above them. They spent long, relaxing moments in the privacy of their pool. Exhausted, they would sit on the veranda and watch the sea.

On Sunday morning, memories etched indelibly, and a love that burned deep in both of them, the fantasy ended as the A350 soared into the sky.

* * *

Wednesday, September 27, started sunny with clear skies and no wind. Nineteen degrees the man said as Andrew watched the ABC weather forecast over breakfast. Trees were sprouting new leaves in earnest, with a noticeable increase in local birdlife. Nineteen still a far cry from Fiji's twenty-eight the week before, but he did not complain. Life felt good and worth living.

Since his return, he felt revitalized, energized, and looked at everything from a new perspective. The wakeup call in his relationship with Adriana settled, he felt emotionally relaxed, keen to direct his energies in pursuit of new ideas and developments. The gravitomagnetic project would keep him occupied well into next year, but that was engineering. He wanted to make a social impact, and Broca Genetics might be a lever he could use to achieve it. His encounter with macrophages and how they cured him, had spiked his curiosity in molecular engineering. Invest in Broca to influence their research? Definitely something to look at.

Adriana's soft tan made her radiant. Their little break had restored something he inadvertently allowed to run down. Things that seemed critical and urgent before were now merely background chores. He intended to do everything to make her happy. With her happy, he could face eternity with a light heart. Nothing else mattered. Without her, he would not want to live forever.

The tram dropped them off at Collins Place, the hurrying throng and constant traffic noises a familiar blanket. He kissed his wife goodbye, promising to meet her for coffee at lunchtime. He had a scheduled board video link at nine, followed by a separate meeting with Sloan, and a catchup with his development team—and she had patients who would keep her busy all day. Busy or not, they arranged to go home together.

Nora greeted him with a cheerful smile as he strode into the kitchenette to snag a mug of tea. He hardly had time to power up the computer when she rang.

"There's a gentleman from Evagen here to see you," she announced, and he raised an eyebrow. His anticipated courier had arrived.

Nelson had not called during his Fiji trip, something Andrew appreciated. When he showed up for work on Monday, they had a lengthy chat that made up for all the missed time. FutureTech had a signed contract with Evagen, Inc. to develop and provide a full-sensor VR flight control prototype with a framework architecture that would enable configuration for any type of gravitomagnetic vehicle. The prototype would be used to validate procedures against Evagen's demonstrator machine currently under construction. On successful trials completion, FutureTech would build a commercial version of the flight control system. Timeframe for the prototype—four months. Evagen expected to announce its demo vehicle in April 2024.

Reynold Parker had already received a copy of the contract that guaranteed Andrew's IP for the design, patent rights, and a two percent royalty for every copy of the flight system sold to Evagen. All he had to do now is get a signed version from corporate and he could officially start the project. Unofficially, he already worked on it.

Another piece of good news—Trans Vis is eager to see the sensor helmet and wanted a demo.

Memory memo to self: Call Sergey and arrange.

"Show him in," he said.

Nora opened the door. "Mr. Leonard Needham."

Andrew stood and held out his hand. "I've been looking forward to seeing you."

The short, wiry African-American gave a small smile as they shook hands. "A pleasure to meet you, sir."

"Just Andrew," he said and extended an arm at a visitor chair. "Make yourself comfortable. Care for a coffee or something?"

"No, thank you." Needham reached into his jacket pocket, extracted a small envelope and placed it on the desk. "Schematics and flight control specifications for our GM demonstrator prototype."

How to deliver the information to Andrew turned out to be complicated. Falzon ruled out flying him in their testbed vehicle to the Phoenix facility to meet the design and engineering team, considering it an unacceptable risk. They thought to download the necessary data to an Internet2 site, more secure than the general Internet network, but Andrew told Falzon Internet2 was also compromised. He dismissed FedEx out of hand, which left only one option.

"When are you heading back?" Andrew asked.

"I have a flight at 11:15 tomorrow," Needham said.

"At least you'll get a good night's sleep," Andrew said dryly. "Is there anything else I need to know?"

"Everything is on the flash drive." Needham stood and nodded. "Thank you for your time, sir."

They shook hands and Andrew escorted him to the elevators.

At his desk, he picked up the envelope and shook his head. Another fourteen-hour flight in two days, including one to Phoenix…despite a layover, the man would be exhausted. This roundabout meeting deeply reinforced the need for impenetrable security. So far, only Nelson and Torres knew about his project. Given the circumstances, they had to keep it secret even from other board members. For the time being anyway. He understood the need, and the unstated implication the board could not be trusted. There were arguments for both positions.

He tore open the envelope and extracted a long flash drive and a card with a password. He logged on to his personal server and created a password-protected directory, 'Flight', not wanting to give even his trusted developers a hint what the thing contained. Under a 'Specifications' sub-directory, he downloaded the encrypted flash drive files, made a backup, then stomped on the black stick until he heard the insides crunch. Even if password-protected, carrying the thing would be far too dangerous.

Memory memo to self: Ask Systems Support to get him another dedicated server.

Something else occurred to him and he winced. He would need his own sensor helmet. Not for a while, though. It would take him a month or so to design the system framework and have it approved by Evagen before he could start coding. A standard VR headset would do fine for initial testing. By January, Mark should be able to build another helmet.

A few minutes before nine, carrying mugs of coffee, Andrew and Sloan made their way into the conference room. Nora had the video links set up with other executive directors, and everybody exchanged pleasantries.

One reason why Nelson did not hold regular board meetings—time zones. Gathering everybody together meant that someone attended in the middle of the night. Andrew had that with his very first meeting. To smooth any ruffled feathers, Nelson staggered conference times.

Juana Medina tapped a glass with her pen and called the meeting to order. She went over the previous minutes, which Regan Price seconded, and Nelson opened with the first agenda item.

"I want to announce that Mr. Sanval Tandul's appointment as acting general manager for the India/Middle East region is confirmed, and he is our new executive director. Welcome to the team, Sanval."

"Thank you, Sergey. I look forward to working with all of you," the tall man replied smoothly in a heavily accented voice.

"TE Flight told me the Chinese are likely to place a significant order for our Boeing and Airbus trainers," Nelson went on. "On the order of two hundred units. They wanted a license to modify the simulators for their local requirements, and TE had to explain why that wasn't possible. The Chinese Commerce Minister threatened to cancel the pending order, and TE told him that would be regrettable," he said dryly, which raised a round of chuckles. "I'm confident they'll do business if they want to stay in the game. They have no choice, unless Andrew is prepared to give them a license."

"I won't grant them a license," Andrew said with a shake of his head. "That would erode our competitive advantage and possibly compromise my IP. They demonstrated repeatedly a willingness to ignore international law on patent and copyright violations. I doubt they could break the macro access locks, but I don't want to give them that opportunity."

Several directors murmured support.

"Well, that's that," Nelson said. "Disney Animation and several other studios approached us again, seeking a license to use your macros, Andrew. I understand Keith talked to you about this. Have you reconsidered your position?"

"I'm prepared to grant any major studio a one-time license for every movie feature with an upfront fee of two million, plus a two percent royalty on the gross take, provided they don't have any link with the Chinese, direct or indirect, regardless how tenuous. Marketing can work the numbers for FutureTech's margin."

This raised a ripple of comments.

If the Chinese simulator sale went through, he would net around five million, and could afford to invest in Broca.

"I doubt Disney or anybody else would try to break my macros and risk compromising their reputation," he added with a wry smile.

With Reynold Parker's help, he looked closely at the movie industry where computer animation had become a major production cost. His 3D macros would reduce that cost substantially and increase profits. With popular movies grossing hundreds of millions, he figured his price reasonable.

"I agree," Dela Torres said. "We'd also kill them with a multi-billion-dollar lawsuit."

"This could be a significant revenue earner for us," Price added.

Nelson gave everybody a quick glance. "Are we all agreed?"

"I second the motion," Sloan said with firm authority.

"Andrew, send me a license agreement and I'll open negotiations with interested parties."

In the background, Juana recorded everything in her tablet.

As Andrew watched Nelson run the meeting, he realized there was more to handling a business than selling and looking at a balance sheet. Intellectually, he knew all that, but being part of the process definitely different from running an MBA assignment. His perspective on many things had also changed. Sometimes, he felt like a much older man staring at the world through eyes of a youngster. His mind had outgrown his body. Where would that change take him? An imponderable question that only time would answer.

"Regarding the dental trainer," Nelson went on. "Keith has secured accreditation from Australian authorities, and Regan is well advanced with the Europeans. The U.S. regulator is on board. How about you, Sanval?"

"Not so good, Sergey. As you know, the Indian bureaucracy is slow to move, but the feedback I'm getting from universities and private concerns is encouraging."

"Light a fire under them," Nelson told him sharply. "Talk to a minister or two. What about the Middle East?"

"Most countries have signed off, and I expect Saudi Arabia and Turkey to approve the app by mid-October. The worldwide promotional campaign is having an effect, and the bureaucrats were forced to act."

"Great. Where are we with South America, Alonzo?"

"Brazil, Chile, and Argentina have certified the application," the regional executive director said. "I'm working with the smaller countries, but it looks good."

"Excellent. Where do you stand with the accounting interface, Andrew?"

"The prototype will be available for initial testing by mid-November."

"Good." Nelson pursed his lips. "At the last meeting, Andrew proposed that we approach General Dynamics to develop a VR trainer for their *Virginia*-class submarines. I later told him I would endorse the proposal. However, Money Manny convinced me not to."

"Sorry, Andrew, but I don't see a plus for us here," Torres said. "It's a one-time deal not worth the investment in time and resources. Even if they were interested, General Dynamics would likely ask for a demonstrator system before they commit themselves, which we would have to build at our own cost. Let's say we got a contract, there simply isn't an ongoing revenue stream for us in this, and there'd be more federal security creeps crawling all over us. It's bad enough having them here for our fighter simulators program."

"I understand your objections, Manny," Andrew told him warmly, and he did. "I considered them myself, and we'd be operating way out of our comfort zone. Only a thought."

"In that case, we'll shelve the proposal," Nelson declared. "I want to briefly raise the full-sensor interface headset program. I'll organize a demo for Trans Vis, and we'll want a timeframe from them to develop a user-friendly version. This is a revolution in the making, and will mean a ton of work for us to upgrade all our products."

"And a ton of money," Torres added dryly, which raised a ripple of chuckles.

Nelson smiled. "Which will also *bring* us tons of money. Remember, not a word to anyone about this, and no speculating on Trans Vis stock, or ours. I don't want to face insider trading charges from the Exchange and Securities Commission, or your local authorities. Okay, where are you guys with new games development?"

That part took some half an hour to sort out.

"Has anyone got anything else they want to discuss?" Nelson asked. "No? In that case, I'll let Money Manny give us our sales and financial position."

When the meeting finished, Andrew had a quick catchup chat with Sloan on the full-sensor conversion program, and touched base with the accounting interface team. Afterward, he welcomed a coffee break with Adriana.

Back at his desk, he opened the specs document for the gravitomagnetic flight control system. He created an issues register and jotted down all the to-do points with related risk factors. He opened Microsoft Project and set up a bare bones schedule with planned/actual time and cost columns. As a professional, he wanted to be in a position to give Evagen real numbers. Anyway, Nelson and Money Manny would want to see a costed schedule.

* * *

Andrew stepped out of the full elevator into a crowded, noisy plaza. Cars crawled along both sides of the street. Two trams passed each other, the drivers clanging bells. He breathed deeply, the hot January air laced with the acrid whiff of petrol fumes. All things considered, still far better than winter's chilly blasts. There, he had the cold *and* the stinks.

Cars, noise, the smells, did not bother him. Nothing bothered him these days. He did miss having lunch with Adriana, but when 2024 rolled in, she decided to spend the last three months of her pregnancy at home. An ultrasound last week showed a growing, healthy boy. They had known for a while it would be a boy. Everything lay ready for him: cot, clothing, and distracting toys that tinkled and clanged.

He had gotten used to the idea of becoming a father, although not overly keen on the sleepless nights bit. He talked to his dad about it, who said not to dwell on it. It was not that bad…later. Disrupting at first, but he would get used to it. It all came with the package, his dad added with a gleeful smile.

Adriana wanted to look after the baby for the first twelve months, then hire a babysitter while she returned to work part-time. A professional, she did not want her skills to deteriorate. He understood that, and they could afford it. His paper worth now over forty-eight million, made largely possible from sale of TE Flight trainers, movie studio licenses, and appreciated stock holding values.

One thing he enjoyed doing when his December royalties came in, was send a check for a million dollars to Professor Harrison Rhodes, Director of the Lyndon Cancer Institute. The old guy, forty-four really, could not thank him enough. Research and equipment cost money, and his donation would help enormously. The Institute saved his life, Andrew told him, was thanks enough.

He weaved between other pedestrians and office workers out for lunch, turned right, intending to eat at the popular Mongolian Barbecue restaurant on Spring Street. Always crowded, they served great meals, and the beauty of it all, he got to pick the ingredients. They had a long buffet-like table with bowls of various meats and vegetables. He would fill a large plate with everything he wanted, hand it to the chef, who would dump it on an enormous hotplate. After a lot of sizzling and steam and addition of various sauces, he would get back a vastly reduced delicious portion.

Two men in blue Telstra coveralls stepped out of a white service van and walked toward him. They suddenly grabbed his arms and bundled him into the van. Before he could yell or defend himself, someone slapped a wet pad across his nose and mouth, and everything faded.

Gradually, feeling returned. He winced at the stab of light when he opened his eyes. A jolt of pain above his abdomen made him gasp when he tried to sit up. A familiar face floated into view and he gaped at her.

"Don't try to move, Mr. Payne," Despina told him firmly.

"What…what happened?" he managed to croak.

"I have no idea. They wheeled you in twenty minutes ago, that's all I know. Here, drink this," she said and held out a glass of pink liquid.

He downed half of it and his head cleared rapidly. With a glance out the window, he was startled to see it already dark. He appeared to be in the same room where he spent weeks waiting to die—at least it looked the same. He gingerly touched the bandage above his stomach. What the hell?

"You rest, and I'll let Dr. Dalton know you're awake," she said and breezed out. All she needed was the meal wagon and he would feel right at home. He remembered that she used to have the day shift. They must rotate them from time to time.

He leaned back, desperately wanting somebody to explain what happened.

Dr. Dalton strode in a few minutes later and stopped beside the bed. "Any discomfort?" her voice and manner detached and clinical.

"My stomach is sore," he complained. "What's going on, Doc?"

"It's sore because someone took a small chunk of your flesh and liver," she said as she pulled up a chair and sat down. "A professional job and you'll recover quickly. We'll hold you here for the next two days to make sure there are no complications or infection. You'll be taking antibiotics for a week to make sure."

"How did I end up here?"

"Witnesses saw a Telstra service van pull up beside the Treasury Gardens on Spring Street. Two men dumped you on the lawn and the bystanders immediately called the police. When the cops saw the Institute emergency card in your wallet, they brought you here. I'm told they found the van abandoned near the Richmond railway station."

Andrew's mind raced as he went over possible scenarios. Only one made any real sense.

"This wasn't your way of getting more tissue samples, Doc?" he asked wryly.

Her mouth twitched. "That's not how I work. Before you ask, it wasn't Broca Genetics either. You see, four days ago, someone made an unsuccessful hack attack into both our computer systems. Broca and the Institute have some extremely sensitive and commercially confidential research material many parties would love to get their hands on."

The pieces fell into place. "It was about me?"

"That's the likeliest explanation. I wrote two papers on you, as did Dr. Ivone Masters. Although we did not reveal your personal details, your case is not exactly a secret in the biogenetic community. Two months ago, DARPA approached Dr. Masters with an offer to fund Broca's research into telomeres and macrophage application. She refused."

"And you suspect DARPA didn't handle the *No* part all that well?"

"Dr. Masters and I are guessing they're behind the attempted security breach, but it might be a competitor. The secrets behind Broca's products are worth billions."

"Whoever did this, how did they know me?"

"Although Broca's research data and the Institute's is secure, they could have checked our admission records, or somebody at Broca talked. If the U.S. government is responsible, the NSA has access to almost everybody's phone conversations and emails, as you no doubt know."

He bit his lip. Her explanation plausible, if somewhat elaborate. Something simply did not fit, but he could not pin it down, although it might have happened as she said.

"Did anybody approach *you*?"

Her mouth twitched. "Like ASIO, you mean? No."

"Remember our weighty chat a while back about the immortality pill? I want to apologize, Doc, for my outburst last time we talked. I was a little upset by your demand for more tissue."

"Don't worry about it. I understand."

"What happened to me today proves that somebody out there is determined to find out how my body is doing it."

"I'm afraid your assessment is probably correct," she agreed glumly.

"What if this happens again? What if I find myself in a padded room kept as a lab specimen? The prospect of a government agency or ruthless competitor experimenting on me doesn't enhance my cool."

"I'm sorry, Andrew. There isn't any way to answer that."

She was right. If somebody wanted to get him, he could do little about it, short of surrounding himself and everyone he knew with security teams, which would not help much anyway.

He gave a long sigh. "That's all right, Doc. I'll just live with it." Something occurred to him and he gasped when he tried to sit up. "My wife!"

Dr. Dalton stood up. "She's waiting outside. I'll send her in."

"Doc? Thanks for looking after me."

She gave a small smile. "Don't make it a habit," she said and closed the door after her.

Adriana walked in, gave him a worried look, rushed to his side, and her arms went around him.

"There, my sweet. Everything is okay," he told her softly, stroking her back.

She sniffed, stood, and sat down. "I could have died when Dr. Dalton called. What's going on, Andrew?"

He quickly filled her in. Hands in lap, she sat there taking it in.

"This is awful," she said at length.

"I'm not thrilled about it either," he admitted. "We'll continue our normal life, that's all we can do. There isn't much point stewing over it."

Her fingers were twisting themselves into a knot. "I thought we left this behind us, and now…"

"We'll handle it."

She gave him a searching look. "You're trying to cheer me up, but you're worried about this, aren't you?"

"I am…a little. Not that it might happen again, but the fact it happened at all. I also thought this to be in my past, but whether

I like it or not, I must accept that I'm different. Somewhere out there is a lab trying to find out how my epigenetic clock became frozen. My fear is that one day, they'll find out."

"And use that knowledge to make themselves immortal?" she added softly, and he nodded.

"The self-appointed elite would rule for untold generations until chaos destroyed everything in factional rivalry."

"That's pretty gloomy."

"Whoever organized my kidnapping proved it wasn't done for my health."

"Let's not talk about this, okay? Are you in any pain?"

He did not want to dwell on it either. "A little sore, that's all."

Her eyes took on a mischievous sparkle. "I saw that cute little nurse come out of your room. Is she looking after you?"

"Despina? I'll be asking her to tuck me in later."

"Dupe. How long will Dr. Dalton keep you here?"

"A couple of days to make sure I don't get inflammation drooling over her."

She laughed, which lifted his own spirits. "On some days, you shouldn't be allowed out of the house."

"Today was the day, all right." He reached for her hand and squeezed. "I wish I could be home with you."

She pursed her mouth and nodded. "I know. Can I bring you anything?"

"My laptop. I don't want to stare at that thing all day," he said, hooking a thumb at the wall TV.

"Tomorrow. Do your parents know you're here?"

"I haven't had a chance to call anybody. This might be a big deal for us, but they don't need to know everything that's going on in our lives."

They chatted about nothing in particular for another half hour, and she left, taking the sunshine with her. Shortly afterward, Despina rolled in the meal wagon, and he almost laughed.

Nothing had changed.

As he ate, he decided that things *have* changed. His world view had changed, and not for the better. What happened this afternoon disturbed him more than he cared to admit. Would they keep hounding him to find the secret of his immortality, if in fact he was immortal? Would he ever have peace? And he might be making too much out of this, but like they said, just because you're paranoid did not mean they were not after you.

The next morning after a fitful sleep—he could not help tossing the incident in his mind—a nurse fed him two pills. She removed the bandage and stared at the wound. The surrounding area still a little tender and inflamed, but no scar, only threads from two sutures. She took one look at him and rushed out. She returned a couple of minutes later with his favorite doctor in tow.

After some prodding around the wound, Dr. Dalton cleared her throat.

"It looks like your macrophages are still very much alive and looking after you. How do you feel?"

"Only a little sore," he told her. "I had no trouble doing my bathroom things when I got up."

"Mmm. Nurse, remove the sutures."

The nurse swabbed the area with alcohol and snipped away the threads. A simple Band-Aid covered the spot.

"Remarkable," Dr. Dalton murmured. "Given your condition, I don't see any reason to keep you here. I'll write a prescription for some antibiotics, and you can pick it up at the nurse's station on your way out. I'll see you at your next scan appointment." She walked toward the door shaking her head.

Andrew knew how she felt.

"I'll bring your breakfast," the nurse said uncertainly.

When dawn broke, and hydraulic pressure forced him to attend to it, he only felt mild discomfort from the wound. He always healed quickly after a scratch or cut, but this rapid recovery came as a surprise. Dr. Dalton clearly thought so.

He thanked the fates and left it at that.

Outside the Institute, he called an Uber cab to take him home. The sky clear and the air warm. Victoria Parade a noisy crush as always. Feeling grand, he tapped an icon in his Contacts list.

"Hi, Andrew," Sloan answered immediately. "I tried to get hold of you all afternoon yesterday. What's going on?"

"I'll fill you in later, Keith. It will probably be around lunchtime before I can come in."

"Are you all right?"

"Everything's fine. Talk to you later," he said and hung up.

Waiting for the cab, he decided that everything *was* all right. Adriana would definitely be happy to see him home early. He did not mind it either.

Whoever took his piece of liver, he hoped his macrophages would jump out and bite him.

* * *

A VR headset snug on his head, Andrew glanced at Masina who wore the sensor helmet, and nodded. He would not experience the full range of responses, but good enough to follow what she was doing. She touched a little red icon at bottom right of the view. In front of him, displayed in faintly pulsing orange font, were menu bars that enabled selection of a personal or passenger craft, and whether he wanted atmospheric or space mode.

"Please state your command or press menu selection," a pleasant female voice asked. "To exit, press the red icon or say 'Exit', or 'Help'."

She touched the PERSONAL/ATMOSPHERE bars. They registered the touch with a brief glow…and he found himself in a different world. A 360-degree view showed a large metal hangar, a concrete apron all around, and a vividly pristine sky. In front of him at knee level, a light green panel displayed a 3D schematic and ship status.

"All systems nominal. State your destination."

"Los Angeles," Masina said.

"Flight plan filed…approved. Are you ready to depart?"

"Depart."

The ground fell away and the Arizona Industrial Park's sprawl with the surrounding Phoenix suburbia quickly became hazy as the craft rapidly gained altitude. Around him, he saw broad color bands sweep the sky—military, civilian, and weather radars. A transparent vertical screen before him displayed pulsing green dots and lines of aircraft moving away from his position. Red lines showed approaching aircraft. At 6,000 meters, the ship stopped its ascent and went into horizontal flight. Another 3D screen showed a genuine ground view, their starting position and distance traveled as a black line. A white line linked the eventual destination and time remaining.

"Exit," she said, and he was again in his office.

Over the next four hours, she tested every manual and voice command option in all flight modes, including warnings and emergency procedures, ticking off each item against an extremely lengthy checklist. She also went through the help options, which in effect instructed the pilot how to operate the craft. The personal/atmospheric mode relatively simple, but a little more involved in the passenger/space mode. Compared to a B787, a GM vehicle was extremely easy to fly. The pilot did not need to worry about trim, ailerons, stabilizer, engine status, and a myriad other things aerodynamic flight demanded. A GM ship did not have to worry about storms, downdrafts, ice or rain. It just flew. That is what Masina said anyway.

She exited the simulation, took off her helmet, looking somewhat dazed. Andrew smiled at her expression.

"Well, what do you think?"

"Damn," she said softly and placed the helmet on the desk. "This is unbelievable. Frankly, I never expected anything like it. I ought to try your *Fighter Combat* game to see what it's like. I miss bending an F/A-18 around the sky."

He smiled at her. "Evagen doesn't let you bend their testbed vehicle?"

She chuckled. "If I bent it, I better pick a direction and run."

"How did you end up working for them?"

"I was a hot Navy Super Hornet driver. One day, Mr. Falzon found me in a San Diego bar when my carrier had a layover, and told me I could fly something far more exciting than a Hornet. I didn't believe him, of course, but I quickly changed my mind," she said and laughed. "They had me on a fast track for a NASA appointment, but the odds were long that I would ever be in space. With Evagen, I've been there three times already. When our real space-capable vehicle is built, I'll be the first woman in history to walk on the Moon. Personally, I think it's a disgrace NASA hasn't sent one during the Apollo missions." She cocked an eyebrow at him. "Want to come along and plant a flag?"

He could picture clearly the stark gray Moonscape, his boots leaving indelible imprints in that ageless dust. Who would not want to go?

"Deal!" he hooted.

"We'll have fun," she promised, then turned serious. "Your simulation has everything the specs said, and more."

"There are several things I cannot finish until I've installed the software in a real ship and have it fly. How close are you to having it ready?"

"All structural work and power systems are done. Right now, we're putting in the life-support systems and interior fittings. This will take a week or so. However, I think we can upload the flight system and begin preliminary live testing." She frowned. "We've flown the vehicle a few times, mostly within the hangar, but we'll need to take it out eventually to proof everything. We don't dare take it out too many times. Even with its low radar signature, the vehicle's speed will give us away. Arizona is dotted with various military bases and all are loaded radars. We might be forced to leave some things undone until we go public." She looked at him and raised an eyebrow. "Are you ready to take a little trip? Say, six days?"

He smiled. "In your testbed vehicle?"

"I'm afraid not. It'll be the old-fashioned way," she said with a grin. "But you'll enjoy going first class."

He already had one trip in November to proof the initial design framework by Evagen's engineers. If he had to fly somewhere, first class definitely the way to do it.

"Set it up," he told her. "Are you sure you don't want to have dinner somewhere?"

"I'd love to, Andrew, but I can't risk it. The less I'm seen the better. We're being paranoid, I know, but none of us can relax until we go public."

"Is there anything else you want to run through?"

"I could play with this all day, but I've seen enough. You've done an extraordinary job, Andrew. Frankly, it's far more than we expected."

Play with it? Thinking about it, with some tweaking, the simulator would make a terrific game—after Evagen goes public.

"I must admit it's been fun working on it, and I'm looking forward to trying it on the real thing."

She stood and extended a hand. "A pleasure, Andrew. Too bad I can't stay longer and see some of the sights."

"Another time." He shook her hand and escorted her to the elevators.

On the way to the kitchenette for a badly needed coffee, Nora shot him a questioning look, to which he responded with a smirk. He and Masina were locked in his office all day, with only a brief break for lunch, and Nora understandably curious. The rumor mill no doubt ground out some coarse stuff.

Coffee mug in hand, he made himself comfortable and powered down the server. After a knock on the door, Sloan stuck in his head.

"Got a minute?"

"Sure thing. Come on in," Andrew said.

Sloan walked in and planted his fists on his hips. "Who was your visitor? Wait till I tell Adriana that you're making out with another woman."

Andrew laughed. "Go ahead. She thinks the worst of me anyway."

"Seriously, who was she?"

"I'm sorry, Keith. I can't talk about it. All I can say, she's part of a new project I'm involved with."

Sloan waved a hand. "Don't give me that. Spill it."

"I'm sorry, but I can't. All will be revealed in due time. Trust me."

"Does Sergey know about this?"

"Absolutely."

"I won't pester you, but I think it's mean of you not to tell me. We're fellow directors!"

"I hate this more than you know, but once this comes out, you'll understand."

"I'll hold you to that," Sloan said darkly and walked out.

Andrew sighed and sipped his coffee.

Shait.

Coffee mug in hand, he decided he and Adriana needed another break somewhere. An accumulation of little things threatened to overload him, and once their son was born, that would be it for some time. He had gone far in the last two years, perhaps too quickly. As an executive director, Nelson expected him to discharge his responsibilities with sober dedication. Andrew had done that and more, glad not having to manage a region. Sometimes, he wondered how Sloan and the others did it. Well, he *knew* how they did it—years of experience. Only twenty-seven, he never had the experience of those years, but learned quickly.

With a significant slice of Broca Genetics shares in his portfolio, he held a seat on their board without any executive responsibility. Nevertheless, the position took chunks of his time attending meetings and keeping abreast of what they were doing.

Research into macrophage applications had yielded several cancer treatments, arresting, and in some cases reversing, Parkinson's, Alzheimer's, and dementia. Telomere repair promised to extend lifespans up to fifteen percent, but a lot of work remained before a marketable product became available. At the last board meeting, Andrew argued for increased funding in genome research.

How body and cell functions are controlled has been the subject of intense research since completion of the Human Genome Project in 2003. From his reading at the Institute, he found that genes made up only two percent of the genome and were easy to spot, but the millions of on/off switches controlling them were encrypted within the remaining ninety-eight percent. Without these regulatory DNA switches, genes remained inert. Finding them and understanding their function the genetic holy grail.

Broca already had a team working on genes, Dr. Ivone Masters argued. As a sideline activity, Andrew pointed out. He urged the board to intensify the company's research effort. Whoever made significant strides mapping DNA and microRNA switches, would hold a competitive advantage in the cure of human diseases. She built Broca into an innovative company based on visionary research, he told them. That vision had made a significant contribution to human knowledge, and considerable profits, he added wryly. The company could not afford to be sidelined while others took up the challenge. Some on the board resisted investing millions into pure research that might not yield anything marketable for years. Dr. Masters sided with Andrew and agreed to set up a division around the existing core team to research genome switches.

Another piece of their research had him excited. Designer organic nanorobots an old idea, biotech companies around the world were pouring phenomenal amounts of money down that hole. Unable to crack the mechanisms how his macrophages changed him, Broca decided to create artificial ones, let them loose in a test animal, and see what happens. A sound methodology, but difficult to implement. They needed a computerized molecular assembler. There were several on the market, but all were infant technology. Even when created, the nanobot's function and behavior could not be predicted with absolute certainty.

Andrew made a proposal to Broca. What if their scientists could assemble a VR nanobot and test it in a virtual environment? Dr. Masters liked the idea, but countered that such technology did not exist. His research identified a number of companies that specialized at imaging biological processes, and one stood above others—MoleImage. They made graphical short movies that showed how cells divided, how DNA replicated itself, how viruses penetrated cell walls, and what they did once they got in. Lots of things.

He told the board to buy MoleImage, and convert the visuals into interactive VR. Broca would image organic building blocks, assemble them for a specific function, and test their behavior in a VR environment. Once happy their creation did the required thing, an interface to a molecular assembler would create a living nanorobot.

An all-directors CC email last week announced that Broca had purchased MoleImage. This made Andrew excited…and depressed. Excited because Dr. Masters took his suggestion seriously. Depressed because he had another major project on his hands, and limited time to do it without compromising his commitments to FutureTech.

After tossing it around, a simple solution to his dilemma presented itself. He would license his 3D macros to MoleImage and their experts could take it from there, opening a whole new market opportunity.

He had not forgotten the kidnapping incident and the biopsy someone did on him, whether a private concern or some government agency. As a Broca director, he had access to all meeting minutes and research projects. Feeling somewhat foolish for harboring a dark suspicion, he could now lay it to rest. One evening, he logged onto their server and started hunting. He scrolled down the January meeting minutes and bit his lip. They had an attempt to hack their system, which prompted installation of additional security. So, Dr. Dalton had not lied to him. Or had she? Had someone tried to hack the Cancer Institute's system? He ought to call Professor Rhodes and find out.

He entertained an outrageous possibility and perhaps did Dr. Dalton a great disservice.

A piece of good news allowed him to concentrate fully on Evagen's flight control system. The dental trainer and the management accounting interface packages were on the market, and both received enthusiastic reviews from the learned community and CPA organizations. This helped sales and brought handsome royalties for Usque Vision, which would only grow as the products gained acceptance.

Happy with his successes, he nevertheless felt drained. A break with Adriana while she could still travel might be the thing he needed to recharge. After his visit to Phoenix, he decided. Once he installed the system on their demonstrator prototype ship and trained Masina how to use it fully, which should not take long, Evagen engineers would spend some time testing everything and identify functional changes. If he learned one thing in his short career, designers *always* made changes, and demanded enhancements not in the original specs. He would be surprised if Evagen did not come up with their own. A concept design was one thing, but once they mated the software with the ship, actual operation would invariably highlight needed modifications.

Hence the objective of his Phoenix visit. Perhaps more than one trip might be required to ensure everything worked smoothly before public revelation in April.

He could clearly imagine the disbelief of those invited to see the unveiling, and the televised world audience at large. During his last visit to the facility, he had an opportunity to meet Terrance Maceroy, and warmed to him instantly. The quietly intense Evagen founder treated him as a serious adult despite his youthful looks, something he appreciated. Bourbon in hand, they talked about a range of things, including the impact gravitomagnetic vehicles would have on society in general, governments, industry, and the military everywhere. Not everyone would be pleased to see GM craft take to the sky. Least of all megacorps with vested interests to maintain the existing status quo where they controlled technological development and markets. Like it or not, they would have to deal with it, and deal with Evagen. Despite the positives GM vehicles would deliver in the long run, there would undoubtedly be some unavoidable initial social turmoil.

He also understood why the demo must be in the glare of world publicity. A secret viewing to select government and industrial representatives left too many opportunities to have the technology appropriated, and Evagen's people made to disappear. He did not consider this a conspiracy theorist's wild flight of fancy, but a real possibility when trillions in existing investment and infrastructure were at stake. There were examples without number of socially beneficial inventions bought out by vested interests and quietly buried.

Until April, the operating word: trust no one.

* * *

Adriana slipped into his arms and Andrew kissed her.

"I wish you were coming with me," he whispered tenderly.

She smiled and brushed his face with a fleeting touch. "I'm not cut out to be a dull businessman puffing cigars at board meetings. Besides, I prefer Melbourne's summer much more than Phoenix's bracing weather. Don't worry about me. I'll be all right."

The cab driver outside gave a toot. He disengaged himself and picked up his bags.

"I'll see you in a week," he told her, and hurried out, hating to leave. His mom would look after her, but it was not the same thing. *He* wanted to look after her. The poignant reminder how he almost allowed her to slip between his fingers still sharp.

Not in the mood to chat with the cabbie, he gazed absently at traffic flowing around him.

The cab dropped him off at the QANTAS international terminal and he strode quickly toward the first class check-in counter. The economy queue wound around the barriers like a long black snake, most people wearing vacant looks, wanting to get the thing over with. The attendant gave him the boarding pass and he walked toward the security portals. They x-rayed his carry-on with the hard drive and sensor helmet without comment, and let him go. He made his way through the brightly lit duty-free area packed with shoppers and those merely killing time before their flight. Not due to board for another twenty minutes, he snagged a coffee in the Star Alliance lounge.

When he walked into the aircraft, a flight attendant escorted him to his first class cubicle, and he gave a low whistle of appreciation. He had two windows to himself with a little side bench, a large screen to watch movies, and a very comfortable-looking leather seat that could be turned into a bed, everything done in tasteful soft gray. She quickly showed him all the features, and left him to stow his carry-on and make himself comfortable. She returned with a glass of what turned out to be yellow champagne and a plate of hot finger savories. Settling himself in the comfortable seat, he figured he could get used to such travel.

The B787 Dreamliner pushed back and bumped its way along the taxiway toward the runway. It surged into the sky and he leaned back with a sigh. Shortly afterward, the attendant came in, placed a white cloth on the foldaway table and served a basket of rolls, crackers, water and wine, and a plate of cheese and salmon strips as a snack. She nodded, smiled, and left him to it.

"Andrew, my boy, this is the only way to live," he muttered and dug in.

After fourteen hours in the air, enjoying superb meals, entertainment, a relatively good sleep in the made up bed, a shower before landing, he felt ready to face Evagen.

With barely a shudder, the aircraft touched down at 15:35 local a little ahead of schedule at Phoenix Sky Harbor International Airport. He cleared passport control, collected his suitcase from the carousel, and strode into the packed and noisy arrivals terminal. Masina met him with a handshake and a broad smile. They exchanged pleasantries about his flight and cabin service as they drove toward the Arizona Industrial Park, thankfully a short trip, only nine minutes.

"If you want to freshen up, there are guest rooms at the facility," she offered.

"Thanks, but I want to download the flight system first and iron out any interface problems."

"I don't mind seeing the real thing either," she said.

"What do you do when you're not piloting?"

"I'm studying for a master's in advanced materials design at the University of Phoenix. Mr. Maceroy is paying for it. He also got me my house."

"That was generous of him."

"He's done this for all his team, and foots all education expenses for those with kids. He's a driven man, and we're all fiercely loyal to him."

When they got to the facility surrounded by neat lawns, lots of tall trees, including eucalyptus, swaying with the help of a warm breeze, Masina tapped her ID card against the sensor and heavy steel gates slid back smoothly. A camera on each support pillar stared down at them. She drove in and parked beside the four-story office building in the shadow of an enormous green metal hangar and lesser buildings. On the other side of Salt River suburbia sprawled across the desert, and Andrew understood why Evagen was wary showing their ship even at night.

Masina took him straight to the hangar, the inside smelling of oil and burnt metal shavings typical of industrial workshops. Next to a small air car with a bubble canopy rested the testbed vehicle with four attached fans.

After greeting two engineers, he looked keenly at the new ship sitting on thick runners. Landing wheels meant complicated mechanical assemblies that required maintenance and could break down. Apart from four large dummy fans, the vehicle had a new coat of pale blue paint and a white belly. Work benches occupied the entire back wall filled with electronic instruments and all manner of tools hung on wall brackets. A heavy lathe stood in one corner, surrounded by bins, rolls of wire, narrow H beams, plating, and odd leftovers.

He climbed the small metal steps and paused in the hatchway, nodding at the changes inside. The professionally laid out interior, seats for four passengers and two pilots, subdued overhead lighting, a 360-degree view provided by a waist-to-ceiling one-way transparent aluminum bulkhead, made it look like a futuristic airliner cabin.

Outside the ship, Masina introduced Paul Truscott, Evagen's senior systems programmer, and there were more handshakes. Andrew inserted his drive into the prepared server connected to the vehicle by a black cable and uploaded the flight control system. It mated cleanly with the ship's BIOS and ready to go.

He picked up the sensor helmet, turned to Masina, and extended his arm toward the ship.

"Shall we?"

Trying to look calm and professional, her eyes nevertheless sparkled with anticipation. "I can't wait."

Up front beneath the transparent bulkhead, a 1000mm x 500mm black plastic panel held the manual control system. Beside it were two USB and HDMI ports. A touch anywhere caused the palm recognition pad to light up. Andrew pressed his hand against the sensitized surface and Masina added him to the list of personnel authorized to operate the ship. After a second, the pad turned green. The ship knew him.

The panel showed navigation and radar screens, a status message display, a standard keyboard, and a dozen touch-sensitive labeled buttons. Elegant, simple, and functional. Beneath the panel, a handgrip controller allowed steering in six options, including pitch and yaw.

He sat down in the right pilot seat, donned the helmet, and quickly ran through the menu options, most giving audible and pulsing display warnings, still firmly on the ground. He removed the helmet and glanced at Masina.

"The flight system is up and running and you can play with it. Jot down any interface issues. I'll join you in the morning for formal trials," he added and glanced at his watch, almost six.

"We'll have a welcome dinner tomorrow," she said. "You're no doubt beat after your flight."

"Not yet, but I'm fast getting there," he admitted with a grin. Although the B787 first class suite turned out to be extremely comfortable, and he managed to catch some winks, the constant background engine hum and occasional turbulence stopped him from sleeping deeply. The wait in San Francisco to catch a connecting flight and two hours to Phoenix made for a long trip.

"Mr. Maceroy and Byrne asked me to extend their apologies for not meeting you. They're in New York, but they'll be here tomorrow."

Darkness held everything in a firm grip by the time he settled into his third floor guest room. Perhaps not five-star, but still very comfortable. He dug out his cell and smiled as he pressed the ring icon, feeling his spirits lift.

"Andrew!" Adriana yelped happily. "Is everything all right?"

"I'm fine, sweetie. Wishing you were here."

"You sound tired."

"A long flight and a long day. How are things back there?"

"We're having a hot one today. It's thirty-four out there, but the air-con's going. What about you?"

"Cool, but I'll be thinking of you all night. That'll keep me warm."

She laughed. "Goat. Belana came over last night and kept me company. We're going shopping at the Vic Market on Saturday."

"Have fun, and give her my regards. I'll call you tomorrow. Hugs and kisses."

"Love you!"

He cut the connection, his heart lighter. Too tired to eat anything, he showered and crashed out.

After ten hours of unbroken sleep, he woke refreshed and eager to start the day. He dressed in smart casual gear, and went down to the busy first floor dining room to snag breakfast. After a second cup of excellent coffee, he walked out and strolled around the deserted grounds, reveling in the crisp air, his legs enjoying the workout. Dawn broke and the sun peeked behind crimson clouds. He went back in, poured himself another coffee, and turned on the large TV to watch the local news. At 7:25, a knock on the door made him raise an eyebrow. He opened the door and stared at the armed security guard.

"I'm sorry to disturb you, sir, but Mr. Maceroy would like to see you."

"Not a problem," Andrew said, mildly puzzled, not due to see Masina until eight.

They rode the elevator to the fourth floor, and the guard took him to Maceroy's office. He knocked once and opened the door after hearing a muffled 'Come in'.

"Mr. Payne, sir."

"Thanks, Alvin. Please ask Byrne to join us."

"Of course, sir."

Maceroy stood, stepped away from the desk, and held out his hand. "Andrew, good to see you again. Have a seat."

They shook hands and he lowered himself into one of the comfortable leather visitor chairs.

"Sorry that I missed you yesterday," Maceroy said as he sat down. "Business things in New York. Are you rested?"

"I'm ready to start the test program."

"Good. By the way, my apologies for the mysterious way you were dragged here this morning. We had a development last night—"

Falzon walked in and took the other visitor chair. "Hi, Andrew."

"Byrne."

"I'm just telling him about the break-in," Maceroy said and rested his arms on the desk, fingers locked. "Around two last night, a man cut through the perimeter fence without setting off the alarm. He wore some strange body gear that scrambled the security camera images. He somehow avoided tripping the laser sensors—we suspect his camouflage suit had something to do with that—and made a dash for the hangar. Our trembler sensors got him and security apprehended him before he could gain entry. A frisk search revealed an electronic lock pick and a small digital camera. We called the police and they took him away, but we still have his camouflage garment. An extraordinary thing. Somebody is going to miss it and might come after it," Maceroy added wryly, then sighed heavily. "What worries me; this is the second penetration attempt this month."

"You suspect a covert government operation?" Andrew said flatly. An ordinary industrial spy does not usually wear a fancy camouflage suit.

"Whoever is running him, they now know more about us. Too much. A small aerospace firm developing a new air car is likely to have security cameras and guards, but not laser sensors and ground trembler devices. As you know, I've collected some of the smartest physicists and engineers in the country to turn the gravitomagnetic concept from theory into reality. Someone wondered why I need such a group of men and women to develop an air car and decided to find out."

If this were a government operation, Andrew mused, the next penetration would not be a lone intruder, but armed SWAT and FBI teams.

"Last night's incursion has forced my hand," Maceroy said heavily. "Where are you with the flight control system?"

"Masina and I are ready to start formal testing. We'll do as much as we can inside the hangar, but by Friday, we'll need a series of atmospheric flights to test everything."

"You'll take the vehicle out tonight," Maceroy said firmly.

"I know it's not enough time to complete the test program, but I cannot wait. Tomorrow morning at nine, I'll hold a televised press conference and reveal the prototype vehicle. Once we go public, we should be safe, and you can tidy up the flight system. The manual controls work, and that's good enough for a demonstration. Anyway, I understand you don't want to reveal your sensor helmet yet."

"That's right. The control system can be operated quite well using a VR headset and control gloves."

"That's that, then."

"What's to stop the FBI from barging in right now?"

"That's what worries me. At the first sign of trouble, you and Masina will fly the prototype out. In broad daylight if necessary. I already moved the testbed machine to another location. The dummy fans we attached to both vehicles won't stand close scrutiny. If we're compromised, I'll upload everything on the Internet and release a statement to local and international media," Maceroy said and gave a predatory grin.

Andrew saw a man who relished a fight with the establishment. The Evagen founder might relish it, but he had no appetite for such entanglements.

"I should have stuck to designing VR games," he muttered, and everybody laughed.

"Always have your hard drive in the vehicle with you. When coding, make regular backups. Paul Truscott has the server linked to our remote site. The welcome dinner I planned for tonight? We'll hold that tomorrow as a collective celebration."

If we're still around, Andrew reflected.

"This might mean an all-day and night effort. Are you up to it?"

Andrew drew a deep breath and nodded. "I can do it."

"Thanks, Andrew. I appreciate this."

For the rest of the day, Masina worked through the flight system, signing off functions in a tablet, adding observations and comments, including change requests. Some things she ticked off last night, which helped. Still, the first time the software interacted with the ship, and not everything worked properly. Andrew sat beside her, following what she did through a standard VR headset, expecting black-clad men to storm into the hangar at any moment.

The checklist had some red ticks and a lot of blank spaces, but they had to be in actual flight before he could address those items. They had the craft off the ground, dummy fans detached, and managed to sign off a number of items. In many respects, the test program turned out to be far simpler than required for games. In concept, operating the ship turned out similar to driving a car. Most of the time, the driver only worried about the gas and brake pedal and steering. Everything else was engine feedback and environmental convenience.

The ship's simple power plant made a GM vehicle easy to run. It had no moving parts that could fail, and did not require fuel to run, which made it extremely reliable. With built-in safety parameters, it would be virtually impossible to crash such a ship.

Memory memo to self: Ask Masina what happens if the ship did lose power.

They had a lunch break and finished what could be done on the ground around three. Andrew immediately went to work correcting bugs and coding changes. Some required consultation with the engineering team, and he left those alone. He finished around 6:30, made a backup, and headed toward the urn to snag a cup of coffee.

Suddenly, the hangar lights went out and the doors began to open. Masina appeared in the craft's doorway and waved at him.

"The FBI is at the gate! Let's go!"

Shait.

Adrenalin surged through him and he felt blood drain from his face. Heart pounding, he ran to the server, yanked out the hard drive, and sprinted toward the prototype. He did not sign for this! With the hatch dogged shut, he glanced through the transparent bulkhead. The craft had already cleared the hangar. It paused, then surged into a black sky.

He sat beside Masina operating the ship manually, and tapped a glowing pad. A screen showed the facility receding below them. Three black vehicles stood in front of the main gate. The image froze as Masina hovered the ship. A car pulled out of the parking lot and sped toward the gate.

She gave a soft sigh and looked at him. "We should be okay now."

The initial shock over, he took a couple of deep breaths. "How do you know it's the FBI?"

"The guards at the gate called Byrne, and he called me."

It appeared Maceroy had reason for concern.

In the screen, they saw four vehicles drive to the hangar. Light spilled as the doors retracted. After what felt like an eternity, three cars moved down the driveway, headlights stabbing into darkness, and faded down the road. Masina's phone trilled. She listened, nodded, and snapped shut the lid.

"We can come down now."

She entered the hangar and the doors slowly closed. Several engineers were inside watching the prototype settle on its runners. Andrew opened the hatch, waited for one of the men to position the metal steps, and scrambled down. Maceroy and Byrne walked toward him.

"You guys okay?" Maceroy demanded.

"We're fine. What happened here?"

"They were FBI, all right. They couldn't see the hangar from the gate, and didn't see the prototype go up. Lucky for us it's dark. It would have been different if they showed up an hour earlier. They nosed around, checked the dummy air car and went away. I don't think they were convinced. They know something is going on here." Maceroy gave Andrew a hard look. "Are you okay to go on?"

"I need to take a leak," he said and everybody grinned.

"There's hot food in the dining room," Byrne said.

After a dinner break, trying not to think about the FBI raid, Andrew went back to the hangar to finish coding the changes. Around nine, he initiated a manual backup and uploaded the new version into the prototype. After more coffee, he and Masina tested everything again. By midnight and another pit stop, they were ready to take the ship up.

With the hangar darkened, the two halves of the enormous door slid back with a soft grind. Navigation lights, radar, and transponder off, the vehicle silently drifted out. Clear of the hangar, it rose and quickly plunged into heavy overcast. It stopped at three thousand meters and hovered as Masina did a status check, sliding VR display panels back and forth with a flick of a finger. Andrew could not do that without his controller gloves, but her sensor helmet gave her much more flexibility.

Like searchlights, orange air traffic and blue weather radar beams, swept the sky. Broad red bands from Luke Air Force Base added its sweeps. The craft's co-gravitational field deflected the beams, which made the vehicle practically invisible.

Masina took the craft up twenty kilometers, and the American landmass glittered beneath broken cloud. She conducted several speed runs, one pushing through five thousand kilometers per hour, which prompted the system to issue verbal and display warnings. She tested all six movement modes, including pitch and jaw in fighter-like turns, relishing the craft's responsiveness. Once a fighter driver, always a fighter driver, he reflected. Inside the vehicle, he could not feel any acceleration or inertial shifting. Despite earlier fixes, several functions did not work properly due to comms problems with the ship's BIOS interface. Something to discuss with Truscott.

At 2:40 in the morning, the vehicle broke through the cloud layer, hovered as the hangar doors opened, and glided in. Andrew immediately jumped out, walked to the server station, inserted the hard drive, and powered up. He brought up the software editor and started on the first item listed in the tablet. Around five, Truscott showed up and helped him clean up the interface problems. When he finished, Andrew made a backup, dragged the connecting cable into the vehicle and mated it with the input port. After the upload, he sighed and leaned against the chair.

"Good enough for government work," he muttered softly.

He should have felt exhausted after almost twenty-three hours on his feet, but felt too keyed up and buoyed by the successful test flight. He went to his guest room, took a shower, and changed into a suit. He had breakfast with Masina and Truscott in the first floor dining room, surrounded by several scientists and engineers chatting excitedly about the coming presentation.

Around eight, Sergey Nelson showed up and Andrew took him to the hangar.

"Christ!" Nelson growled as he stared at the prototype. "You've flown it?"

"We'll give you a ride later," Andrew promised.

At 8:50, Falzon had everyone assembled outside the hangar. Five TV vans, transmission dishes pointing at a clear sky, formed a background for a gaggle of media reps chatting among themselves, waiting for things to start.

At nine sharp, Maceroy walked out of the admin building and stopped in front of his team.

"Ladies and gentlemen, I welcome you to Evagen, Inc. For those who don't know me, my name is Terrance Maceroy." This generated several smiles from the media. "I gathered a team of extraordinary men and women who had a vision many thought unattainable. Some of them sacrificed careers and reputations in the pursuit of that vision. Today, I want to reveal the product of their genius."

The hangar doors slowly slid back. Like a ghost, the prototype vehicle glided silently into light and hovered above the assembled development team. A ripple of gasps and startled murmurs ran among the media reps. Maceroy gave everybody a moment to absorb what they were seeing.

"Looking at this extraordinary vehicle, I know what some of you are thinking," he said. "The automotive and aircraft industries are dead, as are all space programs. We're facing massive unemployment and worldwide economic collapse. Nothing could be further from the truth!" he declared forcefully.

"There will be undeniable adjustment as industries shift to manufacturing gravitomagnetic vehicles, but that change will take years, which should minimize any negative impact. Instead of massive layoffs, this technology will create a chronic shortage of designers, engineers, technicians, and assembly workers. The world isn't facing economic disaster, but an industrial boom.

"Gravitomagnetic vehicles will end the twice-daily gridlock, smog, petrol price gouging, and free the world from dependence on fossil fuels." Maceroy gave a wry smile. "Admittedly, we might be replacing road gridlocks with air gridlocks, but that's something for the legislators to sort out, and there is much more space up there than on our roads." This generated a ripple of laughter.

"New industries will not be confined to Earth. The Moon and the asteroids are a rich source of badly needed minerals and elements, free for the taking by those with vision, especially rare earth elements, a critical component in manufacture of superconductors. This will also create a tourism explosion. Why settle for a ten-day holiday in Hawaii, when you can travel to Jupiter or see Saturn's rings close up? I'm looking forward to that one myself," he added dryly and lifted his arm.

The prototype slowly rose, picked up speed, and became a black speck. Then it descended and hovered in its original position. Any thoughts that he'd fallen for an illusionist's trick were banished.

"Consider how much valuable land is taken by our national road networks and the enormous cost and time needed to build and maintain them. Land badly needed for growing cities everywhere. Suburban architecture is largely dictated by the need for extensive street networks, which most of the time are deserted. Removing that need will free state and municipal funds for recreational facilities, schools, and hospitals." Maceroy paused and frowned.

"Gravitomagnetic vehicles represent a possible future, a brighter future, but it might not happen at all. The multinationals will see this development as a threat to their existence and profits. They will seek to bury this future, as will some Congressmen who rely on those multinationals to keep their seats by throwing up legal barriers. General Motors and Boeing may choose to ignore the existence of GM vehicles and continue to build cars and airplanes that rely on diminishing fossil fuel reserves. That is their choice. I invite them to look beyond short term profits and see an opportunity for long-term expansion by embracing GM vehicles in partnership with Evagen. However, I will not wait for them to make up their mind. I'll lead them. Evagen will build special purpose GM vehicles from this facility, which will create an economic boost to Phoenix and Arizona."

Three black vans with large yellow FBI letters on their sides roared up the driveway and ground to a stop behind the media gaggle. Doors banged and black-clad men in riot gear, rifles held ready, formed a semicircle. Cameras and mikes recorded everything. Two men in dark suits broke away and walked toward Maceroy.

The taller one held out an identification wallet. "My name is Neil Hauser, Supervising Special Agent. Mr. Maceroy, I have a warrant for your arrest and arrest of your personnel. I'm also confiscating this, ah, vehicle as evidence."

Maceroy smiled, took the proffered warrant and held it up for the media. "It has begun!"

The reporters surged toward him. The armed agents closed in and held them back.

"And what is the charge, Mr. Hauser?"

"Violation of the 2001 Patriot Act. Namely, compromising the security of the United States and aiding and abetting in a terrorist activity."

"Indeed?" Maceroy lifted his arm, fingers splayed. "One..." he said and closed his thumb.

Hauser blanched. "What are you doing?"

"Two..."

The FBI men looked uncertainly at each other. One of them pointed his rifle at Maceroy.

"At the count of five, specifications for my vehicle will be posted on the Internet," Maceroy said. "I doubt your superiors will be pleased. Now, I suggest you take your ridiculous warrant and clear out your men."

Houser scowled.

"Three…"

Hauser drew his automatic. "I'll shoot you."

Maceroy shrugged. "That won't change a thing. Four…"

"Stop!" Hauser snarled and spoke urgently into his wrist microphone. He nodded and glowered at Maceroy. "You got your way this time, Mister, but we're not done." He turned to his men and waved them back. They slowly walked to their vans and drove off.

Maceroy waited for the resulting buzz to die down.

"Ladies and gentlemen, any new innovation has a dark side. The vehicle you're looking at is no exception. It represents peace and prosperity, but there are those who're interested in power, not peace, as Mr. Hauser so vividly demonstrated. To preclude creation of a dangerous geopolitical imbalance, Evagen, Inc. will license the manufacture of gravitomagnetic drives worldwide. If any government agency or corporation attempts to stifle this technology through intimidation of my team or their families, I will immediately publish the engineering specifications. I hope someone in the White House is watching."

Maceroy waited a few moments for this to sink in.

"Before you leave, pick up a media pack that will explain everything more fully. Now, who wants a ride?"

Chapter Ten

Smeared with white whorls, Earth stood against a backdrop of brilliant stars. Reach for it, that's all Andrew had to do and the globe would rest in the palm of his hand. A massive low pressure system smothered the Caribbean and most of Florida, trailing ragged tendrils in its wake. A band of green Aurora twisted and danced around the northern pole. He had seen clips taken from the International Space Station, but they could not compare to what lay below him. Above a sharp horizon, the Moon glared in half phase. He never actually expected going there, except in flights of his imagination. Masina glanced at him, her eyes and head covered by the sensor helmet.

Hogan Walsh, Evagen's chief engineer, scratched his chin. "How does it look?"

"Nominal," Masina said. "We're good to go."

Beside her, Andrew plugged in his VR headset into the HDMI port and put it on.

Walsh turned to Erica Stern, the senior team physicist, sitting in the first passenger row.

She nodded. "Let's do it. Watch for power fluctuations, Masina," she added.

"Right. Here we go."

Andrew felt nothing, and the drive gave no sound as acceleration built and *Evagen-1* streaked toward the Moon.

"Eighteen thousand…twenty-six…thirty-five…The power curve is flattening," Masina announced. "Forty-six thousand kph. It doesn't seem to want to go faster."

Stern checked her tablet. "We're within the expected range for our power unit. We'll manage more with a larger configuration."

"Are we tight?" Walsh demanded.

"No pressure change."

At 46,000 kilometers per hour, they should reach the Moon in eight hours or so. A far cry from three days for the Apollo missions. Stern told him that Evagen had a larger and faster ship already in the design stage, with projected speed in excess of 114,000 kph. It could reach Mars in twenty days at closest approach to Earth. A specially equipped ship with an even more powerful drive would allow Evagen to reach the asteroids. According to observational data, among the many rocks out there, Psyche 16's structure mostly made up of gold, platinum, and nickel. Untold riches free for the taking.

Somewhere in her early thirties, Andrew had not asked, chestnut hair worn short, dark eyes framed by thin eyebrows, and a ready smile, he found Stern easy to talk to. PhDs in astrophysics and quantum mechanics from MIT, she said Falzon lured her from Boston's academia to Phoenix where she and Walsh turned theory into repeatable experiments.

Evagen stole the engineer from NASA's Ames Research Center. He tried to convince everybody to forget electrogravity and concentrate on gravitomagnetic propulsion. Frustrated with NASA's bureaucratic methodology and conventional thinking, he jumped at Falzon's offer to join the Evagen team and build a working GM testbed. According to Masina, a weird mob, for sure.

"Mining asteroids is not a new idea," Andrew said, "but I can see trouble brewing as governments and corporations scramble to stake claims. It will be the old Klondike gold rush all over again."

"No doubt," Stern agreed. "The 1967 UN Outer Space Treaty defines activities of states in the exploration and use of space and celestial bodies, signed by 167 countries. Only a concept then, but it does provide a basic legal framework, and will need clarification to make it workable. The situation is not helped by the

2015 U.S. Space Launch Competitiveness Act, which most countries deem a violation of the 1967 treaty."

"Whatever they come up with, we'll need a policing body to maintain compliance and prevent open lawlesness."

"I'm afraid so," she said glumly. "It's all so pointless, as there is enough out there for everybody. Then there is the impact on Earth's economy if the market is suddenly flooded with tons of gold and platinum. Or what an ice asteroid dropped on the Sahara would do to our climate. Water clouds constitute the most dangerous greenhouse gas there is. Instead of greening deserts, we could end up cooking our planet."

Andrew did not want to think about that, not now. Mankind would either cope or screw itself. He wanted to enjoy this flight.

There were only four of them in the prototype. The Moon mission had a dual purpose: test drive effectiveness as the vehicle traveled farther from Earth, and a publicity stunt to prove to the world that gravitomagnetic ships could open the Solar System. If the drive failed part way to the Moon, boosters attached to the outer frame should enable them to coast back until Earth's magnetic field became strong enough to repower the drive. According to Stern, the drive should not fail, but those calculations were done on a computer Earthside.

Two hours into the flight, Masina reported no loss of power, which Stern noted in her tablet with a satisfied nod.

Andrew got out of his seat and walked to a small box of food supplies tucked against the rear bulkhead. It consisted mostly of concentrated nutrient bars, water, and two Thermos flasks of coffee. Two days before the flight, they were put on a low-residue diet. *Evagen-1* did not contain a toilet, and no one wanted to poop into a plastic bag. The process certain to enrich the ambient atmosphere. They could not avoid carrying urinal bags, though.

He poured himself a mug and offered one to everybody. Back in his seat, he sipped and watched the stars.

Following Maceroy's announcement and the bungled FBI raid, the media around the world went into a predictable meltdown, ridiculing the United States administration for its stormtrooper tactics. The White House press secretary offered an apology, claiming the president did not know anything about the raid, but it caused the government intense embarrassment.

At two in the afternoon, Adriana called. Having breakfast, she said. Come over and share, which he would love to do. All the channels replayed Maceroy's announcement. When she saw him under the saucer, as she called it, she almost dropped her pot of tea, understanding the secrecy behind his latest work. They chatted for a while and he promised to call later.

By evening, nobody raided or bombed the Evagen facility, encouraging for everybody concerned. Andrew did not see himself the stuff of martyrs. The promised welcome party went long into the night. Badly in need of sleep, they had to carry him to his guest room.

The media storm continued to rage. Numerous self-appointed experts predicted economic disaster and global war caused directly by what they claimed Mr. Maceroy's reckless revelation. Other commentators cautiously analyzed the development more rationally. Dow Jones took an initial hit, dragged down 1348 points by falling auto and aerospace sector stocks. By close of business, it went up 415 from the morning's opening once people realized a car did not require wheels to move, and aircraft could fly very well without jet engines. Transport vehicles would have different shapes, but a GM drive did not alter the basic function to move people and goods from one point to another. On the contrary, the concept of flying vehicles within everybody's grasp generated keen interest. It reinforced the truism that markets were driven by perception, not facts, and people liked the idea of having a car that did not need gasoline.

Oil futures took a dive and recovered. GM vehicles might be the future, but they would not appear in significant numbers for some time. Meanwhile, cars and airplanes still needed fuel. Nevertheless, OPEC and oil multinationals would need to rethink their position in the new world as the gush of dollars into their treasuries became a trickle.

NASA, SpaceX, Blue Origin, and Ariane were effectively dead as viable long-term concerns. They still needed to launch military and civilian payloads until GM ships came online, but nobody would spend hundreds of millions anymore designing new heavy lift rocket vehicles. For the first time, the concept of large multipurpose space stations could be entertained when the cost to bring materials into orbit no longer a limiting factor. Zero gravity manufacturing now a viable prospect.

The geopolitical mood still to sort itself out as countries and their industrial military complexes evaluated the impact of GM vehicles on existing and planned defense programs. Andrew found defense a curious word in this context, as weapons had only one purpose: destroy an opponent, individually or writ large. China and Russia made cautious murmurs of approval, mollified by Maceroy's promise to license the drive technology, recognizing they had civilian applications other than military. Nevertheless, Andrew feared those regimes would prioritize military development ahead of any other consideration. So would the so-called free world, he mused, as the FBI raid demonstrated. A crappy way to do business.

TE Flight Corp was not amused when they realized Evagen had cut the ground from under their feet. According to Nelson, Mrs. Talbot, head of trainer development, complained bitterly, accusing him of deception and threatened a lawsuit. VR flight trainers continued to sell because the industry saved millions using them. Diversify, Nelson told her bluntly. Conventional aircraft would be around for decades to come, sharing the skies with GM craft. If TE Flight wanted to sue him for Evagen's innovation, they were free to do so. He took a hit also, then told her about the full-sensor conversion program done at FutureTech's cost. Somewhat mollified, Talbot demanded a demonstration, which now landed on Andrew's to-do list.

Six hours into the flight, the drive still hummed happily, and the Moon drew visibly larger. He began to appreciate the face of future spaceflight, which would mostly ignore complex orbital mechanics, replaced largely with line-of-sight navigation.

Masina changed places with Stern and Walsh a couple of times, allowing them to interact with the flight system through the sensor helmet. Like playing an elaborate VR game, Stern said, totally taken in by the virtual graphics. Her comment made Andrew determined to turn the prototype version into a game. It would not take much work, and would serve as a terrific promo plug for Evagen.

At fifteen thousand kilometers, the Moon loomed huge, its cratered surface stark in gray relief. *Evagen-1* slowed as the craggy peaks reached for it, Walsh demanding constant technical readouts. Five kilometers up, they drifted above the barren landscape. Masina kept checking the map display to make sure they were not lost. It would be easy to do, as everything looked the same.

The ship sank to five hundred meters, barely moving.

"My God," Stern cried out suddenly. "There it is."

Tranquility Base looked like any other bare piece of moonscape dotted with craters, except for the Apollo 11 descent stage and the American flag planted nearby in the regolith. Masina stopped some hundred meters from the site and hovered. Everybody stared at the descent stage, Andrew's own feelings mixed.

Armstrong actually walked this ground, he marveled, wishing he could be out there. Regrettably, they did not carry EVA suits as the ship lacked a proper airlock. The new vehicle would have everything required for proper spaceflight, including a toilet, Walsh said.

Evagen-1 slowly descended and touched down with a faint tremor. They might not be able to go out, but the ship would leave its runner lines beside man's first venture to another celestial body. Two contrasts; a hesitant beginning to true space flight.

Andrew began to clap, and everyone joined enthusiastically, which quickly degenerated into laughter and warm hugs. He hauled the bottle of champagne from the cooler bag as Stern handed out plastic cups, and they toasted past and present explorers. He wished Adriana were here to share his moment of intense satisfaction. She would probably be watching this on TV, but not the same thing.

Evagen-1 crossed into the perpetual night side. They watched Earth climb above a jagged horizon and headed home.

* * *

Andrew presented his passport to a severe-looking Immigration lady siting in a little glass-walled cubicle. Her expression suggested she did not like her job, or the long queue waiting to be processed. She placed the passport under a scanner, stamped it, and held it out.

"Welcome home," she said and cracked a small smile.

He collected his suitcase and walked through the Nothing to Declare door into a noisy, crowded arrivals hall. Friends, relatives, and sweethearts pushed against the barrier, waiting for their loved ones to appear. There might have been some enemies there as well, but how could he tell?

"Andrew!" Adriana shouted, waving an arm to attract his attention.

Startled to see her, he broke into a happy grin. He hugged and kissed her.

"I missed you," he growled, holding her tight, mindful of her belly bump. It felt good having her in his arms, feel her warmth, smell her perfume, bask in her radiant smile and unreserved love.

She took a chance with a brash youngster who struggled to be a man and loved him. Before he met her, he thought love was laughter, a few fun dates, some good times, and moments of physical intimacy. A transitory release of passion with little thought of tomorrow. Why think of tomorrow when there were lots of other shells on the beach. When he saw her dark olive eyes for the first time, mouth turned up in a whimsical smile, he found himself floundering in smothering surf of conflicting emotions. Looking at her standing in the doorway, he knew she was different from all the others. He thanked the fates for giving him courage to ask her out for lunch.

"You didn't have to come," he told her and ran a finger across her cheek.

"Silly. It wasn't any trouble. Besides, I also missed you."

He glanced at the slight bump in her belly. "How's the little man?"

"Moving. I think he wants out."

"Tell him to hold his water. Two more months to go."

Hand in hand, they walked out of the terminal into a glaring hot day. The northerly wind felt like something out of a kiln. Cars, cabs, and buses made an unbroken line, dropping off or picking up. The stink of petrol and diesel hung heavy in the air.

They stopped at a crossing that led to the multi-level short-term parking lot, and waited for the lights to change. Some people ignored the lights and dashed across, followed by prolonged blasts from irate drivers. Andrew could never figure out why those seconds beating the lights mattered so much. He saw the same thing in the city. Pedestrians risked life and injury to gain a sense of victory over the system. Somewhat sheepishly, he admitted having done the same thing himself.

"I was surprised when you told me you were flying back," she said. "I expected Evagen to bring you in their saucer."

He laughed. "Tempted, but I'd be entering Australia illegally. Rather than create a problem with Immigration's stuffy bureaucrats, I suffered first class."

"Oh, you poor thing," she cooed.

"No dramas while I was away? You haven't rearranged the furniture, have you?"

"You're a degenerate, Andrew Payne, and mean."

"Just asking."

"I didn't rearrange anything, if you must know." Her eyebrows knitted. "I thought you'd be back a couple of days ago, then I saw the coverage of your Moon trip. All the channels were full of it. What's it like, space and the Moon?"

"Like flying in an airliner, except you see lots of stars."

"They said it took a little over eight hours to get there. It makes the Moon totally accessible."

"Definitely. We landed at the Apollo 11 site and looked around. It's incredible that Armstrong and Aldrin dared come down in such a flimsy craft. After a couple of orbits, we headed back. When I get my own ship, I'll take you there."

"I wouldn't mind that." She looked thoughtful. "Evagen will change transport as we know it. It's exciting and a little frightening."

"Change is always a little frightening," he agreed, "but I feel this change will deliver far more benefits than it causes misery for some, and it will."

"I suppose. People will adapt."

People *would* adapt, he reflected. They adapted when Australia lost its shoe and textile industry to cheap Asian labor. They adapted when in 2017 the country stopped manufacturing cars. There, the industry did it to themselves by not diversifying into global markets and the federal government stopped handing out hundreds of millions in annual subsidies.

The light changed to yellow, and from both sides, people surged across. A cab running the light tooted its horn and swerved to avoid a woman halfway across, which caused everyone to scramble out of the way.

It all seemed to happen in slow motion. Andrew saw the car come at him side on and he instinctively pushed Adriana out of its path. It hit him and he grunted as his arms flailed to keep himself upright. His carry-on and suitcase went flying. He saw the rear end clip Adriana and she crashed against a trash can mounting. He fell heavily against someone, which created a tangle of bodies. Ignoring the pain in his chest, he scrambled to his feet, eyes fixed on his motionless wife, praying she was all right. A sudden silence fell as everything stopped. Then the noise and the stinks returned, and two men helped him to the sidewalk. He knelt beside her and winced when he saw blood oozing from a gash on her forehead. He dragged out a packet of tissues from his pocket, jerked out two, and pressed them against the wound. She twisted her head and moaned. He took her hand and squeezed, wanting to take away her pain.

The cabby got out and looked imploringly at the crowd.

"It wasn't my fault!"

Someone put Andrew's carry-on and suitcase beside him, and he nodded thanks to the unknown face.

The police were suddenly there, directing traffic and moving on the morbidly curious. Then the ambulance came. Everything happened quickly then. The medics put on a neck brace on Adriana and wheeled her in. One of them helped him into the ambulance, and a cop threw in his suitcase and carry-on. The back doors slammed shut. Siren wailing, it pulled out. He watched as two female medics gave Adriana a quick checkup.

"Are you injured?" one of them asked.

"My chest hurts. How's my wife?"

"Her pulse is strong and her pupils are not dilated, which is good. The laceration on her forehead isn't deep."

"What about the baby?"

"Hard to say. We'll know more once they do a scan. From the skin discoloration, your wife has a bruised hip. Perhaps even a fracture."

At The Alfred Hospital, they took Adriana away and he had a full-body CT scan. Apart from a sore chest, he felt fine. An orderly wheeled him to a room in the outpatients ward. When he saw Adriana propped against the bed, huge relief flooded through him. She smiled and waved. He jumped to his feet and rushed to her side.

"I was so worried about you. Are you all right?"

"A headache, but no concussion. My hip and shoulder are a little sore, but nothing broken. Before you ask, the baby's fine."

He kissed her palm. "How long are they keeping you here?"

"They told me I can go in a couple of hours. They want to double check my scans and make sure the baby is okay." She glanced at the luggage beside the bed. "At least you got your stuff."

"Forget my stuff! I went crazy when I saw you hurt."

"What happened to the cab driver?"

"The cops have him. That's all I knew when the ambulance came." He stroked her cheek. "You sure you're all right?"

"I'm fine. How about you?"

"Sore chest, that's all. We were lucky."

"A hell of a welcome home." Her eyes suddenly turned huge. "My car! It's still at the airport. Do you know how much it costs to park there?"

"Forget the damn car. I'll buy a new one if I have to. I'll buy the whole parking lot."

Her cheerful laughter lifted his spirits and he laughed with her.

They took a cab home, a short run to South Yarra. He called Sloan, explained what happened, and told him he would not be in tomorrow.

After a refreshing shower, he changed into light summer gear and went downstairs, thankful Adriana and the baby were okay.

Mug of tea in hand, he sprawled on the couch and gave a satisfied sigh. Adriana sat beside him and wrapped her arms around his neck, favoring her right side.

"I need a cuddle," she declared softly.

He smiled and pulled her against him. "How's that?"

"I missed you."

"Me too. All alone, how did you cope? You never said when I called."

"I must admit it felt a little strange. This is the first time I'd ever been alone. When I lived with my parents, they were always there, and I had my work to keep me busy. Then I lived with you. Suddenly, I had this big house all to myself and not much to do. I couldn't clean and dust all the time. It took me a couple of days to get used to it."

"I'm sorry for leaving you—"

"It's okay. I understand now why you had to."

He mussed her hair, and she squealed as he sought her mouth, relaxing in sweet surrender.

They went to bed early, talked about his trip and the impact of gravitomagnetic vehicles on the world at large. Deep into the night, he turned off the lights and Adriana snuggled against him. He closed his eyes and waited for the dreams to come.

He bounced out of the empty bed as dawn broke, not feeling any discomfort in his chest. A prod at the bruised area, the skin only slightly discolored. Taking several deep breaths, he stretched his arms and felt fine. He took a quick shower, shaved, and padded down the stairs, sniffing freshly brewed coffee.

Adriana messed with things in the kitchen.

"Morning, gorgeous," he said and kissed her cheek. "You're up early."

"I felt restless and couldn't sleep. What do you want for breakfast?"

"A couple of fried eggs will do. Want some toast?"

"I wouldn't mind."

He reached into a drawer and pulled out the toaster. "How's the shoulder and hip?"

"Both are still a little sore, but no headache. I keep wanting to scratch the bandage. It itches."

"Might be inflamed. Let me take a look."

He gently peeled away a corner. When she gave no reaction, he slowly removed the whole thing and gaped. Apart from three suture threads, the skin mildly red, but no scar.

"What is it?" she demanded.

"Your cut is almost completely healed," he told her in disbelief.

She touched her forehead and looked at him. "I hardly feel anything. How is this possible?"

He bit his lip and frowned, knowing exactly what happened.

"Remember the bloodwork Dr. Dalton did on you?"

"She said your macrophages infected me."

"There's your answer. We have the same blood type and Rh factor, and your body didn't reject my macrophages. They repaired your wound."

She reached for her mug of tea and took a large sip. "Goodness." Her head jerked toward him. "The baby!"

He grasped her shoulders. "Relax. If we had a problem, it would have shown up already. I'll talk to Dr. Dalton about your cut, though."

A sunny smile lit her face. "Maybe I should get myself tested again. Who knows, my epigenetic clock may also be frozen."

"Your head is frozen, my sweet!"

If his macrophages healed her wound, they were probably working on her hip as well. He would take her to the Institute for a full scan and find out everything.

She glared at him. "What's the matter? You don't like the idea?"

Startled, he pulled back. "Where the hell did that come from?"

Her face twisted in contrition and she reached for his hand. "I'm sorry. I don't know why I said that."

Did she subconsciously resent that he might live for a very long time while she wrinkled and sagged? Her outburst a simple hormonal reaction because of her pregnancy? *A slip of the tongue,* he told himself, and pushed it out of his mind.

"Let me sterilize the scissors and get those sutures out." He had seen what the nurse did when she snipped away the threads above his stomach. It seemed pointless to bother Dr. Anankos for something this trivial.

* * *

The nurse smiled and placed the cleaned and wrapped bundle into Adriana's waiting arms. Kevin immediately stopped his whimpering and promptly went to sleep. Andrew gave his wife a tender kiss, then pecked his son's forehead. She beamed at him and sniffed.

"Isn't he gorgeous?"

"Because you're gorgeous, my sweet," he told her tenderly.

It took them a while to settle on calling him Kevin. Andrew thought it suitably manly, and Adriana liked it, being her paternal grandfather's name. She ran a finger across Kevin's face. When she touched his lips, he opened his mouth and began to suck energetically. She looked at Andrew with a smile.

"Eager little man."

Kevin was indeed eager. Around six this morning, golden sunshine streaming through the bedroom curtains, Adriana gave a small yelp and pushed him.

"Rapid contractions have started."

He jumped out of bed, threw on some clothes, and led her slowly down the stairs. She only wore a nighty and a robe. The drive to The Alfred took only a few minutes. He did not speed, not wanting to do something stupid to endanger his wife and baby.

In labor for only twenty minutes, although it seemed much longer, the baby came out in a rush. Thankfully, Adriana had not been in much pain, something she confided to him earlier had worried her.

Looking at her, more radiant than he thought possible as she gazed at her son, he reflected on his own feelings. Immensely relieved that she and the baby were doing well, he felt pride seeing new life delivered into the world. Witnessing his son's birth, Adriana's hand in his, had been one of the most moving experience of his life. With the thing over, he unaccountably felt somewhat let down, expecting something more, not knowing exactly what. A natural reaction after the rush this morning?

Over the last two months, both their moms coached her in everything she needed to know about baby care. As far as his mom was concerned, she declared postnatal depression to be a lot of bunkum, something created by male psychiatrists to fleece ignorant young mothers. He wouldn't know. A happy mother made for a happy baby, she said. What a new mother needed most of all was a caring and supportive husband who would be there for her. Andrew took that to heart, determined to spend the next two weeks at home with his wife until she got used caring for the little guy. After that, shorter working days for a while. Whatever work he had, he could do from his home office. He did not want to repeat the mistake he made before.

Adriana's eyes sparkled as she smiled mischievously.

"Want to hold him?"

The idea of handling the little bundle, perhaps dropping the baby, sent him into momentary panic. She saw his reaction, laughed, and thrust Kevin into his arms. Startled how little he weighed, Andrew cradled the baby to his chest and grinned at the slumbering face. Kevin opened his dark blue eyes and stared blankly at him, then went back to sleep. He knew that newborns could not see very far, but he felt his son had peered into his soul.

"A few days of training and he'll be playing soccer," he declared.

"Dupe. Here, let me have him."

Safely in his mother's arms, Kevin continued to sleep.

Andrew reached for her hand. "Are you okay?"

"A little sore, but I'm fine. I feel happy about this. How about you?"

"I'll let you know after the little guy keeps us awake a few nights."

She chuckled and punched his shoulder. "That's mean. He's not going to give us any trouble," she said and gazed tenderly at the baby. "Are you, my little menace?"

Andrew thought that Kevin smiled, but probably only in his imagination. A new baby cannot smile, can it?

Shortly afterward, they transferred her to a private room. She took a shower and Andrew went home to pick up spare clothing and things, and a couple of books. He called his mom and Mrs. Teller and told them the news. They were all excited, having waited for this day with growing anxiety, Kevin decided he liked being in a cozy womb instead of facing a harsh world. He also rang Keith Sloan, who offered his congratulations, reminding him to bring cigars when he came in. Andrew laughed and hung up. He then rang his dad, but Markus was lecturing and he left a message. A call to Amanda Gregory with an apology that he would not be able to attend his scheduled scans finished the administrative tasks.

Carry-on in hand, Andrew took a detour to his study and jotted 9:43 am on the Monday, March 25 calendar page, grateful that Kevin chose a civilized hour for his birth. After a brief chat with Mark and Orwell, who promised to visit, he took an Uber cab rather than take his car to the hospital. Parking around there always a headache. He found a spot this morning only because he came early.

Expecting a son, looking after Adriana, he handled it. Having him actually born into a new world turned to be a different reality. And it was a new world, a changed world.

Maceroy's prediction that multinationals would attempt to block manufacture of GM vehicles turned into harsh fact. Within days of the announcement, powerful lobby groups were active in Washington, calling for a ban on politically, economically, and environmentally dangerous technology. Some claimed that GM vehicles would deplete Earth's magnetic field, leaving the planet vulnerable to solar radiation and cosmic rays. The claim patently ridiculous, but extremists and the gullible seized it to mount protest marches. Third-rate sensationalist media milked it for all it was worth. More responsible papers and commentators presented a measured, and generally positive, analysis.

Congressional members were in a bind. Many had important industries in their districts, and those industries expected payback for their support. GM vehicles would disrupt the existing status quo, and they did not like it. However, Congress was an elected body, put there by the people, and public sentiment remained enthusiastically behind Evagen, relishing the prospect of seeing entrenched multinationals taken down. The shortsighted, resource-wasting industry barons had done this to themselves, profiteering on the backs of expensive products designed to fail on the warranty expiry date.

Congress chose the middle ground and did nothing, allowing market forces to work. FAA and air traffic regulations would need upgrading, but building and use of GM craft did not require new laws. Some reporter wit asked if existing speed limits would apply to air traffic, which clearly needed clarification, but a problem easily managed by setting flight control parameters—once authorities defined them. Parking, one problem GM cars would not be able to solve. Andrew not sure if it could be solved.

Would urban transport survive, replaced by door-to-door Uber-type service? Would airlines survive? Why go through the hassle of getting to an airport, check in, wait for a scheduled flight, when an individual could fly his GM car from Melbourne to Sydney in ten minutes from his home? How would international Immigration and Customs regulations be enforced when that same individual could fly his car to LA for dinner in a couple of hours? Many people around the world were scratching their heads to come up with workable solutions to rapidly emerging issues brought about by GM vehicles.

The U.S. military-industrial complex were more forward thinking, forced to look at GM technology by Congress tired of pouring billions into weapons projects that always went over budget and took years to deploy, lobby pressure notwithstanding. Falzon told Andrew that Evagen already had cautious inquiries from leading auto and aerospace companies to license GM drives, including manufacture of room-temperature superconductor components.

Evagen was no prepared to license drive software, though. To make the drives work, third-parties must purchase BIOS circuit boards and flight control system from Evagen. Falzon admitted that someone would probably attempt to build their own BIOS software that managed the co-gravitational field. It was a business risk. China might be prepared to violate Evagen's patents to do it, but at a huge cost to its economy and international standing. The trade war with the United States had hit them hard, and prompted many industries to decouple manufacturing facilities. He doubted China would relish another round of worldwide sanctions. Still, being an authoritarian regime, anything was possible.

On Monday, March 4, Maceroy listed Evagen, Inc. on the New York Stock Exchange, offering the public fifty-eight million shares at $36.75, with the stipulation that no purchaser can hold more than ten million. This guaranteed that a single multinational or syndicate could not wrest control. Out of the total issue of one hundred million shares, Maceroy wisely kept thirty million for himself. His holding, investment by FutureTech and Evagen employees, gave him a 42% stake. His opponents would find it difficult to mount a hostile proxy takeover. Within two hours, the stock became oversubscribed a dozen times. At end of trading, it closed at $129.17.

Andrew did well for himself from the issue. In February, he netted sixteen million from movie studio licenses, and bought 200,000 Evagen shares at the opening price. He then made an immediate call option purchase of another 200,000, executed within six months, something he would be able to cover easily from game sales and dividends, his net worth now almost $195 million.

On the same day, FutureTech released *GM Flight* worldwide after a week-long promotional campaign. Not a full-sensor version—that would come later, but in ten days, the game sold more than 300,000 units. Everybody wanted to fly a GM ship in their living room. At eighty-six cents per unit royalty, Andrew looked forward to a handsome quarterly return, as did FutureTech, selling the game to distributors for forty-three dollars. With millions regularly coming in, he needed to put in some serious thought how to invest his income.

March 4 had a special, personal meaning for Masina. Piloting *Evagen-2*, she was the first woman to walk on the Moon, and Andrew stood beside her to plant the Australian flag next to the American one at the edge of Shackleton Crater, a proposed Evagen/SpaceX base at the lunar south pole. NASA received an invite to participate, but they were still in a huff sorting themselves out, their manned spaceflight program in disarray, Congress no longer willing to fund an organization that had largely lost its purpose for being. From now on, private industry would reach into the Solar System.

The trip back to the hospital passed with Andrew hardly noticing, his mind on Adriana.

He strode into her room and smiled at the sight of her breast-feeding.

"My little man is hungry," she explained.

He placed the carry-on on the floor and looked at her. "You know what happens after he stuffs himself?"

"You can have the honor of doing his first diaper change," she told him promptly and laughed at his apprehensive expression.

He did not look forward to the experience, or the certainty of many more to come. Part of the package, like his dad said.

"I got you some books."

"Thanks. That was sweet of you."

He pulled up a chair and sat down. "Are you all right?"

"Everything is fine. Women have done this for thousands of years, you know."

"That might be, but it's the first time for you. I called your mom. She said they'd come visiting. So will my parents."

"I know. I talked to her a few minutes ago." She tilted her head. "What about you? Are you all right?"

The question startled him. "Why wouldn't I be? I'm happy that you and Kevin are good, and I'm looking forward to being a dad. Except for the messy bits," he added.

She chuckled. "All part of the deal."

"That's exactly what my old man said."

"He ought to know." She turned serious. "You don't have to spend your time at home with me. I'll be fine, and you've got important things to do."

"Nothing is more important than being with you, sweetie, and I can do most things from my study. We'll talk, listen to music, watch movies, and take care of our son."

"Sounds nice."

A knock on the door and a nurse walked in. "Can you give me a few moments with your wife, Mr. Payne? I need to give her a checkup."

"I'll see you after lunch," he told Adriana and kissed her. He brushed the top of Kevin's little head and strode out.

Outside, the wind had died. Dark clouds were bunching overhead, promising rain. He walked down the steps and made his way along a busy sidewalk toward the taxi rank. Traffic clogged the street, but flowed steadily. A tram clanged its bell and clattered toward St. Kilda Road.

Someone clamped a moist pad across his mouth and he forced himself to hold his breath. It partially worked as his legs became rubbery. Two men dragged him toward a black van and bundled him in. He smelled antiseptic. Somebody after more tissue samples? They laid him down on a plastic-covered makeshift bunk and the van moved. It stopped a few minutes later. Tempted to open his eyes to see, he thought better of it.

"Take off his shirt," a very familiar voice ordered and blood drained from his face. It couldn't be! He had his suspicions, but never thought it would amount to anything. Another mosaic in his perfect world shattered.

Dr. Dalton wiped alcohol over his left side and he flinched when the scalpel bit into him.

"He's not fully unconscious," she observed clinically, voice devoid of emotion. "Make sure."

When he felt the moist pad against his face, he could not stop himself from breathing. Darkness descended and he sank into a bottomless void.

Gradually, sounds and feeling returned, and he blinked. Snug and warm in bed, he did not want to do anything or think about anything. It felt good simply lying there.

"Andrew?"

He turned his head and stared at the face in the next bed. "Adriana?" he managed to croak. He tried to sit up and winced at the tug of sutures in his side. "What happened?"

"They found you outside the hospital. They said someone in a black van left you on the steps. When the attending doctor found out who you were, they brought you here. How's your side?"

"Tender, but I'll recover," he told her grimly.

"What's the matter? You know who did it, don't you?"

"Dalton, my favorite doctor." He shook his head in disgust. "I still can't believe she did it."

After a knock, a nurse walked in. "Ah, awake. That's good. How are you feeling? Thirsty?" She poured him a glass of water and he drank eagerly.

"Let me check your side."

She pushed back his hospital gown and gently touched the area around the pressure pad.

"No inflammation. A clean incision and you shouldn't have any problems, but you'll be on antibiotics for a few days. There's a police detective outside wanting to talk to you if you're up to it."

"Show him in."

She nodded and opened the door. A tough looking Asian stopped beside the bed. "Your case has me puzzled, Mr. Payne. Are you able to make a statement?"

Andrew briefly sketched the events for him. The detective wanted more information, but Andrew could not enlighten him further. The cop placed the card beside his cellphone, wallet, and keys laid on the small bedside cabinet, and walked out.

Adriana stared at him. "Why didn't you tell him about Dr. Dalton?"

"I doubt he would understand epigenetic clocks, and I don't want to complicate things," he said and reached for the cell. He scrolled down the Contacts list, selected an icon and put the phone on the speaker.

"Lyndon Cancer Institute. Veronica speaking. How can I help you?"

"Hi, Veronica. This is Andrew Payne. I would like to speak to Professor Rhodes."

"Nice to hear from you again, Mr. Payne. Let me check if he's available." Background music filled the silence. "The Director will speak to you, sir."

"Mr. Payne? Professor Rhodes. What can I do for you?"

"It's about my case and the work Dr. Dalton did for me."

"Gail and I talk about you often."

"There is something you should know. This afternoon, she had me kidnapped and extracted a tissue sample from my side. This may be the second time she did that. This time, I recognized her voice."

"That can't be possible!"

"She has been collaborating with Broca Genetics to uncover how my epigenetic clock became frozen."

"Yes, I know about that."

"She urged me more than once to participate in her research. I provided blood and skin scrapings without question, but nothing else. It appears, she wanted much more."

"Gail is a dedicated scientist, Mr. Payne, and a key member of the Institute's research team. I cannot believe she would do something like this."

"I found it hard to believe as well, but what happened today cannot be brushed aside. Professor Rhodes, I will continue to support the Institute—"

"Your generous endowment last January has helped us a lot."

"—provided Dr. Dalton is dismissed and the sample she removed from me destroyed, and I'll want proof. If she isn't, the police will get a full statement of both incidents, and the Institute will face a lawsuit for damages. Your standing as a reputable research center will be trashed."

Rhodes gave a long sigh. "I can only imagine how you feel, Mr. Payne, and my apology for this deplorable incident is scant compensation. Let me assure you, I'll look into this and take appropriate action."

"When you do take that action, Professor, I want an email from you to that effect."

"This might take a few days while we follow the due process, but you'll get it, and I appreciate that you chose not to go public with this. If you're able to come and see me, I would like to discuss ongoing research into your case."

"I'll call Veronica for a suitable time. Goodbye, Professor."

"Goodbye, Mr. Payne," Rhodes said and hung up.

Andrew placed the cell on the cabinet and smiled at Adriana. "That should take care of my former favorite doctor. She didn't have to do it like this!" he snarled.

"You like her, don't you?"

"She saved my life, but it appears I was simply a challenging case for her. In her drive to help all humanity, she forgot the individual…me. I might not be her only victim."

"What's going to happen to her?"

He shrugged. "Her career is pretty much done. After this, no institution will take her. She might even lose her license."

"I kind of feel sorry for her."

"So do I, but she did it to herself."

"Do you think Broca Genetics had something to do with this?" she mused.

He bit his lower lip. "An interesting and not very pleasant thought."

How much would an immortality pill be worth to Broca? Cutting him up to find out might be worth sacrificing a little morality and ethics. Faced with the prospect of making untold millions, morality and ethics stood no chance. A decidedly odorous state of affairs, Mr. Payne.

"When is this going to end, Andrew? This time, Dr. Dalton. Who's next? Another company or some government agency? Will you ever have peace?"

He reached for her hand across the space between them. "We talked about this already, my sweet. I refuse to be frightened, but perhaps it's time I hired a security agency to look after us."

"What if they come after Kevin to ensure your cooperation?"

"Let's talk about this later, okay?"

She did not look reassured by his words, and neither was he. *Shait.*

* * *

Hands behind his head, Andrew watched dawn break. Thick silence held him suspended between night and the first glow of day. Nothing moved, as though the world held its breath. Adriana stirred beside him, her face serene and innocent. In the cot next to the bed, Kevin dreamed.

During the night, Andrew also dreamed. The vision eluded him, but he remembered floating endlessly in black deeps against a backdrop of stars. The stars eventually woke him. Unable to recapture the dream, he waited for the one star he knew to shine for him. Suddenly, the shadows fled and golden light flooded the room. He lay there, his thoughts soaring free. Time did not move, because he existed outside time. There was only the now, on and on, forever.

Would he go on forever, unchanging as the world changed around him? He had these moments of introspection before, but as he watched the play of shadow and light, a dust mote drifted into view and vanished. Was he also a dust mote, carried inexorably along the river of life, wondering when it would spill into an unknown ocean? Would he matter once he found himself in those deeps, sinking into perpetual darkness? He would not matter if he simply allowed himself to drift, not unless he cast his own light.

Uncertain what all this meant, he felt a shifting of purpose. What that purpose was, he could not say. All he knew, the things he had done so far were no longer enough. He knew the taste of success, but he felt dissatisfied. There had to be more. Was he really immortal? Would a day come when time would march for him again? It did not matter. He needed a new direction whether he lived forever or only another day.

Adriana sighed and her eyes fluttered open. "You're not sleeping. Problems?"

"Drifting."

She rested her head in the crook of his arm. "Take me to where you're drifting."

He smiled and stroked her cheek. "Everywhere…nowhere. Just drifting."

"Mmm. Sounds deep. You and Mark working on something new? Both of you spent a lot of time in your study lately."

"Tossing around an idea."

"About what?"

"When Trans Vis sent us the final production version of the full-sensor headset, it got me thinking. What if we could take the concept one step further?"

"What do you mean?"

"Connect the headset to a smartphone. Make calls, send emails and text, engage with the Internet, everything displayed in full VR and augmented reality."

"What's that?"

"It's where a VR headset allows a person to interact with projected images while seeing the real world around him. What I would like to do is dispense with the smartphone interface altogether and communicate directly with a cellphone base station. I don't know if this is even possible. It's one thing to stimulate a brain response through a headset, but to control something like a smartphone by thought alone might be tricky. We'd also need new software to make the system Android and iPhone compatible."

"It's a bold vision, Andrew."

"Mark said he's going to look at it, but I suspect it might take a full-blown research team to get anywhere with this. Elon Musk, Mark Zuckerberg, and Jeff Bezos worked on an interface concept for years, but they're looking at brain-chip implants, and there are lots of negative social issues involved with that. What I want is something less invasive."

"Mmm. I like what Trans Vis has done with the sensor headset. It's easy to wear, and I enjoyed playing some of FutureTech's games with it. When are they releasing it?"

They sent him four as a promo gift, impressed with the design. An elegant one-way visor similar to large polarized glasses mounted with audio ear pads replaced the bulky box used to enclose the eyes. A radical improvement from the clunky helmet Mark created when they started.

"Should be any day now from what Sergey tells me. Once it's out there, sale of GM cars and passenger vehicles can take off. The control system won't operate properly without it."

"Sounds like dull business stuff," she mused. "Since we're both awake, might as well have breakfast. You can use the bathroom first."

Andrew showered and crawled into a suit. He went downstairs and got things ready to make toast.

"Do you want scrambled eggs?" he yelled when he heard her coming down the stairs.

"I don't mind."

She placed Kevin in the bassinet next to the breakfast table and pulled two glass jars of baby food from the pantry. Andrew could not believe the kid already six months old. He tried the pureed fruit a couple of times, and liked it. The main meals stuff he found a little too bland for his taste.

Toast and eggs done, he served everything on the table, then prepared tea for Adriana and coffee for himself. Almost seven, he switched on the TV.

"This is ABC Breakfast, October 2, 2024. Good morning to all viewers joining us, this is Paul Norton. In breaking news, a Chinese guided missile destroyer rammed a U.S. 7th Fleet cruiser transiting through the disputed Spratly Islands, which claimed twelve U.S. lives. In response, the U.S. launched a strike against the Chinese Burgos Reef installation."

Andrew sighed and shook his head, not understanding why China persisted pursuing an aggressive foreign policy that only served to alienate the world against them, when cooperation would give them everything they wanted.

Adriana looked at him. "What do the Chinese hope to gain by doing these things?"

"Territory, access to oil and gas, and control of shipping lanes. They won't get it this way."

"Evagen, Inc. launched a ship to Psyche 16. Founder and managing director, Terrance Maceroy, said yesterday, the ship would reach the asteroid in thirty-seven days. It will then carry out a mineralogical survey."

The scene cut to Evagen's Phoenix facility. The craft, perhaps twenty meters in diameter, glided out of the enormous hangar, paused, and shot into a clear sky. Andrew knew Evagen was preparing for this flight, but did not know it would happen this soon. Trans Vis must have given them a batch of new sensor headsets to operate the ship.

"Wow. Thirty-seven days to the asteroid belt, that's fast," Adriana remarked, getting ready to feed Kevin.

"NASA claims the 200-kilometer asteroid is composed primarily of iron and nickel, with significant deposits of gold and platinum. If everything goes well, the ship is expected to return on December 14." Norton turned to his solemn co-host. *"Emilly?"*

Kevin did not appear to care much for the strained mush Adriana tried to shove into his mouth and kept squirming.

"Thanks, Paul, and a good morning to everybody. Mr. Maceroy created ripples of consternation in the energy industry when he announced release of an electricity generator based on a room-temperature superconductor. According to the Evagen founder, these generators will only become available once

we can manufacture cheap superconductors. This development promises to provide almost free power to the world, he said in a media statement, severing forever our dependence on nuclear and fossil fuel plants. Mr. Maceroy indicated he would license manufacture of his generator worldwide. Utility stocks took an immediate hit as investors surged to purchase Evagen shares."

"He has done it!" Andrew said with satisfaction and rubbed his hands, although he considered the announcement somewhat premature, given the chronic commercial shortage of lanthanum needed to manufacture superconductors.

Norton picked up the commentary. *"FutureTech, a leading U.S. developer of interactive virtual reality games, and developers of revolutionary flight control systems, in partnership with Trans Vis, a major VR headset provider—"*

"Hey! It's about you!" Adriana exclaimed, which made Kevin cry out.

"—launched an all-sensor headset, which will give users an experience indistinguishable from reality. The announcement came with the release of twelve all-sensor games. FutureTech and Trans Vis stock prices rose sharply following the announcements.

"General Motors and the Ford Motor Company said they will cease production of all petrol cars by July 2025, with a reduced capacity for commercial vehicles, as both companies prepare to roll out GM models. Volkswagen stated it is considering a similar move."

"Following approval by the U.S. Food and Drug Administration," Emilly continued, *"Broca Genetics, a Silicon Valley biogenetics firm, released a drug they claim cures Alzheimer's, Parkinson's, and general dementia. The drug is also supposed to extend life by up to ten years.*

"The details…"

Andrew picked up the remote and switched off the TV. He took a sip of coffee and turned to Adriana.

"Shait, everything seems to be happening today."

"It doesn't sound like Broca has found their immortality pill," Adriana said.

"And I'm glad."

"Still, it's a wonderful breakthrough. Did you know anything about this?"

"The trials with artificial macrophages were done about two months ago and I knew they were ready to start production. I didn't know they would get FDA approval this quickly." He gave her a speculative look. "You know, those pills would extend *your* life."

"No thanks. I'll let others try it first for a few years and see what happens." She cut a slice of toast in half, spread some of her mom's apricot jam on it, and took a bite. "Anyway, the only time I had dementia was when I decided to marry you."

"Maybe you still have it, since you haven't left me."

Her eyes turned deep green as she looked at him. "If I do, I don't want to be cured."

"We're crazy, both of us. You know that," he said softly as a wave of tenderness threatened to overwhelm him.

She gave him an impish grin. "You don't want to start something you cannot finish."

"So, I'll be a little late for work. Not that I'm thinking about work right now."

"Later. Those Evagen generators. I like the idea. No more power bills."

"You like it because you cannot hear utility execs scream as they jump out of tall buildings," he said wryly, and she laughed.

"Let them. They've been gouging us long enough." Ariana stuck a small glass bottle of highly diluted fruit juice into Kevin's mouth, which he sucked eagerly. The baby happy, she nibbled a piece of toast. "Can they pressure governments to ban them? Utilities must have untold millions invested in existing plants and transmission lines."

"I don't see how. They tried with GM vehicles and failed. Oh, I'm sure lobbyists will pressure politicians demanding protection, but I doubt they'll get far. This will be very popular with people, and it will take a brave government that tries to stifle it. If power companies are smart, they'll plug an Evagen generator into the grid and it'll be business as usual. We won't need long distance transmission lines, that's for sure," Andrew added and forked scrambled eggs on his toast. "We adjusted to GM vehicles. We'll adjust to this."

"I suppose. The greens everywhere ought to be pleased. They've been campaigning forever to abolish nuclear and coal-fired plants."

"They ought to, but don't be surprised if they start protest marches to preserve wind and solar farms. These people will never be satisfied until we turn all farms into prairies."

Adriana snorted and threw a piece of toast at him. "Dupe. Those generators, could they put them into appliances?"

"You mean, things like dishwashers and fridges? I suppose it depends on how much power a small unit can produce, if they can make it small. An interesting thought, though. Anyway, those things won't be around in any numbers for a while. Evagen will have its hands full supplying superconductors for their GM vehicles. Whatever lanthanum stocks China has, they'll want to keep for themselves as a political bargaining chip, unless Maceroy has stockpiled a supply. I would."

"Why don't they mine it from the Moon? You said there are plenty of rare earths up there."

"That's exactly what Evagen wants to do, and why they built their base. Not only to mine rare earths. The Moon is rich in other elements such as aluminum, magnesium, manganese, and things like titanium, oxygen, and hydrogen."

"Is Psyche 16 really made of gold and platinum?"

"I don't know, but it looks like Maceroy is determined to find out."

"What if he brings back a ton of gold?"

"Then he'll be richer than he is now."

"You're a degenerate, Andrew. How can you be so flippant about this?"

"He's not doing anything others won't be doing soon, and it will cost a fortune to set up mining on the Moon. The asteroid belt holds almost limitless resources. Resources Earth needs badly, but they're far away. Setting up a mining operation on the Moon is far more economical."

"Mmm. There's going to be a rush to mine the Moon and the asteroids," she added.

"You're right there. Don't forget tourism."

"I can imagine sitting in a restaurant up there, with Earth hanging above the horizon," she said dreamily. "It would be so romantic."

"When they put one up, we'll be among the first to go there," he promised.

"I wouldn't mind at all." She took a sip of tea. "Last night on the news, QANTAS said they're buying twenty Boeing GM aircraft to service the Melbourne/LA route."

"I haven't heard, but I'm not surprised."

Manufacture of conventional passenger jet aircraft had collapsed, as airlines worldwide canceled orders, preferring to wait for GM alternatives. Freed from complex design constraints imposed by aerodynamic flight, Boeing and Airbus were gearing to provide genuine passenger comfort instead of creating noisy cattle trucks everybody loathed.

Surprisingly, FAA and AESA did not hesitate to issue Level D certification for GM craft. Conventional aircraft are a nightmare of moving mechanical parts, all prone to failure. A GM ship by comparison was simplicity itself, needing only cabin climate control and waste disposal systems…more or less. One thing regulators were quick to jump on—control of international traffic. GM vehicles could only depart or arrive into a recognized geopolitical area from a designated Immigration and Customs point. It turned to be a relatively simple software upgrade to Andrew's flight control system. Years into the future, he envisaged immigration controls abolished altogether. Bio quarantine on the other hand a beast with different horns.

"I feel sorry for all those pilots who'll lose their jobs as passenger jets are phased out," she said and sipped her tea.

"They can always switch to driving GM ships," he said. "They probably won't get paid as much, as flying a GM vehicle is easy, but at least they'll have a job. There will also be a great demand for pilots once spaceships start rolling out. Bus drivers, actually."

"The world has changed a lot in the last six months," she reflected. "Evagen and SpaceX building bases on the Moon and Mars, GM cars and aircraft, and now free power. It's all good, I suppose, but it also created its share of misery. Jobs lost, businesses closed…"

"It's a price we always pay for progress," he mused.

"Sometimes, I feel the world is so heartless and uncaring."

"I can't argue with you there, because it is."

"Your full-sensor headset is likely to be a hit."

"I must admit, Trans Vis has done a great job for us. They didn't price it out of reach."

"At $325, I think it's pricy," Adriana said.

"It's not, and it will come down once they ramp up production. Remember, the headset is also needed to operate GM vehicles, not just games."

"You said that you and Mark get two percent from every headset sold?" Her eyes grew round. "With game and GM vehicle sales, you'll be looking at a monstrous income."

"We won't be doing badly out of it," he admitted and brushed Kevin's cheek. "Will we, buddy?" His son gave a happy gurgle and waved his arms. "He doesn't think so."

"How much is Usque Vision worth now?"

"Oh, around three hundred million."

She gaped at him. "Three hundred? What are you going to do with all this money?"

"It's not the money, but what you can do with it. Our portfolio gives me a voice in Broca Genetics and FutureTech. In time, it will allow me to invest in social programs. There are still a lot of people out there who don't have shelter or food, and water shortage is a growing problem everywhere. If you have ideas to help expand dental services, we could definitely look at it."

Adriana shrugged. "I'm wary of aid programs. Most of them fail because of corruption in the supply chain. It's all politically motivated anyway."

Andrew raised an eyebrow. "I didn't know you were so cynical."

"Dupe. You know what I mean."

He sighed and took a sip of coffee. "I'm afraid I do. We'll simply must find a way to help people directly. We need to support efforts where they can apply local knowledge to lift them out of the poverty trap."

She glanced at Kevin, fast asleep in her arms. She placed him in the bassinet and looked up, eyes bright.

"I have some news of my own. You're going to be a daddy again. I checked myself this morning."

Andrew felt a rush of heat surge through him, followed by a feeling of immense satisfaction. He stood and gathered her in his arms.

"I love you, gorgeous, and I couldn't be happier. Kevin will like having someone to play with," he said and kissed her.

"I'm glad you're happy about it. You'll know how to handle the next one better," she added mischievously.

He pulled back in mock surprise. "You mean, changing Kevin's diapers didn't cut it?"

She laughed. "You did all right. Anyway, he didn't give us much trouble."

It was true. There were some sleepless nights to begin with, but Kevin managed to sleep through most of the night after two months. There were occasional walking around sessions when a little out of sorts, but generally, he had been a healthy baby. Andrew understood why. When he infected Adriana with his macrophages, she in turn passed them to Kevin, and they were looking after him.

She jokingly thought that her epigenetic clock might be frozen, but a test at the Institute dispelled that once and for all. His macrophages were keeping her healthy, but she would have a normal lifespan. He had not changed at all, still looking like a twenty-five-year-old. He may look like one, but he felt old inside. He had done and experienced things others would not until their thirties or more, and his world view had become jaded with disillusionment. Jaded when he saw powerful leaders act like kindergarten kids, which led to disillusionment that sanity might never prevail. Knowledge and understanding merely served as a convenient cloak for the aggressive savage underneath, the club replaced by a missile. Would mankind survive to enjoy the fruits of his genius, or would mushroom clouds dance on the landscape?

"What's the matter?" Adriana demanded. "Why the long face?"

"Sorry. I wondered what kind of world we're going to leave our children."

"All we can do is make our little corner better," she said gravely. "If others do the same thing, in time it might not be such a bad world."

"I know, but I cannot help feeling that we're staring doom in the face."

"I refuse to believe that. Things are changing, and our generation is responsible for that change. The old reactionaries now in power, wedded to bankrupt ideologies, will eventually die and we'll take over."

"I want to believe that, but as long as parents keep indoctrinating kids with hotheaded beliefs, hatred will feed hatred."

She gave him a puzzled look. "You've been despondent and moody for a few days now. You're not having a relapse, are you?"

He smiled and shook his head. "No, it's not that. Just the opposite. Perhaps for the first time, I'm beginning to realize what it means to live for a long time, and I'm not sure I want to live forever, not when it means losing you, Kevin, our unborn child, and everyone I know. You'll be gone and I'll keep living and living. I don't want to, not without you."

"That was sweet, but you're missing the point," she said softly.

"What point?"

"We must live today like tomorrow might never happen. We love each other, and that's all that matters. You cannot assume the burden for the whole world. You have to leave a little room for yourself and us, for as long as either of us shall live."

He stared into her eyes. "You're wise, did you know that?"

"Because I'm also changed."

He gaped at her. He should have realized it before. His macrophages were roaming through her body, repairing, rebuilding, in the same way they were doing for him.

She nodded. "I tested myself. My IQ is up fifteen points," she said and grinned. "You're married to a genius, Mr. Payne."

"I've always known it," he murmured. "Did I tell you that I don't deserve you?"

"You did, but I decided I'll hang onto you anyway. It's kind of fun being with you."

Fun? If only she knew. He still could not get those mushroom clouds out of his head. Then again, perhaps he should give mankind some credit. The problem, he could not, remembering what the world did with GM ships. Instead of promoting social benefits, they weaponized the things.

Despite Adriana's bright outlook, he could not shake off the feeling that men were bastards. That's all there was to it.

Okay, so what are you going to do about it? Do? Go somewhere else.

The Moon…Mars perhaps, but men were there as well.

* * *

Christmas lunch at Adriana's parents' place left everybody bloated and giggly. A tall pine tree in the lounge room corner blinked colorful lights, branches festooned in cotton wool, glass baubles and hanging bonbons completed the decorations.

Over drinks, coffee and cakes, Andrew watched his dad argue passionately how the urban landscape would change when everybody owned a GM car. Adriana's dad countered energetically that things would remain the same for a long time. People liked their six or seven-hundred-meter blocks and distance from neighbors, and streets made that possible.

Andrew recalled a discussion he had with his dad about a paper to calculate safety parameters for construction materials used in high-rise buildings. His dad claimed that many architectural firms used dated tables and took safety and integrity shortcuts to satisfy builders' budgets. Thinking about it, he realized he had a market niche FutureTech could exploit.

Memory memo to self: Talk to Dad about creating a VR design package.

Kevin explored the living room in bursts of fast crawling, pausing when something entertaining caught his eye. The three moms quietly talked, Belana providing an occasional outrageous remark that would set them off.

A spiced rum in hand, he watched his family enjoying each other's company, and felt content. He had everything in life he could possibly want. He once offered them a million to retire on. They thanked him gravely, but refused. They were independent and provided for themselves. Should they need anything, they knew he would be there for them. Both accepted a hundred thousand, though, and took extended holidays, everything first class. They did not mind that at all.

Belana was equally difficult. He offered to buy her a house or luxury apartment anywhere she wanted. She turned him down, preferring to live at home for the time being. Independent and determined—it ran in the family—pursuing a career, she wanted to make it on her own. He approved and taught her how to invest in the stock market, encouraging her to buy FutureTech, Broca, and Evagen shares. She would never lose out, he told her, glad to see she converted her five million trust into stocks.

After several aborted affairs, she now went out with a young chemist. From what she told him, it might be serious. Andrew hoped it was, wanting his sister settled and happy like him.

On reflection, he realized he *was* happy.

Adriana lifted her head and their eyes met. She gave a faint smile and gathered Kevin from her mother.

Later that night, they did not say much as they lay together. Nothing needed to be said, their spirit one spirit. They had three weeks together before both returned to work. Only two days a week for Adriana until Kevin became used to having a babysitter look after him.

2025 rolled in with the usual fireworks display over the Yarra River and the city, accompanied with midnight revelry, hugs, and stolen kisses.

Adriana snuggled against him and he held her tight.

"Happy New Year, Mrs. Payne," he whispered. He fancied he saw her smile in the dark bedroom.

"Happy New Year, Mr. Payne. I hope it'll be even better than the last," she murmured, rolled on top of him and took him in.

A lingering, blissful time later, he sighed. "Can I do anything for you this year?"

"You just did." Her sharp fingernails marched playfully across his chest.

"Apart from that."

"I'm looking forward to our Hawaii trip in a GM aircraft. Honolulu…Waikiki Beach…Mauna Loa volcano…palms…hot beaches…"

"Not long now, my sweet. On Saturday, we're jetting off."

"You know, we should get ourselves a house in Cairns or somewhere like that. Much nicer than spending miserable winters in Melbourne."

"Not a bad idea. I'll talk to somebody and get one built."

"Remember the house we had in Fiji? Something like that."

"Done."

She propped herself on one elbow. "You mean it?"

"Why not? And you're right about Melbourne. There's no reason why we should freeze our butts here. Once we get our own GM car, we'll be able to get there in fifteen minutes."

"I'm still finding it difficult to wrap my mind around how air travel has changed. I won't miss check-in queues or waiting to board."

"It's still happening for international flights, but it's not as bad as it used to be."

"Smuggling will be a much more serious problem when someone can literally drop out of the sky."

"Well, not really. We'll fit every GM vehicle with a transponder that constantly transmits the driver's ID from the palm imprint. An update I did for Evagen. Authorities are able to see where it's going and who's driving it."

"I remember you saying something about that."

"Stealing a GM vehicle will be almost impossible. Some people won't like that feature, claiming Big Brother is always sitting beside them. You can argue it from both sides. One thing Evagen resisted, and I agreed with them, not to allow air traffic control and police forces the ability to take over the vehicle. That would take things a little far. It might happen if people don't rise up to check growing authoritarianism."

Adriana fell asleep, head on his shoulder. Andrew dreamed of swaying palms and black sands, with Pele standing over a belching volcano.

During breakfast, he chatted with Mark, while Adriana had a giggle with her longtime friend Susan, confirming their lunch date for tomorrow. Orwell called and they exchanged pleasantries, begging off on the lunch date at Mark's place. Somewhat sheepishly, he admitted he had a planned engagement. When Andrew pressed him for details, Orwell said he planned going to Apollo Bay for some surfing with someone he met two weeks ago at Anglesea on the Great Ocean Road.

"That someone a girl?" Andrew wanted to know.

"As a matter of fact, it is, and it's none of your business."

Andrew hooted with delight. "Of course it's my business. Go for it, man. It's about time you found somebody. Bring her over sometime, okay?"

He hung up, pleased that his friend might finally be settling down, and not be the odd one in the group.

In the background, the ABC presenter filled the lounge with background noise as Andrew helped Adriana clean up.

"Da!" Kevin yelled, waving his arms at the TV.

"What's the problem, little menace?" Adriana asked, wiping her hands.

Andrew leaned over the breakfast bench. "Listen."

"*...employed two GM strike fighters and bombed a Chinese radar facility constructed illegally on the* Bolshoy Pelis Island, *part of the Rimsky-Korsakov Archipelago in the Peter the Great Gulf, south of Vladivostok. For several months, China has sortied fishing boats into the Gulf, escorted by PLA Navy Coast Guard vessels, in an attempt to assert its claim over the Muravyov-Amursky Peninsula, citing that Vladivostok belongs to China, repudiating the 2008 Sino-Russian Border Line Agreement signed by both countries. Following the attack, Moscow positioned additional forces along the disputed southern border, warning Beijing that further encroachment into Russian territorial waters by Chinese fishing vessels would be met with deadly force. The details...*"

Adriana shook her head and sighed. "Great. What a way to start a new year. Turn it off, will you? I don't want my day spoiled with more stupidity."

A heavy frown on his face, Andrew picked up the remote and switched off the TV. It might be idiotic stupidity by China to annex more territory, but taking it from Russia a huge mistake.

Last September, Russia made angry protests to Beijing when the PLA began construction on Bolshoy Pelis Island, and the situation had been escalating since then.

Vladivostok used to be part of China in the Qing dynasty, until annexed in 1860 by the Russian empire after the Second Opium War. Despite several agreements, the latest in 2004, where China received numerous islands in the Peter the Great Gulf, apparently not enough. Andrew knew all this, as did everybody else, because of ongoing media coverage.

With almost free power and growing prosperity around the world, the Chinese Communist Party appeared bent on pursuing an aggressive foreign policy. A standoff between two ideologically intransigent nuclear powers not a welcome development for anybody.

Andrew preferred not to think about the consequence if either side pushed it to a confrontation. It would only give him nightmares.

Predictably, Russia and China were the lunchtime topic of discussion at his parents' place, which gravitated to looming water conflicts. The two-year-long drought still held northern Africa firmly in its grip. Egypt and Sudan were demanding that Ethiopia increase the discharge rate from its Renaissance Dam into the Nile to relieve a severe water shortage in both countries or face retaliation. Ever since construction began in 2011, the dam had been a source of increasing regional tension, without an acceptable solution in sight. Something else Andrew did not want to think about, determined to enjoy his lunch.

After a round of hugs and promises to visit soon, he drove to Fawkner Park and left the car opposite the oval. A warm northerly stirred leaves and branches. Young families clustered beneath trees, enjoying their picnics. Kids chased each other, yelling and screaming. A group played a cricket game.

Adriana looked at him, Kevin on her hip, a handful at nine months. "Any special reason why we're here?"

He glanced at his watch, almost three. "You'll see," he said and walked toward an empty clearing.

Suddenly, kids stopped chasing each other and pointed at the sky. He glanced up and smiled at his wife's puzzled expression.

Evagen-2 descended slowly, paused, and rested on her runners some four meters away. The hatch opened and he tugged at Adriana's arm.

"Let's go."

Several youngsters began to run toward them, with some adults following.

A familiar figure stood in the hatchway and smiled. "Hi, I'm Masina, the bus driver. Nice to meet you at last, Adriana," she said and took Kevin from her hands.

Andrew climbed in after his wife and the hatch cycled shut.

"Happy New Year," he said and pecked Masina on the cheek.

She hugged him. "Likewise. It's good to see you again." She opened the inner airlock door and they strode into the cabin. "Welcome aboard," she said brightly, then laughed at Adriana's confused expression. "Please sit down and we'll be on our way." She took the left pilot seat and put on the sensor headset.

With a clear 360-view through the transparent bulkhead, Andrew saw a small crowd gathered around the craft. The ship lifted a little and everybody fell back. With a surge, they were streaking through a clear sky. In moments, it turned purple, then black, and Earth curved beneath them in glaring brightness.

"A supply run," Masina explained cheerfully and hooked a thumb at cartons and metal boxes packed behind six passenger seats.

"Supply run?" Adriana asked, tearing herself from the view, Earth fast receding.

Masina glanced at Andrew. "He didn't tell you?"

"Tell me what?"

"In two hours, we'll be on the Moon."

Andrew wished he had a camera to capture his wife's expression. He remembered his cellphone and took a couple of quick snaps.

She fisted his shoulder and glared. "You're a degenerate."

He shrugged. "I thought you would like to have dinner on the Moon. Breakfast really, as the base is on Greenwich time."

"We'll be there around eight o'clock," Masina added.

"I can't believe you did this to me," Adriana groused, but she could not hide the gleam of excitement in her eyes, then her face froze in consternation. "What about Kevin? I don't have anything for him."

Masina smiled and pointed at a brown leather carry-on beside the airlock. "Everything you need is in there, including warm milk."

Adriana glanced at her son, who observed his surroundings with intense interest.

"He doesn't look like he minds taking a little trip into space," Andrew remarked. "Do you, my man?"

Kevin gurgled and waved his arms.

"I didn't think so."

"Come up front, Adriana," Masina prompted.

"Shouldn't we clear Immigration or something?" Adriana queried.

"I took care of things at Melbourne Airport. Technically, you're not making an international flight, so clearance isn't called for, but I'm sure they'll get around to flights like this sooner or later. Before we know it, we'll be hip deep in regulations."

Adriana put on the headset and gasped at the full-sensor view.

Andrew left the two women to chat while he entertained his son.

He watched the Moon grow, then shift as the ship headed for the Shackleton Crater. The reason they built the base there, Masina said, the crater had ice pockets, which made managing the base much easier. *Evagen-2* slowed and drifted above a gray, pockmarked moonscape toward the terminator. Four white interconnected habitat blocks nestled against the crater wall. One ran a connector straight into the wall. Beside them, a half-clad skeleton of a much larger structure cast black shadows. Two suited men were maneuvering a wall panel suspended from a crane. They paused and looked up.

The ship moved toward a lit landing pad and settled. Not far off, he saw two small excavators move regolith into conical piles.

"We had to use *Evagen-3*'s cargo hold to get them here," Masina explained. "We'll be bringing up larger equipment in a few days for serious mining."

"What are they doing?" Adriana asked.

"Sampling surface material for minerals. This site is particularly rich in rare earths and light metals. Until the electric smelter is built, we'll ship ore to Earth for final processing. SpaceX is constructing a bulk carrier for us. Setting everything up is a little more complex than digging iron and nickel from Psyche 16."

Adriana stared. "You were there?"

"An interesting trip."

"They said you brought back two tons of gold and platinum."

"Plus a few other things, but the reports are right," Masina said with a grin. "This place still needs a lot of investment before it becomes a full-blown commercial facility. Mars is also rich with rare earths deposits. That's why we set up a base there, but it's at the end of a very long logistical pipeline, and the Moon is much closer."

"Those workers, they're up early."

"The crew, six men and five women, work two five-hour shifts, starting at six. They're here for ten days, with five off on a rotating schedule. Once everything is built, this place will house thirty. Plans are already on the drawing board to build Evagen Resort to house technical staff, administration, and tourists, but it won't happen for a while."

What looked like an airport air bridge rolled toward them from the crater and mated to the hatch with a clang.

"The four habitats out in the open are mainly storage and workshops facilities, courtesy of SpaceX. We dug the living quarters into the crater and covered everything with a layer of regolith as protection against micrometeorites and radiation. Without the connecting tunnels, it would be a nuisance having to suit up all the time." Masina stood and walked to the airlock. "Let's go."

The habitat manager and chief engineer, who reminded Andrew of Dr. Erica Stern, met them inside the lock, and led them to what they jokingly referred to as the dining hall. Everything had a rough, unfinished look, but the manager gushed enthusiastically about the facility. Others began to drift in, and introductions were exchanged all around. The women crew clustered around Adriana, cooing over Kevin, who appeared nonplussed by all the attention.

Everybody welcomed the lavish brunch brought by Masina, and conversation flowed freely, as did the wine. Andrew was surprised that nobody showed much interest in the latest events on Earth, much more enthusiastic about their own work and getting the facility fully operational.

Watching them, he saw a group of young men and women filled with enthusiasm, vision, and determination to succeed. They had a new world to mold, and nothing would stop them. For them, this was tomorrow, not the mundane day-to-day things and silly politics back on Earth. Most said once they built the Resort, some would not mind relocating permanently.

After a couple of hours, Andrew and Adriana said their goodbyes. Cargo unloaded, *Evagen-2* decoupled and they headed Earthward.

"They're very nice people," Adriana told Masina.

"SpaceX helped us getting crews. They already had a highly motivated group of employees who wanted to see the company lead manned spaceflight. Our GM vehicles left them understandably shattered. Everything they worked on for years suddenly meant nothing. When Mr. Maceroy proposed a partnership to build and man his Moon and Mars bases, they never hesitated."

"Some said they were prepared to live permanently on the Moon. Are they serious?"

"It won't happen for a while, but once the Resort is up, and the place becomes more self-sufficient, I wouldn't be surprised if some of them decided to stay for a few months at a time," Masina said and smiled. "They might love the challenge, but Earth is still home."

Evagen-2 landed at Fawkner Park to a warm night. After the canned habitat atmosphere, Andrew enjoyed taking several deep breaths of scented air. Adriana and Masina hugged, and the ship vanished among the stars.

With Kevin slumbering in his arms, they walked across the grass to where they left the car. Adriana slipped an arm around his waist and leaned her head against his shoulder.

She did not have to say anything else.

Chapter Eleven

Cool water slithered up golden sands and receded with a hiss. Gulls glided overhead looking for scraps thrown their way. When someone tossed a morsel, they would swoop down with screeching cries and a tangle of wings until one of them snagged the tidbit and took flight, with others in squawking pursuit.

The air still and hot, St. Kilda Beach offered an oasis from everyday bustle and city grind. Only mid-morning, the shore had filled quickly. People staked out their piece of sand with colorful towels and broad umbrellas. Coolers and hampers provided refreshment after a brisk swim or frolic in the shallows. Behind the beach, cars and an occasional tram clattered along Jacka Boulevard lined with hotels and condominiums. Far on the right, Melbourne's spires climbed into a clear sky.

Kevin splashed in a little pool Andrew dug for him in the sand, spluttering occasionally when salty water got into his eyes and mouth. The first time he had ever seen the sea, smelled iodine-laden air, and attempted to toddle through rippling surf, Andrew holding his arms. After a hesitant start, he decided he liked it.

Adriana waded through the shallows, striking in a white bikini, not showing a belly bump after only three months. She patted down her platinum hair, and flopped on the towel beside him. He smiled at her, then yelped when she flicked cold drops over him. He longed to be out there with her, fooling around, enjoying the feel of water running over him, but someone had to look after their boy. In the shade of a beach umbrella, clad in trunks and shirt, he watched his wife embrace the sea and felt her delight.

Kevin dropped his little orange bucket and crawled toward her. She picked him up and held him high. He crowed enthusiastically, his little legs kicking the air.

"Your daddy taking care of you?"

Kevin glanced at Andrew and extended his hand, making pleased gurgles.

"How's the water?" he asked.

"Nice. If you want to go for a swim, I'll look after our little menace." She nuzzled the baby's chest. "Because you're a menace, aren't you?"

Kevin agreed with a broad smile.

Andrew stood, patted sand off his trunks, and ran into the water, spray flying everywhere. Once up to his waist, he plunged in, his powerful strokes taking him out quickly. When he started to feel the strain, he turned on his back and stared at the sky. It seemed endless, going on forever. High above, the Moon shone as a thin sliver of white. The sea cradled him and he allowed himself to drift, wanting nothing, because he already had everything. After a time, he slowly swam toward the shore.

He knelt beside Adriana and gathered her hot body against his cold skin. She gave a squeal of protest and pounded his back with small fists. This drew indulgent smiles from people around them. Kevin gave a little cry, not sure what happened. Andrew let her go and picked him up.

"Don't worry, my man. We're just fooling around."

Adriana slapped his arm. "Dupe."

He lay on the thick towel, hands locked behind his head, and listened to the screeching gulls and the chatter of beachgoers.

"Da!" Kevin yelled and sat up. His little man content, continued to make a mess of the sand castle on the edge of his little pool.

Adriana rummaged through the hamper. "Want a drink?"

"Sure," he said, and she held out a plastic bottle of fruit juice. Kevin saw this and immediately lifted his arms. "Da!" Adriana picked him up and stuck the nipple of a small bottle into his mouth.

"Greedy guts," she murmured fondly.

They walked to the end of St. Kilda Pier and gazed at Melbourne's skyline. Fluffy clouds hung low on the western horizon. Several adventurous fishermen were trying their luck, but judging from the empty buckets, the fish were not in the mood to cooperate.

With Kevin straddling Andrew's neck, kicking his chest, they made their way back to catch a tram into the city, not wanting to be late for their lunch date at Mark's place. As they approached the boulevard, away from the sea breeze, the air became thick and hot, laced with the stink of petrol.

They joined a group at a crossing opposite the tram stop, waiting for the lights to change. A young couple started to walk when they turned green, and he automatically turned his head to check for traffic and heard a car horn blare. A battered blue sedan swerved to avoid the couple and roared through, the laughing young driver giving them the finger. The girl next to him also thought it hilarious.

"That idiot could have killed them!" Adriana protested in outrage.

Andrew shook his head, not trying to understand it. Some youngsters saw driving as a license to cause mayhem, oblivious to the consequences should someone get maimed or worse. What concerned him, they did not appear to care, thinking it was all a game.

A tram clanked its bell and sighed to a stop. Andrew tapped his Myki against the sensor and eased himself down on a seat in the almost empty car. Adriana sat beside him, took Kevin off his hands, and shivered.

"A little cool in here. I hope Kevin doesn't catch a cold."

The air-conditioning seemed determined to turn everyone into an icicle. The doors snapped shut and the tram moved off with a whine. Whether on automatic or the driver turned it down, the wintry blast subsided to a comfortable whisper. They changed trams at Chapel Street, which took them to Toorak Road. From there, a short walk home. A shower and a change, and they were good to go.

With Kevin safely strapped into his seat, Andrew reversed his Mazda 3 out of the garage, and they were off. Adriana fiddled with the radio settings and settled on some FM jazz. With all his millions, he could get himself a gold Lamborghini if he wanted. The thought repelled him. His comfortable Mazda worked fine and served him well. A Lamborghini would not get him around any quicker, not in the city. He could not see the point of having a car that could go more than two hundred K an hour, when he could not drive it that fast anywhere. A stretch of ruler-straight highway did exist between Alice Springs and Darwin in the Northern Territory that did not have a speed limit, and hotheads used it. It seemed pointless for him to drive all the way up there simply to kill himself, or have someone smear him across the desert. Besides, a Lamborghini had concrete seats made for show, not comfort.

He would stick with his reliable Mazda until he got himself a GM car.

The roads were almost deserted, most people having fled for a holiday destination. On Saturday, only two more days, he and Adriana would be doing the same thing.

It did not take long to reach Elwood. Andrew turned into Beach Avenue past the golf course and motored at fifty along a quiet, stately street lined with terrace houses, 1930s brick veneer residences, and modern condos. He entered a broad driveway of a recently renovated double-story mansion and stopped in front of a large garage. They got out and smelled the sea, only a couple of hundred meters down the road.

Mark opened a heavy polished wood front door and beamed.

"Welcome to my humble abode, guys!" He gave Andrew a tight hug, pecked Adriana on the cheek, and made cooing noises at Kevin, who smiled indulgently at this juvenile behavior.

Susan appeared and wrapped Adriana in her arms. "Glad to see you." She smiled at Andrew and gave him a hug. "And how's the little menace?" she asked, taking Kevin into her arms.

"He's had an exciting morning at St. Kilda Beach, and I expect him to crash out soon," Adriana told her.

"Let's get out of the heat," Mark said and pulled at Andrew's arm.

With the two million he got from FutureTech, and another million from Andrew for an extra helmet, plus ongoing sensor headset royalties, Mark and Susan were doing well. Not in the same league as Andrew, but his friend had never shown any resentment that Andrew had considerable wealth.

Adriana glanced at her friend. "How long now?"

"Ten weeks. The little monster is kicking and wants out."

Adriana laughed as they walked into the spacious open plan lounge. Similar to Andrew's place, except here the kitchen lay on the left side.

Mark and Susan made a contrasting pair. Tall, he towered over his wife, a slim, petite woman. Looking at them, Andrew could tell Mark was totally devoted to her. If Orwell could find someone, their get-togethers would be boisterous parties every time.

Kevin crawled happily on the floor, exploring every cranny. Susan pulled Adriana into the kitchen and the two lost themselves in girl talk.

"Can I get you something?" Mark asked, standing beside the liquor cabinet. "Bourbon or rum, I have both."

"Make mine bourbon, no ice," Andrew said as he settled into a leather couch.

"Too bad Orwell couldn't join us," Mark said.

"A hot date, I understand. Do you know anything about her?"

"Only her name; Romana." Mark held out a crystal tumbler and grabbed a seat opposite him. They clicked glasses and Andrew took a sip. "Did you see the news this morning?" Mark queried.

"I haven't been watching. What's going on?"

"Egypt attacked Ethiopia's Renaissance Dam with a flight of MiG-27 Floggers."

Andrew sat up in surprise, wild images of destruction and flooding cascading through his mind. "You're shitting me."

"Made a mess of the electricity generating plant and damaged three release gates. Water's pouring out unchecked."

"Shait. A hell of a way to start a new year."

"That's not all. Ethiopian Air Force jets retaliated with a strike against the Aswan Dam. The dam is okay, but they pretty much flattened the surrounding infrastructure, which is going to leave half of Egypt without power. According to the news, the Ethiopians lost three of their Su-27 Flankers."

Andrew sighed and shook his head. "Somehow, I always knew this would happen. With a prolonged drought over there, Sudan and Egypt were pleading with Ethiopia for months to release more water."

"They needed the water for themselves. After the spat between Russia and China near Vladivostok, the world's gone crazy," Mark added glumly.

"Two weeks ago, the United States demanded that China dismantle all remaining bases created on artificial reefs in the South China Sea, or the 7th Fleet would do the job for them."

"I wish them luck. After what happened in the Spratly Islands last October, things are hotting up. The world has grown weary of China's belligerent international policy, and everybody is happy for the U.S. to do the dirty work, knowing the Security Council will never do anything about it."

"That's all we need," Andrew said. "More brushfire wars."

Mark wagged a finger at him. "What happened in Ethiopia a little more than a brushfire, my friend. The loss of generating capacity will hit them and their neighbors hard. Looks to me like we're at a major escalation tipping point, especially if the U.S. follows through on their threat to clean out the Chinese out of the South China Sea."

"It won't come to that," Andrew mused. "The Chinese will make a deal. They'll have to. The West has dismantled hundreds of manufacturing plants over there, finally realizing that short term profits aren't worth giving away their technology and intellectual property rights."

Mark snorted. "Too little, too late, I'd say. The Chinese don't need to steal Western technology anymore, when their cyber hackers were getting it for them. Evagen hasn't exactly done the world any favors by giving away the GM drive to everybody."

"They had no choice, Mark. Either that or risk creating a very volatile geopolitical climate."

"I guess, but it still sucks."

Susan walked in from the dining room. "Enough of this gloomy talk, you two. Lunch is ready."

Andrew walked in and sat beside his wife, with Kevin in a baby seat next to her, sucking on a bottle. Susan placed a tureen on the table.

"Pumpkin soup," she announced. "Help yourselves to the croutons," she added and nodded to Andrew. "Please…"

He filled his plate, added crispy croutons, and had a taste. The crunchy croutons added a nice burnt flavor to the pumpkin's nutty taste.

"This is great."

"She uses different pumpkins to change the flavor," Mark explained, helping himself, and leaned toward him. "She can't make much else."

Susan threw a crouton at him. "You'll pay for that, you brute."

"Andrew likes…" Adriana began, and her face lost all color. Blood oozed out of her nose and she slowly toppled to the floor.

Andrew jumped to his feet and knelt beside her. She lay on her side, which removed the risk she might drown in her own blood. He snatched the napkin off the table and pressed it against her nose.

"Call an ambulance!" Susan yelled at Mark and grabbed Adriana's hand. "Her skin is icy, and the pulse is erratic."

Kevin sensed something wrong and began to cry.

Andrew picked up his wife, carried her into the lounge, and placed her on the couch. Susan rushed in and covered her with a blanket.

"Has this happened before?" she demanded.

He shook his head. "Never."

"Looks like anaphylactic shock."

Her words struck a memory chord. "Has she eaten anything unusual while you two were in the kitchen?"

"Well, I mixed some marzipan into a cake filling and she had a bite. She also had some almonds. Oh, God, you don't think—"

"She isn't allergic to almonds, but they're not something she eats," he said. Why now, my sweet, he asked himself. The festive atmosphere, being with her friend, she probably forgot.

"She never told me—"

He patted her arm. "Don't worry about it." He looked down at Adriana and bit his lip. Although she had a slight flush, no visible swelling around the lips or a rash. He tucked the blanket higher under her chin and stroked her clammy skin. His heart hammered with concern, helpless to do anything for her.

He heard a wailing sound, rapidly coming closer. The ambulance pulled into the driveway and Mark rushed to open the front door for the female paramedic. Her partner opened the back door and pulled out a gurney.

"What happened?" she asked, checking Adriana's pulse, then took her temperature with a scanner.

"She started to bleed from the nose and fell unconscious," Andrew told her.

"Any history of seizures or other neurological problems?"

"Nothing."

Her partner wheeled in the gurney and Andrew helped him put Adriana on it. He dug out his key ring and held it to Mark.

"I'm going with her. Can you take care of Kevin for me?"

"Of course. We'll be right behind you."

Andrew turned to the paramedic. "Where are you taking her?"

"The Alfred."

Inside the ambulance, the paramedic fixed an oxygen mask over Adriana's face and hooked her to a monitor. The siren's sharp wail set his teeth on edge as the ambulance raced down the street. He took Adriana's hand and stroked it.

The drive to the hospital seemed to take forever. He wanted to take his wife into his arms and hold her against him, wanting his strength to flow into her, wanting her pain to be his pain. The thought of losing her knotted his insides. He did not want to live if it meant empty, lonely days without her.

He glanced at the monitor tracing wiggly lines. "How is she?"

The paramedic frowned. "Her pulse is weak, and heart action is irregular. I gave her an epinephrine shot, which stabilized some of her vitals, and the oxygen has eased her breathing."

The ambulance pulled into the Emergency parking ramp and they wheeled Adriana inside. Andrew stood there feeling somewhat foolish. An orderly in green garb walked toward him.

"They took your wife to Intensive Care. Please come with me and we'll sort out the admission procedure."

He got the formalities out of the way, made easier when he told them Adriana had been a patient, and they advised him to wait in the outpatients' room. Only then he noticed other people coming and going, all wearing grim expressions. Well they might.

The air had a sickly antiseptic smell, and he wrinkled his nose. He turned and began walking toward the waiting room.

"Andrew!"

Mark and Susan hurried toward him. Kevin's face lit up when he saw him.

"Da!"

Andrew took him from Susan's hands and held him close.

"What's going on?" Mark asked.

"She's in Intensive Care. That's all I know." Andrew grasped his friend's arm. "Thanks for coming. Sorry to spoil lunch for you like this."

"Don't be a schmuck. I only hope it's nothing serious," Mark said, clearly concerned. Susan looked like she was about to cry.

They found seats in the crowded room, attracting normal looks of vacant interest. More victims.

"Look, guys, I don't know how long this is going to take. You don't have to hang around, you know."

"We want to know what's going on too," Mark told him gruffly and held out the key ring. "We came in your car. If we hadn't, you'd have no way of getting into your house."

Andrew managed a faint smile. "Thanks. You removed my number one worry in life."

Sometime later, he did not know when, an elderly bald man wearing rimless glasses walked into the waiting room.

"Mr. Payne?"

Andrew looked at Susan. "Would you mind?"

She took Kevin off his hands. "He'll be fine with us."

Andrew nodded and walked quickly toward the man.

"I'm Dr. Bremmer," he said and held out his hand.

Andrew shook it. "My wife—"

"She's resting comfortably, but she is still unconscious, which is of some concern. Her EEG shows she is not comatose, but we cannot bring her out of it. I consulted with two colleagues, and the only conclusion that makes any sense is that your wife is suffering from an autoimmune response. We're doing bloodwork which should tell us more."

Andrew told him about Adriana's aversion to almonds.

Dr. Bremmer frowned and pushed up his glasses. "Her symptoms aren't indicative of a severe allergic reaction, but we'll test for that. This is not conclusive, as we haven't finished our tests, but Pathology said your wife has unusual macrophages in her blood. Do you know anything about that?"

Andrew stared at him. Were his macrophages attacking her for some reason?

"In 2021, I contracted polypoid melanoma," he said slowly. "I was cured with tailored macrophages, which I later passed to my wife."

Dr. Bremmer's eyes went round. "Broca Genetics, right? I read articles about your case. This could explain her condition and gives me something to work with. Mr. Payne, I don't know how long it will take to analyze the tests, but you might as well go home. I'll call you when we have something."

"I want to be with her," Andrew told him bluntly.

Dr. Bremmer nodded. "Very well. Come with me."

"One moment." Andrew walked to Mark and Susan. "Adriana is stable for now. They're running some tests, and it might be a while before they know more. I'll call my mom, and she'll take care of Kevin."

"We don't mind looking after him," Susan said.

"Thanks, I appreciate that, but my mom is used to having him around, and she has all the stuff to look after him."

Kevin reached toward him with both arms, and he took him. "I'll call you as soon as I know anything," he promised.

"You do that," Mark said. "Take care."

Andrew shook hands and gave Susan a hug.

Dr. Bremmer took him to the fourth floor ICU room and pulled back a yellow curtain. Adriana lay on her back connected to a monitor and a drip tube, a mask over her face.

"Da!" Kevin cried when he saw her.

Andrew stared at Adriana's pale features for a long time before he pulled a chair and sat down. He dug out his cell, scrolled down the Contacts list, and pressed the call icon.

"Hi, Andrew. How are you?" his mom answered cheerfully. "Your dad and I are in the backyard having cold drinks. Why don't you two come over if you're not doing anything?"

He took a deep breath and exhaled. "I'd love to, Mom, but I have a situation on my hands. It's Adriana. She's in Intensive Care at The Alfred. Can you come over and take care of Kevin for a while?"

"What happened?"

"The doctors are trying to find out. She's okay, though."

"We'll be right there."

He stared at the phone, then pressed another icon. It took tree rings before her crisp voice answered.

"Dr. Masters."

"It's Andrew Payne, Ivone. My apologies for disturbing you this late, but there's an emergency."

"What's going on, Andrew?"

He quickly sketched out the situation for her. "What I need to know, could the macrophages I passed to my wife have triggered this adverse immune system response?"

"She hasn't shown any negative reaction to the macrophages in over two years, but it's possible that a mild allergic reaction by her body when she ingested the almonds probably elicited an aggressive response when the T lymphocytes were activated. I'll call Dr. Bremmer and discuss the case with him."

"I don't know how to thank you, Ivone."

"If her macrophages are responsible for the autoimmune attack, The Alfred might not have the necessary facilities to treat her."

"The Lyndon Cancer Institute has."

"They have the facilities, but not the expertise."

"If necessary, I can have my wife flown to Sunnyvale in a couple of hours."

There followed a moment of silence. "Your relationship with Evagen? Let me talk to Dr. Bremmer and I'll call you."

"Thanks again," he said, and she hung up.

He sat back and sighed, pushing back worst-case scenarios. No use trying to understand why Adriana's macrophages went into such an aggressive mode, if in fact they were responsible. It might be something else altogether. He had seen her eat almonds before, or had he? They ate all sorts of nuts every now and then, but as far as he could remember, they did not have almonds in the house.

Kevin squirmed in his lap, wanting to be let down. Ordinarily, they allowed him to crawl anywhere in the house or at Mark's place, knowing the floors were clean. Here, only gods knew who walked through this place.

He saw his mom and dad come in and called out. Kevin happily snuggled into his grandmother's arms.

"This is so awful, Andrew. Any news?"

He shook his head. "Nothing, Mom. It's driving me crazy."

"What happened?" his dad asked.

"We were at Mark's place having lunch when Adriana suddenly went pale and keeled over unconscious. It could be an allergic reaction to some almonds she ate. The doctor here doesn't know and they're running tests to find out."

"I guess you won't be flying to Hawaii on Saturday."

"Looks that way. She so looked forward to that trip. It's a delay, nothing more. I'll reschedule. Sorry to spoil the day for you guys, dragging you here."

"Pfui! Don't be silly." His mom waved a dismissive hand. "We weren't doing anything anyway."

A few minutes later, Dr. Bremmer walked in and Andrew stood up.

"I have your wife's results, Mr. Payne, and I just finished talking to Dr. Masters. She could not tell me definitively what may have triggered your wife's autoimmune response, but her suggestion to apply an inhibitor to block T lymphocyte signals confirmed my own diagnosis. I administered a corticosteroid, which had an almost immediate relieving effect. Your wife is conscious and you can see her. We'll keep her in intensive care for the next twenty-four hours to make sure her immune system settles down completely before moving her to a regular ward for observation."

"How long will she be here?"

Dr. Bremmer adjusted his glasses. "If she continues to improve, I could discharge her on Sunday."

Andrew stuck out his hand. "Thanks, Doc. I appreciate what you've done," he said as they shook hands.

Adriana smiled broadly when Andrew walked in and opened her arms. He leaned over her and she held him tight. A lingering kiss dispelled the mists of anxiety around him, his heart dancing to see her smile.

"You gave me a fright, you know," he murmured tenderly and brushed her cheek.

"I still don't know what happened. One minute, I was having soup, then everything went gray." She waved to his parents. "Hi, Ethel…Markus."

"How are you, dear?" his mom asked.

"Tired, like I've run a marathon and then someone beat me up." Kevin gurgled and flapped his arms. "Come here, you little menace."

"Da!"

Adriana wrapped her arms around her son and cooed to him.

Andrew's phone went off and he pressed the accept icon. "Hi, Ivone."

"How's your wife, Andrew?"

"Dr. Bremmer gave her an immune inhibitor and she's much better, thanks to you."

"I discussed her condition with two of my colleagues. We think we understand what happened, but not why. We're working on it. If you can arrange it, I would like you to bring your wife to our facility for testing. We need to understand why her macrophages overreacted, and if possible, do something about it before they cause a potentially fatal response in the future."

Andrew did not relish turning his wife into a lab specimen, but appreciated the need to find out the cause.

"I'll get the hospital to send you before and after blood samples, and I'll talk this over with her," he told her.

Dr. Masters laughed. "Are you still afraid that I want to experiment on *you*?"

"The thought had crossed my mind."

"Don't worry, Andrew. Broca has given up trying to replicate your macrophages. Seriously, though, your wife might still be in some danger, and I would like to do a complete workup on her."

"Thanks again for everything, Ivone."

"My pleasure. Talk to you later," she said and hung up.

Andrew turned to Dr. Bremmer. "I suppose you heard?"

"I'll courier the samples to Broca right away. This has been a most enlightening case. If you don't mind, Mr. Payne, I would welcome an opportunity to discuss your situation at some depth."

"I don't know what I can tell you that you haven't already read. If you want to find out more, talk to Dr. Masters."

"I tried, but she was very reserved. Probably protecting proprietary research."

"Probably. I also want to thank you, Doc, for what you did."

Dr. Bremmer nodded and walked off.

Andrew pulled up a chair and took Adriana's hand. "Everything will be all right now."

* * *

His December dividends came through, and forty-three million from the Psyche 16 proceeds. Sale of twenty-eight film licenses and some change from a film that hit the cinemas, netted him over sixty million. When he added returns from his games and full-sensor headsets, it enabled him to purchase another substantial block of Evagen shares, and he took a call option for more. Once personal GM cars started to sell in volume, he would be doing very well indeed.

Time to think seriously what to do with all his wealth.

According to one ABC breakfast report, Evagen had gone back to Psyche 16. It took money to build Evagen Resort, establish a viable foothold on Mars, and begin serious mining operations on both worlds, Falzon reminded him. It was not all about profiteering.

Maceroy hit it right when he said space tourism would surge, and it did. Aerospace companies around the world were scrambling to build passenger ships for Earth orbit and Moon overflights. Evagen did not bother entering that market, focused on setting up their Moon and Mars habitats to one day make them self-sufficient. It would not happen anytime soon.

In a rare show of unity, the UN Security Council members passed a resolution authorizing formation of a Space Defense Force. How would such ships enforce space law? Until laser and particle weapons were perfected, lidar missiles and old-fashioned rotary cannons, which worked very well in space, plus superior speed, would need to carry the day. That still left a lot of room for enterprising individuals, companies, and governments to mount clandestine operations.

Andrew did not worry about things he could not control. It would sort itself out.

Their belated Hawaiian holiday ended up filled with pure magic. Still feeling some lingering aftereffects of her illness, she expanded like a tropical orchid as they walked hand in hand along the shore early every morning, gentle surf rippling between their feet, before holidaymakers flooded the place. In the evening, they would watch a bloated sun sink into black water, the palms whispering to them a siren's song. Her color came back and she tanned easily. They did all the usual touristy things, which left Kevin exhausted. They liked to find a deserted spot somewhere and simply enjoyed the scented air, watched the gulls circle overhead hoping for a morsel, and allowed tranquility and peace to fill their souls.

The one thing both of them agreed not to do was watch the news or read the local papers. If the world ended, someone would send him an email. Otherwise, he did not want to be bothered. He did get an SMS from Dr. Bremmer, but refused to read it. After ten dreamy days, it had to end. Adriana wanted to take up part-time work, and he keen to push his smartphone/sensor headset project to FutureTech.

Just because he did not want world events to spoil his moment in paradise, it caught up with him when they got home. Another altercation between the U.S. Navy and China, this time serious. According to news bulletins—the chair experts still pompously pontificating on possible ramifications—China fired two hypersonic anti-ship missiles at a U.S. carrier group transiting through the Spratly Islands for supposedly violating Chinese territorial waters. One missile sank a screening cruiser with the loss of most of its crew. The U.S. Administration immediately launched a retaliatory strike with B-2 Spirit bombers based in Guam against three Chinese-occupied atolls with fuel-air munitions, obliterating the installations. Following the strike, the CCP Standing

Committee vice chairman mounted a coup against General Secretary Xi Jinping in a power spill. Not everyone in the Party happy with the General Secretary's persistent provocative policy. The country had achieved too much to risk a hot confrontation with America. Above everything else, the Chinese were pragmatists. Tensions between the two countries remain high. At least the mushroom clouds were not blossoming, and there appeared hope for tomorrow.

When he read Dr. Bremmer's SMS, he took Adriana to The Alfred. Broca had identified the problem and devised a treatment. Her macrophages *had* responded aggressively to a mild allergic response when she ate the almonds. The culprit turned out to be the second receptor added to his macrophages. They were designed to bind with T-cells to enhance his immune system's ability to trigger a faster than normal response against cancer cells. With the cancer eliminated, the macrophages reverted to their cell-repair state, but the second receptor remained to help ward off any pathogen invasion. When Adriana ate the almonds, his macrophages stimulated a massive attack against the allergen, which sent her into shock.

Dr. Bremmer wanted to administer an injection of tailored nanorobots he received from Broca that would seek out the modified macrophages and block the second receptor. Broca suggested that he also take the shot, but he declined, not wishing to mess with something that appeared to be working smoothly. Before agreeing to the treatment, he called Dr. Masters to clear up several concerns.

"Our tests did not show any negative immune response to the nanorobots," she told him.

"They were not regarded as foreign antigens?"

"The nanobots block macrophage and T lymphocyte recognition receptors and prevent ingestion. Without an inflammatory response, the immune system considers them 'self'. We tested this thoroughly, Andrew."

"I'm not convinced Adriana should have this."

"Your wife recovered from her episode because Dr. Bremmer administered a corticosteroid to counteract her macrophages. In event of another attack, it could be life-threatening. She may need to carry an EpiPen wherever she goes. Administering the nano-bots will be a permanent solution."

"How permanent?"

"What do you mean?"

"The nanobots will block the second receptor on macro-phages she currently has in her body, but what happens when we have intercourse and I pass on more macrophages?"

"We thought of that. The nanobots will remain potent almost indefinitely. If your wife exhibits any negative reaction, the nano-bots can be removed by administering a Cephalosporins antibi-otic. I briefed Dr. Bremmer on this."

Andrew disliked the idea of interfering with Adriana's physi-ology. There were too many unknowns when playing with some-thing new, as his unique condition vividly demonstrated. At the same time, he recognized that she risked death if her condition remained untreated.

He talked it over with her, pointing out his concerns. Short of carrying an EpiPen filled with corticosteroid everywhere she went, the nanobots appeared to be the only viable solution. Since Dr. Masters said they were safe, she said, she agreed to have Dr. Bremmer give her the shot.

He had an anxious half-hour wait for a negative reaction to rear its head, but apart from an initial slight flush, Adriana seemed fine. Dr. Bremmer kept her under constant observation for twenty-four hours to make sure, something Andrew appreciated.

* * *

Sergey Nelson gave each general manager a quick glance. "Does anybody else have anything? No? In that case, the floor is yours, Andrew."

He placed his coffee mug on the table. Given the current events, did anything they did matter?

Dawn had broken over Melbourne, and he was minus on sleep, having to get up early for the conference. Beside him, Keith Sloan stifled a yawn. For Nelson and Dela Torres, lunchtime, which also suited Alonzo sitting in his Sao Paulo office. Somewhat late in London for Regan Price, but better than middle of the night for Sanval Tandul in New Delhi. Andrew wondered how the man survived the stifling pollution that perpetually blanketed that city.

"What I would like the board to consider is to enhance the Trans Vis full-sensor headset to interact directly with the Internet for all data searches, email, phone, and message functions."

The general managers looked at each other to some clearing of throats.

"To achieve this, my proposal comes in three parts. The first and easiest is to connect the headset to an Android or iPhone. The phone output would be displayed on the headset's visor. To enable virtual interaction with the phone would require modification of the Android and iPhone operating systems, which means going to bed with Google and Apple."

Regan Price shook his head. "I don't like the idea of partnering with those monsters. We would do all the hard work to make this possible and they would take the largest piece of the profit pie."

"Agreed, and that's where the second part of my proposal comes in," Andrew said. "FutureTech should buy a software company who would build us an independent operating system."

"What about compatibility with existing Android and iPhones, not to mention the thousands of apps out there created for them?" Tandul pointed out.

"Why worry about compatibility? If people can do everything a smartphone can by wearing an enhanced headset, apps developers will flock to us. They don't like Google and Apple's predatory business practices anymore than we do." Andrew raised a finger. "There is a major downside to the first two options, and that's to do with aesthetics."

"Care to clarify that?" Alonzo queried.

"The Trans Vis headset is a neural transmitter and antenna for a computer-brain link. It enables the wearer to interact with our games and operate GM vehicles."

"We're all aware of that," Alonzo said.

"The point I want to make is that to use the headset as an interactive communications device that retains all smartphone functionality, means a person must wear the headset all the time. The headset also needs a power pack. It wouldn't consume as much compared to a phone's LED screen, but I'm sure that existing button batteries would not last a day of continuous usage. Moreover, they're not rechargeable. People wouldn't buy our headsets because of the high running cost. There is one other thing. Can you picture people wearing them all day with visors over their eyes? They would look like zombies!"

This raised a few chuckles.

"You wouldn't be making this proposal unless you had a solution," Nelson said.

"I do. Do away with the headset altogether."

Sanval Tandul snorted. "You're talking about a brain-chip interface, aren't you? A lot of people sunk millions into researching this concept, and all came up against an immovable wall—signal degradation. There simply isn't any way to connect all the required brain areas to exercise full sensory interaction. Not without major invasive surgery, and perhaps not even then."

"That's no longer true, Sanval," Andrew said softly, and everybody waited. "You may be aware of the work done by Broca Genetics on organic nanorobots. What I propose is a chip device with an Internet communications module, and a brain interface for input/output, connected to the cortex with artificial axons built by nanorobots."

"An interesting notion," Price mused. "How would you power this device?"

"The brain is an electrical organ. We'll simply be adding another component for it to manage. I talked to Broca, and they said it might be possible to create such nanobots and tendrils. Elon Musk and his team did a lot of research into brain-chip interfaces with his Neuralink program, and we're already involved with SpaceX. They might be receptive to a collaborative project." Andrew leaned forward. "Picture it, gentlemen. Communication and device control by thought alone. This would be worth billions to FutureTech."

Money Manny already had dollar signs in his eyes.

Nelson sighed and shook his head. "Even if this is technically possible, I can see a number of serious social issues."

"So can I," Andrew agreed. "Big Brother in bed with us 24/7. Lots of opportunities for totalitarian regimes to control their populations even more. Even our so-called democracies could easily slide into autocracies. Civil liberty groups would march in protest, urging legislators to ban the technology. We can prevent that if we encrypt all communication and global data clouds."

"Security agencies and police forces everywhere would never go for it," Sloan interjected immediately. "How can we protect the people if we cannot monitor what they're doing? It might be a tired cliché, but still an effective one."

"Don't forget one thing, Keith," Andrew said. "People are also voters. The one thing uppermost in every politician's mind is to keep his seat once elected. If this means snubbing surveillance agencies and the police, they might go for it. I wouldn't bet on it either way, though. Despite the potential social negatives, there are overwhelming benefits to pursue this. I would rather see this project abandoned than give governments another tool to continue evolving into autocratic regimes. The decision is yours, gentlemen."

"You've clearly been thinking about this, Andrew," Nelson said, looking thoughtful, as well he might. "Let's break this down. Who's in favor of approaching Google and Apple to provide a simple smartphone link?"

Nobody said anything.

Nelson snorted, "Apple haters, right? Next, buy a company and build our own operating system?"

Price, Tandul, and Alonzo raised their hand.

"The motion fails. Now for the big one. Do we proceed with the brain-chip interface proposal?"

"With one caveat, Sergey," Price interjected. "Build a proof of concept device only. Once we have that, we resolve the social and political dimensions before we consider any sort of public release. If we cannot guarantee total personal privacy and data security, I don't want anything to do with this."

"I second that," Sloan said immediately. Others murmured approval.

"Carried," Nelson said.

"For this to work," Andrew pointed out, "we still need an independent operating system."

"Have your team research a best-fit company, or we hire communications specialists to build the thing in-house." Nelson gave everybody a glance. "If there is nothing else, this meeting is adjourned."

* * *

A scorching July sun beat down from a clear sky on the media gaggle assembled outside the Ford Company's new Kansas City plant. The complex had a deserted feeling without a constant stream of new cars coming out for shipping to dealers. Most manufacturers around the world had ceased production of standard vehicles and were retooling for GM cars.

Perry Adams, the company's president, stood behind the lectern and raised his arms to quell the tide of excited media commentary. Behind him were seated senior corporate execs, a couple of political luminaries, Sergey Nelson, and Terrance Maceroy. Andrew found it flattering to be included, although not quite sure what he was doing there. He tried to pump Sergey about it, but the FutureTech founder refused to say, a smug expression on his face. With his daughter Anita only nine days old, Andrew wanted to be with his wife.

Even now, the memory of watching her being born, Adriana clutching his hand, made him misty-eyed. Anita came into the world with barely a whimper and snuggled contentedly into Adriana's arms. The next day, Andrew brought Kevin to see his new sister. His son still to decide whether he liked the idea, no longer being the center of attention.

Some three meters from the lectern a tall, slim woman dressed in a blue business suit guarded a mound covered with blue cloth. Andrew suspected that most males present were studying her rather than watching Adams.

"Distinguished guests, ladies and gentlemen, I want to thank you all for coming," the Ford president announced gravely. "In January 2024, Evagen, Inc. set off a transport revolution the world has not seen since the steam locomotive and the Model T. The sounds of that revolution are still reverberating, and many in the auto industry have not recovered. Life would have been much easier for Ford if Mr. Maceroy had kept the thing to himself," Adams said dryly, which generated a predictable ripple of laughter. "Since he didn't, we were forced to choose whether Ford wanted to be part of this revolution, or sink quietly into obscurity.

"I am proud to say that Ford will be at the forefront of GM cars and commercial vehicles, as our new plant in front of you demonstrates. July 1, 2025, marks the day when the Ford Motor Company launches full production of personal GM cars. This plant and others like it around the world will roll out six hundred cars a day. This will increase as we build capacity. Dealerships will showcase them within the week. From October 1, Ford will also roll out its first run of small and medium commercial vehicles."

He turned to the statuesque lady and nodded. She smiled and pulled back a red cord that revealed Ford's personal car. A collective gasp came from the media.

Andrew admitted it was a lovely thing. Elongated, a transparent dome gave the driver and occupants total view. The dark blue gloss finish had lines along the curved side that marked the doors.

"Ladies and gentlemen, it is with immense pride that I announce the release of the Ford Adriana sedan in honor of Mr. Andrew Payne, responsible for development of the GM control system."

Everybody stood and clapped and cheered. The Ford president turned and smiled.

"Mr. Payne…"

Andrew stood in total shock, torn with conflicting emotions. He wanted so much to share this overpowering moment with his wife, hoping she was watching. He also felt immensely elated at what Ford had done, seeing Maceroy and Nelson's hand in this. He gave a long exhale to steady himself and walked to the lectern. He shook Adams' hand and held it a few seconds longer than strictly called for.

"Thank you for this undeserved honor, Mr. Adams. I am overwhelmed by your generous gesture, and I want to thank the Ford Motor Company for naming their first GM model after my beloved wife, who I'm sure, will be equally touched. If it were not for her love and steadfast support, I would not be standing here now. I hasten to add that I am merely one small part of a dedicated team who made the GM control system possible. If there is credit to be handed out, it should go to Mr. Sergey Nelson, founder of FutureTech." Andrew turned toward his boss and clapped. Others joined him with enthusiasm and prolonged whistles. He turned to Adams and nodded. "Thank you."

The Ford president smiled and stepped to the lectern.

"There is one more thing I want to do before I let you all take a closer look at Adriana and enjoy a demo flight. Mr. Payne, it is with real pleasure that I present to you the very first Ford GM car made anywhere in the world."

Everyone clapped and surged around Andrew to shake his hand. Genuinely overcome, he could only mumble in reply to the many questions thrown his way, fighting to hold back his emotions. Surrounded by friends and people who openly cared for him, left him with a satisfied glow. Perhaps there was hope for this world, and living forever might not be such a bad thing after all.

After a smörgåsbord snack, a smiling Terrance Maceroy sprung another surprise. Masina landed *Evagen-3* in front of the factory, and a Ford technician flew the car into its hold. Everybody hooted with delight, which left Andrew bemused. He *had* wondered how he would get the thing home.

The luxurious mansion he had built at Trinity Park near Cairns, overlooking the ocean, now *would* be only ten minutes away. Adriana loved the area at first sight, and he looked forward to escaping Melbourne's biting winter. Once he got GM cars for his friends and family, they could all use the place to reenergize until he built something for them at whatever retreat they favored.

Memory memo to self: Talk to Adams.

Epilogue

Earth hung low above a gray moonscape in full phase, a blue marble smeared with white blobs. It looked small and fragile, a decorative glass bauble. That is what many people said from Loona Inn—Lunatic Inn to the locals—when they saw it. The restaurant also served as an informal transit lounge for departing passengers returning to Earth or going farther into the system. When a ship broke Earth orbit, people could see the planet fill the sky against a black backdrop, but that view lacked the emotional impact when seen from the Inn window. They could not grasp that Earth looked small and insignificant after appearing huge and indestructible from orbit.

Andrew sipped his coffee and gazed at his world from the same seat he watched it for the last eight years, since December 2025, when Evagen Resort only had three geodesic domes. Now, a complex of eight served the Shackleton Crater base, and not the only one. The UN had two bases that serviced the Space Defense Force, and all the major powers had their own facilities, doing whatever they were doing. By and large, private concerns had colonized the Moon and Mars.

Those who came to stay, or spent a few months working, were smart and generally polite. Living in a vacuum environment, or the near-vacuum of Mars, sometimes hazardous to health for an overbearing boss or budding totalitarian administration. China tried to run one on strict Communist Party lines, when a mishap demolished one of the dome habitats. Beijing said it was an accident, all true—for the Party hierarchy who happened to live in that dome. Some men liked absolute power and tyrannical rule, whether sponsored by a government or multilateral conglomerate. Human nature cannot be suppressed.

"Would you like anything else, sir?" Dephane asked politely.

Andrew looked up at the Inn manager and smiled. "Another round, please."

"Certainly, sir. I trust everything is satisfactory?"

"Everything is fine."

She nodded and withdrew.

The restaurant staff and most of the base personnel knew who he was, of course—The Forever Man. That is what one reporter wit dubbed him when the story broke a number of years ago. Bound to come out sooner or later when he could no longer explain his persistent youthful looks as simple dieting and exercise. Somebody said something innocent at The Alfred or Broca Genetics, or deliberately leaked. It did not matter how it was done.

No CIA or Russian FSB team tried to snatch him and turn him into a lab rat. When the news broke, Broca published their work into macrophages, and global pharmaceuticals scrambled to replicate the results. So far, the immortality pill everybody wanted eluded them, much to Andrew's relief and satisfaction.

Broca were the first to offer treatments that extended life by up to fifteen years based on telomere repair, but others followed. Curiously, after the initial rush by the mega-wealthy and the powerful to secure for themselves even partial immortality, the desire to live to 110 seemed to taper off. Those in their nineties who had the treatment found that living beyond their allotted time not what they thought it would be. Their minds remained active and alert, but the treatment could not restore their bodies to youthful vigor, which they really wanted. What use having a long lifespan when confined to a bed or wheelchair? They wanted what Andrew had, something still beyond Broca's reach. He was a genetic accident born from a combination of factors impossible to replicate. Eventually, they and others gave up trying.

His parents were somewhat miffed that he did not confide in them, but after talking to them, they accepted, but did not like, the reason for his reticence. His closest friend, Mark Sanders, also felt slighted at first, but got over it, as did Orwell. They still went out together occasionally for a stag dinner to chew over the good old days. When he saw what time did to them while he remained young, it made him depressed. They envied and secretly resented him, hiding their discomfort behind cutting humor.

Andrew sipped his coffee and stared at Earth.

Eight years…a lot of change, and most of it good. GM vehicles snaked over cities and landscapes—they were still to solve the parking problem—and for the first time in history, mankind had unlimited, cheap, non-polluting power. Villages in the Sahara and the high Andes who never had an electric bulb, finally knew a measure of comfort.

One change that swept the world, perhaps more significant than GM vehicles, was secure personal communication and data storage, which directly contributed to Andrew's six billion dollars net worth. Google and Microsoft were still around, but Apple, a specialist phone and tablet provider, never recovered when in 2028, FutureTech rolled out its Personal Communications Device. This also led to the demise of Trans Vis and full-sensor headsets, an unavoidable side effect of progress.

Countries, including the U.S., tried to ban the technology when FutureTech refused to hand over the master encryption key, but when the Supreme Court ruled it a violation of the First Amendment, the effort died. The government still hated Future-Tech, but were mindful of voter backlash. People were prepared to take only so much from governments before they rose up and swallowed them.

At thirty-five, he faced a minor life crisis. He had done almost everything he wanted in life. His business empire encompassed many things, among them genetic research, quantum computing, space industries and resorts, and VR entertainment. A thriving market existed for full-sensor escapism for those wishing to forget the burden of reality. Despite his corporate and philanthropic interests, he realized he needed something new to capture his imagination. A project so complex, it might take half a century or more to implement. A project that produced substantive social benefit, and he had the perfect thing.

Technology had transformed Earth and made life easier for billions, but war still existed, including starvation, sickness, and international rivalry not much changed from the start of the century. Mankind needed to advance and mature philosophically and ethnically. It all came down to a simple question. What did he want out of life, a life that might last for a *very* long time?

One thing he never tried was enact social change. He could not hope to make every person on Earth prosperous and disease free. There were far too many cultural, economic, religious, and political barriers for that to be possible, but gradual change could be achieved, given time and resources, and he had plenty of both.

He would enter politics.

Not as an elected representative, though. He would become a background player and mover. This promised to be a game that would keep him amused for some time. Not exactly virtual reality, but close enough.

First, he intended to enjoy his vacation.

Masina walked in, sat down and smiled. "The cargo is secured and the passengers are tucked in. We lift in fifteen minutes."

He finished his coffee, connected to the restaurant's billing system with his PCD, paid the bill, and added a lavish tip. He stood and glanced at the barren moonscape, Earth hanging fixed above the horizon, and smiled at Adriana.

"Shall we?"

"Let me round up our two little monsters."

After his Mars vacation, he would reshape Earth. He figured the project should keep him busy for about half a century or so. After that? His gaze drifted toward the wide plate window.

Lots of stars out there…

About the Author

Stefan Vučak has written twenty-one novels, which include eight SF books in the Shadow Gods Saga. His *Cry of Eagles* won the coveted Readers' Favorite silver medal award, and his *All the Evils* was the prestigious Eric Hoffer contest finalist and Readers' Favorite silver medal winner. *Strike for Honor* won the gold medal.

Stefan leveraged a successful career in the Information Technology industry, which took him to the Middle East working on cellphone systems. Writing has been a road of discovery, helping him broaden his horizons. He also spends time as an editor and book reviewer. Stefan lives in Melbourne, Australia.

To learn more about Stefan, visit his:
Website: www.stefanvucak.com
Facebook: www.facebook.com/StefanVucakAuthor
Twitter: @stefanvucak

9 780648 552840